THE SOVEREIGN

By Pearson Sharp

D1501626

The Sovereign
ISBN-13: 978-1515102021
ISBN-10: 1515102025

Published by Pearson Sharp
Third US Printing, July 2015
www.pearsonsharp.com

Printed in the United States of America

To My Parents

To my Father, for all the worlds I discovered
in the books we read together.

To my Mother, for teaching me
to believe in magic.

Acknowledgements

There's no such thing as writing a book by yourself. There are numerous people who are involved in putting it together, even if you think you're the only one, or at least the most important one. There are so many who have helped me get to this point, and without their feedback and guidance, this really wouldn't be the book it is today.

Megan, without your tireless efforts to read, reread, and re-reread my manuscript, this would be a different book entirely. Your support and encouragement helped make Errolor the incredible place it is.

Pat, I'm not sure there's a world record for how quickly my book has been read, or how many times, but you'd doubtless be the champion. Thanks for all your feedback and diligent, insistent, tireless, dogged, and unrelenting persistence in helping me finish writing the book.

Introduction

I don't believe that an author, or any artist for that matter, should need to explain their work. An artistic creation should stand on its own. So I won't do that. But I will admit to being a reader of science fiction, and even fantasy on occasion, and there are times when it can be unnecessarily confusing. Complicated words, pronunciations and getting lost with characters or places got to be a real problem when I was writing this book. So I had to make a list for myself, just to keep track of all the things I'd invented.

I've included this "Encyclopaedia of Errolor" in the back of the book to help you out. It's not the complete list—I've saved a few things for later. But every odd name, place, and creature you find in this book you hold in your hands is there in the back. If you're like me, you'll find it a relief not to have to keep track of everything yourself.

There, that's it. That's all. Read away—and I hope—get lost in the world of Errolor. But if you find you get too lost, there's always a guide.

Oh, and "ch" is pronounced with a "k" sound. Usually.

Contents

ONE

THE MALEFACTOR

Aldric twisted the controls of his fighter, spinning through a dizzying loop. Swallowing the nausea in his throat, he shook his head and pulled the yoke back to its limit, hammering into full throttle. The nose of the Starling went vertical as fifty two gravities rammed him into his seat. His vision went black and he gasped, unable to breathe, his lungs fighting against the sudden force. The blood rushed out of his brain faster than his suit could compensate and for a moment the sounds around him faded and he was floating in a dark, empty room.

Aldric's adaptive flight suit and AI gelseat quickly adjusted to the pressure, and he sucked in a deep breath as the weight was suddenly lifted from his chest. His vision returned, colours fading in through grey, followed by his hearing, growing above the ringing in his ears. Bio-readouts in his helmet flashed red, but he ignored them. The fighter's twin engines roared just beyond the cockpit to either side, their penetrating whine growing fainter in the thinning atmosphere. He could just now see the stars, still vague among the hazy clouds above.

The clouds began to thin, and suddenly the full moon burst into view directly overhead, dancing over the silver wings. Blackness once again crept into the corners of Aldric's eyes, a dim fog shading the world, throbbing with the drumming heartbeat in his ears. He was nearing the threshold of his suit's tolerances, and systems were beginning to fail. He heard the creak and flex of the hull adjusting to the pressure, felt the pulsing vibrations of the engines through his seat and the controls: his ship, his body, pressed to the limits of endurance. Only moments remained before he broke atmosphere and left gravity behind.

But time began to change, seconds growing into minutes, hours. Aldric's face tingled as his suit tightened, struggling to repressurize and regulate his vitals against the staggering forces around him. Dazzling ice crystals crawled inward towards the centre of the cockpit's ferranite glass nosecone—small, silvery tendrils that edged their way closer and closer, obscuring Aldric's forward view until only the moon remained in the very middle. Clenching his jaw, he concentrated on the moon, fighting his growing faintness. The cabin was hot, his suit constricting, the AI gelseat straining to cushion him against pressures that would crush his body. He felt his hands tingling on the yoke, his fingers numb and distant.

He saw numbers, lines, scrawling across his visor in vivid green—meaningless, blurring together. He felt sluggish, dull, his reactions delayed. You could be trained to tolerate high gravity situations, he knew, but there were limits. A mere sixteen gravities was fatal after only a minute without proper gear—your brain would starve of blood and oxygen. Now his suit visor read sixty-two gees, more than he had ever trained for. The supple gelseat cradled his body, yet under this gravity he now weighed nearly forty-eight hundred kilograms, almost five tonnes, and neither Aldric nor the gelseat could tolerate much more. Willpower didn't matter—his suit and his fighter and his body were at their very limits and his brain simply didn't have the chemicals to remain conscious anymore.

He struggled to blink, feeling remote, far from himself, from the cockpit, from the controls. He tried to recite the Valorí mantra for courage. *You... an... errant?* He couldn't remember it. He couldn't remember anything, his mind was empty. He tried harder. What was the mantra? What was anything? He didn't know. Nothing was anything. He felt drunk, his mind swimming, drowning.

He heard the engines howling, so close, straining; the gelseat absorbing his weight, the ice crystals, the canopy, the glowing console, flickering green numbers, green, red, the moon whirling, his heart thudding, the blood roaring in his ears, the glowing console, dull pain, acrid taste in his mouth, the stars above, the moon, the stars, the crystals and the moon and the stars.

Aldric jerked forward into his harness and then felt nothing. The sensation of forward motion stopped suddenly as he left gravity and the atmosphere behind. The ringing in his ears grew louder as the roar of the engines was silenced. The ice crystals receded from the canopy, the moon glowing beyond in a blanket of stars. He rose against the padded straps, and he let his hands fall free of the controls, floating in the air.

It took Aldric a moment to come to his senses, realising he had broken orbit and was now sitting here. He shouted suddenly, shaking his fists in the air, at the moon, at everything. Emotions rushed through him, releasing the stress and joy and euphoria that had been building inside the past few moments, hours, days. He flicked the locks on his stuffy helmet and let it float away. Rubbing his eyes, his skin tingled with the increased blood flow as his suit relaxed its grip. Adrenaline lit up his nerves. His vision and awareness returned with a dull throbbing, and he could feel his pulse beating in his temples. His head ached, but he didn't mind.

A grin spread across his face and he laughed, savouring the moment. This was his release, ridding himself of all the tension he'd been carrying for what felt like forever. Taking his personal Starling fighter for an early morning flight purged him—it was his escape, and he cherished these fleeting moments of freedom.

Aldric twisted the yoke, whirling the ship into a reverse spin that brought him around to face the planet Errolor. Cutting the power, he sat without moving, gazing at the clouds massing serenely below. Aldric had never broken atmosphere in a Starling before, the elation was overwhelming. He'd also never climbed vertically under that kind of gravity. Even with both the gelseat and his suit compensating, he'd nearly lost consciousness. It was a personal triumph.

His hands felt sweaty through his gloves. Tugging them off, he flexed his fingers, shaking the numbness out of them. Running a hand through his matted hair, he pulled long, jet-black strands away from his face. He tasted blood. Gently dabbing his lip, his finger came away red. *Must have bitten it on the way up*, he thought.

Clicking his release lever, he floated away from his seat. The dimly glowing cabin enclosed him, a dark nest among the stars. There was absolute peace. He breathed for a moment, drifting weightlessly above the swirling scene below. The nightline cascaded across the clouds. It gathered the landscape into its dark folds as the planet spun, passing over hazy mountains and twilit vales. The ocean's endless waste poured out to the grey horizon, its leaden waters touched mutely by the golden sun.

Breaking orbit, sitting here above Errolor, these were things he had done many times since he was a boy. And yet it remained a sacred experience. *This is where the gods sit,* he thought, marvelling at the vastness of the scene. The cabin was cooling rapidly, but he was still hot, still sweating, and the coolness felt good. The air in the cockpit felt close, heavy, stale— redolent with a biting metal odour, ozone, his sweat. His helmet floated up beside him, bumping into his shoulder. He stowed it beside his seat and took a long, satisfying pull from a water tube in his flight suit. The water tasted hard and coppery, and he swished it around, trying to rinse away the tang of blood. *If I sit with the gods, am I not god-like?*

A pair of sapphire streaks blazed bright into the upper atmosphere, twin trails glowing coldly through the lurid clouds. The trails vanished and a glimmering silver dart raced towards him, starlight glinting on its metallic hull. He recognised another Starling fighter; short but elegantly sweeping wings and a smooth, tear-shaped body and conical canopy, nestled between two sloping chrome engine pylons. It slowed as it approached his ship, finally coming to rest some twenty metres beyond his nose. Three small white jets fired in intervals along the hull, and the other ship matched Aldric's orientation.

The pilot removed his helmet. Through the receding frost on the fighter's canopy, Aldric saw the familiar features of his younger brother Arem. Dark hair framed Arem's face, and the keen blue eyes Aldric knew so well were merely dark points from this distance. They regarded each other for a moment, Arem's round, youthful face contrasting with Aldric's square chin, broad forehead and strong, high cheekbones. Aldric's dark eyebrows and long, straight nose were hallmarks of the Danarean line, a feature he shared with both Arem and his father. The similarities ended there, however, for two brothers could not have been more dissimilar.

Aldric was not overly tall, though he could meet most men in the eye, and looked down on many others. His trim muscles filled out under fair skin that was tanned from riding apalas bareback in the plains outside of Chaldrea, as well as much training in the outdoor temples of the Asaani. His deep-set, penetrating grey eyes and full, softly curled lips lent him the sensual aspect of a poet; yet a sharpness in the lean angles of his features suggested he was no stranger to hardship, noble born though he was.

While Aldric looked more mature than his twenty-five years, Arem looked much younger than his own twenty-three. He was short, and though he was not out of shape, there was a visible softness to his flesh that combined with his pale skin to recommend a life spent comfortably indoors. Arem shared his brother's hard, aquiline gaze, and though he was often expressive and animated, there was something in his blue eyes hinting at a secretive nature. The sharp lines of his cheekbones and jaw were lost beneath his soft, ruddy cheeks, and his full lips were ever turned in the faintest of pouts.

Aldric watched his brother's fighter drift towards him, a drop of quicksilver above the turbulent clouds below. Arem tapped his finger to his ear and Aldric nodded, switching on his com-channel.

There was silence for a moment, then, "I lost consciousness." Arem's voice sounded thin over the channel, but Aldric could read the bitterness.

"It was stupid. I barely made it," Aldric admitted, his neck muscles still aching from the strain. The two ships drifted closer, close enough for Aldric to see tension on Arem's face.

"I read fifty eight gees before I blacked out."

Aldric nodded. "I read fifty four," he said, lying.

"You blacked out too?"

"No," Aldric said. He saw Arem look away, and he wished he'd lied about that as well.

"*Arrus Athaban*?" Arem ventured. He said it jokingly, but Aldric could hear the tightness in his brother's voice and see the resentment on his face. Aldric knew if they began a race for the orbital station *Arrus Athaban* that he would only be encouraging Arem's competitiveness. This rivalry had existed since they were boys, growing evermore hostile and creating a rift between them in recent years.

"Not today," Aldric said, knowing even his refusal would provoke Arem. "I'm going to meet Bahir at the Temple this morning," he said, pulling his mesh gloves back on. They were still damp with his sweat, and he struggled with them, tugging them on a finger at a time. "Honestly, I shouldn't even be here," he said. "Not today. I just needed to get out."

He looked out to Arem's ship, feeling the scorn in his brother's gaze. Arem never lost with dignity, yet losing to his older brother was especially hard. Aldric was simply a better pilot, and they both knew it. These little games they played were tiresome and Aldric tried his best to discourage them. He'd been alone when he got into the Starling and left the palace this morning. It was only too late when he'd realised Arem was following, and he'd resented the intrusion.

Aldric waited, but Arem said nothing. "I don't really know why I came up here at all," he said finally, almost speaking to himself. Arem's silence was irritating.

"Another time, then," Arem said.

"Another time."

A red light flickered on Aldric's console, and he glanced at his screen. A warning indicator, collision detection. A display overhead showed a large mass object careening towards them at high velocity.

"Arem, there's—"

"I see it," Arem said, cutting him off. Aldric watched as Arem powered up his ship, diving back through the clouds in a plume of white fire. *He didn't wait to see what it was,* Aldric thought briefly, switching on his Lantern drive. It seemed odd, but he dismissed the thought and floated down into his seat again.

Grabbing the yoke, Aldric darted a dozen kilometres away, spinning the Starling around to face the incoming object. It wasn't yet visible, but his computer told him he was now well clear of its path.

Inbound ships always identified themselves, especially entering Home Space, but this one hadn't, which made him uneasy. *Corsairs?* No, the Raeth wouldn't dare an open attempt on Errolor. *And it's too big to be the Raeth, they don't have any ships that large...* He glanced over the port engine pylon to where the yellow star Daedrus was rising over Errolor's horizon. He knew the orbiting battle station *Arrus Athaban* would be coming into view shortly. The Attendant Fleet was in orbit as well, and if it *was* corsairs...

Aldric squinted, scanning the star field ahead for any tell-tale signs of stream space distortion. A faint blurring in a cluster of stars told him where the ship would arrive. The little patch of stars shimmered gently, and an instant later a ship emerged. It appeared suddenly out of the black wall of space, like rising out of a pool of water, and moving so fast Aldric's eyes couldn't follow. It slowed rapidly as it approached the planet, and in a moment Aldric relaxed, leaning back into his seat. The graceful lines of an Adamant-class Imperial destroyer glided towards Errolor.

But something was wrong. Aldric peered forward, examining the destroyer as it slowed. As the lines of the silvery hull became distinct, he noted blast marks and places where explosions pocked the superstructure. A gaping rift split one of the operations towers in half, and Aldric could now see that only three of the massive engines were working.

A sudden twinkle of light beyond his port wing caught his eye—three ships approached from around the horizon of Errolor. Aldric powered his Starling and raced towards the wounded destroyer.

The other three ships came on with lightning speed, rising into relief from their shadowy silhouettes. Two Imperial dreadnoughts and a super battleship made straight for the destroyer, their vast bulks casting long shadows through the streaming sunlight behind them. As Aldric drew near, the extent of the damage to the destroyer became clear. He couldn't believe its Lantern drive still worked at all. *The Raeth*. This must have been a convoy escort, he surmised, and the convoy had been attacked by the corsairs known as the Raeth. That was expected though, that happened all the time. But he'd never seen an Imperial destroyer take such damage. *Raeth don't have the firepower.*

Aldric closed to a few hundred metres and switched on his communications. He tried hailing for a few moments, but there was no response from the destroyer. Keeping a safe distance from the huge ship, he drifted over the bow and made a visual scan. A gash twenty metres in length and trailing debris cleaved through the destroyer, all that remained of the control tower. *That explains the radio silence.* The bridge seemed intact, and Aldric manoeuvred forwards until he could look across to the narrow slit of windows of the command deck. Scorch marks marred the silver skin of the destroyer, but the heavily armoured bridge appeared otherwise undamaged.

A shadow fell over the gleaming hull, and Aldric looked up to see the Imperial warships settling into position above the crippled destroyer. Any craft entering Home Space undeclared was cause for alarm, and the three warships had immediately come to investigate. But this was clearly a rescue operation now, and there was little enough a dreadnought could offer in support.

Aldric pulled away. There was nothing he could do, either. Salvage and escort ships would be arriving soon, and the wounded destroyer would be towed to the orbiting dry dock for repairs. He wondered what had happened. Powering away from the scene, Aldric drifted abaft of the massive destroyer. INV *Malefactor* was scrawled across the curving stern of the ship. She was newly commissioned, only a few years old, a first rate ship-of-the-line.

As he watched, the top port engine began to falter. It flickered briefly, and then extinguished. *It's losing containment.* A brilliant blue light erupted from the engine, and beams of jagged energy rippled down the rear quarter of the ship, slicing the hull wide open as they went. Aldric shielded his eyes from the intense blast, instinctively pulling his ship further away. Miniature explosions danced along the hull as superheated blue-green plasma vented into space. *One of the cores breached,* he thought in horror. If the breach cascaded into the main reactor, the entire ship would go.

The explosion knocked the *Malefactor* from its course, sending the ship into a sidelong roll towards the planet. The aft section tumbled in a slow motion arc, wheeling out of control as tiny eruptions stabbed through the silvery skin of the hull. The whole scene played out in terrible silence, adding to the dread awe as Aldric watched helplessly. *Another minute or two on this course and she'll fall into the atmosphere,* he thought desperately. Swathes of detritus trailed behind the spinning destroyer, some of it floating past Aldric's canopy as he followed behind. He noticed the three warships had moved off a distance, anticipating a cataclysmic explosion.

A ripple of lights coruscated down the length of the hull. Tiny jets of white gas blew outward, and little silvery darts burst away from the ship. *They've launched the escape pods. They're abandoning the ship.* Whatever the situation on the *Malefactor* was, it had reached a critical point. Abandoning the ship meant there was nothing else they could do on board, and that they believed the ship lost. *Only a matter of time,* Aldric thought.

Aldric watched the little silvery flecks race away from the destroyer as it tumbled towards Errolor. The thousands of one-man pods glittered like chaff in the sunlight. They would be picked up by the nearby rescue ships, and then hopefully a story would emerge from this disaster. But that would come later. What could be done now to stop the *Malefactor* falling into the planet? Besides the loss of an invaluable destroyer, it would be devastating if it landed in a city. It was too large and armoured to break up on entry, even in its damaged state. There might also be people trapped on board, he thought—*people who couldn't evacuate.*

Aldric stopped, holding his breath. The thought caught in his mind and he inspected the ship. Were there pods that hadn't ejected? Every warship was equipped with spare evacuation pods, but as Aldric studied the destroyer, he could see hundreds of escape hatches that hadn't been blown. Were those intended for crewmen killed in battle, dead already? Or were people trapped and unable to get to the pods? *There are survivors,* he thought, not sure why he felt so certain. *Gods, where are the salvage ships?*

Abruptly, the three Imperial warships began turning in unison, their vast bulks heaving to present a broadside at the destroyer. Each of them levelled on the *Malefactor,* imposing rows of cannons coming to bear in a direct line for firing. *Hahka! They wouldn't,* Aldric thought. Yet he watched as the great deck guns were brought about and steadied at the *Malefactor.* The dreadnought's long, sleek lines looked menacing as the last of its massive guns trained on the destroyer.

Aldric targeted the nearest dreadnought, flagship of Attendant Fleet. "This is Prince Aldric Danarean, respond."

There was a hiss, then, "Your Grace, this is the *Imperial Naval Vessel Crucible,* responding."

"What's the *Malefactor's* situation? Does anyone have a plan to stop her?"

"My Lord, we've been ordered to destroy her before she can enter the planet's atmosphere."

Aldric was stunned. "You've been what? Where are the salvage ships?"

There was hesitation in the operator's voice. "They were deemed incapable of stopping the *Malefactor's* free-fall. Before more time is lost, we're to—"

"No, listen to me," Aldric cut in. "There could be survivors on board, she has a lot of escape pods that haven't launched."

"Yes Lord, we noted that as well. Yet the likelihood of survivors has been judged acceptably low."

"Acceptably low?" Aldric said, incredulous. Who was making these decisions? "That ship is heavily damaged, there are no communications. It's possible, probable, people couldn't escape. You *will not* destroy it."

"My Lord, we've been ordered by the Admiralty, we must proceed."

All three warships had swung about, bringing their broadside guns to bear upon the helpless destroyer. Their deep, wedge-shaped prows seemed to cut through space itself, trailing backwards in lethal, graceful lines. Their hulls bristled with deadly cannons and only moments remained before the great guns opened up and obliterated the *Malefactor.*

"I'm countermanding *all orders.* Do you hear me? *You will not fire on that ship,*" Aldric said.

"Your Grace, the Admiralty, in body—"

"If you fire on that ship, I'll have every officer on the *Crucible* pilloried before the Citadel and imprisoned for treason, do you understand? *Hold your fire.*"

"Yes Your Grace!" the man stammered. "I will repeat your orders to Attendant Fleet."

Aldric watched in breathless silence, waiting for a sign of confirmation. The *Malefactor* continued to fall, but the three warships held their fire.

Aldric's comm light flashed. "Prince Aldric, this is Commodore Blakely. My pennant master informs me that you've ordered us to hold our fire."

Aldric's chest flooded with relief. "Yes, I believe there are survivors—we can't destroy that ship."

"My Lord, our salvage ships aren't able to stop her falling into Errolor. We estimate she'll fall over central Galinor, a populated area seems probable. What do you suggest we do?" The Commodore's voice was urgent but even. *He needs orders,* Aldric thought.

What could they do? Aldric glanced towards the stricken *Malefactor.* In less than a minute, she would plunge into the atmosphere—a deadly, irrevocable descent. If he were wrong about the survivors, it would be too late for the warships to fire and destroy her, she couldn't fragment in time. All of their larger weapons would rain lethal fallout, as devastating as anything the plummeting *Malefactor* would do. Whatever was to happen, it would be over in minutes. Time was running out. His mind raced, considering scenario after scenario, each impossible.

Communications on board had been disabled, but even if they hadn't, there was clearly no one able to respond or they would have evacuated with everyone else. The destroyer still had two functional engines, and despite the damage to her hull, she might yet be piloted down. *I need someone on board to guide her down.*

Aldric smashed his fist into the arm of his seat, his eyes widening at a sudden possibility.

"Commodore, can you tap into navigation on the *Malefactor?*"

Aldric felt the pause before the Commodore responded, knew the realisation. "We'll try, Your Grace."

A tense moment passed before he replied. "Lord, the navigation computer is online, but it's too damaged to operate at this distance."

"What do you mean, *at this distance?*" Aldric asked. "Are you saying if the signal were closer?"

"My Lord, the signal is so weak, an uplink would need to be impossibly close—there are no ships that could get within range."

"*How close?*" Aldric felt desperate, there were only moments left before the *Malefactor* would enter the atmosphere.

"For a successful uplink, we estimate no more than a hundred metres, my Lord— possibly much less. Our capital ships can't follow her down, not at those ranges, no ship can."

Aldric cursed. His mind darted through the situation. There were so many outcomes. So many possibilities he didn't have time to consider. *Hesitate, and all is lost.* Aldric strapped on his helmet, he would need the display. "Commodore, relay your information to authorities in the threatened cities, do what you can to ensure all civilians are protected. Raise the Royal Air Wing, get them active—tell them to be prepared to destroy the *Malefactor* on my command."

"My Lord, the Roy—"

"Commodore, these are your orders, there isn't time. Alert the regional Siege Batteries, tie them into the orders for the Air Wing. If I give the signal, I want the *Malefactor* destroyed," Aldric said.

"Yes, Your Grace," the Commodore said.

Aldric switched off the channel and launched the Starling towards the *Malefactor*. Instantly all three warships fell behind as he raced for the tumbling destroyer. She lay dangerously to starboard, listing with her port side facing Aldric, the rift above her ruptured core pointed upward and spewing neon plasma. If she entered the atmosphere at this angle, she might break in half, and there'd be no hope of bringing her down safely.

Switching his navcomp on, Aldric prepared the uplink. Every ship was fitted with a navigational computer that could be activated to guide the ship in an emergency. The *Malefactor* was too damaged to use her own, but ships could be linked together, and Aldric hoped he could slave the *Malefactor*'s crippled systems to his own, allowing his navcomp to take her in. *A hundred metres,* he thought, trying not to consider everything that could go wrong at that distance.

The destroyer rolled through billowing clouds of plasma, fragments of the hull tearing away from gashes as Aldric dodged through chunks flying past him. The sun was rising above the horizon, and the white clouds below contrasted with the flaming destroyer. Aldric closed to five hundred metres, close enough to see the individual windows and hatches on the destroyer's sleek hull. Her graceful wings seemed pitifully helpless, unable to keep the wounded ship aloft. Yet even fatally damaged, the destroyer was beautiful, and the silent scene felt almost poetic.

He manoeuvred closer, watching the heads up display in his visor. His computer was attempting to link with the *Malefactor*, but he still wasn't close enough. *250 metres.* Any second and the *Malefactor* would enter the atmosphere. Errolor loomed over his forward view, white clouds swirling over blue ocean and green swathes of jungle. He edged the Starling closer, drawing up to the bow of the destroyer. A deep blast mark scorched through the prow, cutting the stencilled name in half: INV *Ma-tor*. Bitter anger welled up through Aldric's concentration. He was touched by the loss, the tragedy of the falling destroyer. The *Malefactor* became personified, and he felt a deep sense of injustice at her demise.

150 metres. Link! Gods, link. Aldric thought furiously. His ship shuddered at the first eddies of atmospheric current. There was no more time left. *100 metres.* The destroyer rocked, buffeted as it descended into the atmosphere. Without warning, gravity returned, and Aldric sank forward into his harness. The whine of the engines suddenly pierced the stillness with a deafening shriek. That was it, they had entered the atmosphere, and the

Malefactor was still falling sidelong into the planet. It lurched and swayed, rolling precariously from side to side. Flames erupted from the underside, and pieces of the silvery hull began to kick off in sheets, whizzing dangerously past Aldric. *If one of those comes through the canopy*...60 metres.

The uplink status blinked off and on, trying to establish connexion. *This isn't going to work*, he thought desperately. *And there might not be any survivors—I've put everyone in danger for nothing.* Yet he could feel that there were. Somehow, he knew there were people on board. His ship bucked wildly, tossed on the invisible turbulence. Flames leapt over his nose and wings, roaring, screaming as he plummeted with the falling destroyer. *30 metres.* The flames pouring over the bow of the *Malefactor* began leaping up over his own canopy, blinding him. He guided the Starling merely with the raw data fed to his visor, watching the distance between himself and the destroyer quickly tick away. *Approaching stratosphere: 75 kilometres to surface.*

The uplink suddenly winked into solid green. *Online!* Aldric quelled his excitement and focused on the controls. *25 metres.* He couldn't believe the destroyer was still in one piece. *Navlink established, awaiting command.* He dialled in the command which would slave the *Malefactor* to his fighter. *Command received: awaiting telemetry.* It had worked. Synching the computers, Aldric allowed his nav-system to direct the *Malefactor*, acting as autopilot for the crippled ship. *Entering stratosphere: 52 kilometres to surface.* He couldn't even see. The giant silver, wedge-shaped bow of the *Malefactor* eclipsed his entire view. Gingerly he eased the Starling laterally under the destroyer's prow; *25 metres, I can't lose the link.*

With a sudden lurch and groan that Aldric heard above the roaring wind, the destroyer's two remaining engines kicked into life. For a sickening heartbeat the bow of the ship heaved up towards him as the computer tried to regain control, coming within mere metres of Aldric's nose. He reflexively pulled back on the controls as collision lights blared angrily at the corners of his vision. *30 metres.* The uplink light flickered. *No!* he thought fiercely, pushing the fighter closer again.

The *Malefactor* began righting itself, the starboard flank fighting down and into the thick atmosphere to face the planet. Aldric guided the Starling tediously alongside the bow as the massive destroyer began to level into a more controlled descent. *90 degrees, 85, 80, 70, 60, 50...* The angle became gentler and Aldric dared to breathe. The bow of the destroyer threw off powerful eddies, violently battering and tossing the Starling as Aldric fought to keep his critical distance. With precious care, he eased the fighter up and behind, letting the destroyer pull in front of him. He watched as the smooth, subtle curves of the command towers passed beneath him like silver waves in the glinting sunlight, noting each rending blast in the hull.

The uplink between his computer and the *Malefactor's* was actually working, and the giant ship began to slow. It would be impossible, Aldric realised, to land her properly—but a controlled crash somewhere in the open would be better than letting her fall headlong into a city or mountain range. The earth below was just visible now through the thinning clouds. Long rivers of gold glowed across the landscape, winding down through snow-capped mountains and shadowed jungle forests. Looking below, the plains of Lannachlor were bathed pink in the morning sun. *Where can she come down?*

42 degrees... the computer was struggling with the descent. 42 degrees would be a hard landing, there wouldn't be much left at that angle.

His eyes flickered over the hull. *I've got to reduce her incline.* He keyed into the *Malefactor's* computer, quickly scanning her systems. If he could give the last two engines more power, there was a good chance the computer could level her out. The list of systems still operating wasn't long, but there were a couple he could cut. *Life support? We'll be down in minutes, don't need that.* He deactivated the system, watching his visor's readout. *40 degrees, 39, 38...* What was left? He'd need at least a 15 degree incline for any hope of landing the destroyer intact.

A sudden updraft rocked his ship, rolling him sharply to port. A moment of terrifying confusion rushed through him as his ship twisted in the wake of the destroyer, spiralling upside down, whirling him through a full spin. Aldric dangled upside down from his seat as he tried to keep his control and not fall out of range, his fighter lurching and quaking in the titanic eddies. Bringing himself around, Aldric righted the Starling, falling back into his seat. He drew up again to the mirrored hull, glancing at the uplink. The connexion glowed solid green: it was stable. *Unbelievable.*

The sun climbed steadily above the horizon over his starboard wingtip, the ground now tinged a golden yellow. The vast continent of Galinor stretched out below Aldric's canopy, out beyond the furthest view in all directions. The snows of the Enowyrth mountains glowed purple and pink in the dawn's light, and Aldric surveyed the landscape, searching for a suitable landing site. Scanning the terrain in his visor, he found a barren heath beyond the Carrac Fold, directly in their flight path. Kilometres of open moors and farmland, all the way up to the Lyndron River. It wouldn't get any better than that. But he had to bring down the angle of descent to fifteen degrees or less, or it wouldn't matter where he landed.

He looked through the list of available systems again. *Atmospheric Compensation; Reactor Control; Auxiliary Manifolds...* He shut down a handful of systems, watching the angle of descent for each one. 31, 28, 24...

Almost. He went through the last of the list. He caught his breath. *Weapons Systems.* That would be a massive drain, and it certainly wasn't needed anymore. *Deactivated. Weapons Systems: Offline. Diverting power.* He watched the declinator. *20, 19, 17... 15...15.* He sighed. That would have to be enough. He'd hoped it would fall further, but in any case—*13, 12, 10. 10 degrees!* He almost shouted with relief. 10 degrees gave him as gentle an incline as he could have imagined. The *Malefactor* would certainly take some damage, but she'd be in one piece.

Aldric gripped the yoke tightly, gliding through the turbulence with ease now. *Entering troposphere—22 kilometres to surface.* Both ships had levelled out their descent, and the plunge through the clouds was breath taking. The *Malefactor* thundered on only two dozen metres away, her silver hull glowing brilliant orange in the new light. Water beaded and streamed in rivulets across the canopy as he passed through a cloud layer, remnants of the night's storm. The cloud was dense, the destroyer vanishing in the haze. Aldric could still hear the powerful engines booming behind him, feel their vibrations over those of his own ship. Still, he took a reassuring glance at the readouts in his visor. *27 metres: ok.* A moment later they broke through the cloud cover, and the sun bounced off the destroyer's body in wondrous yellows and golds.

The last challenge would be dropping their speed. *10 kilometres per second—Hahka! She'd disintegrate on impact.* The *Malefactor* was too destabilised to deploy full brakes, and Aldric doubted she even had all her brakes remaining. *16 kilometres to surface.* At this angle and speed, Aldric estimated another three minutes before they landed. Tapping into the *Malefactor's* computers, he scrolled through the operational systems. Half the airbrakes had been damaged beyond use. The magnetic array was still functional however, and he could also reverse the engines—*carefully.*

The landscape was still hazy from this height, but he knew very soon it would get a lot bigger. Keying into the central systems, Aldric began the manual application of the braking structures. Reversing the engines would be the hardest on the ship, he'd try that last. Keeping an eye on the destroyer, he told the computer on the *Malefactor* to begin deploying the forward airbrakes. He watched as a series of hydraulic fins began extending outward, vaporous contrails fanning off their leading edges. *Stable.* He keyed in the next row of brakes. One jammed, only rising half-way.

As he entered the command for the next row, one of the fins in the first row twisted, the hydraulic piston snapping, sending it whirling down the length of the hull, tearing off two more fins before careening over Aldric's canopy. There was a terrible thud as it collided with his port wing, tipping his fighter towards the destroyer. Aldric banked hard to starboard, sweeping mere metres above the destroyer's hull. He straightened out on the other side, checking his systems: miraculously, the fin hadn't caused serious damage, the sturdy armour of the Starling protecting him. *Gods,* Aldric thought, *and a prayer to Daor.*

All the airbrakes were deployed, and the *Malefactor* had slowed to a kilometre a second. *Ten kilometres to surface.* He checked the magnetic array, it looked solid. Hesitantly he gave it thirty percent power, watching the *Malefactor* for any uncertain signs. Contrails plumed off of the airbrakes, but she seemed to be holding. Stress levels were tolerable. He increased to fifty percent, sixty, seventy, eighty... The hull began to shudder, tiny tremors fluttering through the fins. Aldric eased the power down. *75 percent.*

The magnetic array slowed their speed significantly, yet it was still too great. *Five kilometres to surface.* East of Lannachlor, great black mountains wound jaggedly north, their angry peaks vanishing into clouds. He was roughly level with the snowy Enowyrth to his right, hurtling into the wide valley of Erioth. He could see glittering cities and small parish towns below, wondering if the people there knew the certain death that roared so close above their quiet homes. Lush jungle forests and rolling green plains rose up to greet them as they sailed ever lower into the valley. *This will be bad.* Taking a deep breath, he gave the command to reverse engines.

The misty trees of the Cwarri Glour ranged out on Aldric's right, while the ancient mountain fortress Craic Morran rose in front of him. And, just beyond that, the empty heath of the Carrac Fold. The droning thunder of the destroyer's great engines suddenly grew quiet, masked by the wail of the wind. Aldric coasted beside the destroyer, gliding peacefully over a sleepy landscape that hadn't quite woken up. Aldric's heart thudded in his chest, his mouth dry. He flexed his fingers on the yoke, all his muscles tense. There was nothing more he could do. If the engines couldn't handle the strain, they would explode, and the destroyer would be toppled off course—and at this range, it would probably take him with it.

A booming roar suddenly cut above the wind, crescendoing in a mechanical howl that reverberated through Aldric's ship. He watched his visor's readout—*the engines are reversing.* The *Malefactor* began shedding speed dramatically. *Hold on, hold on...* Aldric quietly prayed to himself. The immense bulk of the destroyer quivered under the terrible forces, but it was too late to halt the reverse. *They'll either hold, or they won't,* he thought, clenching his jaw tightly. *One kilometre to surface.*

The ground seemed very close now. The forest streaked past beyond his starboard wing, the destroyer blazing on his port. *Seconds left...* He would have to pull away at the last moment, making sure the destroyer kept its even approach as long as possible.   The fortress city of Craic Morran rolled distantly past, hazy in the morning fog. From here it was all open heath, stretching out before them in leagues of barren wetlands. His comm light flashed.

"We're on your wing, Spectre One," a voice crackled through. It was his personal call sign, and Aldric looked up to see five Starlings streak overhead, their silver bodies blue and gold in the morning light. The Royal Air Wing.

"Good to see you, captain," Aldric said, turning his attention back to the destroyer.

The ground blurred below, green and brown, black water, yellow fens and marshland, one continuous stream of colour. Pulling back slightly, Aldric could see the deep prow of the destroyer whizzing just above the ground. *This is it!* Aldric jerked the yoke back, his fighter veering up sharply, throwing him back hard. He pulled up and away, going into a steep climb, blue sky above. The navigation uplink flickered off.

TWO

PARALLELS

Arem pulled off his helmet and let it drop beside him, clattering dully. He removed his harness and leaned forward, resting his face in his hands. He breathed deeply, inhaling the stale air of the cockpit, feeling the ache in his shoulders, the soreness in his neck. Dim blue light from the hangar trickled in through the canopy, casting shadows through the cockpit. His suit made a soft wrinkling noise as he stretched.

He smashed his fist into the console, kicking his helmet and sending it clattering into the canopy. *Hahka! I blacked out.* He wanted to be angry with Aldric, but he couldn't. It was his failure, his shortcoming. *These Starlings,* he thought. They didn't handle like the old fighters, like the Signet. You could *feel* what you were doing in those ships. With this new fighter? He huffed. You couldn't feel your limits.

Anyways, Aldric wouldn't tell me if he had *blacked out,* Arem thought, recalling his brother's haughty, superior voice. He was so dignified and composed for the palace courtiers and those damned Valorí; he saved his condescension for Arem. *I shouldn't have said anything.* He didn't know why he'd told Aldric, what did he care? Aldric had won, the reason didn't matter. He always won. Arem felt childish, obsessing over something he knew Aldric wasn't even thinking about. Aldric never thought about these things. So why did he? *Because I lost. Gods!* how he hated that, it got through to something deep inside, wormed its way into his gut and wouldn't let him forget.

He tried to recall his training with the Valorí when he was younger, tried to remember the mind-composing techniques that suffused those warrior druids with their formidable battle calm. *"Denial is the root of all unhappiness,"* he remembered. What did that tell him? *Nothing.* He continued. *"Acceptance of pain and fear is the path to self-actualisation. No person is only one thing: he is many."* He felt his mind wandering, tried to focus. *"Change is my armour, adaptation my weapon."*

He folded his hands in his lap, controlling his breath. His head throbbed, lingering pain from his flight. He tried to ignore it. *"Pain and fear, these are the bed-mates of joy and peace—their contrast is the measure of their worth. When one is at your side, the other waits for your return. Suffering arises from loss, from attachment to things that pass—to things we do not control.*

But suffering is the herald of joy, because you would feel no pain at a thing's departure if it were not dear to you. Suffering tells you that you are human, and that is a good thing to be reminded of."

Arem pulled his gloves off and undid the straps of his breast flap, letting it fall loosely over his chest. *"Feel your hesitation: unbind it."* He stood and climbed to the rear of the Starling, releasing the hatch and dropping to the tarmac below. *Unbind, hell!*

Heat radiated from the engine pylons above his head, the metal ticking as it cooled. The hangar was carved from the rock of an immense cavern deep beneath the Imperial palace, its darkened walls stretching hundreds of metres into the gloom above. The hangar entrance was at the far end of a long runway that opened onto a sheer limestone cliff face high above Lake Nimaine. From that distant mouth, wan grey light filtered into to the murky hangar, mingling with the mellow blue of the low-hanging service lights. Arem's boots clicked on the concrete, echoing off the listless hulls of ships in their berths.

Unbind! he thought. It was the mantra of the Valorí, the creed that accompanied their every action. "Unbind, reduce, objectify. Certainty is death," he said aloud. *I couldn't have done anything differently, anyone would lose consciousness at fifty eight Gs.* His face twisted. *Aldric didn't.* He clenched his fists, then unclenched, feeling foolish. He'd always thought revealing your anger was weak, and anytime he let it escape, he *felt* weak. Anger happened inside, and that's where it should stay. *Control. Unbind.* Despite himself, he swore. It was louder than he wished, his voice reverberating through the hangar. He shook his head, resisting the urge to look around and see if anyone had heard.

Arem passed glowing berths where mechanics stooped low over their torches, silhouetted grotesquely under arching fountains of blue sparks. Ships rested in their berths, their magnetic repulsors suspending them a few metres in the air; to Arem they looked like nothing so much as insects, poised and ready to strike. He took a deep breath. The air was musty, grimy, the chalk smell of wet limestone. Even through the steel reinforced walls, Arem could smell the dampness of the jungle seeping in through the cavern walls. Humidity was everywhere on this world.

From the darkened heights above him, Arem caught dim voices, and looking up he saw a few pilots on the gantries above. They were gathered around one of the Starling fighters, and he could hear their laughter at intervals. The First Wing of the Royal Flight Corps—called the Emperor's Hammer—was routinely on exercise, permanently stationed at the palace.

Arem had flown with them a few times, but he found the repetitive drills boring. He thought of Aldric then, who had spent days and weeks training with them when he was younger. Last year, when the Starling had replaced the aging Signet fighter, Aldric had been asked to perform a demonstration with the Corps—Aldric, but not Arem. *I don't need to waste my time stuck in a cockpit,* he thought dismissively. *It isn't as if* I'll *ever go to war.*

Observing Arem's approach, a nearby controller stood straighter and saluted, clutching his right fist above his heart. He was a middle aged man with sandy hair and a lean face, Arem recognised him.

"My Lord," the man said genially. He was standing over a stooping mechanic who had his back turned to them.

"Hail, Gavin," Arem returned. He jerked his thumb over his shoulder, "Will you have someone take a look at my Starling? The controls felt sloppy, I don't like how it responds."

The controller nodded his head apologetically. "At once my Lord."

Arem thought he detected a patronising note in the controller's voice. He'd never liked the man; he seemed too dignified for his position. What did he have to be proud of?

Arem decided to let it go, maybe he was just tired. He looked down at the mechanic. He was wearing a large helmet that enclosed his entire head. A concentrated glow outlined the man as he used a torch to mend a panel beneath an aging shuttle. The shuttle was at least thirty years old, its bulbous belly bathed in blue light. The mechanic hadn't noticed Arem's approach and continued to work.

Following Arem's gaze the controller looked surprised and reached to tap the mechanic on the shoulder. Arem put a hand on the controller's arm and shook his head. "Forget it," he said. "Inform me when you've finished the repairs."

The man nodded and saluted again. "Of course my Lord."

Arem made his way towards a service lift that would take him up to the Imperial Palace. Or maybe he should go to the Talos Quarter? The girls were there always happy to see him. *Gods of the Abyss! I need to forget about this, about everything.* He felt the weight in his shoulders and flexed, twisting from side to side. *Soon, things will be different.*

Without warning, the hangar lights flickered red and klaxons began wailing. Mechanics dropped their tools and stood, looking around. He turned, searching for a deck commander. He spotted one running to the aft of the hangar, down the long runway.

"Commander, what is it? What's happened?" Arem called, catching up and falling into pace.

The man saluted respectfully despite his exertions. "My Lord, there's been an accident. We don't have the full details, the Royal Air Wing's been raised."

"Why?" Arem asked, alarmed. The cavern was growing lighter as they approached the mouth of the runway. The air was heavy and wet, clinging to him as he ran. "There isn't an attack, is there?"

"No my Lord, we don't think so," the man managed between breaths. "A destroyer jumped into Home Space, she was badly damaged, she's fallen into the atmosphere."

"She's *what?*" Arem asked, nearly halting mid stride. "Has she crashed? Why didn't Attendant Fleet stop her?"

They were nearly at the entrance now. Several dozen people were already gathered on the protruding catwalk, officers and pilots and deck crews, all talking loudly. "My Lord, Prince Aldric ordered Attendant Fleet to stand down. The Siege Batteries are tracking the destroyer, and we now await his word to fire."

Arem sneered. *Smug bastard. Thought he could save the day, did he?* They stopped at the end of the runway on a gantry that extended out away from the cliff, personnel parting for Arem as he made his way to the front. The air was denser outside, though a slight breeze rushed up the cliff from the lake below. Lake Nimaine shone stilly as the sun rose higher in the sky, small yachts and cargo vessels reflected in its dark waters.

High in the atmosphere Arem caught sight of a blazing ball of light, a falling star crawling through the pale western sky. It was much too slow to be a meteor, though Arem knew the deceptive speeds betrayed by those brilliant flames. In a few moments it disappeared into clouds, and then vanished from sight.

"Clear the deck!" A strident voice called out. "Launch pattern in progress!" It was a deck commander, standing tall at the end of the gantry in a dark blue service uniform. He waited until the deck crews and other spectators had cleared beneath the lee shield.

Arem stepped in last, keeping his eyes fixed on the last point he'd seen the flaming destroyer. A faint glow rolled through the clouds, almost like lightning. The deck commander nodded to the launch controller and ducked under the shield next to Arem. A moment later a Starling fighter screamed out of the hangar, followed seconds later by two, three, four more.

Arem watched them go, their distinctive howl fading away as they dissolved into the sticky morning air. *Are you up there, dear brother?* He thought, his forehead furrowing as he scanned the pale skies. *Are you in danger?* He couldn't suppress a smile.

THREE

A PALACE IN THE CLOUDS

Circling above the destroyer, Aldric thumbed his comlink. "Are there any survivors?" He reigned in the Starling and dropped his speed, banking low over the sagging hull of the *Malefactor*. He glanced backwards at the seething trough the destroyer had carved through the heath. Trailing wreckage smouldered as small grass fires burned away from the remains.

Rising from the east, the sun poured thick and golden through the haunted hollows over the Carrac Fold, driving away the lingering morning mist. The damage to Aldric's wing was worse than he had first thought, the flying debris tearing through control systems that were now failing. He struggled to keep his altitude, fighting the yoke hard to keep the Starling from spilling over into the heath.

"We're not sure, we believe so, my Lord," the captain of the lead salvage ship responded. "We're containing external fires now, it'll be a while before we can get teams in there. Scans are having trouble making a clear reading, but it looks like there may be survivors trapped deep inside."

Exhaustion crept over Aldric, and he did his best to shrug it off. "Very well, captain. My ship is damaged, I'm returning to the palace. Keep me informed."

He made one last pass over the hull of the destroyer. Dozens of rescue ships had already landed and were busy putting out fires. Aldric was amazed at the response time. There were already hundreds of people on the ground around the destroyer, wading through the marsh and setting up support tents and emergency triage centres.

Aldric wanted to rub his head, his temples were pounding with the latent strain of his flight. Keeping the Starling airborne required both of his hands though, so he settled for sitting up straighter and flexing his back muscles, relieving some of the tension. At a fifth of his normal flight speed it took Aldric nearly forty-five minutes of strenuous manoeuvring to finally reach Lake Nimaine and the jungle city of Chaldrea, capital of the Vassaryan Empire.

Aldric wrestled the controls, circling up around the royal palace that was perched atop an island plateau in the middle of the lake. "Spectre One this is control—you seem to have taken some damage Sire," a concerned voice chimed in from the conn-tower.

"I did, but I'll manage," Aldric said. Landing would be tricky. "Have the cables out, I'm aiming for the maglev chute. And clear the deck, my wing's hit and I can't keep it straight."

"Spectre One, chute four is prepped for your landing, deck is cleared and catchers are standing by," the controller said. "We have the grav-net armed."

The palace radiated in the morning light as Aldric rounded the island to approach the cliff side hangar. The bay entrance was carved about three hundred metres above the lake and directly into the white limestone cliff face. It was a large opening, capable of handling an imperial corvette if needed, but it looked smaller than ever as Aldric tried to steady his Starling.

"Control to Spectre One, your approach is high, drop point-ten."

Cutting his ram drive to a tenth power, Aldric let his tail fall as he held his nose up, drifting down below the mouth of the hangar. "Control I'm coming in manual, I can't keep her lined up." His wing was pulling hard to port and he struggled to keep it lined up with the runway. He had a moment of grim humour as he imagined sailing past the chute and straight into the cliff face—the irony of demolishing two ships in one morning.

"Spectre One we're tracking you in, the pen is hot. Bring your tail up point-eight and fall off port-five. Stretch her legs."

"I've got it Control," Aldric said, dropping his landing gear. He was using every last ounce of strength and concentration to control the little fighter. He watched as the heads up display in his visor swayed and rolled as the Starling teetered from side to side, adjusting his course to stay in line with the runway. The display mapped a course in front of him that looked like a virtual tunnel, with green lines for a good approach, yellow for corrections needed, and red for a probable failure. His screen was glowing solid red.

"Spectre One, you're under the pen, pitch up one-seven and mark the roll." The controller's voice was steady, but Aldric could hear the tension. This could still go either way. But it was getting harder and harder to handle the little craft. He couldn't make another pass if he didn't get this right. He'd either hit the cliff, or have to swerve and ditch the Starling in the lake.

"I've got the pen under gun," Aldric said, nosing the Starling dead centre on the approach. He was just a little low, but right on course. That was good, but he knew it wouldn't mean anything if he came up under the deck.

"On sight, on sight Spectre One, spotter has you in the pen. Dump the foils and bring her in," the controller said.

Aldric dropped his foils, giving him some extra lift as he closed on the runway. The hangar bay yawned in front of him, and at the final moment he gave the engines a kick of power, launching himself up and over the lip of the protruding gantry and into the chute. But he overshot the deck, clipping his port landing strut and skidding into the hangar wall, dragging the wing against the bay through a storm of sparks. He was sure he missed the tail hook, and he saw the flash of light as the grav-net descended, feeling the maglev suddenly grip the fighter, the hull vibrating and humming as it jerked to a stop. The smell of burning metal was overpowering.

Aldric shook his head, fumbling with the latches under his chin and tugging off his helmet. He blew out a long breath, his heart pounding. The engines whined, spooling down and sounding like an angry swarm of insects. His pulse thudded in his ears. He couldn't really believe he'd landed, or that he was sitting here right now and everything was ok. The realization came flooding through him and he felt dizzy.

Aldric watched airmen and ground crews rushing to his fighter, emergency vehicles surrounding him in seconds. He tried to slow his breathing, clenching and unclenching his fists. He watched the crews swarming around his ship and he braced himself. Wrenching the hatch open, he hopped out of the Starling, steadying himself as his legs wavered. A roar of cheers and applause burst from the deck crews and officers. In a moment he was surrounded, rescue teams shouting and clamouring around him until he couldn't move. He might have welcomed the celebration another time, but he was too fatigued to meet the jubilant crews with any enthusiasm.

A quarter of an hour later Aldric arrived at the operations center, where he was met by a sobering council of the Admiralty. Military attachés from the Royal Navy joined the chiefs of staff from the Circle of Amren—the Danarean secret intelligence agency—and their grim faces were a stark contrast to the greeting he'd received moments before.

Looking around the operations room he marvelled at the pandemonium. The once peaceful command centre was now a swarm of activity, buzzing with communications and tech officers, junior staff and others Aldric couldn't even name, all flying frantically around the room trying to make sense of the situation. Aldric made his way to the senior staff gathered at a large command table in the centre of the room. A strategic overlay was illuminated with the numerous fleet deployments highlighted in glowing green, and suspected Raeth deployments in sinister red.

Time blurred as Aldric gave his debriefing, recounting the morning events in excruciating detail. Yet after he had finished, no one could arrive at a consensus. No hard data had been recovered from the *Malefactor*, and the convoy it was escorting had vanished. Everyone's best guess assumed it was an attack by the Raeth.

Chaos ensued as the general staff and Admiralty argued over where to deploy the fleet, what kind of weapons had been used, whether proper escort procedure had been followed and a myriad of other bureaucratic minutiae

Aldric found pointless. And of course foremost on everyone's mind seemed to be who was responsible for the disaster. *Someone will lose their commission over this,* Aldric thought, though he doubted the real culprits would ever be found. Clearly no one had been prepared for this. Aldric was as shocked as any of the top military leaders, and although he was eager to know what had happened, there simply wasn't enough information to act on. The fleets would be put on heightened alert and convoys would be under lockdown. But these were defensive measures. For now, there would be no retaliation.

With his debriefing finally over, Aldric left, aching for some peace and quiet. He knew the day would be long, and it had already been a restless night before he'd given up on sleep and taken his fighter out this morning. The members of the Admiralty hadn't dared rebuke Aldric for countermanding their orders about the *Malefactor*, but it was obvious they weren't pleased either. He couldn't really blame them. He'd just proven to a room full of ranking senior staff that they'd been dead wrong in their assessment of the destroyer.

The lift from the bowels of the operations room brought Aldric speedily up through the many floors of the palace, opening with a quiet whoosh before a lofty veranda. Polished stone floors in interlacing patterns of black agate curved away to both sides, and yawning windows set in heavy stone were framed with deep purple curtains that gathered in thick mounds on the floor. Aldric stepped out onto a terrace near his room on the top level.

Leaning on the balustrade, he looked out over the cliff below, his grey eyes scanning the jungle out to the ragged ivory shore. Leafy green ivy embraced the stonework, its leaves hanging stilly in the warm dawn air as the sun climbed greedily into the sky. Sweat was already beginning to bead on his forehead. The morning air was sweet, and he relished the moment, looking out to the lake beyond.

The palace and capital city were built on three large islands near the centre of the lake. The Imperial City Chaldrea was built on Callas Andunn, the largest of the three. It was the oldest city in Galinor—possibly the oldest on the planet. It rose on a gradual plain from jungled shores to a summit several hundred metres above the water, with a steep cliff on the highest side. The city was built on the slope in seven fortified terraces, each smaller than the last, rising with the island. The highest tier on the hilltop was butted up against the cliff, the fortified walls resting atop the sheer limestone rock face.

The next island was Callas Baltan, a long, low, flat island with many farms and plantations where the aristocratic Erolan kept some of their vast estates. The third and smallest island, Callas Waith, was the home of the royal palace Dur Enskai. White cliffs jutted up from the lakebed to create a craggy pinnacle nearly five hundred metres high, and ten times that across. The palace and the lush grounds spread out over the plateau, surrounded by a formidable curtain wall that braced the cliffs on every side. Connecting each of the islands was the ancient bridge Gaeliath, a colossal stone relic as old as Chaldrea itself.

Hearing a rustle of leaves Aldric looked around. A jet-black razorcat leapt onto the balustrade and padded over to him, tail held high, muscles rolling under lustrous fur.

"What's up Cipher?" Aldric said, reaching out his hand. The razorcat paused and squinted, sniffing Aldric's fingers, pointing his tufted ears backwards. Apparently satisfied, Cipher rolled his head under Aldric's palm, purring loudly. Aldric scratched his ears and the big cat flopped down onto his side, sunlight revealing iridescent stripes so dark they looked purple. Aldric rubbed his belly as Cipher nipped at his fingers playfully. Even when playing, Aldric was wary of the four centimetre claws. Cipher looked up when Aldric paused, making a low whuffling sound and grasping his hand with his big paws.

"Come here buddy," Aldric said, picking Cipher up and lifting him away from the edge of the balcony. It was a straight drop to the shore half a kilometre below. He stroked the big cat, smiling and feeling some of his stress dissolve as he cradled the purring bundle. Cipher was just over thirty kilograms of muscle, but he still liked to be held, and he licked Aldric's hand with his rough tongue, his green eyes blinking slowly.

Only days ago Aldric had ridden out through the fells near Bailynn, with Cipher sitting there in his lap on the apala as they trotted along. Aldric had never known any cat, even a razorcat, that wasn't afraid of apalas—from their massive hooves and horns, to their whinnying and sheer size. Yet Cipher had to be wherever Aldric was, and seemed to like the adventure. When the prince was at the palace, the razorcat traded the open moors for the gardens and jungles around the lofty island plateau, hunting at his leisure. He often left his trophies outside Aldric's door—or on occasion—in his bed. More than once Aldric had woke to find his sheets covered in feathers, or to discover a bloody corpse of some mangled creature beside him with Cipher nearby, panting happily.

Leaning on the balustrade Aldric let his head drop, closing his eyes. This morning had been a trial, but he knew the real ordeal would come later when he met with his father. He was certain the emperor wouldn't look favourably on his interference with the *Malefactor*, or its destruction. Added to the humiliation of having no one to blame, Leopold would be in a black mood indeed. His father would regard this as a personal affront and would be more concerned with how it affected his image, rather than what it meant for Vassarya and his people. He would take action, but it would be from a position of indignity, not justice. *Vanity seldom submits to reason,* Aldric thought. But all that would come later.

The last several days were trying, on top of what had been the most strenuous months of Aldric's life. It was the eve of the Dhemorgal festival, and he was to champion the Imperial House in the grand arena of the Coliseum. He'd spent every day for months training at the Asaani temple in Chaldrea with Bahir Danu. Bahir was a Valorí battlemaster and captain of the emperor's royal guards, as well as Aldric's mentor in the ways of *craidath.* There was no one more skilled in the ancient fighting techniques of the Valorí than Bahir, and under his rigorous lessons Aldric had sparred and battled and grappled for many hours each day, retiring only after utter exhaustion.

His muscles ached and his temples were throbbing. That would pass, and so he drove it from his mind, stroking Cipher. *We may only grow in opposition to resistance,* he recited to himself as he avoided the fatal mind-trap of self-pity. It was a quote from the Valorí mantras, one of his favourites. He let his mind fall into a meditative calm, releasing endorphins, sending his muscles signals to relax. He detached himself from his surroundings, falling into a light trance as he recovered depleted energy.

Despite his upbringing in the bustling city of Chaldrea, Aldric was most at peace in nature. *Man is an animal of nature; let his soul be rekindled in the woods of his fathers. There is company in the forest where no man dwells, and society where no path leads.* The cheerful calls of kala birds floated up from the cliff side where they nested, and Aldric could clearly see their garish orange and blue and green plumage in his mind's eye. Cipher perked up his ears too, listening intently. The Asaani called this internal awareness *aina,* or clairvoyance, but Aldric wasn't so sure. He'd always had a vivid imagination; that didn't mean he had a preternatural gift. Sighing, he straightened up and let Cipher jump down, wincing as sharp claws dug into his chest.

Someone coughed and cleared their throat behind him. "I received word," said a rasping voice, "that one of our ships was lost this morning, and our beloved prince risked life and limb to bring her safely down."

Aldric turned around to see a robed figure, silhouetted in the doorway. Chiron, the Palace Seneschal, bowed and stepped forward. "It was a princely thing you did, and very rash," he said, moving to Aldric's side. "What are the crew of a destroyer to the life of a prince?"

Aldric straightened. "Then there were survivors?"

Chiron inclined his head slightly. "There were one hundred twenty-six people still on board, trapped in the stern. Seventy-five of them are alive and are being treated."

"Seventy-five?" Aldric's head whirled and he had to lean against the rail. "I knew it," he said under his breath.

"Oh?" Chiron said, arching his bushy eyebrows. Though he was old beyond reckoning, Chiron never seemed to age. His was a long, sallow face, with deep set eyes above prominent cheekbones, and mangy black brows that curled inwards. His protruding chin, high forehead and narrow, pointed nose reminded Aldric of an old grey fox; wise in the ways of the world, and yet somehow sad. His bronzed skin was a leathery patchwork of wrinkles, yet he did not look old: merely well-travelled.

Chiron was like a grandfather to Aldric, and as far as Aldric knew, had been the seneschal since before his own father was even born. Myth was robed in dark legend, and secrets followed Chiron wherever he went. He served as the emperor's most intimate advisor, yet was invisible when not at his side. He was never seen in public, and his personal habits were a mystery to all save the emperor. Yet he'd been Aldric's private tutor for many years, and Aldric had come to rely upon his judgement, and even his friendship.

Aldric noticed the lingering pause and looked up. "It was just a feeling," he said. "I couldn't *see* anything, I just noticed all the remaining hatches and figured something was wrong." He shook his head. "It just felt... wrong."

"*Aina* is intuition first, my Prince—vision second." Chiron's voice was rich and gravelly, with deep undertones that sometimes made Aldric's eyes well up. "The crews of Attendant Fleet also saw those hatches."

"I don't have clairvoyance, Chiron. I just don't, I never have. Having a hunch is different, everyone has those."

"Not everyone risks their life on a hunch, my Lord." He removed his cowl and looked out over the lake. "Though," he said, casting a disapproving eye towards Aldric, "Even with *aina,* I would still think you were impossibly reckless."

"*Stupid* is the word you're looking for, I think," Aldric said.

Chiron tut-tutted. "It's not my place to put words in the prince's mouth."

"Chiron, I can't put myself above my subjects. A life is a life, and one life for seventy five isn't a foolish gamble—it's an obligation."

"You have your grandmother's audacity, my prince," Chiron said coolly.

Aldric smiled. That was a compliment, at least. He'd never known the Empress Dowager Alexandra, but she'd accomplished many daring triumphs during her reign. Far more than his own father had, he thought.

"Yet you lack her strength and clarity of vision," Chiron said, reproving Aldric's smile.

Aldric ignored him. "Chiron, that destroyer... it was brutally attacked," he said. "I've never seen any of our ships so badly damaged."

Chiron stared out towards Chaldrea. It radiated opulence, yet with none of the vulgarity of other capital cities. The purple heights of the Enowyrth

Mountains rose behind the city, eternally capped in snow. It was a striking contrast: the oppressive green heat of the jungle and the austere, boreal climes of the mountains.

"The Raeth are resourceful," Chiron said finally.

Aldric shook his head. "No, no this wasn't resourcefulness, this was total devastation. None of our ships have ever come back like that. Our spies have never reported anything with that kind of firepower." He slapped his hand on the balustrade. "It's a miracle it came back at all. What do the Raeth have that can do that to an Imperial destroyer?"

"The mark of survivalists, especially against great odds, is innovation, and the unexpected. Consistency is extinction," Chiron said.

"Don't quote Valorí Mantras at me, Chiron," Aldric said. "I want to know how a band of pirates in dilapidated freighters could destroy an Imperial warship."

Chiron shrugged his shoulders. "They adapted."

"That isn't an answer." His nonchalance was irksome. "The Raeth are getting out of hand," Aldric said. "This must be dealt with."

"How, my Prince? Our great fleet—the Sciphere—is deployed, we have no more ships."

"And now we have one less," Aldric said. "And the crew..." An Adamant class destroyer was manned by over four thousand officers and crewmen. How many hadn't made it back?

"A prince must learn to accept sacrifices," Chiron said without emotion. "Nothing of value can be maintained without sacrifices. How many live in the Imperium? Are their lives not worth a sacrifice? Not worth one destroyer? Is that not the very purpose of our Navy? Of our marvellous war-machines?"

"You treat the matter too lightly. Should we write it off, ignore it, just because it was a necessary sacrifice? Lost in the line of duty?"

"Not at all," Chiron said. "But you are suffocating yourself with thoughts of vengeance, of victimisation. This is an impossible state in which to govern. React from logic, not from feeling. This is not an injustice."

"Life isn't weighed on a scale, Chiron. It's ineffable, invaluable, inca—"

"Your idealism is hubris, my liege." Chiron interrupted. "A degoll will gnaw off its own leg before dying in a trap. It is a sacrifice, survival. The degoll is not indignant to trade a limb for its life." He turned a thoughtful eye on the young prince. His dark hair shone in the sunlight. "You will be crippled by your humanity if you cannot see the distinction, my Liege."

"Lives are not resources, not bartering chips. I will not consider my subjects as leverage," Aldric said. He didn't approve of Chiron's amoral approach to government.

"Oh ho!" cried Chiron. "And how do you presume wars are won, Your Grace? How did your grandmother defeat the Illarien invaders, defeat your great uncle Aethric's army? Did she will them away? No? Perhaps she gave them lessons in the ideals of humanism and virtue, eh?" His tone was sincere, open, but Aldric knew better. Chiron never sided with Aldric, on any point, no matter his own personal views. He would argue simply to challenge an opinion.

"No," Chiron barked gruffly, answering his own question. "No, she used her *army*. She used brute strength, because man is an animal, and he doesn't understand words; he understands being beaten bloody—beaten until he has no choice but to submit. Man understands *violence*." He emphasised the word, hissing out the final consonant. "She *leveraged*, as you say, the lives of her soldiers. She protected the body, by cutting off the hand." He raised his hands in the air, turning them about. "And see, the body lives. And the hands are regrown, and the wound is forgotten."

"Soldiers are different," Aldric argued. "They contract warfare, it's their profession."

"Ah, how gallantly you sacrifice your subject's now," Chiron smirked. "You see? You don't even believe what you're saying, you say it because you are afraid of appearing heartless."

"You're twisting my words," Aldric said.

"Am I? Or am I showing you your own inconsistencies? If an army is different, then why do you mourn the loss of this one destroyer? Did those crewmen—those soldiers—did they not contract warfare also?" He ran a hand over his face, rubbing his chin. "An empire is no different than nature, my Prince."

"No," Aldric replied, seeing the turn of the conversation and knowing he would find no peace. "An empire is founded on philosophy and human nobility. It is the opposite of nature, it climbs above the animalism of nature," he said. "It imposes rules, and order, and alleviates the chaos of human greed."

"How you malign nature," Chiron said. "Very well. What is an empire then, Prince Aldric?"

"It is a monarchy," Aldric said, knowing the answer was insufficient, but not wishing to elaborate.

"And what is a monarchy?"

"It is a hierarchy, it is the nobles born to lead the rest."

"No no, what is it literally? What does it look like—what is the shape of it, the structure?"

Aldric thought for a moment. "It is the most powerful at the top, the supporting class beneath. It flows from top to bottom, bottom to top, the few leading the many," he said, drawing a triangle in the air with his finger.

"Ah, I see, very good," Chiron said, nodding. "So tell me, my prince, what is nature?"

Aldric stopped. He realised he was trapped. He cursed inwardly, trying to think quickly. "'All animals function according to their purpose—so does man think, and thereby achieve his distinction,'" he quoted.

"The *Dol Regas* will not spare you an explanation. You cannot avoid the question because you don't want to be wrong," Chiron said. "You will learn nothing this way." He studied Aldric for a moment, the tenseness in his shoulders, the distant look in his eyes. He said finally, "What do you gain by your reluctance? I am not your judge, I am the curator of your mind; I must prune the aberrations before they take root. A prince cannot afford to think such things. I would expect this of your brother, but you should know better."

Aldric felt the truth in his words, but his pride would not let him concede.

"'Certainty is death,'" Chiron said dryly. "...If you insist on quoting scripture."

Aldric pursed his lips together and blew out, wondering if his admission would satisfy Chiron. "An empire is like nature because the few, the powerful, claw their position to the top, ruling over the rest fiercely...violently when necessary. Yet they cannot survive without the herd animals—the people—beneath them."

"People must be ruled," Chiron said quietly.

"People must be ruled." Aldric intoned.

Chiron nodded approvingly. He looked over the young body, the broad shoulders, strong back, lean contours; the prince had the potential of a brilliant leader. If only his mind could be brought back from the decadence of his father's reign, rid of these pitiful vanities and his own festering self-doubt.

"Anyways," Aldric said, standing, unzipping the collar of his flight suit to mid-chest and revealing a skin tight mesh fabric beneath. "The real question is if they have these ships—whatever they are—where did they get them? Where did the money come from?"

Chiron allowed him the change in topic. "Their wealth from raiding convoys can't be significant enough. Fleets are expensive."

"It's taken two decades and the revenue of an entire empire, half a dozen planets, to field a fleet the size of the Sciphere and equip them with enough firepower to destroy a moon. Where could a nomadic band of asteroid dwelling scavengers raise such capital?"

"Where indeed," Chiron said.

"They're being supported, then? An organisation here on Errolor, or perhaps Allria?"

Chiron cast his eyes downwards in thought. "There are many who would benefit by a change in regime, or from the profits of the stolen cargo. Bribes, kickbacks, it's all possible."

"Yes, but who stands to gain the most?"

"Who would benefit most from your father's death?"

"Mal'Dreghen," Aldric said, feeling anger at the thought.

Chiron nodded. "I wouldn't be surprised to learn that he sponsored the Raeth in some way. It's the perfect weapon to wield against the emperor. Mal'Dreghen can declare the emperor is ineffectual while the Raeth are killing Vassaryan citizens."

"And all the while he appears compassionate and concerned," Aldric said, the weight of the realisation growing inside him.

"It's a position which costs him nothing."

"His profits from the Dhemorahn church must be staggering," Aldric said, chewing on his lip. "But he must realise that if anyone considered this, he would be one of the first suspects. There aren't many who could support such an operation."

"The Erolan."

"I thought of that too," Aldric said. It wasn't hard to imagine, though if it were true, the ramifications would be terrible.

"The wealth and influence of the Erolan is vast. What they lack now in military power, they make up for ten-fold in political ambition. They own the land, they own the wealth, and anyone can be bought. The aristocracy have fed on their resentment for half a century, plenty of time to fabricate some labyrinthine plot of revenge," Chiron said.

"If the Great Houses united against the emperor…" Aldric trailed off.

"It would be the bloodiest civil war in the history of the Vassaryan Empire."

"The Houses wouldn't stand a chance," Aldric said. "That was the whole point of the War of the Dukes: they have no military, nothing to counter the Imperial Navy and the Sciphere, let alone the Grand Army."

"That's what's troubling," Chiron replied. "They wouldn't make their move unless they were confident of success. So where will the strike come from? Which hand holds the dagger?" Chiron waved his finger. "We've already had a taste of their power, and clearly we were unprepared. What else lies in waiting?"

"If the Erolan can't be trusted, then what's the alternative? Destroy the aristocracy completely and leave a tyrant king in their place—a dictator for an empire? The triangle of power would become a pillar," he said, drawing a line in the air from top to bottom.

"No, my Prince," Chiron replied. "The answer is to understand the nature of people, and not to allow the situation to disintegrate as your father has.

The Erolan is necessary—their dominance over the people permits the emperor in turn to dominate them; there are rulers at every level, and the people don't feel so oppressed," Chiron said.

"Still," Aldric said, "I don't believe the archduke is involved."

"No, curiously enough, Archduke Raynard has been quite loyal to your family. He is one of the few the Erolan hasn't been able to reach. Being the archduke of Allria is a temptation that would drive most men to commit rebellion. Yet Raynard has been a faithful ally. Such loyalty is uncommon in my experience."

"You don't trust him, then?" Aldric asked.

"I do, but he's an anomaly. And in politics, anomalies are highly suspect. Honest men are often more worrisome than dishonest men, because honour is not a quality that can be bought; its rewards are immaterial."

Aldric considered what might happen if the archduke defected. He ruled Errolor's sister planet, Allria, as regent under the emperor. That kind of power put him in a position nearly equal to the emperor himself, and if Raynard chose to side against the throne… Aldric swallowed. Yet he was a battle hardened veteran who the emperor had trusted and relied upon more times than Aldric could remember. The emperor owed his life to Raynard, as did Aldric and Arem.

"If he can't be trusted, then does my father have any allies at all?"

"Oh, he can be trusted. And your father does have allies, but they will be of little use should he lose the support of the Erolan."

"Gaiban Morrigan," Aldric said, though he knew she was of no political value.

"The High Lady of the Rock would not intervene except to save your father's life. Calling pacifists to war is a… well, I think that might actually be the metaphor I'm looking for."

"If Mal'Dreghen influences half the empire, then she must influence the other," Aldric replied.

"The Asaani look to her as a spiritual leader. She is no warlord, nor would the Asaani rise up and take arms should the blast of war sound through these green hills," Chiron said, waving his hand expansively. "The Valorí are sworn to protect the emperor, and they will. But there are only a thousand of them."

"I should rather fight with a thousand Valorí than a million dragoons," Aldric said defiantly.

"Be that as it may," Chiron said, continuing, "we may not look to her for aide should the need arise."

"This is an absurd position to be in," Aldric said. "Removing the Dhemorahns from parliament wasn't enough: the entire religion should have been disbanded. It's the perfect platform for war-mongering demagogues like Mal'Dreghen to take a stand against the emperor."

"The Empress Dowager was wise to remove the Dhemorahns from their seats of power, but you can't stop people from having their private thoughts. The Dhemorahn sect is very old, as old as the Asaani, and hardened by aeons of practise. There are many who oppose your grandmother's decision even now and it's no secret Mal'Dreghen uses this to his advantage."

"Chiron, he's just a man. Twenty years ago, who was he? Had anyone even heard his name? He gets up on his pulpit and shouts and waves his arms about and puts on a good show, but you'd have to be a fool to believe anything he says."

"Yet people *do* believe," Chiron said. "Is there anything more powerful than religion for holding people in thrall?" His eyes ran over Aldric's face, searching for understanding. "There has never been a king or emperor to contend with man's fear of eternity."

"Then perhaps we should make them," Aldric said.

Chiron watched him for a few moments. He spoke quietly then, changing his tact. "The wise ruler affects a great show of religiosity. It is far better to be perceived as a god *and* a king, than just a king."

"Our state has no religion," Aldric replied.

"But the people do," said Chiron. "The old monarchy was impotent from excessive simony and indulgence. Empress Alexandra was able to cut Dhemorahn ties and influence, but it cost her dearly, and the empire was nearly destroyed in the War of the Dukes. Emperor Leopold has been too lenient, too permissive—too forgiving—with those who oppose him; he prefers tolerance and peace."

"They dare not challenge him," Aldric said.

"They dare not? But my prince, they do." Chiron replied. "The emperor represents ultimate power. Power is never secure, never safe. People are close to him to take his power, not support him. Your empire is overgrown with weeds."

"A ruler is never carried by those beneath him: he elevates himself by standing on their backs," Aldric said, gazing out towards Chaldrea. It was one of the first lessons Chiron had taught Aldric when he began studying politics. It underpinned all of his other philosophies.

"Exactly," Chiron replied. "The people must be ruled, but they never wish to believe they are being ruled. Every man thinks himself a king. Your father has forgotten this; his mind is on festivals and celebrations, content to ignore Mal'Dreghen's fetial overtures so long as no one interrupts his parties. Corruption festers everywhere, my Prince," Chiron said. "The kingship is in peril. Mal'Dreghen will try to take that power for himself, of that you may be sure. Stability does not exist; it is a comfort-illusion. Only the weak persist in its belief, and they are kept weak by it."

"Yet the empire endures," Aldric said, turning once more to face Chiron. He could not tolerate the idea that the Fatherland was so vulnerable.

"Aldric, my Prince... You *will* be the emperor. That *will* happen." Chiron said, folding his hands beneath his robes. He patiently wet his thin lips. "Mal'Dreghen is not merely a whim of the people. He has become a fixture. Your father has done nothing to curb his ambition. Your birthright is in jeopardy."

"I would never submit to his authority, nor would the Erolan, despite what they may believe now, and the Mal is nothing without their help."

"Neither is your father," Chiron replied. "You see the danger of his position."

"The Erolan owe fealty to my father, Mal'Dreghen has no power of his own."

"Ah, yet you can already see his power. While the emperor hesitates and loses the confidence of the people, Mal'Dreghen incites more and more to his cause. The dukes will support your father as long as they can because he has been good to them. But the emperor is weak, and weakness doesn't inspire loyalty. If another magnate should appear, I'm afraid you might find yourself inheriting a throne under siege."

"The emperor has the only standing army in the system, let them rally outside the city walls and shout if they like."

"Armies can be crushed, Prince Aldric: influence isn't as easy to destroy. Besides, it is much safer with the people on your side. A defensive position always weakens the defender," Chiron said. "If the people are against you, it doesn't matter how thick your walls are. And the Valorí can only protect you, they cannot fight a war."

Aldric snorted, massaging his hand tiredly. "If the dukes and other lords owe so much to my father, then their gratitude ought to be worth something."

"Lords who are bought are not reliable, my Prince." Chiron said. "The emperor has been generous with his bribes, but that can only buy him peace. And as we see, peace is an illusion, merely the breath taken between axe strokes." Chiron paused, clearing his throat. "There is also the problem of the army and the Old Guard."

"They are obedient to the emperor," Aldric said.

"Perhaps," Chiron said. "But what does your instinct tell you?"

"That the Erolan has filled the army with officers who live in palaces, not barracks."

"Precisely. The Erolan doesn't need its own army: they have the Grand Army. And they remember all too well how your grandmother disarmed their families. The Old Guard may be officers of the army, but they're noble born, and ambitious."

"There's Craic Achran," Aldric said.

"Yes, but the Naval Academy was the Grand Marshal's idea, and your father took nearly twenty years to do anything about it. I told him many years ago that he needed a military academy to train officers independent of the Erolan. But the military has always been an institution of the aristocracy, one of the noble pursuits, and he wouldn't listen. Princes love to put on their polished suits of armour. Now I fear it may be too late."

"What an honourable world to inherit," Aldric said.

"You are the scion of a thousand generations, my Prince. This is their eternal legacy to you."

"And yet, I want nothing to do with it," Aldric said, anger rising in his voice. "When I sit in council, when I speak with the emissaries and lords, I think, my god! What liars are all around! What liars. I am here, in this palace, this royal place of my ancestors, spending my life learning to treat with liars and beggars... pretenders all! And oh, how sweetly they'll kiss my hand, and how low they'll bow, and they'll swear allegiance—their damned, undying allegiance. And I am so disgusted by every one of them. Where is the *nobility* in these nobles?"

"It is in *you*, my Prince," Chiron replied. "You must be the nobility they aspire to. You must be that greatness. Do you understand, Your Grace? The Imperial Seat is always but one emperor, *one life*, away from desolation—from vanishing."

"If I should fail, Arem would resume the kingship," Aldric said.

"Prince Arem is not ready to take the throne," Chiron said carefully. "His cares lie elsewhere, I fear."

"But I'm not *ready*," Aldric said, unable to express to Chiron the fear he felt. What right was it of his to govern? He was no better than the people he ruled, than any of the thousands of faces he passed daily in the streets as he rode through in his royal carriage. The universe would keep spinning if he were standing there in the streets instead, watching another face looking down on him from the carriage as it passed him by, from nowhere to nowhere again yet master of his doom from birth till death. Was he the chosen of the gods? Did the bloodline of Aronach the Great run through his veins?

What if it did? Aldric didn't feel any wiser, any more sure of himself or confident that he had an answer to the problems of his kingdom. His people looked to him for surety in themselves. How could he give this to them when he felt sure of nothing he did himself? The terrible loneliness only grew as he contemplated his obligations, what his father expected of him, and how his brother despised him. He couldn't win, no one was pleased and the isolation was maddening. Chiron might understand, but what difference did it make? The burden was his. How happy he would be to pass on his birthright to Arem, to anyone, and leave everything behind him. Duty was unavoidable. Damnable, crushing duty. His chest tightened as he tried to see a time when he would be free.

Aldric looked back to the jungle. He hadn't earned the right, and he didn't know what to do with it, nor did he want it. He tried to push the thoughts from his mind. Slowing his heartbeat, he took a long breath, calming his nerves. All he wanted, the thing he longed for most in the world, was to escape. The throngs of people, the adoration, the pomp and fanfare and honours... Aldric gazed out to the green fields of Callas Baltan, remembering mornings spent wandering through the drooping lullabane trees, their branches trailing in the water beside the sprawling plantations. Picking handfuls of wild grass and feeding it to the urocha and riding long legged apala bareback over the hills. He let out a sigh. That was his dream, to be free of the rigors of his office. He didn't deserve it, he didn't want it, and he felt trapped.

The memory rejuvenated Aldric, and he smiled despite his fear. When this was all over, he promised himself, he'd take the time to relive those moments again, his father be damned. There was so much of this world he loved, so much green and living. The goddess Ertu called to him, and he heard the voices of his ancestors harkening him back to the forests and jungles they'd once called home. He would answer that call when this was over.

Aldric nodded, pleased with his resolution. The morning fog was vanishing from the lake and Callas Andunn stood in green prominence above the waters. Aldric was reminded of the legend of the Tir Annath, those ancient tribal people from the north who had settled the region a thousand years before the line of emperors began.

The legend said that a mighty giant had swum into the middle of the lake in search of pearls for his wife. While he was searching, his wife had stolen away with her lover. Yet the giant continued to look for the pearls, even to this day, and the islands in the lake were the ridges of his mighty back as he stooped, peering through the deep waters. It was said that one day he would tire of looking and would rise again, and that Chaldrea would then be thrown into the water, sinking forever to the bottomless depths. Aldric hoped the giant didn't know there were no pearls in Lake Nimaine.

"I'm prepared, Chiron," Aldric said finally. "I don't want to be emperor, but I'm ready, and I will serve my people."

"Unwillingness to serve is no mark of ignominy, my Prince," Chiron said. "Emperor Magnus did not take up his mantle willingly, either." His eyes wrinkled softly. "Yet Chaldrea would not exist without his guidance, and the warring kingdoms might have remained forever divided."

"It will still be many years before I am emperor, but it will be with the memory of your words that I will rule," Aldric said, squeezing the old man's shoulder.

Chiron smiled, a strange expression on his sallow features. "My Lord, kingship is but a small task, in comparison to what you will face tomorrow."

"Oh gods," Aldric said, cringing. "The Dhemorgal." He shook his head. "I'd nearly forgotten."

The seneschal nodded. "It is a troubling matter for many, my Prince. You do not suffer alone."

"Oh no?" Aldric smiled. "Then I suppose I can count on seeing you next to me in the Coliseum tomorrow, eh? What's your weapon then, the darrac? Falcata? Tamka? Or will you mesmerise them with your incredible powers of senility?"

"My martial prowess is legendary," Chiron said, raising his fists in mock combat. "But if I defeated Mal'Dreghen's champion for you, it would look very bad indeed."

"That's alright, I don't think they could find a suit of armour that fit you anyways," Aldric said, patting the seneschal's belly.

Chiron drew back, feigning indignity. "It would be a shame," he said, drawing out the words, "if some fire sand from Erzog Koth were to find its way into your armour tomorrow."

Aldric laughed. "Wouldn't it? It would also be a shame if my father were to discover where his private stash of Skogmarra honey disappears every month."

Chiron's eyes grew wide. He tapped his chin thoughtfully. "A stalemate, I see."

Aldric smiled. He hopped onto the balustrade and let his legs hang over the side. The cliff was sheer, dropping straight down to the thin stretch of jungle below. Beyond the trees and a margin of beach, the cerulean waters of Lake Nimaine glittered, and he breathed in the fresh air.

"What a festival," Aldric said. The pennants and colourful banners that streamed from every street and building in Chaldrea could be seen from all the way from the palace. Celebrants had even festooned the mighty Gaeliath bridge that joined the three islands, its white statues decked in brilliant ribbons.

"Celebrating the defeat of the Asaani gods by the prophet Desedar…" Chiron trailed off thoughtfully. "A thousand years has passed since the last festival, I never imagined I'd see it revived. It is a powerful tool for the Mal."

"I don't understand why the Asaani don't do something," Aldric said. "The Dhemorahns would never just sit around quietly and let the Asaani insult them like this."

"But the Asaani don't care what the Mal does," Chiron said. "Their rights are not infringed upon, not yet, and so they continue as they always have."

"If only the Gaiban would protest, there would be a justification to intervene. The concerns of half the empire's citizens aren't trivial."

"If Gaiban Morrigan protested it would be an invitation for religious war."

Aldric looked at him, unbelieving. "There may be more Dhemorahns in the Chaldrea, but surely the minority isn't irrelevant."

"The outspoken will always overcome the passive. And what could she do, my Prince? She might be High Lady of the Rock, Seeress of the Asaani, and Mother of the Starborn, but the Mal would welcome her confrontation. Nonaggression is a powerful tool, and her reticence has incommoded the Mal many times."

"She won't petition the emperor either," Aldric said. "She hasn't even requested an audience. It's as though the Asaani are content to suffer whatever happens to them."

"The Valorí may be Asaani, but they care only for the emperor." Chiron said, touching the side of his chin with his forefinger. "This festival is nothing to them. The Valorí record time in lineages and kingdoms and epochs. This festival is but one short day, and for them it will come and go and all that will remain is their sacred duty to the emperor."

Aldric stood, stretching. "I hope it's just one short day for me as well," he said, feeling the soreness creep back into his muscles.

"Will you repair to your chambers then, my prince?" Chiron asked.

Aldric shook his head, heavy with fatigue. "No, I don't think I'd be able sleep if I did." At his full height, Aldric was nearly a head taller than the seneschal. He looked down on the old man, feeling a fondness there that surprised him. He realised then how much he relied upon the seneschal's judgements and how valuable these conversations were. Aldric wondered what he would do when he was gone. "I always feel certain of my beliefs until I talk with you, Chiron," he said.

Chiron plucked a leaf from the vine in front of him and lifted it to his face, turning it over in the light. "I only offer another point of view, my Liege." There was genuine humility in his voice, and he looked at Aldric intently. "If we believe anything without question, we begin to settle into the morass of our own delusions, and for most people, there is little chance of recovery." He held his palm open and blew on the leaf. It rolled off his hand and fluttered in the air briefly before sinking below the verge of the balcony.

FOUR

REVELATIONS

Emperor Leopold Danarean II looked up from a display buried in his desk. "Has there been any word from the forward patrols?" He was reading a report detailing the loss of the INV *Malefactor* and the events of the morning. His usual council of ministers had been interrupted to bring him news of the destroyer's fate. He left the meeting in a fury.

He turned to the dark haired man before him. The man wore the black, high collared uniform of the Royal Landser. On his left collar in gold were the crossed spears of the Household Guard; on the other, the prancing apalas of the royal family, hooves held high. Bruce Ramsay, Grand Marshal and coordinator of Imperial Security returned the emperor's gaze.

Bruce Ramsay had the classic appearance of the aristocratic Old Guard. His close cropped, dark brown hair was greying at the temples, but age had stolen none of his vigour. Above a hard, angled jaw, dark eyes looked out with the intensity of a hawk. Daily training with the Valorí had stripped his flesh of any softness, and his fair skin was drawn tight against sharp cheekbones.

"We've had no word from the convoy, Your Eminence." Bruce said, clearing his throat. His low, curt voice cut through the sombre atmosphere. "I've conferred with the Admiralty. All convoys are grounded and we're systematically scanning the surrounding areas. The Fifth Fleet has been recalled from *Torr Archus* and is rendezvousing with the Sixth and Eighth fleets at the battle station *Naedras Marr*." Bruce compressed his lips, drawing them into a thin line. "There's a chance we might catch them yet, but the advantage is theirs."

"The advantage is theirs?" Leopold repeated. His voice was very soft. He studied the Grand Marshal for a moment, then, "How can the advantage be theirs!" he shouted. "The entire navy is looking for these ships, they cannot escape."

Bruce shrugged. "They caught us off guard. Forward listening posts reported sensor ghosts around Argoth, but scouts found nothing. Carrier Battle Group *Tempest* has already swept the sectors around Aera."

"And?" Leopold asked. The other viziers in the room had shrunk back to the walls, fearing their emperor's wrath. In his early fifties, Leopold retained all the ferocity of his youth. From behind pale eyes gazed a wild animal, predatory and keen. The depth of that gaze was measured beneath a broad, determined forehead. The long, regal nose that was his gift to his sons was set in the midst of a proud face framed by jet black hair worn long in the manner of the Thedarran aristocracy. A short cropped beard did nothing to hide the angular jaw and fine bone structure of his handsome features. His lips were full, and as gracious as they were cruel. It was this fickle gaze he now turned upon the Grand Marshall.

"And we've come up empty handed," the Marshal replied in a gruff baritone. Bruce Ramsay's voice had been ground down to a hoarse growl after years of shouting orders on the battlefield. "This appears to be a calculated hit and run. I doubt we'll find anything this time."

"What do you mean, *this time*?" Leopold asked, his voice so low the Marshal had to strain to hear it. A tense quiet filled the room. Slatted windows let in some of the early morning light, but the dark woods and thick tapestries drank in the golden rays and filled the room with an oppressive closeness.

"I mean that this was a successful operation on their part, and there's no reason to believe they'll stop here. The only hope we have is to shore up our defences and attempt to tighten the convoy escorts. It might mean cutting back on convoy shipments from the outer planets, but I think..."

"We're not reducing shipments, Bruce," Leopold interrupted. "I won't allow these *renegades* to interfere with our mining operations in this system."

"Your Grace, we lack the resources to adequately repel their incursions. Even with ten carrier battle groups, we are spread thin, and there is no way to ensure the defence of the convoys, especially if the Raeth can bring down a destroyer now."

"This empire relies upon the timely arrival of shipments from our mining planets. What of the new super-carriers? Weren't they commissioned for precisely this reason?"

"My Lord, the first of the carriers is still in drydock at *Torr Archus*, it won't be finished for months, and there aren't enough ships in the Sciphere to form a battle escort without taking them from other groups."

"I want you to take the Sciphere through the asteroid field rock by rock, if you must. Scan every moon, deploy more sensors—send scouts to Kor, but *find those rebels and destroy them*." The emperor glowered at the Grand Marshall. "The Raeth are making a mockery of my forces, Bruce, and it must end."

"Your Grace, we *don't have enough ships* to do that." The dignified Grand Marshal was having a hard time keeping his composure.

"Then we'll build them," Leopold said. "Speed up production if necessary, we have five shipyards, we should be able to produce a new carrier fleet in a year's time if we redirect our resources."

"Ignoring the fact that we don't have enough skilled labourers to build that many ships, we also don't have the crews to man them. Craic Achran is barely two decades old; half the instructors there were students when it was founded. We can't just *will* more ships into existence."

"Perhaps we won't have to," the emperor said, folding his arms over his desk. "I've been reviewing the reports from the Admiralty concerning the captured Raeth fighter. It appears genuine. I believe the Raeth are fully committed to their plan, and that our previous fleet deployment must be doubled. The entire Sciphere is needed, and if we are successful, hunting Raeth through the asteroid belt will never be necessary again." His voice was sinuous in the gloomy light of the council chamber.

Bruce started at the suggestion. "My Lord," he said, stepping forward. "We're overextended already, there's no place left to draw on further ships—not if we wish to keep the Core defended."

Leopold regarded the Grand Marshall for a moment, returning his gaze to the screen before him. He considered the information there. Only a few days ago a Raeth ship had been crippled and captured, its computers mostly intact. When the files were decrypted, analysts discovered a plan which detailed an imminent attack upon Drusus, one of the central mining planets. So far the intel appeared genuine, and in just two days' time the Raeth would launch an assault on one of the richest shipping convoys in the system.

The Admiralty had expected a Raeth fleet of no more than fifty ships, and those nearly a century old and held together by spit and fibre bonding. However the seized files indicated there would be over *three hundred* warships in the Raeth armada. And judging from this morning's incident, they would be well armed. The Admiralty had been floored. Where had such a fleet come from?

Leopold thought he knew exactly where they had come from, and though he didn't have proof yet, he was certain Mal'Dreghen was at least partly responsible. What he really wanted to know was how this had been kept a secret from him. He knew everything. His informants were in every corner of the empire. Chiron had spies in all the Great Houses of the Erolan. There wasn't a trade guild or consortium that didn't operate without his knowledge. The entire Aethian System was under his all-knowing, all-seeing gaze. So where had such a fleet been hidden?

Of course his empire wasn't what it had been. While the noble Old Guard was stripping him of his power, Mal'Dreghen was stripping him of his prestige. If the reports were true then someone close to him was feeding him false information. He cursed inwardly. Take away the ducal armies, and they infiltrated the imperial army; remove the religious zealots from power and they threw festivals mocking his impotence.

Not a month ago the emperor had sat stony faced and silent in Aldon Court with Aldric and Arem by his side while he listened to a speech from Mal'Dreghen. The Mal had arranged the chamber so that the emperor's throne was at the back of the room, and while he did not turn his back to the emperor—which would have been an outright insult—he frequently addressed others in the audience before the emperor. He had called the Gods' City, Chaldrea, a blasphemy to all mankind.

He shouted at the top of his lungs, calling the "shepherds of our times" prophets of wickedness and betrayers of man. The hall had been silent as he spoke, his red face and raven hair whirling around wildly in his pulpit. "What justice is there when the infirm, the weak, and the morally corrupt offer guidance to the glorious sons and daughters of Desedar?" The high, domed ceiling and black marble pillars of Aldon Court reverberated with his rich, clear voice. His performance had mesmerised his audience, including the emperor, who realised then what a mistake he had made in not silencing this madman years ago. It was too late now.

Many in the emperor's highest council suspected that the Raeth were receiving funding from anti-Imperialist groups on Errolor, even within Chaldrea. A few of these groups were known already and Chiron's spies kept the emperor well informed on their activities. Yet none of them commanded the necessary capital to raise a fleet capable of dealing a blow to the Imperial Navy. That kind of money could only come from dissenters within the Erolan, such as the Old Guard, or the Dhemorahn church itself. Contributions to the Dhemorahn coffers were staggering, making Mal'Dreghen the wealthiest man outside the royal family. Not even the mighty dukes of the Erolan were as well funded. Along with his thinly veiled hostility, this wealth placed the Mal at the top of the most likely suspects.

However, actual Dhemorahn spies were impossible to get. All the highest priests and those closest to the Mal were men bred to their positions and handpicked by the Mal himself. Intelligence inside these circles was non-existent, and Mal'Dreghen trusted no one. And with the Mal's ever present Inquisitors, Leopold's clairvoyant Augures couldn't tell him anything.

Leopold shook his head. "The Core Planets aren't their target," he replied. "Errolor, Landas, Allria—these are heavily defended from orbit, I don't care if the Raeth can field a thousand ships, nothing can penetrate our web of defences. *Arrus Athaban* alone could handle a fleet the size of the Sciphere, and that's supposing the Raeth have even a hundredth of our firepower."

"Your Grace, the destruction of the *Malefactor* alone demands that we rethink our entire strategy. We've been operating on the idea that the Raeth command an antiquated fleet of refit cargo vessels. Nothing like that could have brought down a destroyer. We must re-evaluate our tactics."

"I will not sacrifice our convoy shipments on the notion that the Raeth have suddenly acquired some mysterious, advanced fleet of ships able to confront our armada head on. The *Malefactor* is nothing more than a fluke, and we will press onward with our plans to surprise the Raeth at Drusus. This means we will need to divert stationary battle groups from around the Core to rendezvous with the Sciphere around Argoth, and head the Raeth off in a decisive first strike."

"If we're wrong, my Lord, that would leave Allria and Errolor helpless. It is entirely possible this is exactly what they expect us to do." The strain on the old general's face was clearly visible. "With respect, we cannot sacrifice the Attendant Fleet, not for any convoy, no matter the cost of its loss."

"Bruce, this convoy represents over a year's mining of thadium, among other metals, without which our industry will grind to a halt. It's not simply the cost of the convoy, it's what it will cost the empire if it's lost. The Raeth cannot possibly have the ability to destroy both the Sciphere and our home fleets. If they could, they would have done so already. No," Leopold said, stabbing his desk with his finger. "We must fully commit to this operation and wipe them out in a single blow."

"I've spoken against our dependence on Drusus, my Liege," Bruce said. "Relying so heavily on one planet puts us in danger—as we see now."

"Drusus is the closest core planet, it's easily mined. Without the thadium it provides, our fleet would be immobilised. Argoth and Hellas are too far away, too hard to mine, and too dangerous to transport to and from. No", Leopold said, shaking his head. "The situation is what it is, Bruce. We must deal with it." He was not convinced sacrificing Attendant Fleet was the right choice either, but he wouldn't lose the priceless cargo carried by the convoy. "We cannot afford to lose this shipment." His tone and expression would brook no argument.

Bruce nodded, clearly trying to work out a solution. "My Lord," he said after a moment, "perhaps there's another solution. Couldn't we delay the convoy? We don't need any of the materials immediately, and if we can postpone their shipment then the Raeth would have nothing to attack and we might avoid this entire situation."

The emperor shook his head. "Delaying the convoy doesn't eliminate the threat posed by the Raeth. Having such a large fleet of corsairs massed above Drusus is the same as losing the convoy—perhaps much worse."

Bruce frowned. "You think they would attack the planet?"

"I think if the reports are accurate then they have the power to lay siege to Drusus and confiscate whatever they wanted—hostages, mining equipment, the orbital refinery; they could infiltrate the entire operation. We can't let them manoeuvre into such a position."

"My Lord, Drusus is a barren rock—they have no place to retreat. It's an untenable position."

"They wouldn't need to occupy the planet," Leopold said. "If they cripple the facility it would be worse than losing the convoy. No, Drusus must be protected."

"My Liege, send the entire Sciphere, send every ship in the fleet, but I ask you to heed my council. I have served you faithfully for many years, and all my experience tells me that it is a grave mistake to leave Errolor *entirely undefended.* If you must take every last ship in the fleet, at least leave Attendant Fleet behind. Three ships could not turn the tide of the battle at Drusus, but they might be invaluable here at home." The lines in his face deepened as he stared at the emperor. "I will say nothing more."

Leopold steepled his fingers beneath his nose thoughtfully. He worked his jaw side to side, trying to decide if it would be a show of weakness at this point to concede his Marshal's request. "Very well," he said, leaning forward. "Attendant Fleet will remain behind. But I will make no further concessions on this point. I want our fleet above Drusus to be as armed and prepared as possible. Every ship is necessary in this fight, we must cripple them here and now."

Bruce Ramsay breathed a sigh of relief, straightening himself up. "As you command, Your Grace."

Leopold nodded and leaned back in his supple chair. "I want you to coordinate with the Admiralty and complete the sector sweeps of the system; I don't want any surprise visitors showing up on our doorstep. If there are Raeth lingering about and unattached to the main force headed for Drusus, I want them found. If not, so much the better. But either way the armada must be assembled and prepared for the strike at Drusus within the next sixteen hours."

"That doesn't leave us much time to secure the Core, my Lord," Bruce replied.

"We cannot afford to miss this opportunity. We must cripple the Raeth. If they are committing their entire force to this action, then we must as well; I don't want to leave anything to chance."

"As you wish, Your Grace."

"Excellent," Leopold said, clasping his hands together. "So what do we know so far about this business this morning?"

"The reports from the recovered crew are conflicting," Bruce replied. "The convoy was attacked four hours after leaving Argoth when they stopped to pass through the asteroid belt. The crew says the attacking fleet wasn't large, but there were several smaller ships which they couldn't identify."

"Meaning?"

"Meaning they were unclassified."

"Could these ships represent some kind of new weapon? Are they responsible for destroying the *Malefactor*?"

Bruce furrowed his brow. "I don't believe so. From everything we've gathered those ships weren't large enough to inflict that kind of damage. It would need to be something much larger, but no one saw any ships large enough to be suspect."

"So what then?" Leopold asked, growing impatient.

"I'm not sure, Sire. The captain and most of the commanding officers were killed when the bridge depressurised, so the reports we have aren't based on exact information. Several of the crew recall what felt like impacts before the *Malefactor* escaped."

"Impacts? As in phase cannon fire?"

"No, they said it felt like the ship was hit by something."

"Ballistic weapons?" Leopold asked.

"Doubtful, the ablative armour of the *Malefactor* can deflect any ballistic weapon known," Bruce replied. "From what I've heard, it looks more like it was smashed, by a rock or a meteor."

"Then what points to the Raeth?"

"The crew all claims they were attacked by the Raeth. The convoy was ambushed, and there's Raeth cannon fire all across the hull. But," Bruce said, pausing as he chose his words. "There were gouges into and through the ship, and remnants of rock has been found deep inside the inner decks."

"Well it tore up half of Lannachlor when it crashed," the emperor said.

Bruce pursed his lips. "But that wouldn't leave the kind of rock fragmentation we're seeing here. Again, we still don't know everything and the reports I have are conflicting, but some of the crew do claim they were hit by an asteroid."

"That doesn't make any sense," Leopold said, his frustration mounting.

The Grand Marshal shrugged. "I can't tell you any more yet, it crashed barely an hour ago, and crews are still putting out fires."

"Bruce, I need answers, this is getting us nowhere. A state of the art man-of-war was destroyed, and we have absolutely no idea how."

"We're trying to salvage what we can from the computer files, but the databanks were pretty badly fried. The nav-computer records being attacked, but doesn't give any specific information on where or how. We have our best teams on it my Liege, and the rest of the crew is being debriefed as they're discharged from the infirmaries. If there is anything there, we'll find it."

"Very well," the emperor said. "We must formulate a response for the time being." Glancing at the viziers, Leopold inclined his head towards the door. As one, the darkly robed body of counsellors rose and bowed, filing towards the chamber door opened by two waiting lictors. They left wordlessly, the doors closing with a quiet thud in their wake.

It was decadent, Leopold knew, retaining servants where machines would function as well or better. Sensor doors were common in every home across the empire; yet they lacked the eloquence of human subservience. Electronics, machinery—these would serve anyone, and they were cheap. Humans, though... Obedience was the privilege of royalty.

And while the wealthiest families might pay for servants, royal lictors were a special breed reserved only for the emperor. Born and raised in the Palace for a lifetime of devotion to the Royal Family's every whim, each lictor was a deaf, mute, male eunuch. Women had proved too great a temptation in the past, even to emperors at times. Males had as well, though not quite as frequently. Many courtiers and others of the Erolan saw the practise of raising handicapped servants as barbaric, but Leopold enjoyed the distinction. No one else could afford such an outrageous liberty.

"Such a strategy implies central authority," Bruce resumed.

Leopold stood, composing his deep purple robes. He walked to the nearest window and pressed a disguised button in a panel below the sill. The window slats began to angle downwards, revealing a flagstone paved courtyard below.

"I will not suffer this, Bruce," Leopold said. "Mal'Dreghen mocks me at every turn. Even as I gather my power, he eludes my grasp."

"My Lord," Bruce said uncomfortably.

"He must be made to pay. Each of these outrages is building towards something, I can feel it. I can feel it as much as the changing of a season, it is there. If I had heeded your words so long ago, this could have been avoided."

It was a rare moment of candour for the emperor, and Bruce was at a loss for words. "Your Grace, the situation isn't lost. There's tomorrow, and the next day. We won't sit idly by, there are many steps still to be taken..." He trailed off.

Leopold turned to face the Grand Marshal, a startling intensity in his blue eyes. "He presses the Dhemorgal upon me, and now picks apart my fleet, my convoys, as if it were nothing. Yet where is he vulnerable? Where can I strike at him, that the empire won't retaliate against my brutality? There are too many webs, Bruce—too many delicate strands binding me to everyone, and everyone to him. I can't move but I upset the littlest of them, and then I am vilified."

"You are the emperor," Bruce said.

Leopold regarded him. The man had a troubling way of putting words to his doubts, of making him see the obvious nature of his complaint. The Grand Marshal's battlefield demeanour was often a source of consternation. Yet he valued it. "I am the emperor," he said.

At least Aldric didn't seem to share Leopold's uncertainties. What Aldric lacked in ability as an orator, as a politician, he made up for in popularity with the people and a natural talent for leadership and command. When Leopold had learned of Aldric's involvement this morning it had shocked him at first. But on further thought, he found it didn't really surprise him. Aldric never balked at taking such risks, as he had proved in the past. Leopold only hoped that this gathering storm would not end in the loss of his throne. He had never feared for his position before. Now, however, he felt the first pangs of uncertainty.

He strode to Bruce Ramsay, his thick robes shuffling. "Would it have been too much to ask that Aldric let the destroyer fall into the Ziggurat?" He said. "How poetic it would be."

Bruce did not smile, instead said, "Retribution is not enough, my Lord. If we are to strike, Mal'Dreghen must be destroyed completely. There can be no chance for retaliation, for raising a force against us."

The emperor nodded. "Tomorrow, Bruce," he said, turning back to face the gardens. "Tomorrow I will show the people what kind of *prophet* they worship.

FIVE

APOTHEOSIS

Not half an hour after speaking with Chiron, Aldric received a summons from a furtive palace messenger to attend the emperor's audience chamber. He'd been lying in his bed, unable to sleep but still enjoying the peace when an envoy had brought him to the door. He realised then there'd be no rest this day. Aldric knew what to expect, and didn't relish the coming encounter. He thought of the growing distance between himself and his father. When he was younger, Aldric had anticipated leading much the same life his father did—rich in pageantry and celebration.

Yet as he'd grown, Aldric began to see faults with his father's careless indulgence. The empire was decadent, lavish. It had become gluttonous under his father's care. This was as much to blame on the influence of the Dhemorahns as his father, Aldric thought with scorn. The cult of Mal'Dreghen had become infamous for its hedonism.

Bahir Danu, the captain of the Valorí Guard, had said once that the pursuit of pleasure, in the guise of happiness, had long been a tool of tyrants. 'Distract the people with games and wine,' he had said, 'and they will forget their sorrows.' While Aldric had been old enough to understand it at the time, the words were now a lesson he witnessed daily. 'You can steal anything you like from the people so long as they are entertained.'

'Even their freedom?' Aldric had asked, incredulous.

'Especially their freedom,' Bahir had replied. 'Pleasure is an excellent substitute for liberty. It has all the taste of freedom, yet it is never filling, and leaves only the desire for more. A capable ruler will always have an abundance of pleasures to dispense for his people, lest they look too deeply into his principles.'

The long corridor leading to his father's chambers was filled with deep shadows. These were stabbed at intervals by silvery beams of grey light which poured in through towering windows on either side. Tall windows, high ceilings, long hallways...*It's meant to make you feel small,* Aldric thought, not for the first time. Secret eyes were watching him as he walked, he knew—eyes were everywhere in the Palace. There was no movement unseen here.

He passed two Valorí guards in féthabban phase armour and white cloaks. They bowed as he entered, silver armour gleaming, spear points dipping low. The spears harkened back to the ancient days and the function of the Valorí as the emperor's defenders, but they were also deadly in close combat, supplementing the sabre-rifles they carried. In all the empire there were no more than a thousand Valorí, and from sparring and practise sessions in the Temple Aldric had met all of them at one point or another. He considered many of them his friends. Yet when they donned their mirror-finish helmets, with only a darkened slit in their visor, it was impossible to tell one from another. There were no badges of distinction among the Valorí.

Aldric stepped through the large carved doors and squinted, his eyes adjusting to the gloom. His father had always preferred dimly lit rooms. Leopold enjoyed the sombre, restful atmosphere of a dark chamber, and he seldom held audiences under full light. Aldric thought it suggested a weakness in character. Hiding in the shadows, deliberating in the darkness— that was how Aldric always found his father. He rarely left his chambers these days, and the long rides they used to take together were nothing more than a memory. It revealed inaction, self-indulgence, and even self-pity: *The world is threatening, I'm going to hide.* It was decay.

His father had been there as Aldric expected to find him, seated behind his enormous desk in a deep chair of leather uroch hide, framed by elaborate carvings in the dark wood. Before Leopold was an immaculate presentation of breakfast on a silver platter, with little silver serving dishes and steaming bowls. The emperor eyed his son quietly over the extravagant breakfast, two lictors in sheer white robes waiting patiently behind him. Aldric hadn't eaten yet, and his stomach grumbled in protest at the savoury aromas. A fragrant bowl of yellow ghinni peas was set out beside boma eggs, spiced porridge, a platter of fruit, and sweet brown sticky buns.

Aldric stopped before the great desk and gave a slight bow, folding his hands behind his back. His father was wrapped in his purple robes, his strong frame hidden in their folds. Aldric found the idea of such clothing distasteful. It seemed artificial to him, and he glanced out the window to the palace gardens beyond. Not four metres from where the emperor sat, the drenching humidity of the jungle would make such an outfit unbearable. But here in the cool darkness of the royal chambers it was just another of the self-indulgent luxuries that set the emperor so far apart from his people. Aldric's own clothing was subdued and adaptive to most environs. The light fabric was particularly suited to the sweltering heat of Thedarras, the tropical southern province of Chaldrea.

Aldric shifted uncomfortably. Every meeting with his father reminded him of how far the rift between them had grown. *A battle of wills.* He didn't like the sensuality of his father's rule. To Aldric, it seemed no better than the hedonism of Mal'Dreghen. Yet Mal'Dreghen was one of the people. He was a commoner, no royal title or inherited lands. He was no better than any other citizen. The emperor, however, was likened to a god. His pleasures were seen to set him apart from the people, having rare privileges unattainable by anyone else. *You can't have this, but I can. I am what you can never be.*

Mal'Dreghen, on the other hand, was the voice of a religion, the centre piece in an idea that gave the people hope for something better. His luxurious lifestyle was a crucial part of his religion. It said to the people 'Look, look! *This should be yours*; you have a right to this! Take, indulge, *rejoice.*'

This elitism was a flaw with all monarchies, Aldric thought. But perhaps it was necessary to keep the people controlled. Perhaps they needed to believe in the sanctity of their rulers, it gave rulers legitimacy and unquestionable authority. Aldric's training with the Valorí had taught him about the perils of luxury. Aldric would never deny how much he enjoyed his heritage. But he had never been deluded into believing that it was his right. Or worse, that it made him superior to those he ruled. This set him apart from his father and brother, who quite enjoyed the myth of their divinity.

"Please, sit," his father said, lifting a spoonful of peas to his mouth.

Feigned disinterest: So that's how it'll be, Aldric thought. He sat, keeping his back upright and away from the chair.

"Would you like something to eat?" his father asked, gesturing at the food.

Aldric shook his head. "I already ate," he lied, knowing his father would probably know that. The stubbornness he was feeling would make this conversation more difficult, but he couldn't shake it off. He knew this would turn into a reprimand somehow. His father never "summoned" him otherwise.

The emperor dropped his hand to his lap and swallowed. He regarded Aldric for a long moment. "I'm proud of what you did this morning, Aldric." Leopold said.

Aldric was taken aback. His father never praised him. "It seemed like the only choice," Aldric said after a moment. "The commander of the *Crucible* said they were ordered to fire. I couldn't let them destroy the ship, not when I was sure there were people still on board."

The emperor narrowed his eyes thoughtfully. "You were *sure*?"

Aldric shrugged. "It wasn't *aina*, if that's what you're thinking. I just... I knew something wasn't right. All those unfired escape pods looked out of place." He looked up at his father, still anticipating reproach.

Leopold said nothing, however. He took another bite and set his fork down, chewing quietly. He studied his son with what Aldric felt was an uncharacteristic look of fatherliness. "You created quite a disturbance," Leopold said, swallowing. "The Admiralty are not accustomed to being countermanded."

Aldric stiffened. *There it is.* "I am the crown prince of Vassarya. I decided what was best in that situation—I was there, in my ship, sitting next to the *Malefactor* when it exploded." He flexed his hand beneath the table. "I don't remember seeing anyone from the Admiralty there."

Aldric knew what his father was thinking, how tedious his relationship with the bureaucracy was: ruffling feathers, overturning the status quo and complicating the emperor's job. Even as supreme dictator—perhaps especially so—people liked to believe they had some power, some influence. Things did not go well when that belief was shattered. But dammit, there were still the seventy five survivors on board. Nothing changed that.

"Aldric, if you had been wrong—"

"It wouldn't have mattered either, because I am still the prince. They cannot gainsay me." *That felt haughty. Let him argue with that.*

His father sat back in his chair. "That is true," Leopold said, conceding the point. "But what *would* you have done if you'd been wrong?"

Aldric frowned. "Nothing, it still wouldn't have mattered. Nothing was lost, in any case, and at least I made the effort. No one else did."

"The Admiralty aren't peons, Aldric," the emperor said firmly. "Many of them are members of the Erolan, the Old Guard even, highly influential at court, and—"

"What do you care for the Erolan?" Aldric asked. "You are the *emperor*. They do *your* bidding. This isn't a popularity contest or vote by majority— you are *irrefutably* master and lord of all the empire. *You* were chosen by the gods, not the Admiralty or the Erolan."

Leopold's eyes widened and he started to speak, thought better of it and instead took a drink from his tea. "You don't realise how wrong you are, son," he said, setting down his teacup. "This is very much a position of popularity. Have you forgotten the lesson of the Empress Dowager? She thought as you do, and the empire was driven to war."

"Yet, she acted like an *empress*. She was not cowed by those she ruled." Aldric's tone was icy. He felt bitter resentment towards his father's weakness. It made him sick to see the emperor succumb to the wishes of sycophants and politicians. "This is exactly why Mal'Dreghen is a problem today, because you were *afraid* to do the right thing when you had the chance. Now he's too much for you."

The emperor's face blackened for a moment. Aldric could see he'd gone too far. It passed, however, and Leopold dismissed the comment, tossing his hand flippantly. He took a long sip from a slender silver chalice, condensation trickling down the sides.

"You were speaking with Chiron earlier," the emperor said, forcing a casual tone into his voice.

Aldric remained quiet. He couldn't tell if it was a question or a statement. He decided it didn't matter. He'd let his father direct the conversation and recover some of his ground. His pride was fragile. Aldric was sure his conversation with Chiron had been recorded and passed along to the emperor anyways. Very little that happened in the palace escaped the emperor's attention, and certainly not where his son *and* his seneschal were concerned; at least Aldric couldn't fault him for that.

The emperor set his glass down and studied Aldric. "It makes no difference," he said. He raised his hand and gestured at a lictor standing nearby. The man nodded mutely and opened the door. From the deep shadows near the entrance stepped a robed figure. He pushed his cowl back and bowed respectfully towards Aldric.

"Seneschal," Aldric said, hiding the irritation in his voice. Chiron was at the emperor's bidding, but he disliked his father spying on him.

"Chiron and I have been discussing the situation," Leopold said. "As you've noted, I'm in a rather delicate position." He directed a fixed stare across the table at Aldric. "With Mal'Dreghen at my front, I am well to keep the Erolan at my back. I may have the only standing army in the system—but I wouldn't last very long if I had to use it against the whole empire at once. The Mal has turned the people against me, even as I permit them their little festival." He pursed his lips and raised an eyebrow quizzically. "This morning's events have set into motion something that cannot be stopped."

"Your Eminence, if I may," Chiron said, moving to the emperor's side. His long face was deeply creased in the dim light. "This situation must be contained. Your Grace ought not to let Mal'Dreghen turn this against you."

"I'm listening," Leopold said, sipping from his chalice. "I may control the media, but I can't pretend a destroyer hasn't simply fallen from the sky and landed in the middle of the Carrac Fold."

"Quite so," Chiron said. "However, rather than allowing the Mal to paint you as inept and unable to protect your people, we should use this as proof that you are valiantly defending the Fatherland. The brave souls that perished on board the *Malefactor* were heroes, and they died protecting the empire they so loved," Chiron said, moving around the table to stand between Aldric and the emperor.

"Before they were ambushed by a hundred Raeth ships, they defended the convoy and singlehandedly brought down forty of the corsairs before they were overcome by sheer numbers. We will compare it to the Brythonic warriors at the Gates of Helas," Chiron said.

The emperor absorbed the words, rubbing his chin. "And Aldric was a hero as well," he said, looking up at his son.

Aldric cringed inwardly. He felt as ever that he was not his father's son, but rather a game piece to be manoeuvred.

"Oh, our prince was the greatest hero of all," Chiron said, lifting his arms in adulation. "The emperor's son risked his own life to protect those of his people. He is our modern Anaxarian."

Anaxarian had long ago given his life in defence of the first emperor and had become the model and champion for the Valorí ever since. He was a hero to all, Dhemorahn and Asaani alike, and his tales were told by fathers to their sons, generation after generation. "We must paint our beloved prince as such. The Mal cannot contest such a claim when it follows this valorous deed."

"Really, that's a bit far," Aldric began to protest.

"No, Chiron is right," Leopold said, his eyes intense. "It's exactly what we need, and it couldn't have come at a better time."

Aldric sat back in his chair, feeling forfeit. It made sense to him, but it also made him very uncomfortable. His princely image was heavy enough, he already didn't feel like half the person others saw in him. To be compared to an immortal hero of the empire was entirely more than he wanted.

"The Mal may have orchestrated this catastrophe," Chiron said, "but he couldn't have anticipated that Aldric would rescue the destroyer."

"And the timing is perfect," Leopold replied. "The Dhemorgal was meant to disgrace me. But when Aldric enters the coliseum tomorrow and faces the Mal's champion, he will not only be the prince of the people, but he will also be their saviour."

"The people will be in a frenzy," Chiron said in agreement. "Even before he wins, Aldric is a hero."

"And if," the emperor said, turning a considerate expression to Aldric, "if you are defeated tomorrow, the Mal's victory will be hollow. He will have beaten a hero, it will be an insult to the people, and he will appear heartless and cruel."

"I will not fail," Aldric said deliberately, though he suddenly felt more uncertain than he ever had before.

"Of course you won't," said Chiron. "There is no one more capable of *craidath* than you, dear prince."

"That's not actually true," Aldric said. "But it doesn't matter. His champion cannot win. I won't allow it." He felt suddenly angry. He didn't know why. This was all too much for him to process. *Unbind,* he said to himself, trying to calm his nerves. *Hear the sound of no-thing.*

Leopold smiled, appraising his son. "No, you will not fail."

Aldric felt sick. He could see the wheels of the emperor's mind turning over, all of the gears fitting into their proper places. Aldric could almost feel himself being pushed into a slot, aligning with his father's expectations. It felt inhuman, and he blinked away the feeling before it could grow.

It didn't matter what his father expected, Aldric knew what must happen. The empire depended upon him. He must vanquish this creature of the Mal and prove that the finest thing the Mal could produce—the champion of his religious order—was inferior to the Asaani. And to Aldric. The Mal must be put in his place. The empire needed to show him where he stood. *The empire? Or me?* Aldric wondered. *Or my father?*

"I recommend that we broadcast images of the destroyer in all public venues throughout the Five Cities and especially Chaldrea," Chiron said. "Include footage of Aldric's Starling and some clips of him guiding it down, and then receiving congratulations from the Admiralty afterwards. My Prince," Chiron said, turning an expectant eye towards Aldric. "You must gather yourself for this coming ordeal. The people of Vassarya will be watching you."

Aldric returned his gaze and found softness in his eyes. Chiron might insist upon the gallant image of the invincible prince and his eternal empire, but he knew Aldric, and he knew this was taking a heavy toll on him. "I'll do what I must," Aldric said.

The emperor appeared not to have heard them. "We must magnify this," he said, eagerness growing in his voice. It appealed to his vanity. "A hundred and fifty survivors, rescued by the emperor's son. Mal'Dreghen will be furious if we distract from his beloved festival."

Aldric ignored the exaggerated number. It would be part of the illusion his father was creating. "The people will see their prince as hero," Leopold continued, "and that is all that matters."

"And the Raeth?" Aldric asked, changing the subject.

"The Raeth are still a concern," Chiron said. "And we know less about them now than we did this morning."

"I've spoken with Bruce Ramsay and the Admiralty," Leopold said, coldness coming back into his voice. He enjoyed the pageantry and ceremony of making his son a hero. More than that, he enjoyed the attention it would bring him. The rest was details. "The Sciphere is gathering in a day's time around Aera, where they will then proceed towards Drusus. We will hopefully take the Raeth by surprise." He cleared his throat, adjusting himself in his seat. "The Attendant Fleet will remain behind. All other ships will be joining the Sciphere at Aera." He glanced towards Aldric.

Aldric couldn't hide his surprise. "You read the transcripts, you saw the recordings taken by the monitoring stations this morning—we need more protection, Attendant Fleet won't be enough to stop whatever brought down that destroyer," Aldric said, disbelieving.

The emperor waved his hand dismissively. "We have *Arrus Athaban*, and there are a dozen warships docked at Craic Achran which will be placed on standby. Believe me, son," he said. "If the Raeth are foolhardy enough to assault Errolor, they will be handily dealt with."

Aldric exchanged looks with Chiron. Chiron remained ever inscrutable. "Have you learned nothing from this morning?" Aldric asked. "We were totally unprepared for what happened. We know nothing of their full capabilities, save that they brought down an Adamant class destroyer, and we don't even know what *their* casualties were. If they bring that force to Errolor, do you think three dreadnoughts and a battle station can withstand them?"

"They won't attack Errolor," the emperor said, "because they're going to attack the convoy at Drusus."

"And if they don't? We've never had the good fortune of finding a single ship of theirs before now, let alone one that's intact. They *want* us to go to Drusus."

The emperor frowned. "Really, Aldric, you're far too concerned. We're in no danger here. The *Malefactor* was a coincidence, possibly even just the error of her captain. Errolor is safe, rest assured."

Aldric was incensed. How could his father be this blind? He wanted to shout but he knew it wouldn't matter.

"My Lord," Chiron said, addressing the emperor. "I think the prince is concerned about our lack of knowledge here. Where could they get the technology, the resources, for such an attack? If we had some idea, we might better prepare ourselves to make these decisions."

"The Raeth aren't the real threat," Aldric said. "They're just a tool. The real threat is wherever the money is coming from. That's what we need to be concerned about."

"Strike at the hand that wields the sword," Chiron said, nodding approvingly at Aldric's observation.

"Mining operations alone couldn't fund them," the emperor said. "The profits from captured convoys, logistically, must barely sustain them in their meagre asteroid outposts. It couldn't outfit a new fleet, or pay for such weaponry as brought down the *Malefactor*."

"Mal'Dreghen." Aldric said in a low voice.

The emperor looked at him narrowly. "That is the word that comes back to me from all quarters, even among the Erolan," he said. "I am not surprised that he would conspire against me, but his audacity is startling. My Augures have tried to observe him, but they detect nothing. If he is responsible, he's taking extra measures to protect anyone who might know. All his closest associates are being followed by his damned Inquisitors—*aina* is impossible."

Aldric leant on the arm of his chair, cupped his chin in one hand. He stared at the whorls in the darkly grained wood of the desk. Black slivers intertwined within deep reddish brown pools. The problem was enormous. Beset upon all sides, with very few allies. He was reminded of Chiron's words earlier this very morning.

There was nothing more he could do here. His father and Chiron began a lengthy debate about the best way to go about promoting Aldric's heroism, and Aldric slumped in his chair, drifting in and out of the conversation. Eventually he left, deciding he would try again to get at half an hour of rest. Glancing out the window at the early morning light, he could tell it was going to be a long day for the Hero of the Fatherland.

After Aldric and Chiron had left and Leopold was alone, he stood in thought for a long time. Why did he fear this so? No sense of urgency had ever impressed itself upon him as this did. Something unimaginable, intangible—a waiting menace beyond his vision. Like his sons, Leopold was not gifted with *aina*, though he did occasionally feel a suggestion of something more than he could explain. The Dhemorgal gave him this feeling. An unpleasant awareness, a tingling pulling at the back of his mind—a vague hint of something ominous stirring.

Was it the Mal? Something Chiron had said? Aldric? That seemed to trigger something. He felt queasy of a sudden, and he put a hand against his desk to brace himself. It passed in a moment, but its effects left many questions in his mind. *Am I afraid?* He found with irritation that he couldn't answer the question.

Standing, Leopold walked to the high, slatted window and peered out at the well groomed gardens beyond. One of the low clouds that frequently rolled in over the lake had begun to creep through the forest and was pouring over the high curtain wall surrounding the gardens, draping itself like a living thing over the hedges and flowering trees. Gardeners could be seen poking their heads above the tops of bushes, pushing around wheelbarrows piled with trimmings. Green, green, everything was green. Watching the gardens calmed him. The Mal could not withstand his might, not even at this late hour. He was the emperor, after all. Nothing could oppose him and remain for long.

This thought comforted him. With a hand signal one of the waiting lictors brought him a hot cup of sooling tea. Its warm vapours enveloped his senses, lingering exotic spices filling his pallet. What would be the first step? *The Dhemorgal.* He must perform the Dhemorgal before his people, present to them an image of implacable composure—the imperious sovereign, master of all. Whatever the Mal thought he knew, he must not see the emperor's uncertainty. And he mustn't be allowed to gloat. A victory could not be permitted to fester here, the Mal must be uprooted. Resolution filled Leopold's mind. He would muster his forces, and show the world the true power of the emperor.

SIX

THE SPLENDID CITY

The streets of Chaldrea burst with colour. Aldric rode through the thoroughfare in an open carriage, driven by two snow white apalas and a surly coachman in garish royal livery of blue and gold. Cipher rode beside him in the carriage, his iridescent fur shinning in the sun. He swivelled his tufted ears, panting and hopping from one side of the carriage to the other as his long tailed swished. He liked being outside, liked the energy and smells and excitement and Aldric liked bringing him.

It was a festival day, and the city rang with lights and laughter, vibrant with energy and celebration and growing each day as Dhemorgal approached. The apalas whinnied as they drove under the walls of the seventh terrace, alabaster fluttering with banners and kites, balloons swimming in skies of lapis lazuli. Cipher chirruped eagerly, ready to get out, bracing his paws on the carriage and panting. Aldric laughed, rubbing his back.

"Soon enough!" Aldric said, gazing around. Phaetons whizzed overhead, catching the morning light and flashing the streets as they passed. Small aerials flitted over the concourses, but there really wasn't much room for them today with all the crowds. Nobles and members of the Erolan still insisted on being coached in their gilded phaetons, but even the more nimble open topped aerials couldn't squeeze through the throngs of people.

Even on good days the upper terraces of Chaldrea were too narrow and flooded with pedestrians for the modern flow of traffic. They were built instead for carriages like the one in which Aldric rode, or for single riders on apalas in ages long before modern phaetons and maglevs and aerials. It imbued the old city with tradition and romance. *Chaldrea is nothing if not a city of aesthetics,* Aldric thought. A living, breathing piece of artwork, passed down through the ages.

Subterminals were still active, out of sight and in keeping with the pristine appearances, but Aldric preferred the sunshine. Besides, Cipher got nervous in the confining terminals, and Aldric would have missed the sights if he'd ridden underground. And there were a lot of sights today.

Men and women jostled together in flowing colours, diaphanous saris and skirts and dazzling jewellery. Many women wove the rainbow feathers of kala birds and the fire red, fantailed feathers of the hoji into their hair, setting off turquoise stones around their necks. Others tied threads of gold and silver into their hair that glittered in the sun.

Both men and women wandered the streets topless, their fair skin painted and stained with ancient symbols of the festival. The first Dhemorgal in a thousand years, but no one had expected such an orgy as this. Aldric felt like a pilgrim tossed on a roiling sea of colours and faces. The late morning was growing hot and already the sun was near its zenith when Aldric stepped down from the open carriage onto the flagstone street.

"Ride on to the Citadel," Aldric said to the driver, walking up beside one of the fidgeting apalas. "I don't know how long I'll be, and this one looks like he's had enough for the day." The apala flapped its lips and tried to nibble his hand as Aldric playfully cupped its mouth, patting its glossy white neck.

Larger and with bigger chests, the royal apalas were the only pure white apalas in the empire. They were said to have been bred from mythological stock that once pulled the chariots of the gods. Aldric admired the animal, its long mane braided and spiralling horns capped in gold. They were graceful creatures, even if technology had made them unnecessary. The apala stamped its hoof, powerful muscles rippling down its leg to flowing fetlocks. Aldric patted him again, nodding. "I know, I know. Off with you," he said, as Cipher leapt from the car and landed at his feet. The driver saluted and pulled away into the crowd, people parting respectfully for the royal carriage.

Aldric stretched from the long ride. After changing earlier he had sat in quiet meditation, refocusing his body's energy. It was one of the first techniques of *craidath* the Valorí had taught him. It couldn't sustain him forever, but it was a good alternative if sleep wasn't an option. In battle, minutes of meditation could replace sleep for several days if necessary, and Aldric felt energy returning to his limbs, his mind clearing. He would need sleep tonight though, or he would suffer tomorrow in the Coliseum.

Normally busy streets had become impassable. Aldric had avoided the city for the past week, swarms of people were uncomfortable and the crowded avenues felt claustrophobic. However today he decided to walk up Bael Dunmar.

Meaning 'the street of heavy steps' in the Asaaran tongue, Bael Dunmar ran from the Citadel to the Great Gate at the entrance of Chaldrea, connecting the entire city through all seven terraces. It was the biggest street, and always the busiest. Aldric tried to walk up the centre of the broad avenue where it was only slightly less crowded, Cipher weaving around his legs. It would take a while to get to the Temple, but he was enjoying the sights today.

In the past few months Aldric spent a dozen hours a day honing his skills and sparring with the Valorí in the Temple of Daor. Representing House Danarean in the Dhemorgal would mean going up against renowned masters in martial combat. Among the nobility, swordplay was revered as an art form. Those who could best their opponents with daring tricks of the blade won great renown across the empire.

The greatest swordsmen might even gain an audience with the emperor himself, and there was never a shortage of seats at feasting days for honoured masters. It was physical artistry of the elite, and every great house struggled for a champion to best their rivals. To master the old arts was a mark of pride for the ancient houses, modern weaponry lacking the finesse and sophistication of a fine blade. There was poetry in swordplay, while firing a rifle could be reduced to no more than the pull of a trigger, decimating an opponent without ever engaging him.

Aldric had been brought up with a sword as part of his classical training, and was comfortable holding his own against some of the best swordsmen the empire could produce. But to add to this, he would be challenged by a champion of the Dhemorahn Sect. They were called the Draugor, and they were Mal'Dreghen's finest acolytes. The Mal knew what an excellent opportunity this was, and Aldric's opponent would likely be handpicked for the purpose of defeating him. It wouldn't be a commonplace fight, and Aldric's loss would be perceived as impotence of the Imperial Throne.

Aldric dismissed the thought. He couldn't dwell on the politics. *Focus, channel energy, observe the course,* he told himself. *Become the path.* It was his favourite aphorism. Whichever direction he chose, it fell to him to create the path. He repeated this as he pushed his way through the crowd. Cipher helped somewhat, people parting nervously for the razorcat. At least his opponent wouldn't be trained in *craidath.* As part of the sacred religious practises of the Asaani, it was forbidden to be taught outside the Temple of Daor. Only the vaunted Valorí—Imperial Guardians of the emperor—knew its secrets.

Called 'the soldiers of man' in the old tongue, the Draugor were instead instructed in *gho,* a fighting style unique to the Dhemorahns. They were chosen from boyhood by Dhemorahn priests to embody the rigorous physical philosophy of the Sect. Contrasting the subtle artfulness of *craidath,* the Dhemorahn techniques encouraged brute force and ferocity. It was the perfect counterpoint to Aldric's training, and deceptive in its simplicity. *The rock to my sword,* Aldric thought.

Aldric breathed in the perfumed air. The Festival of Dhemorgal had turned the serene shops and markets of Chaldrea into crowded centres of chaos. The entire week preceding the festival saw the city's population trebled. People from all across the empire travelled to the city, wanting to be a part of the historic celebration.

Aldric tried to convince his father that allowing the festival was a violation of the beliefs of countless people on Errolor—including his own royal guards, the Valorí. Not only that, it was a flagrant insult to his power. Yet the emperor was unwilling to intervene. He couldn't maintain a secular position by showing favouritism to one religion over another; nor could he keep the peace of the people.

"It isn't about being fair or just," Aldric had said. "When you support those who don't support you, your ruin will follow." His father had merely shaken his head, unable—but more unwilling—to take the necessary steps. He would not be the first emperor whose complacency might cost him his empire, Aldric thought.

The Erolan was mostly indifferent, many being far too occupied by their own politics and internal rivalry to give any heed to a religious festival. However several of the Great Houses had pledged their support in favour of the celebration, demonstrating a surprising disrespect for the Imperial House. Yet perhaps it wasn't really that surprising after all.

The Dhemorahn Sect actually embodied a lot of noble ideals, Aldric thought, encouraging the collectivism of humans: people gathering and working together, striving to achieve human perfection through great works of art and music and cultural splendour. Cooperation was one thing, though. Elitism was something else. As such, Dhemorahns tended towards cities and metropolitan living, places where large numbers of people were concentrated, facilitating their philosophy to the greatest extent. And as Chaldrea was the capital of the Dhemorahn Sect, the people here were largely Dhemorahn.

The Asaani celebrated the natural world, worshipping the earth and forests and seldom settling in large cities. Villages and agrarian communities saw much greater gatherings of Asaani followers, particularly near the many old temples that still remained scattered around the continent. Although the Temple of Daor in Chaldrea was the spiritual centre of their faith, many Asaani chose to live outside the city where they could be close to the lake, in Bailynn or Balimaar. Since the last Dhemorgal, this peaceful coexistence had endured for many generations. Aldric wondered if that was about to change.

The emperor had a good point, and Aldric knew he couldn't openly choose sides. But the vulgarity of the Dhemorgal was too much for him. Mal'Dreghen knew the emperor wouldn't stop him, and was openly flaunting his power. Aldric had never felt so trapped before. He was the prince, the son of the Golden emperor of Errolor, successor to the Fael Danarean kingship and heir to the supreme power in the Aethian system. Next to his father, Aldric's whim was law.

Yet he felt totally powerless. More than once he'd considered leading a squad of the Valorí and personally ridding the world of Mal'Dreghen. But that would be suicide, real and political. The people would rise against the emperor, and like Chiron said, no stronghold can protect you when you're hated by your people. *Maybe it'd still be worth it,* Aldric thought. *Maybe sacrificing a corrupt empire is worth destroying the Mal.* Someone would just step in and take his place, he thought dryly. The world was never short on corruption.

Aldric stumbled as a child crowded past and knocked into him. The youngster didn't turn or stop to apologise, but kept running, his friends close behind him. Aldric ducked under a darkened awning to escape the fray, Cipher dropping to the ground next to him, tail swishing.

There would be no way to successfully remove Mal'Dreghen. And the Mal wasn't interested in money or bribes; that had been tried before. The Mal had just made the bribe public, and turned the scandal into popular support for his cause. Fortunately it hadn't been linked to the Imperial House—the emperor had been wise enough to protect himself in that event. But there was talk, and even without proof, it looked bad enough. *More foolish talk, where direct pressure is needed.* That was the trouble with the emperor: he was a politician first, and a leader second. Aldric tried not to dwell on where "father" fell in that list.

A lean, elderly woman with coppery hair approached Aldric and bowed. She wore a sheer sari of bright blue, and Cipher sniffed at her, taking interest in her skirt. The woman smiled, proffering a bronze urn with the image of the prophet Desedar carved upon the side. "Twenty guilders, my Lord," she said in a faltering voice. Aldric returned the smile and shook his head politely. The lady bowed again and walked off, offering the urn to another passerby.

Sheaves of incense smoked and billowed in braziers along the wall, fragrances from the far corners of the empire filling the air. The pitted white stone walls of the ancient buildings loomed over the street, their doorways and colonnades blooming with wreaths and golden plates featuring Desedar, his lean arms raised above him triumphantly. Lattices arched between buildings over the street, dangling clusters of violet flowers swaying in the summer breeze. People of all ages dressed gaily in sarongs of yellow and orange, red and purple, and every shade of blue and green.

Enormous banners had been raised to celebrate Aldric's triumph in rescuing the crew of the *Malefactor*. It was part of his father and Chiron's scheme of propaganda, their attempt to portray Aldric as Chaldrea's dashing saviour. The banners were four metres high and featured Aldric standing proudly in his flight suit, helmet under one arm and the rising sun behind. The portraits had been raised this morning after his talk with his father, and

Aldric was surprised to see they were already hung on every block and corner. *"The Prince of the People,"* the banners proclaimed. *"Hero of the Fatherland"*, read others. Aldric had to admit he looked quite heroic in the pictures. He didn't feel it, however, and the blatant evangelism made him uncomfortable. He wondered if anyone else was buying it.

It was on all the news channels and on the government controlled netspan. Every household in the empire with a transcaster would see it, and before the games tomorrow his legend would be that much greater. They broadcast interviews with Aldric and the Admiralty, lots of shaking of hands and exaggerated numbers. Nearly three hundred people now owed their lives to Aldric. 'Controlling information is the first part of controlling an empire,' Chiron always told him. 'Knowledge is the privilege of the elite. Whatever else you do, never lose control of the flow of information.' *Lesson learned*, Aldric thought, stepping beneath a flapping yellow banner of himself.

A sudden blast of noise startled Aldric. Looking down the street he saw four great aurancs, their wide horns bellowing loudly. The aurancs were twisting horns of bone and wood as large as a man—a native instrument older than anyone knew. The low sound reverberated off the walls, and Aldric moved nearer for a better look. As he got closer he saw four old men sitting together in a circle, cradling the aurancs between their bony legs. Red faced and sweating, they pursed their lips over the silver mouthpieces, skilfully fluttering their cheeks. Cipher stood tensed against Aldric's leg, wary of the noise.

Drawing out haunting moans from the giant horns, the men squeezed their eyes shut, their faces glistening under the sun. They seemed to travel to another world, rocking back and forth, back and forth, leaning into and away from the sound. The music created a wide circle where people set down whatever they were carrying and swayed together to the rhythm. A woman from the crowd joined in and began to sing, and Aldric recognised the strange, melancholy mixture of sounds as Elcaern mouth music.

Another young woman with a five stringed arba picked up her bow and began to play, the instrument high and lilting against the droning aurancs. She danced before the men, whirling in circles as she fiddled, her bright hair bouncing in the sunlight, her feathers bobbing and bracelets and rings jingling and glittering and the sun glowing in the warm red wood of the arba and her blue skirt twirling and her bare feet pattering on the pavement. It was a very old sound, and Aldric's spine tingled at the melody, and suddenly he was carried away to the misty moorlands of Galhane and the gypsy travellers and twilight folk that haunted those ancient fells.

A topless girl wearing a flowing green skirt danced towards Aldric, catching his eye as she passed. She flashed him a tantalising smile, her dark eyes twinkling. Aldric smiled back, admiring her body as she twirled around, following the roll of her hips and her sweetly curving breasts. She wore a glittering necklace of gold, and her dark hair set off creamy white skin that glowed in the sun. She whirled around, arching backwards, her hair spilling down and her soft breasts rising and falling as she danced, beads of sweat trickling down her neck and chest.

The girl looked back and saw him watching her and she grinned, beckoning him to join her in the circle and dance. Aldric felt his pulse quicken at her glance. What he would have given to not have been a prince just then. Aldric knew he couldn't be seen dancing in the streets with a half-naked girl—even if it wasn't above his brother. He smiled at her in answer, shaking his head, and he noted the sharp look of disappointment in her eyes. He wished he were someone else.

Aldric left the circle of music and dancing and walked on, through people with painted faces who danced and sang, and mongers of every kind peddling antique carts through the streets. Assorted food stands crowded together under the archways. Game meats cooked over roasting spits, rich brown sauces dripping and sizzling into the leaping flames below, and Cipher yowled and looked longingly at the meat cooking on skewers as they passed. Fruits and sweets of kinds Aldric had rarely seen garnished every corner. Men crowded together sharing wineskins filled with arak, and pipes fumed with spiced tobacco as old men nodded sagely and told stories of how the world used to be. Fireworks exploded day and night, and every building was hung with brilliant banners and buntings of red and blue, the colours of the Dhemorahn Sect.

As he walked through the streets Aldric felt oddly out of place. In the garish atmosphere, his beige, high-collared uniform was sombre and stood out against the vivid colours around him. Many in the street recognised him and respectfully bowed and made way. Trying to avoid a scene, he slipped through the crowd without much disturbance. He found that much of what he had been taught by the Valorí had many practical uses in daily life.

Walking down several more noisy blocks, Aldric finally left Bael Dunmar behind. He paused to wait as two massive urocha bellowed past him hauling carts of laughing, jeering people. At sight of the giant beasts Cipher crouched down, growling quietly as the hackles on his back rose. Aldric patted him reassuringly. The people leaned out, shouting and waving, throwing flowers and candies to the onlookers in the street. Dancers ran in front of the urocha, taunting them, the urocha bellowing and shaking their muscled shoulders in irritation. The big bull urocha wore garlands and wreaths as well, their leathery black hides painted all over.

Aldric passed numerous gendarmes, their rifles slung over their shoulders and standing at ease. Small riots and drunken brawls broke out now and then, and of course merchants were accused of marking up prices. Yet the celebrations were peaceful, the gendarmes content to let most infractions pass in the spirit of the festivities. The Imperial Army was also on alert should anything become serious between the Asaani and the Dhemorahns. In truth, many of the Asaani simply stayed in their homes, and others found excuses to leave the city entirely. Even Bailynn and Balimaar, nearby towns on the shore of Lake Nimaine, had swollen with Dhemorahns making the pilgrimage to see the first Dhemorgal in a thousand years.

Aldric looked around. Everyone was happy. Everyone was smiling and laughing, drinking and singing. It was difficult to maintain his stoic disapproval amidst such gaiety, yet Aldric wasn't just an ordinary citizen, and the troubles of his office weighed heavily on his mind.

He rounded a corner to an empty side street, glancing down the way as he did. Two young men in red and blue robes stood with their backs to him, their attention focused on something in front of them. He couldn't see past them, but something about it felt wrong. Cipher tensed up as well, his ears swivelling as he sniffed. The men were speaking harshly, and Aldric moved closer to hear what they were saying.

By their manner it was obvious they'd been drinking. One of the men stepped to the side, and in the gap between them Aldric glimpsed an older man in distinctive grey robes. *An Asaani Elder.* He moved closer and positioned himself in a nearby alcove. He glanced around, but there were no gendarmes in sight. *Typical.*

"They left!" slurred one of the young men to the Asaani Elder. "They left, and d'you know whyyy?" He asked, jabbing his finger at the man.

"I have nothing to give you," the Elder said. "All I can offer you is this bread, would you like some?"

"Bread?" said the other man, grabbing the Asaani's shoulder and shaking him. "Whadda we want bread for?" He slapped the basket out of the Elder's hands, loaves of bread spilling onto the flagstones.

"I asked you *a question.* Where'd they go, eh? Where? Your gods, your little gods, all of them, where? Poof!" the first man said, tossing his hands in the air. "They vanished! Cause they're *schlec,* and everyone knows it."

"Everyone, but you," said the other man, taking a step forward and shoving the Elder again.

There was no expression on the old man's face, but he took a few steps backward. "There's no need for this," he said. "Come back to the temple with me, let me make you some tea."

The first Dhemorahn seized him roughly. "You think we want *tea?*" he asked.

"I wish I had more to give you," the Elder said apologetically. "Here, take these." He stooped to remove his sandals. "You are barefoot, and these will keep your feet safe." He offered them to the first man.

"I don't want your sandals old man," the Dhemorahn said, swatting the sandals away. "We want you gone!"

"Then I will leave," the Elder replied, turning to go.

"Whoa hey hey now," the first man said, grabbing the druid's shoulder. "Not so fast, we aren't done with you. You go around, all the time—I see you. You and the others, you far-sighters, you *watchers*, watching. You're always watching! And what are you watching, eh? What? What are you watching? I want to know! I want to know... what you're watching! What do you seeeeeee," he said, twisting his finger into the man's forehead. The Elder wore a delicate circlet of silver above his brow, and the Dhemorahn flicked it with his finger. It made a small ringing sound.

The Elder looked down, almost sadly Aldric thought, but he said nothing. Aldric looked around again. *Dammit! Where the hell are the gendarmes?*

"Well," the young Dhemorahn said haughtily. "If you see so much, you old *gazer*, did you see this?" He raised his hand to strike him.

"Hey!" Aldric shouted, stepping out of the alcove. The two men whirled around, forgetting the Elder for a moment.

"Who the hell are you?" The first Dhemorahn asked.

"Are you enjoying the celebrations?" Aldric asked, ignoring him as he walked closer. Cipher walked beside him, ears back and tail down.

"Hey, he asked who you are," shouted the second man again, echoing his friend.

"Yeah, and what are you doing, coming about here, anyways?" asked the first, taking another step towards Aldric. Their faces were painted red and blue, and their robes were stained and torn in places. Their long blond hair was braided over their shoulders in the style of the Thedarran upper class. *Rich Dhemorahn brats drunk and looking for a thrill.*

"This street's a little quiet, eh?" Aldric said, again ignoring them. "Why don't we head back to Bael Dunmar and have some more drinks? They're on me."

"No, I wanna know why you think you can come 'round here and poke your nose in where you please," the first man said, taking another step closer. Aldric tensed, but remained motionless. He could hear Cipher growling quietly, but the two men didn't seem to notice the razorcat. The man was within striking range, but Aldric would give him another chance.

"We was 'avin a good time, right, and you had to come 'round here and muck it up. This *gaetha* was putting on airs, right?" he said, pointing back at the Asaani Elder, who was nowhere to be seen.

"Oy!" the Dhemorahn shouted. "After him!" His companion turned to run after him when Aldric caught him by the wrist and twisted his arm behind his shoulder, kicking the back of his knee so that he fell over, landing hard on his bent arm. A look of utter astonishment flashed over the first man's face. He made a fist and sluggishly lunged at Aldric.

Aldric blocked his swing and drove his fist into the man's gut, winding him. The man fell over coughing and hacking. Aldric stepped back and watched. The first man had staggered up, but before he could get back to his feet a blur of black fur was suddenly on his back, and the man screamed as he stumbled over, Cipher landing on top of him.

"Cipher hold," Aldric said, and the razorcat froze, his teeth clamped on the man's neck. The man whimpered and started to try to get up. "I'd stay down if I were you," Aldric said. The man lay back down.

Aldric looked around at the other Dhemorahn, who was also trying to get up. He made it to his knees before he threw up, retching loudly on the street. He rolled over onto a pile of hay next to an uroch cart and lay gasping. He waved his arm at Aldric, swinging his hand around. The effort was too much for him, and he dropped his arm heavily. His head sagged on his chest and he closed his eyes, covered in his vomit and breathing deeply.

Aldric looked down the street to find the Elder, but he had long since disappeared. In the scuffle, however, the circlet of silver had fallen from his head and lay in the street. Aldric bent over and picked it up. It was a *clamael*, a piece of traditional jewellery worn by elders of the Asaani. It was said to enhance the clairvoyant powers of *aina*. Aldric didn't know if that was true, but it was incredibly valuable nonetheless. Whoever that man had been, it just wasn't his day. *Probably hasn't been his week, either,* Aldric thought, tucking the *clamael* into his breast pocket.

He returned to the two men who were lying where he had left them. Cipher hadn't moved, and the young Dhemorahn was sniffling piteously, tears rolling down his red face. Yet Aldric felt neither pity nor anger, though a keen sense of foreboding had been stirred by the encounter. *This is what it will be like,* he thought. *The entire city, turned on itself.* He wasn't sure why he felt that way. In a city with tens of thousands of people all drinking and celebrating, there was bound to be a fight or two.

Yet this was different. This touched him deeper somehow. If he had been concerned before, he was now openly fearful for the Asaani who remained in the city tomorrow. There would be other festivals held across the world, he thought—even on Allria, Errolor's twin planet in the system.

But the great Ziggurat with the Divine Hall of Man was here in Chaldrea; the Temple of Daor and Gaiban Morrigan, the Seeress of the Asaani, were here in Chaldrea. And Mal'Dreghen was here. Aldric shook his head. Walking down the street he turned and whistled. Cipher released the man's neck and bounded down the street towards Aldric, ears up and tail held high.

SEVEN

EIDOLON

The gas giant Victus towered overhead. Purple clouds the size of planets swirled in veins of gold and yellow gas like ripples on a pond. The monstrous planet haunted the outer wastes of the Aethian star system, terrible and lonely. It was the last planet in the system before the great rift of nothing beyond.

The Archduke Raynard Sinclair watched the bulk of the planet whirling noiselessly above. Standing on the bridge of a small Imperial sloop, he watched the titanic storms and vortexes raging nearly a hundred and fifty thousand kilometres away. Even at this distance, the planet still engulfed the forward view. *You could squeeze all of Errolor between here and Victus, ten times, and there'd still be room left over,* he thought to himself.

The gas giant appeared weightless, suspended among the stars. Yet beneath those boiling purple clouds, Raynard could imagine the crushing pressure and heat of a thousand atmospheres swallowing his little ship without mercy. Across the soundless void, he had the strangest feeling at times that he could somehow *hear* the planet. It was a low, throbbing groan that echoed through the gulf—*almost like a growl,* he thought uneasily.

Raynard clasped his hands behind his broad back. The reflection that stared back at him through the reinforced panels of ferranite glass was tall and imposing, though it wasn't what it had been in years before. The wrinkles about Raynard's eyes had deepened with age and the rigours of his office: as the archduke of Allria, Raynard was second only to the emperor, and nearly a suzerain in his own right.

He'd fought on many battlefields in his day, and the thickly corded muscles beneath his enormous shoulders were still prominent. Years of comfortable living had added some girth to his giant frame, and his once trim waist had rounded out nicely with age. He was sixty-five, and since his years of climbing in and out of trenches and leading battle charges under fire were long over, Raynard didn't see the sense in a man worrying about his figure at his age. Hell, he figured he was living on borrowed time anyways, and he might as well enjoy it.

His fiery red hair hadn't faded with age, though there were more than a few wires of grey bristles speckling his bushy red beard. A broad nose, thick eyebrows, ruddy complexion and powerful jaw imbued him with a rugged ferocity, intimidating both foes on battlefields and in staterooms alike. Combined with his deep, basso voice and the intensity of his green eyes, Raynard was a Gal Galheal warrior from out of the oldest myths and legends of his highland ancestry. In another era, he would have been a clan chieftain, and in any era he seemed destined for command.

He shrugged his shoulders and stretched his neck, longing for a hot shower. It had been a very long voyage from Allria to *Torr Archus*, the military shipyard orbiting Victus. The little sloop they had travelled on didn't have the advanced stardrives of more modern military vessels. It was limited by its Nebrian drive, and travelling at roughly one twentieth the speed of light, it had taken almost ninety hours to reach Victus. Even with a transfer to a faster sloop at Ahran, he'd spent three days confined in the tight quarters aboard a vessel not designed with a man of his stature in mind. He breathed deeply and put it out of his mind. He was here now, and he anticipated some peace and quiet at the station before rejoining the fleet.

"Sire, we're approaching *Torr Archus*," a technician reported from the crew pit below the quarter deck. "Approximately 10k kilometres and closing."

"Proceed on thrusters and slave the navigator to the port authority," Raynard said. He turned to see *Torr Archus* twinkle into sight beyond the narrow bow of the sloop. At this distance it was no more than a dot of light in the crawling umbra of Victus. Yet as they closed on the station, it began to take form against the night. A dozen minutes later it loomed before them, and Raynard watched as his crew guided the little sloop towards the docking bay.

Torr Archus was an immense station, home to thousands of people. It served as both military shipyard and research station. Its remoteness in the system kept most traffic away, but Raynard still noted a few civilian shuttles here and there. Most were scientific vessels on survey missions around Victus and its many moons. However, a few were passenger transports from Errolor for the brave few who made the decision to live with their families stationed here at the edge of oblivion.

"Sir, the harbourmaster is requesting permission to take us in."

"Granted. Proceed," Raynard said without turning around. A small, one man craft settled above the bow of the sloop, dim blue contrails funnelling under its waffling engine skirts.

Drifting in tow behind the pilot, Raynard surveyed the wide, flat structure of the station, the purples and golds of Victus reflected on its silver skin. *Torr Archus*, or The Tower of Archus in the old Asaaran language of the Asaani, resembled an elongated arrowhead with a hollowed centre that functioned as the dry dock, while the inner sides of the ring housed numerous ships in recessed bays.

The slumbering bulk of an enormous warship glittered in the starlight, hanging idly in the dock as crews swarmed its hull. Its chrome body was illuminated in the bay lights, and Raynard knew this must be the future INV *Armistice*—a new class of super-carrier that dwarfed anything in the Imperial Navy to date. It looked to be almost as large as the station, and was barely contained by the dock. Its sloping turrets and drooping double prows looked like ominous fangs in the darkness. Raynard wondered who the Admiralty had in mind for command. His eyes darted over the rest of the station quickly, yet he didn't see the *Eidolon*, the newly commissioned cruiser he'd come here to retrieve.

A shadow passed over the bridge as the harbourmaster released the sloop and drifted up and over the command deck, falling gently to the port side. The sloop floated forwards into a circular bay where crews in white suits operated loading machinery. Scores of technicians and naval personnel watched from an observation deck suspended from the ceiling at the fore of the hangar. A shudder ran through the ship as it sidled into place and the magnetic locks engaged.

"Well done," Raynard said, congratulating the crew with his usual brusqueness. "Crew rotation begins in one hour, evening watch is on duty." He surveyed the crowd of officers shuffling about the bridge. Standing at the gantry to the quarterdeck was a sandy haired man in his late forties wearing a trim, grey, high collared uniform. The man had white captain's piping on his epaulettes, polished black boots, and a small outstretched wing on either side of his collar. He was addressing a junior officer.

"Captain Achres," Raynard said, raising his voice above the general hum.

Achres dismissed the officer. "My Lord?" he said, nodding curtly. He was a slender man, dark of hair with a pale complexion and aquiline nose that betrayed his Illarien heritage. He possessed thoughtful blue eyes and a small mouth that seemed forever drawn rigid in disapproval. Yet he was reliable, intelligent, and cautious, and Raynard valued his abilities as an officer immensely.

"I'd be grateful if you'd oversee the necessary preparations on board the *Eidolon*," Raynard said. "I have business with Admiral Harding, and I'm not certain how long I'll be."

The captain nodded, his mouth tightening into that familiar line. "At once, my Lord. Are there any special arrangements you'd like seen to?"

"No, the rotation should be routine enough, and everything else should have already been taken care of, but double check with the *Archus* quartermaster." Raynard folded his arms. "I didn't see the *Eidolon* as we came in—as soon as I speak with the admiral I'm going to find her. If you could get things under way for now, I'll meet you when I'm finished."

"Of course, my Lord."

"Then I'll leave you to it captain," Raynard said. He paused. The captain's eyes flickered to the side briefly, staring uncertainly somewhere over Raynard's shoulder. "Was there something else?" Raynard asked, trying to hide his exhaustion.

The captain frowned. "My Lord, I wanted to meet with you privately to discuss this, but I see we have no time now," he began.

"Let's have it captain," Raynard said, his patience slipping.

"This is the largest task force ever assembled; with all our ships deployed to this one sector, I am concerned at the tactical disadvantage we're placed in elsewhere."

Raynard was well aware of Achres' concern. In many ways it reflected his own misgivings about the operation. "The Raeth have never marshalled a substantial fleet against us. It's been hit and run until now. Nothing about this is routine," Raynard said, agreeing.

"I've read the briefings and the Raeth's posture is alarming." Achres lowered his voice, his tone still urgent. "I'm afraid the Admiralty underestimates the manoeuvrability of the Raeth—after this morning, we can be sure of nothing. They may yet have a force we're unaware of, something they've been keeping hidden for the right moment."

"The Raeth have never mustered anything with enough strength to contend with the Attendant Fleet, let alone *Arrus Athaban*." Raynard studied Achres. He appeared calm, but after serving with Achres for two decades, Raynard had learned to trust his instincts. After all, the reports from the morning were shocking. *An Adamant class destroyer,* he thought.

They didn't even know the whole story yet—perhaps something else had been involved; they'd have to wait until the ship's data was recovered to know. Eye witness accounts varied dramatically, some claiming they had collided with a rogue asteroid. *Asteroids don't leave blast marks.* Besides, data transmissions were five and a half hours behind events on Errolor. Any number of developments might have been made in that time; it was too early to speculate. They might make a more informed decision once they were en route to rendezvous with the armada around Argoth.

"I agree, captain," Raynard said finally. "But our best projections indicate this is our chance to break the backbone of their fleet. I've been in touch with the emperor, he is insisting that we take every available ship from every strike force and wipe out the Raeth once and for all." Raynard drummed his fingers over his folded arms. "Frankly, I'm astonished he decided to leave the Attendant Fleet behind, that must have taken some convincing on Ramsay's part."

"My Lord, if their fleet is as large as the captured data indicates, it's entirely possible they might take this chance to cripple us instead. It would be the perfect opportunity."

"Captain Achres, what would you suggest? We can't possibly leave the facility on Drusus to the Raeth. The ore the convoy carries is priceless. Damn the politics, our fleet can't operate without thadium. And if they captured or destroy the facility itself...?"

Achres looked away uncomfortably. He didn't seem to like his position in the matter, but he wasn't willing to outright argue with the archduke. "I advise caution, my Lord," he said stiffly. "In such a situation, we are terribly exposed. On your command, two or three dozen ships could remain as a rear guard—"

"I recognise your position, captain," Raynard said. "But two or three dozen ships represent a sizeable portion of the fleet. I can't risk losing that on the off chance that the Raeth would be crazy enough to attack Errolor. And I won't countermand the Admiralty—or the emperor. Three warships, captain, are all I can spare. I won't be unprepared at Drusus. Our mining interests are too important—Drusus is invaluable."

"With respect, Your Grace, it is a mining facility. There are several thousand workers there, and it could be recaptured, or at worst, rebuilt," Achres said. His firmness surprised Raynard. "*Athaban* is home to twenty thousand, and the gateway to Errolor. If we lose control of the space over Errolor..." he trailed off, trying to find his words. "If something happened, it would be hours before our fleet could even regroup there."

"Captain, I cannot commit to another course of action at this point. All I can say is that I am going to speak with the vice admiral. I'll let you know my decision after I've had some more time to consider." Raynard ran his hands together. "And eat, and change my uniform, I should think."

Achres nodded, relaxing somewhat. "Very good, my Lord," he said.

Raynard raised an eyebrow. "Now—anything else?"

Achres shook his head. "No. I simply wanted to be certain all possibilities had been weighed. I know you will do what's best."

"I appreciate your confidence, captain," Raynard said, giving the captain a half smile. "The ship is yours, then."

Passing down sky lit corridors, Raynard marvelled at the giant above. Victus, "the Wandering Chaos", was named after an ancient god of the Asaani who feasted on the madness of those about to die. *Aptly named,* Raynard thought, still feeling that dread growling somewhere in his subconscious.

Four Valorí surrounded Raynard, marching quietly in step, preceded by his envoy. Aside from the emperor and his sons, Raynard was one of the only people in all the empire granted an escort of Valorí. This was due more to the fact that he had saved the emperor's life in the War of the Dukes than it was his political position, which he had also received for his efforts in the war. The others were his wife and daughter, who Raynard insisted were also afforded escorts. The old archduke slept much easier on his long tours away from his palace on Allria knowing there were Valorí watching over his family.

The narrow corridors leading from the docking bays opened suddenly onto a broad plaza, curving away both directions into the distance. Raynard could see hundreds of people milling about the various shops and restaurants in the concourse. Potted trees lined the plaza and large water fountains bubbled cheerfully. At first glance the enormous concourse resembled the indoor mall near the Citadel in Chaldrea. Technicians stood discussing plans, officers in high boots clipping smartly past, marines marching together on the lower decks and mechanics skimming above the steel deck plating in sleek cargo lifts. The air was a little chilly, stirring with the faint hum of lofty spaces.

Despite its nature as a military space station, *Torr Archus* exuded extravagance, flaunting the critical imperative of conservation in space. *Torr Archus* boasted luxury and expansive living comforts, and the impression was not lost on Raynard. *Archus* wasn't just a station; it was a home to thousands of people. The human psyche demanded certain niceties, and being enclosed, confined—*trapped*—tended to make populations unproductive or rebellious. *Beautiful,* Raynard thought. *And wasteful. Like much of the empire these days.*

Raynard paused to gather his bearings. The winding steel hallways all looked the same. And he was tired. All he wanted was to soak under a hot shower. When had he slept? He couldn't remember. It'd been at least a day. The tiny quarters aboard the sloop were intolerable. He gave up and allowed the envoy to lead the way, his eyes dropping to the floor as he fell into thought, lingering on the fringes of the envoy's flapping white cloak.

He'd considered the attack on Drusus was a diversion. Attacking Errolor wouldn't offer the bounty that taking the convoy would, but it would be a devastating blow to the Imperial fleet, and it would force the navy to reassign its forces around the system, giving the pirates a free hand to manoeuvre around the shipping lanes. *If the station really* was *their target,* Raynard thought.

Of course they would need to disable *Arrus Athaban* and Attendant Fleet, but they might also attempt to attack the capital from orbit. *Why not? Never get another chance like it.* Chaldrea was protected, and supporting fleets could be raised from the planet's surface. But it would take time to assemble, even on standby—and if Achres was right, they wouldn't have that time.

Gods, but he was tired. His back ached from standing stiffly on the bridge for hours, and he could smell the stale sweat on his uniform. And he was hungry. *Famished, more like,* he thought to himself as he tried to ignore his grumbling stomach. He reminded himself he'd faced much worse in his campaign years. But those were merely distant memories now. *Look how soft I've become,* he scolded himself cheerfully.

He glanced at the Valorí to either side. He didn't know how they maintained their composure. Well, he did, but their unfaltering demeanour never failed to astonish him. Raynard never saw them eating, performing toilet, or anything else considered commonly human. Their mirrored-armour close-helmets and precise movements complimented their super-human mystique. They would stand at his side as stiff as statues for hours without moving, yet be ready at the slightest hint to spring into action. He'd seen them do it before, and it was uncanny how quickly they moved. *I'd rather have a dozen exhausted Valorí than a company of fresh Imperial dragoons,* he thought.

"Wait here for me," he told the Valorí as they stopped outside Admiral Harding's command room. The Valorí silently took up station on opposite sides of the door with quick, mechanically precise movements. Their phase armour was dialled to achromatic silver, reflecting dully the steel grey walls and floor. The darkened eye-slits of their visors betrayed nothing. They might have been statues.

"My Lord?" his envoy asked, hesitating at the door. His envoy was a small man who spoke indirectly, and Raynard found his peevishness tiresome. He tolerated him because he was talented at managing his affairs, but his obsequious mannerisms grated on Raynard's nerves. He had clearly expected to announce the archduke's presence to the vice admiral, a responsibility of some prestige, but ultimately unimportant. Raynard wasn't in the mood for decorum, and he knew the admiral didn't really care either.

"Wait here," he repeated, letting his irritation show. The envoy bowed his head, nodding.

Inside the steel doors a sparse office stretched away towards floor-to-ceiling ferranite glass walls overlooking Victus. The cosmic view was spectacular, and Raynard fancied anything else must seem claustrophobic after being stationed here. A dark haired man in a high collared, naval grey uniform sat at a desk at the far end of the room. He looked up, his light-coloured eyes keen as they took in Raynard's robust figure.

Raynard didn't wait to be greeted, walking over and grasping the vice admiral's forearm in both hands as he stood from his desk. "You look comfortable, Alasdair," Raynard said genially, some of his fatigue lifting at seeing his old friend.

"I'm busy," the admiral said, returning Raynard's grip. There was a brief pause as they both sought to crush the other's hand. The admiral was a strong man, and met Raynard's intense gaze with an impassiveness that only an old warrior could muster. Yet he was nowhere the size of the archduke and finally succumbed, gently releasing his hand from Raynard's massive paws.

"I'm unbelievably busy," Alasdair said, massaging his arm behind his back. "I suppose you think I have nothing to do out here but wait for fat old men to make house calls when a ship needs picking up?"

Raynard chuckled, levity overcoming his weariness. "Now then, I can't imagine them putting you in charge of anything too important," he said, dropping into a chair opposite Alasdair.

"You know it's lucky your daughter's as pretty as she is. If she inherits your charm, she'll need something to fall back on." Alasdair's dark beard offset his pale complexion in the wan light of Victus. Raynard couldn't place his ancestry, though his high nose and broad face spoke of Brythanic stock.

"You always did prefer the company of ladies," Raynard said. "I was more at home on a battlefield doing real work, but you were more comfortable, well," he said, waving his hand across the expansive carved wooden desk to Alasdair's luxurious high backed recliner. "I suppose those papers won't shuffle themselves."

"Oh enough," Alasdair said, sitting up a little straighter. "Did you come in here to show off what passes for your wit, or do you have something worth my time to discuss?"

Raynard smiled. "It's good to see you Al," he said.

"How is your daughter anyways?" Alasdair asked, unbuttoning the top facets on his collar.

"Oh Evaine? She's well, thank you. I wish I got the chance to be with her more often. She's grown so much the last year or two, really come into her own. I think she'll make a better politician than I ever have. She's a lethal quick study of the mind. But she'd sooner cut throats than bandy words. She'll make an excellent Grand Duchess," he said, his eyes twinkling proudly.

"Does she still train with those Asaani druids?" Alasdair asked.

"The Valorí? Yes, she does. She hasn't much in the way of *aina*, though she's far better than I am. She's devilish in *craidath* though. A few months ago I made the mistake of thinking she was still my little girl when she asked me to spar with her," Raynard said, leaning forward. "She might've killed me if I didn't have ten stone on her." He laughed. "I was sore for a week! I'm glad my men didn't see that."

"Floored you then, did she?" Alasdair asked, not concealing a grin.

"Oh no," Raynard said waving his hands. "I pulled through. I don't even think she knew how bad off I was. But it wasn't pretty Al—black and blue all over my chest, and Eleanor scolded me something fierce. Now I let her spar with those warrior druids of hers, I don't dare make that mistake again."

He drew his hand over his face, smoothing his beard. "Whoever takes her hand someday better be sure he does it gently," he said.

"Yes, well I hear Prince Aldric has been spending some time at the Temple himself these days," Alasdair said. He glanced at Raynard from under his brows as he rearranged some papers.

Aldric and Evaine seemed an obvious pairing to everyone in the Erolan: a union bringing together two Great Houses and uniting the planets. Aldric was only few years older than Evaine, and it would be a monarch's match made in heaven. "Evaine's never forgiven the prince for what happened at that gala. When she does, perhaps there's a chance," Raynard said. "I'm not noble born, and I've no mind to force her into the trappings of the Erolan."

"That was years ago," Alasdair said.

"When have you known a woman to forgive intemperately?" Raynard asked.

Alasdair shook his head. "Well, in any case, give her my best when you're home next, I can't remember the last time I saw her."

"Just before you first came out here," Raynard said, gazing upward as he thought back. "Four years ago, I think?"

"Four and a half," Alasdair said, nodding. "It's a wonderful assignment, Raynard, but it does feel a bit out of the way."

"Hell it took me three days on a Nebrian drive," Raynard said.

Alasdair nodded, brushing down the breast of his uniform absently. "The Raeth never venture out here, nothing for it! So I sit here, aging gracefully. I just can't help but feel some regret. The Ascendancy seems so long ago."

Raynard smiled to himself. Alasdair could be such a sentimentalist. A man of the utmost capability, but given to bouts of melancholy if left to himself, which was most of the time out here.

"It was a long time ago," Raynard said, breaking Alasdair's reverie before it turned sour. "But it looks like all that's about to change."

"Yes, the Raeth. Of course I've heard," Alasdair replied.

"We all have. It's the damndest thing Al. They've never done anything like it."

"Never could," Alasdair said, steepling his fingers beneath his nose.

"Exactly my point. Where did it come from?" Raynard asked.

"I think we know where," Alasdair said dryly. "Or at least, have our hunches. But that doesn't matter for now. A captured ship with that kind of information is troubling enough. We can worry about where the money came from later."

"Yes... the captured ship," Raynard said. It was a troubling piece of evidence. "The Raeth can't possibly have a fleet that large."

"A hundred, two hundred ships? It's possible," Alasdair said.

"*Three hundred,*" Raynard corrected him. Alasdair raised his eyebrows. "And if they can match the firepower that brought down the *Malefactor* this morning, then we'll need the entire Sciphere to engage them."

"On the defensive, Ray," Alasdair said. He was one of a small handful who could use such a familiar tone with the archduke. "I don't like it. They're dictating, we're responding."

"And they know it. They must. This isn't a solo operation, there's someone who knows what we're doing and is keeping them informed." He leant on one arm, wagging his finger at the admiral. "And wherever we *aren't*, I have the surest feeling that's where they *will be.*"

Alasdair's eyes narrowed as he nodded, absorbing the thought. "We're over extending our resources," he said. "The Navy just isn't that large. Securing one sector leaves another open, no matter how we play it."

"It's too big an opportunity to second guess," Raynard said. "There's too much at stake. The Raeth have never been so bold—if they gamble and fail, which, even considering the odds, must seem like a possibility, their back is broken. They'll be finished."

"Perhaps not," Alasdair said. "I admit it seems unlikely they'd throw it all at this one convoy, but everything points to something bigger. If they failed, it might be a calculated loss, and the real target might be elsewhere."

"You really think they're going after Errolor?"

"Or Allria."

Raynard shook his head. "They wouldn't, there's nothing on Allria. You can't sack an entire planet with a handful of ships. Besides, Allria isn't developed, and they couldn't hold it even if they did capture it. The military is on Errolor, they'd be sitting targets. They don't have the force to entrench themselves."

"That's true, but I can't imagine a single convoy, no matter how rich, being worth risking their entire fleet. It isn't logical. They know they can't go toe to toe with an Imperial battleship, let alone a dreadnought or carrier, which would be the normal escort for this operation." The admiral reached into his desk and produced a plain black bottle and two glasses. He measured out two clear drinks and pushed one across the table to Raynard.

Raynard drank his quickly and set the glass down harder than he meant. It was crisp and clean and biting, and it rolled down his throat and burned his empty stomach. Alasdair's words reflected his own fears. Yet the Admiralty's briefings were so convincing. First hand intelligence reports, discussions with freighter captains from the convoys during the past week, hidden listening posts deployed among the asteroid belt and around the system, communications intercepted from the mining colonies themselves—it all pointed to a massive gathering at Drusus. But it had never been done before. Never even attempted.

It made sense on paper, and seemed exactly like the obvious move. But that was what bothered Raynard. The Raeth knew about the listening posts and the reports the Navy would be receiving. They couldn't suppose such a move would be executed without the Navy learning of it and taking appropriate countermeasures.

"I spoke with my captain just before coming here, he felt as you do," Raynard said. "I admit my own doubts are eating me up, the whole thing is too obvious. We've never been able to anticipate an attack ahead of time, except that larger convoys make larger targets."

Alasdair poured another drink. "The emperor has his best advisors' assurance..." he said quietly. "If he's given the order, the military has to assume that all other avenues have been explored."

Raynard had been looking out the window, but there was something subtle in the admiral's voice that made him turn to regard Alasdair intently. "It's oversimplified," he said. "What if it's a feint?"

"What if it isn't?"

"Their numbers make them vulnerable. Even with three hundred ships, we still have a superior force—better crews and ships than they could ever hope to field."

"Our immobility makes *us* vulnerable," Alasdair said. "We're still defending, they're still attacking."

"Their position is tenuous at best, they have no guarantee this would work, why risk it?"

"Because our attention is diverted. They must believe their plan will succeed without a doubt," the admiral said, his baritone voice grinding out the words. The reflected light from Victus cast shadows over his face, drawing out the narrow creases around his eyes as he studied Raynard. "The emperor feels our strength alone will be enough—that a show of force will subdue any possible threat. I think he hopes it won't though. I think he's itching for a fight."

"I think he is too," Raynard said. "The problem is, we have one old strategy, and it's wearing thin. Mal'Dreghen has the emperor's attention with the Dhemorgal; he's locked between the popular view of the Asaani and the Dhemorahns, and the Erolan won't miss the opportunity either." *What's a pirate raid on a dead planet millions of kilometres away, to political chaos on your doorstep?* Raynard thought. *But oh, deny the people their little luxuries, let the commodities begin to trickle and cinch up the purse strings, and you'll feel their wrath.* Never mind what having no fuel for the fleet would do to his Navy.

"He's never been a tactician," Raynard said, folding his arms across his chest. "Gone are the days when our leaders would ride out onto the battlefield with their troops. Aronach the Great, Siegfried Söderström—all the other great emperors of the Vassarya's Golden Era. Leaders are politicians now, their battles take place in Aldon Court. We're the old dogs left to sort out their messes when their hubris meets reality," Raynard said.

"To old dogs," Alasdair said, raising his glass.

Raynard downed his drink quickly, the bitterness lingering in the back of his throat. He rolled the rim of the glass around the table. "Do you suppose the trade consortiums might have terms with the Raeth?"

Alasdair looked up. "It would make sense," he said. "Our patrols can't catch everything, and sometimes the Raeth take our escorts by surprise."

Raynard nodded. "If they formed some kind of agreement, it might explain how the Raeth have managed to elude us this long, and why we were totally surprised by the attack this morning."

"Merchants might see it as a better option than simply depending on our protection. Giving up a percentage of your goods for safe passage?" Alasdair swallowed. "Seems like a good deal to me."

"But cargo is checked and accounted for at destinations," Raynard said. "Anything missing would be noticed."

"Not if it was never recorded," Alasdair said.

Raynard whistled. "The consortium guildsmen—in league with the Raeth." He pushed his glass towards Alasdair for a refill. "The goods would arrive at the warehouses, but they'd never be logged in the books. They could buy protection and the wares would never be missed."

Alasdair had the mind of a superb strategist, outmanoeuvring superior forces on more than one occasion. Like Raynard, he didn't have a taste for the untrained, academic theories that were somehow translated into orders through the foggy minds of politicians. The military offered clear options in a situation, highs and lows, advantages and disadvantages, real strategies of terrain and numbers and strength. Politics was another kind of war, a war of opinions and feelings and internal struggles for power. *Far costlier, in many ways,* Raynard thought. A battle might take several thousand lives, but a war between politicians might drag on for years, deplete a nation of its power and strength, and cost hundreds of thousands of lives in the pursuit of mere vanity.

It hadn't been this way twenty years ago, and Raynard blamed Mal'Dreghen for the current state of chaos that plagued the empire. Prince Arem and his father Leopold were more alike than Raynard cared to think, their love of idle luxury drowning any sense of duty. Raynard wondered about Prince Aldric, who so far seemed dedicated to his station. He spent much of his time training with the Imperial Army, the Valorí, and even commanding the Naval escort of a recent convoy. He acted more like a general than a politician, which Raynard supposed might serve him better in the end, though it certainly wouldn't make him any friends of the Erolan. *Or of Mal'Dreghen*, he thought musingly.

"We have to come to a decision, Alasdair," Raynard said. The admiral nodded, but said nothing. Raynard rubbed his temples. "Despite the reports, this doesn't feel like everything; we're missing something. It's too organised, the evidence is too easy to interpret. It's a trail, leading away from *Arrus Athaban*."

"It's easy to see shadows," Alasdair said. "Perhaps we've been looking in the wrong places. Perhaps the dukes still resent losing their armies."

"Or they're being encouraged to resent it."

Alasdair merely nodded.

"Emperor Leopold is the only reason the Asaani can still show their faces outside their homes. There'd be a pogrom if the emperor were eliminated."

"You have a dark turn of mind, Lord Sinclair," Alasdair said. "But I share your suspicions."

Raynard absently rubbed the pale embroidery on his cuffs between his thumb and forefinger. "Suppose for a moment, Alasdair," he began, his voice low. Alasdair regarded him closely. "Suppose for a moment that there is something altogether deeper in this?"

"Beyond what we already suspect? A feint within a feint?" Alasdair said.

"We are looking beyond the assault on *Arrus Athaban*, or on Errolor. There is nothing to argue against something much, much grander in ambition here. The stage is set, the situation for the emperor is precarious at best, the Imperial throne challenged from all corners—Mal'Dreghen, stirring common opinion against him and inciting anger between the Dhemorahns and the Asaani, as well as the Erolan, who perceive the emperor's indecision for the weakness it is."

"But isn't this taking it a bit far?" Alasdair asked.

"Is it?" Raynard said. "Oh I don't know. Someone is coordinating this. The Raeth aren't organised, they're pirates, corsairs—they don't work with each other. They smash and grab and beat it back to their bases in the asteroid belt or the moons. Bringing them all together like this would have to mean they'd agreed to cooperate and someone was leading them, someone who'd managed to bring them under one banner."

"Why not an ambitious commander somewhere? A warlord who's finally united the colonies? It's not unheard of—nomadic tribes converging around an authority figure. In fact, I can't think of a single time when, given a large enough population, that hasn't happened. Just look at the plains chieftains during the Warring Kingdoms."

"You're right Alasdair," Raynard said. "But this, plus the Dhemorgal, and the *Malefactor* this morning, it's all too unlikely."

"The Mal."

"A revolution, Alasdair," Raynard said. "Overthrowing the monarchy. It's happened before, and I'll be damned if this isn't the perfect opportunity for someone to try again."

Alasdair considered the archduke for a moment, twisting his glass back and forth in his hands. "That wouldn't be the first time I've heard that suggested," Alasdair said.

"Rumours all the way out here, eh? It must be worse than I thought," Raynard said, raising his eyebrows ever so slightly.

"There's been rumour for some time now," Alasdair replied. "Nothing substantial, but my friends in Amren have mentioned the odd report from scouts every now and then. Nothing concrete, mind you, but there's evidence that something sinister is happening beyond our listening posts in this system."

"The Aethian System isn't infinite," Raynard said sceptically.

"It's big enough," Alasdair said, wiping the water rings from underneath his glass. "Besides, there's always Kor."

He hadn't really considered the planet before. Its eccentric orbit ran perpendicular to the rest of the system, and its rotational cycle was somewhere around a thousand years, if he remembered. "Kor? Well I suppose anything is possible." He rubbed his hands together thoughtfully. "For now, however, I want to see my ship."

EIGHT

CRUCIBLE

E vaine could feel him watching her. With effort, she could even imagine herself through his eyes, seeing what he saw. A small, athletic girl standing there in the sandy ring, legs planted, loose in the knees, arms tight at her sides. She composed herself, poised to strike. This vision of herself wasn't quite *aina,* but it felt close. She kneaded her toes into the sandy arena, *no coolness there.* Panting, she listened, trying to slow her heartbeat and catch the sounds that her blindfolded eyes could not show her. There was the faintest crunch of gravelly dirt to her right; she didn't betray she'd heard anything. *A decoy.* Attack now, and she would be thrown to the floor.

With effort, she recovered her breathing, deep lungfuls of dusty, biting air as oxygen depleted cells rushed to her lungs, back through her muscles, replenishing lost stores. She breathed in with her stomach and her chest, maximising her capacity, feeling her heart rate slow. Mere moments, and she was ready again.

The old blindfold was itchy, its coarse fibres scratching her cheeks and eyes. *A distraction.* It didn't hold back her hair either, long golden strands clinging to her face and neck, drenched in sweat. Another slow, hesitant crunch of dirt: this time behind her and to the left. Evaine tensed inwardly, while making a neutral shift in her hips to disguise the minute twisting of her left foot as she prepared.

Her legs burned from bending for so long, her back muscles aching in her strained position. But she pushed these reports from her awareness, focusing all her attention on the sounds in the little ring. No telltale breathing sounds, he wouldn't be that sloppy. *Calm. Awareness. Calm. Listen. Breathe. Listen.* A scratch. *A rolled heel.* Then the slightest double-tapping sound, as of two steps lightly in the sand. *Now.*

With incredible speed, Evaine spun around and dropped her right knee to the sand, kneeling as she leaned forward into the sound. Without waiting for contact with her assailant to reassure her of her decision, she hooked her right foot into the sand and powered upwards, swinging her right arm above her in a smooth arc. All at once she felt a heavy weight collide against her shoulders, slide onto her back, carry onwards behind her as she stood and threw the body over her shoulder, turning as she stood.

As the body passed over her, Evaine followed the man's arm with her left hand, catching his wrist and pulling it back into her, knowing precisely what position he'd be in. She landed beside him as he fell, driving her head hard into his chest. Locking his arm in a painful hold she sat back, smashing her knee into the tender ribs at his side, her other heel squeezed under his jaw, jamming his head backwards.

"*Anda,*" the man said, his voice a choking rasp. Evaine pulled off her blindfold and stared down at a dark haired man, his face contorted in pain. She released him and jumped up, hands akimbo, feeling a triumphant smile force its way through her guard.

With deliberate slowness, the man stood, attempting to regain some of his composure. The redness faded from his face, replaced by a look of stern appraisal. He stretched himself up, towering over Evaine, her head barely reaching his collarbone. His dark brown *kilpi* had loosened at the waist, and he was a moment straightening it and retying the fibrous wraps about his arms as he recovered his breath.

"You are a spindly little creature," the man said, massaging his shoulder. Evaine knew it for the compliment it was.

"And you're an oaf," she said, smiling. "I don't need my eyes to hear you lumbering, Vasya."

He nodded grudgingly. "I am too big."

She rolled her eyes. "Lighten up. I only knew what to do 'cause you've used that same move for years. Honestly, a child knows the *medara*," she said, jabbing his ribs with her knuckles playfully.

Vasya winced, putting his hand to his ribs. A pained expression came over his face and he looked at her unhappily.

"Vasya," she said, feeling sorry. She reached out to touch his ribs. With a blinding motion Vasya swept out his hand and locked her head into the crook of his arm, gathering both her tiny wrists into his giant paw. She was stunned, unable to move, gasping for air, pressed against his massive chest. He looked down at her, struggling, legs flailing uselessly. Yet each kick forced her entire weight onto her neck, and as she choked she stopped kicking and stood there glaring up at Vasya from the corners of her eyes. A look of hatred glazed over her face.

"Does a child know the headlock?" Vasya asked.

Evaine's face was turning purple, her lips still pouting defiantly. He held her there, waiting for her to submit. He frowned as her eyes started rolling back in her head.

"Fine," he said, letting her go. She collapsed at his feet in a pile, sucking in huge gulps of air. Her body heaved, and Vasya thought she would be sick, but after a few moments she collected herself and sat back on her haunches, regarding him ruefully.

"That was pathetic," she said. "If you have to trick me to win—"

"You forget, my Lady—fairness is not part of combat. Nothing is unfair. Nothing is *pathetic*. Winners need no excuses."

"We weren't fighting! I'd beaten you," She said, wiping spittle from her mouth with the back of her hand. "And I actually felt bad for you. A big man like you, beaten by a *spindly* girl."

"Apparently not," Vasya said, grinning.

Evaine sat in the dirt, breathing hard. Lifting herself up she joined him on the wooden bleachers in the shade of a darkened awning. Her small, heart shaped face had begun to tan in the spring sun, drawing out freckles across her cheeks and nose that were disguised by the dirt and grime smeared over her face. Gentle curves barely disguised the course of sinewy muscles beneath. She had a body like her mother's, born for winning kingdoms, and a mind like her father's, born to conquer them.

The afternoon light poured down into the little arena, golden rays glancing over swirling dust motes. It was a small ring, no more than six metres across, enclosed by a high wooden palisade. Leafy green branches drooped over the edges of the arena from outside, flowering petals falling through the warm air.

Voices in the yard beyond came muffled over the wall, and the smell of baled hay from the fields mixed with the pungent animal odours in the nearby stables and the musty smell of dirt and sweat in the arena. Heady aromas of nature and the earth, and Evaine closed her eyes, the burning in her muscles and the aching of her head beginning to subside.

"I wasn't going to say anything," she began, pulling her flaxen hair back into a ponytail. "But after that little trick, I don't think I'll mind telling Gaiban Morrigan how I laid you out flat on your back," she said.

Vasya cast her a quick glance, her thin yet muscular arms tugging her wet hair into a braid. Her slender neck was bruised in several places, and a deep purple gash below her right eye told of when she connected with his elbow earlier. Dirt from the training yard stained her *kilpi* a rusty brown. The *kilpi* was the traditional training uniform of the Asaani, and Evaine's hung loosely where it had come undone during their sparring. She tucked the corners into her belt and retied the wraps around her forearms and calves. Gathering her bright hair off her neck, she turned her sharp green eyes onto Vasya, expecting a defence.

"You would embarrass me, my Lady?" He said, chuckling softly. "I think the High Lady of the Rock would be happy to hear how well I've taught you."

Evaine tried to conceal her disappointment.

"After all," he resumed, his rich voice full and merry. "I am only Valorí—yet you are to be the archduchess. If I am lost, what of it?" He held up an empty hand. "The hopes of an empire are carried in *your* little heart," he said, tapping her chest gently.

She jabbed him hard in the ribs with her elbow.

"*Ooph*," He bent over holding his side. Glancing at her sidelong he laughed. "I hope my Lady shows her enemies the same compassion as she shows her friends," he said.

"If you weren't such a brute, I could've taken you," she said. "Just because you're a walking wall of meat doesn't mean you're a better fighter than I am."

He sat back, rubbing his side. "That's very true." Deep, bubbling laughter. "But your Ladyship again confuses justice with reality. If you're ever in a real fight, you'll not have the luxury of choosing your opponent. A *walking wall of meat,* or a dainty little thing like yourself," he said. "You must prepare for them all."

Evaine bit her lip, thinking; a habit she'd no doubt acquired from her father, the old archduke. There was boldness in her eyes, and the arrogance in the set of her jaw contrasted with her innocent beauty. When she smiled, an impish glint flickered in her eyes, like a thief making off with treasure in the night.

"You reveal much," Vasya said.

Evaine turned to look at him. His brown eyes twinkled. She released her lip and folded her hands in her lap. "Nothing gets through to you, does it?" she asked.

"I am content," Vasya said, shrugging his big shoulders. That was his answer for everything.

Evaine considered him for a moment. "Go again?" she asked, hopping up. "And this time, no *magael*," she said, tossing the blindfold to the side. "I don't want you to tell me you went easy on me because I couldn't see."

"If her Ladyship wishes. Though, you'll never master *craidath* that way, " Vasya said, goading her. He heaved himself up off his elbows.

"That's what *you* think," Evaine replied, jumping down into the arena.

Vasya shook his head. "No, that's what *you* think. My Lady, you fight with instinct, with passionate aggression. You were lucky this time—you've fought me before, you anticipated my attack. That's my fault, I should be more inventive." He stepped gracefully down into the arena, almost floating over the bleachers to her side. "If you would only focus your *aina,* it would not matter who you fought, or even if you wore the *magael.* " He touched her forehead lightly with his finger. "You must see here." His deep brown eyes softened with concern.

"You are all anger and ferocity. You attack with passion, with all the rage of your Gal Galheal ancestors in your heart. Remove yourself from the moment, sense your surroundings—your eyes will betray you. Practise your every minute awareness. *Aina* is another sense: just as you are handicapped without your sight or your hearing, think how much you lose by ignoring what your *blind sight* can reveal."

Evaine glared at him. "You're stalling," she said, a fiery glint in her eye.

Vasya shrugged. "As my Lady wishes." He walked over to the bleachers and picked up the *magael*, tying it over his eyes.

"No, don't," Evaine cried, rushing to stop him. "I don't want—" she reached out to remove the blindfold but Vasya caught her arm mid-air.

"You are stubborn. Rocks are stubborn. They do not move unless something else moves them. I will move you."

They squared off, standing a few paces apart. "*Faegrid,*" Vasya said.

"*Imbralad,*" Evaine returned.

They began circling each other. Already this was different from moments ago when she had worn the *magael*. Vasya was moving, sensing her, *seeing* her. Evaine had simply responded to what she'd heard; Vasya moved in real time, as if he were watching her without the blindfold at all.

Evaine stepped forward, then feinted to her left, her right leg arching upward in a crippling blow towards Vasya's face. In one motion Vasya reached out and deflected her attack with his right arm, throwing her leg away from him in a follow-through that sent her sprawling face down in the dirt. As she landed she felt him suddenly on top of her, his big arms sweeping over and under her shoulder, gripping together under her stomach, forcing her into a constricted ball. Her face was smashed painfully into her own knee, her arms pinned beneath her. It was like being crushed by a wargren, and she lay snorting in the dirt, sucking in mouthfuls of sand and grit.

"Get off," she gasped.

"Submit," Vasya said in her ear.

"*Get...off!*" she cried, furious, unable to contain her frustration. Vasya leapt up instantly. Evaine was surprised, she hadn't expected him to listen. She heaved herself to her feet, her back and legs stiff. "You think because you—" she began, but was cut short.

"Evaine!" A thin gasp of astonishment. A woman's voice. Evaine knew that voice very well.

She saw Vasya bow his head in a respectful gesture, but knew it was also to hide his embarrassment. *He sensed her coming,* Evaine thought. *Not soon enough.* Evaine turned to find the Archduchess Eleanor Sinclair standing in the bleachers above the arena, a look of horror on her face.

Evaine fidgeted in her chair. The Imperial Physician tried to hold her head still as he applied a fascia stimulator to her injured cheek. It tingled and she batted his hand away.

"This will take much longer if you *don't hold still*," he said, suppressing irritation.

"You can do it without *touching me*," she growled.

The physician straightened, frowning at her. He turned a helpless look towards the archduchess who stood in the doorway to her daughter's chambers. Clear light from high windows filled the room, reflecting off the pale blues and whites and giving a general airy impression. The room was clean, efficient, uncluttered. It was at odds with much of the rest of Cnoc Baegan, the ducal fortress on Allria, and far less sumptuous than Dur Enskai on Errolor.

"Evaine, if you don't comply, that will be the last time you ever train with the Valorí." Eleanor's voice was calm, peremptory—tempered from many years of giving commands and seeing them obeyed. The archduchess strode into the room, her green and white gown ruffling faintly. Evaine looked up at her lean face, her high cheek bones and supple, sensual lips. Eleanor's blonde hair had begun to silver, enhanced by the sunny glow of the room and complimenting her light complexion. Yet her eyes were icy crystals as she gazed down at her daughter.

Evaine knew when it was useless to argue. She could badger the palace servants, soldiers, official dignitaries and representatives—even her father couldn't resist her when she really wanted something. But it was futile with her mother. Eleanor had been just like Evaine when she was younger, and understood exactly how to apply pressure to make Evaine fall in line. There was no bargaining, no compromise, and no chance for subtle manoeuvring. Evaine could wrestle men twice her size to the ground and survive for weeks in the wilderness—yet a few words from her mother and she was powerless.

Evaine sat still. The physician raised his eyebrows at her and she nodded, turning her cheek to him. He picked up the silver stimulator and she heard a faint hum as a violet light began tickling her bruised skin.

The archduchess walked around her and sat lightly on the foot of Evaine's bed, watching her. Evaine knew already what she would say, numbing predictability already dulling her attention.

"It has absolutely nothing to do with us," Evaine said, attempting to pre-empt her mother. "The festival is a waste of time, a pointless extravagance... actually it's quite insulting."

Her mother sat silently, studying her. Evaine waited for some response, but her impatience got the better of her. "It isn't as if I'll be missed—or any of us, really. Father isn't even going to be there." Evaine couldn't directly see her mother from this angle, only her shape from the corner of her eye. The green and white figure didn't stir, her mother remaining motionless. *She's waiting me out*, Evaine thought. *Damn her.*

The silence between them built, Evaine's frustration growing as the physician quietly ministered to her. The breeze from the open windows fluttered the white curtains, sending them floating up to the ceiling in long ribbons, twisting there, settling back down in the gentle air.

"I haven't been to Chaldrea since I was eighteen, that was four years ago. It's too... much," Evaine said finally.

"Exactly," Eleanor replied quietly. The perfect moment, she'd waited for her to say something impetuous. "All the Erolan will be there—the dukes, earls, counts, barons—and all their families, noble sons and daughters."

"Let them go," Evaine said. "That's *another planet*. Only the emperor matters, and gods know he doesn't care for this charade."

"Evaine, you can't honestly be that dense."

"Why do I feel like it's the other way around?" Evaine muttered.

Her mother stood, walking to her side. She lay her hand gently on Evaine's head, smoothing her tousled hair. The physician continued to work, deftly ignoring their conversation. The angry purple gash above her cheek had subsided to a puffy red welt, and he was now attending a long scrape that ran from her shoulder to mid-bicep. She winced, glaring at him as he rubbed the area with a clear, sweet smelling unguent.

"The people there are boorish," Evaine said. "They are petty and jealous and consumed with vanity, I don't see—"

"I know you don't," Eleanor interrupted. "These vainglorious charlatans are immensely wealthy, powerful, and devious. Do you really think you're beyond their scheming? Do you really think that the lure of ruling Allria, an *entire planet*, is without appeal?" her mother asked, stroking her hair. Eleanor picked up a brush beside the nightstand and began combing out the tangles. Evaine felt smothered under all the attention.

Eleanor continued. "And do you think that you will gain any ground when you are archduchess by boasting your superiority? Flaunting your removal, your disdain for their ways? Oh, it's quite apparent when someone thinks they're above it all. And nothing is more repellent than someone who won't share any of your vices. The virtuous have few friends in this world, my dear."

Evaine squeezed her eyes shut, her hair tangling painfully. "But I really *don't* have anything in common with those *baesach*," she said.

Eleanor tut-tutted. "We're all in the same pyramid of power. The Imperial continuum encompasses us, as well as them, and so we are vulnerable to the same dangers they are. Your father is a loyal man, and abides the emperor's command. Unless he were to rebel, then he is also a part of the continuum, of the political interplay. There are no isolated pieces in the game."

"It's so tedious," Evaine said. "I think I'll do what father did, and set up a proxy to manage affairs of state."

Her mother stopped brushing her hair. She set down the brush lightly on the table. With a wave of her hand she dismissed the physician. He bowed low and retreated from the room, closing the door behind him. Evaine regretted her words as soon as she spoke them.

Eleanor walked around and knelt by her daughter's side, her face so close to Evaine's that she could smell the fragrant spiced tea on her mother's breath. She took her daughter's hand firmly in hers. "What you do not understand will always control you," she said in a low voice. "There is no place for such naivety here, Evaine. Power is not static—it never ceases to change hands. Words behind closed doors, favours here, secrets leveraged there. You are never safe. Complacency will destroy you." The archduchess looked into her daughter's eyes, and Evaine saw something there that made her swallow. "We remain unchallenged because the emperor remains unchallenged. It may not always be so.

"The archduke delegates his affairs because he was a general, he knows men, he knows who to trust and who is dangerous. His reason for political removal is that he is far too abrasive to be friendly with these plotting sycophants—not because he can't be bothered and doesn't see the relevance." Her mother's stern eyes cut through every wall Evaine tried to hide behind.

"You have been allowed to toy with other interests—to pursue your training and practise and learning at your leisure. Perhaps that was my mistake, thinking to spare you what I've known all along would be inevitable."

"Mother, I—" Evaine began.

"Shhh," Eleanor said, squeezing her hand. "Perhaps I have also allowed it to continue because I want you to be independent—the throne of Allria is rightfully yours, not your husband's, whoever he may be. I don't want you to ever rely upon the judgement of another, or feel coerced because you are a woman." She chuckled, glancing over Evaine's wounds and touched her cheek gently. "Somehow, I don't think that's something I need to worry about."

Despite her irritation, Evaine smiled. "It's always been something I've hated," she admitted. "I suppose I've thought that I could just avoid it somehow. But it still seems very…trite."

Her mother looked at her, patience filling her pale green eyes. "It will always seem so," Eleanor said. "But you must learn to guide yourself. Your father is the first archduke—there has never been another. There are dangers ahead that no one can see, and forces to contend with that you alone will face. Your father has carved his regency from nothing." Eleanor waved her hand about the room. "All this? It wasn't here a hundred years ago—fifty years ago. This is what your father has done." She released Evaine's hand. "Will you keep it?"

Evaine looked down, hesitated, then, "Yes," she said, returning her mother's gaze.

Eleanor nodded, her lips tightening in firm resolve. "Good," she said, standing. "Good. Then clean yourself up. I'll send in the physician again. We leave for Dur Enskai in the morning, and the Lady Sinclair can't look as though she were ambushed by highwaymen on the way to the Dhemorgal."

Evaine laughed. When her mother had gone, she sat quietly while the physician tended to her arm. She stared out the window, over the dry grass hills that stretched away to farmland and budding orchards. The brown, sun baked tiles of the Graf's manor were just visible beyond a hillcrest, shimmering in the morning heat. The sky was a high dusty blue, winds from over the mountains far to the west stirring up the basin flats. The warm smell of earth floated in through the windows, the spring wheat ripening in the valley fields below Cnoc Baegan.

It was so difficult to imagine that all of this was part of something bigger—that this world didn't belong to itself. What an alien concept. Seeing beyond the immediate, the beige walls of the fortress, the city in the valley below, past the distant rim of the blue mountains: that was the world, that was real, and changes could be measured from day to day.

To think that this was only a small portion of what existed, that everything happened simultaneously, beyond her awareness and understanding. She felt diminished. An instrument clattered on the tray beside her as the physician picked up another tool. Her wounds were superficial, but she smiled to think how she might have appeared before the Erolan, trophies of a life she knew was real. How many of the ladies at court had ever been punched in the face? How many had ever felt their ribs break, or winded men who stood head and shoulders above them? How many could see with their eyes closed?

She would suffer through this: Chaldrea, the glitz, the glamour, the preening and adulation. Because really, it didn't matter. What did it cost her? A few days inconvenience. And Evaine could see the necessity, if she were really honest with herself. She spent so much time arguing for a life that didn't exist except in her mind. It wasn't denial, it was... *regret,* she decided. *What a useless sentiment.* At least she could visit the Temple of Daor. Gaiban Morrigan always welcomed her, and perhaps she could spar with someone new, learn something she could bring back to Vasya.

Standing, Evaine dismissed the physician. Most of her injuries were treated and she couldn't sit still any longer. She needed a shower, she needed to close her mind and just be alone. As the man collected his instruments and closed the door quietly, she walked to the vaulted shower room at the rear of her chambers and undressed. The *kilpi* was still tightly woven around her, and she unwrapped it from her arms and legs, breathing a sigh of relief as she finally pulled off the snug fitting tunic.

The Asaani tailored cloth was made specifically for Valorí warriors, and was usually quite comfortable, even in combat. But women were not Valorí, and so it wasn't made with them in mind, and occasionally it pinched or constricted her chest and made it difficult to breathe. Evaine had several custom made *kilpani* of course, but those were torn and so squeezing herself and her bosom into a standard *kilpi* wasn't always easy. With two fingers she massaged the tender muscles under her breasts, kneading the knots away. She sighed, stepping into the shower as four fountains of water splashed down from the high ceiling, filling it with steam.

As the water poured over her, washing away the dirt and grime from the day, Evaine looked down at her naked body. Little cuts and scrapes ran along her arms and down to her hands, and there were bruises along her ribs. She would be better next time, she promised. She could almost see the muscles under her skin when she flexed her arms, or tensed her abs. There was softness there, it was a woman's body, she thought gladly. But she knew there was steel there too, beneath the supple contours and gentle swell of her breasts there was firmness that belied her delicate appearance.

Just a few days and it'll all be over, Evaine thought. Peace settled over her, and lightness came into her chest. She breathed, deeply, filling her lungs and taking in the hot shower air, feeling the cool tiles beneath her toes. She turned off the water, wringing out her hair and tying it behind her. Reciting mantras of the Asaani, she knelt on the cold patterned marble and began a calisthenics routine. As her breathing echoed through the shower, her mind began to drift, and she felt the tension melt away. *Just a few more days, and it will all be over.*

NINE

THE TEMPLE OF DAOR

Bahir folded his arms over his lean chest. "No more today," he said. Aldric wiped his brow, leaning forward on the stone bench and resting his elbows on his knees. His black hair dangled in his face, the tips dripping with sweat. The slap of hands against bare flesh and the rasping scrape of the *kilpani* cloth grinding together mixed with grunting shouts from the arena. Fat stone pillars surrounded a large, rectangular training yard, its sandy floor open to the sky.

Thick trunks of creeping vines grew down from the roof of the temple, clinging to the pillars, spreading out their veined fans to catch the sunlight. Every hundred years or so they had to be cut back. A shadowy walk ran behind the pillars and around the arena where Aldric and Bahir sat recovering their breath. Cipher sat on the thick stone balustrade between them and the arena, patches of sunlight falling over his dark fur. He blinked at Aldric, then lay back and closed his eyes.

Two young men in faded brown *kilpani* grappled in the sand. They had been sparring for nearly half an hour without rest, their strength so spent they couldn't even stand. Now they wrestled on the ground, fumbling, grasping, rolling over and under, finding a grip and gaining the upper hand, succumbing to exhaustion and losing the advantage.

Through his own sweat and aching muscles, Aldric smiled to see two so dedicated to their craft—a reminder of his early days here. What point was there unless one was willing to move into and through exhaustion? To exist there, that was the thing; for rest to feel unnatural, uncomfortable—to desire and long for exertion.

Memories of training with his brother when they were children flashed before Aldric's eyes. Arem stamped his feet and refused to wrestle, faking coughing fits so he could sit out, where he would watch Aldric and sulk. Arem never liked the feeling of exhaustion, like most people he feared it. Most people feared the dull ache and nausea of fatigue—would do absolutely anything to avoid it—and there was nothing for them unless they stopped fearing it and wanted to move beyond that feeling.

One of the first lessons at the Temple had been to gain an awareness of his own desire for limitation. Self-repression was a natural and even helpful tendency among humans: it kept them from being reckless and stupid, endangering themselves or others. Being tired and exhausted was hazardous in nature. Energy was precious, and taking risks could be fatal. But this timidity had to be overcome, endured, and welcomed as the harbinger of triumph and the conquest of fear.

"I think any more training today, and you'll spoil yourself for tomorrow," the Valorí battlemaster said. Bahir's light brown hair clung to his cheeks, and he pushed it aside. His deep brown eyes were narrow like a hawk's, and the skin around them was wrinkled from years of squinting and some smiling. His small, round face tightened as he watched the two wrestlers. His hard jaw was set in that old way that Aldric knew so well. Aldric had learned to mistrust that bony jaw, for Bahir would bury it painfully into his side when they wrestled.

Bahir's skin was very brown from many years in the sun and the dry, high plains of the Pyrric Waste and the Arran Kuth far to the west where he was born. He was a good natured man, Aldric found, with much humour and patience. Everything happened, and that was all, and he accepted it without expectation, except of himself and occasionally Aldric.

Whereas the emperor had taught Aldric to be mistrustful of others, Bahir had taught him to trust himself. Aldric had learnt from him to rely on his intuitions, his instincts, and this confidence had built into him a subtle ferocity not easily overcome. Aldric knew this about himself, and though he took care to temper it, he was proud of his strength.

Bahir unwound and adjusted his *kilpi* below his knee, tightening the fabric that was almost black with his sweat and the grit from the arena. He gazed at his hands as if they were very far away, things almost unseen. He was a pensive man and Aldric respected him and was quiet when he saw that look in his eyes, understanding the need for inner solitude himself. But sometimes Aldric didn't notice and would begin speaking and suddenly realise his mistake, and it always made him feel bad, as though he had broken something sacred.

Aldric watched him for a moment and then averted his eyes. It was odd to see a man so completely withdrawn. He'd noticed it many times with others of the Asaani, especially those of the Valorí. It was part of their discipline to be removed, and Aldric observed their calm even as he had begun to experience it himself. Yet with Bahir it was different. Aldric felt that if Bahir had not been Captain of the Guard that he would have been a poet.

Aldric leant back against the mossy stone, shifting so that a rough edge wasn't digging into his back. His head rested between two grooves in the rock and he breathed deeply. The sound of bubbling fountains filtered in from somewhere out of sight. He began reciting mantras in his head, watching the two acolytes grappling in the arena. *Listen to the sound of no-thing. Fill your mind with no-thing. Be no-thing.*

"You fought well today, *Solani*," Bahir said, rousing Aldric from his meditation.

"Did I?" Aldric asked, smiling at the traditional title the Asaani gave to the prince. *Solani.* It meant something like "redeemer", or "champion of the gods", and Aldric didn't hear it many places outside the Temple. So many of the old ways were being forgotten.

Bahir nodded, slapping his calf where the *kilpi* was tied, watching the fibrous cloth cinch together. "Your head is everywhere, which isn't good," Bahir said, glancing at Aldric. "But your body knows what to do, even if you aren't thinking about it." He squeezed Aldric's knee. "It would help though, if you could focus your attention."

Aldric screwed up his face. "So much is being tested, Bahir," he said. "There's so much being watched and weighed, I'm not ashamed to admit I'm struggling with my role in all of this."

"Don't," Bahir said. "It is, you are, I am—and tomorrow comes, and tomorrow goes."

"For some people, yes," Aldric said.

"For all people! *You* are some people, *Solani.* You are everyone on Errolor—here, in this city, *you* are everyone. And best of all?" he said, his eyes bright, "you are *no one.*"

"You know Bahir, when you say a lot of things that don't mean anything, you end up saying nothing."

"That's usually the best thing to say."

Aldric shook his head. "I should sit you down with Chiron, let you two talk about nothing for a while."

"That would be *something*," Bahir said.

"Wouldn't it?" Aldric laughed.

"Really, though, Aldric," Bahir said, stretching his arms. "Really—it doesn't matter. What matters is kingship. And you will be emperor, and tomorrow will not matter."

"Bahir, reputation isn't meaningless. The people won't forget an emperor who was beaten by a religious zealot—someone who obviously hates everything my father and this empire stand for. And when I'm emperor, he'll do the same to me. I have to win."

"Then it is simple," Bahir said. "You must not fail."

Aldric shook his head. He liked Bahir. He was absurd, and that made Aldric smile. It was a good quality to have, Aldric thought, in such absurd times. He glanced into the arena. The boy in the darker *kilpi* had won, and was helping the other boy onto his feet. They could hardly stand, and limped shoulder to shoulder out of the sandy ring, laughing as they went.

"So what should I do?" Aldric asked, not really expecting an answer.

"You should fight," Bahir said.

"I will fight."

"Then that is good."

"But my opponent will also fight," Aldric said.

"You must fight harder."

"I will."

"Then that is also good."

"And what if I fail?" Aldric asked.

"You must not."

"And if I do?"

Bahir finished stretching and stood to his full height, letting his muscles relax. He turned to Aldric and looked down at him, his open features betraying no emotion. "Then the people of Chaldrea, of Errolor, of the Vassaryan Empire—they will all lose respect for you. Mal'Dreghen will be seen as the hero of the empire, whom not even an emperor of the Fael Danar could oppose, and your father will be shamed. The fabric of the dynasty will crumble, and your throne will be taken from you." He sat down next to Aldric. "Also, I will not be your friend."

Aldric folded his arms. "You should stick to *craidath*," he said.

"And you shouldn't ask ridiculous questions." Bahir's northern accent was still strong after all these years, giving his words a harsh, crisp quality. He walked over to the railing where Cipher was sleeping and scratched his ears. The razorcat flopped his tail and stretched.

"You can pretend to be wise, but I know you're just a little Ordanian who likes to fight," Aldric said.

Bahir shrugged. "At least I'm not confused about that," he said, walking back to Aldric's side.

Aldric laughed.

"You, what are you?" Bahir asked. He cuffed Aldric below his ear and feigned the other ear when Aldric tried to block him, then cuffed him again. "Are you a prince? Are you a fighter? Are you a druid, a wandering vagabond? Are you a fish monger? Do you want to sell fish in the market, from your cart all day, by the docks in the sun and the breeze? You wouldn't have to be a philosopher or a prince then, only know how to sell your fish. Could you do that?"

"How would you like that Cipher, selling fish all day?" Aldric asked. Cipher glanced up, blinking lazily. "Those fish mongers are a wily lot; I've had some good conversations with a few of them."

"Of course you have, they know what they are. It's you who are confused." Bahir massaged his chest and leant against the stone balustrade facing the arena, stroking Cipher.

Aldric scoffed, turning his back to the ring.

"Well it's what you wanted to hear, isn't it?" Bahir asked. "That this is the most important event of your life, and that the empire hangs in the balance?" He turned to Aldric, his small eyes becoming smaller. "Think of all the perils the empire has faced, my Prince. Think of the thousands of years of history passed down to you, built around you, piled on top of you and in you and in every corner of your mind and every recess of your genes. Do you think nothing like this has ever happened before? Do you believe you are the most important person in the history of the empire? That what happens tomorrow will forever alter a civilisation older than your deepest ancestral memory?" He paused, and his eyes softened. "The sun sets, *Solani*. But the sun also rises."

It was a fine afternoon with the sun just past the zenith in the sky and the light shone directly down into the arena where small insects droned in the still air. After the two boys had left the sparring yard and their voices no longer echoed down the long stone corridors, the ivy clad walls filled with warm silence, broken by the murmur of trickling water. Aldric couldn't believe just a few hours before he'd been fighting for his life as a destroyer plummeted through the atmosphere. He was reminded of an old Asaani expression, "There are many days in one."

Bahir breathed, stretching and Aldric watched the little man flexing his muscles. He was like having a dog around, Aldric thought, and you could never be really cross with a dog. There was a certain sort of honesty that Aldric felt made a man easy to be around and let him be comfortable without worrying of what he would think or say of this or that, just like a dog. When a man was honest with himself he would be honest with you as well.

A procession of *maedes* in drab green robes with cowls back marched through the stone archway at the other end of the small arena. The girls broke to the right in single file and followed the path around the outside of the ring with their heads bowed so that their faces were difficult to see in the shadows. They made their way in a line past Aldric and Bahir, who did not move, and through the archway behind them. Cipher sat up, sniffing at them as they passed, his whiskers twitching.

Aldric smiled at the girls, who were all very pretty with their hair pulled into long braids that he thought sat very sweetly on their shoulders and who each wore circlets of silver above their foreheads except for the last girl who wore none. He smiled, hoping to catch one of them looking at him, but none of them did, and in a moment the swishing sound of their robes and padded rope soled shoes had faded and was gone. The faint scent of flowers and crushed leaves followed their passing and Aldric leant back against the stone, feeling disappointed.

"Is there any pleasure in it for you?" Aldric asked. "In fighting, I mean." He brushed his hair from his face and folded his hands in his lap.

Bahir chewed his lip for a moment. "In fighting? No. I don't think so. I think maybe it's good to release your tensions, but you can do that running, or climbing, or something else like that."

"So it doesn't feel good?"

"Sometimes, but not hurting someone. It feels good because I know it is difficult, and because I know I can do it well. I guess that's why it feels good, because I know how hard I have worked, and how much of my blood is there in that sand," he said, nodding towards the arena. "But perhaps it would feel as good to be a great artist."

Aldric smiled, trying to imagine Bahir as a painter. It actually wasn't that difficult to see the little man behind an easel.

"And because it is my duty. There is much satisfaction in knowing that you have been entrusted a duty, and that you are performing it well." Bahir swallowed. "But beyond this? No. Sometimes it feels quite bad, and then I wish that I hadn't fought at all and that I could take it back," Bahir continued. "But this feeling goes, and then I just know that I've worked hard and done as much as I can and that everything will be alright. It doesn't feel good when there's anger though, or fear. Then you get a lump in your stomach and your heart sinks and your face feels numb and you know what you've got to do but you don't want to do it, and then you do it anyways. Then it doesn't feel good. Then you are only happy that you have survived, and that you aren't as badly hurt as the other, but sometimes you feel as though you are."

He looked at Aldric and rested his hands on his knees. "That isn't why we are trained to fight, my Prince," he said. "*Craidath* is finding the balance between your body and your mind, and understanding how to use them both in the present. When you can see what is happening inside yourself, inside your opponent, when you can see his movements in your mind and with your eyes at the same time, see what your eyes cannot see, move your body with awareness that defies the mortal senses, then you will understand yourself and the world and others in a way that you never could have imagined, and you will find a peace in solitude and a comfort in companionship that was never there before. It is for richness of existence that we train so hard, not for pleasure of combat."

Aldric furrowed his brow. "So persecution of the Asaani and protection of the emperor's household have nothing to do with the most fearsome warriors of the Fatherland?"

"Perhaps," Bahir said, raising an eyebrow. "Of course *craidath* has its uses, my Prince. That is what I mean by duty. And I won't pretend for a moment that it hasn't been crucial to the survival of the Asaani over the millennia. But I think you'll agree that we are not a warlike, aggressive people?"

Aldric nodded.

"We train for a fullness of spirit and mind, my Prince, and all else is secondary."

"Even at the threat of your extinction?"

"What good is living if you must live in betrayal of your beliefs?"

"So why fight at all? If violence is so abhorrent, why ever fight? Why not allow yourself to be killed, rather than take a life?"

"Because we do not fight to save ourselves."

"You're protecting the royal family," Aldric said, considering his words.

Bahir nodded, turning to look Aldric solemnly in the eye. "I fight for you, *Solani.*"

"But why?" Aldric asked. It was an odd moment, and he felt uncomfortable in the intimacy of its admission.

"Because you are the chosen of Daor. In the last days of the Aínír, the emperor sheltered the gods from Victus, the Wandering Chaos, and in repayment, Daor decreed that the Asaani would protect the emperor and his line from all harm, forevermore."

"But you don't really believe that, Bahir? That mythical gods actually came down from the heavens and gave the Asaani a divine commandment?"

"Can you think of a better reason?"

Aldric started to protest, but then couldn't honestly think of a response. He closed his mouth. Religion, any religion Aldric thought, had a tendency towards the mystical, the poetical, and the vague. That was where it got its power, by being indefinable. If you couldn't prove something, then you couldn't disprove it either, and so many religions had survived long after science found answers for the questions they posed.

Yet Aldric knew better than to press Bahir on this point. A man must have his beliefs, Aldric decided long ago. If they didn't make sense to him, well, that was between a man and his gods. As long as a man was happy, then Aldric felt he didn't have any right to judge. And what did it hurt? Happiness and peace was all that really mattered in life. And happiness was easy to see in someone's eyes. He decided to let the matter go.

"As long as I defeat the Mal's champion tomorrow, I don't really care why I'm doing it, or if I feel pleasure. Seeing the Mal beaten is worth any cost."

"That is an empty thing to say, *Solani,*" Bahir said. "Victory at all costs can be ruinous."

"Loss, in this case, will be ruinous."

Bahir shook his head. "For all of your lessons, you still cannot see this most basic point. Loss, or victory," he said, weighing his palms in the air. "They are no different."

"I guess that's a lesson I'll have to learn another time," Aldric said.

"You will, or you will not." Bahir said. "You are too concerned with the myth of self. You believe in your own aura, your own fable. You are afraid, but fear is good. To fear is to know the truth. You are not what everyone sees—this grand prince, this doer of great deeds—do not believe the stories. You are only a lens, a singular lens through which light passes from nothing to nothing again. What is on either side of the lens? Who can say? All that exists is the light, the life, inside the lens for that brief, impossibly short moment, and then is gone. Focus this, direct it, absorb it—but do not interpret or demand anything from it. This only clouds your lens, turns it black, so that nothing can pass through."

Aldric tried to visualise this, seeing a lens in his mind's eye, floating in a black void of nothingness. The lens was clear, full of white light, suspended in darkness like a star. He tried to understand the light inside the lens, and he saw it blacken and dim, fading from view. He let go and allowed himself to swim into the lens, trying to imagine one side as the end of his life, and the other the beginning, creating a timeline between. It seemed so linear that way, such a narrow understanding of what Bahir was saying, and he let this go as well. He was left with just the image of a brilliant lens, floating lonely in the dark, waiting to extinguish.

"If happiness is our aim, then what is tomorrow? To be good, to feel the sun shine, to laugh... this is enough," Bahir said. "After all, what is life, *Solani*? Is it your time here on Errolor? Is it how many breaths are in your lungs, or beats of your heart? Is it how many enemies you defeat, or how many battles you win?" He paused. "Is it how many girls you will love?"

"All of them, I suppose," Aldric replied.

Bahir shook his head. "No, *Solani*."

"Then what is it?"

Bahir breathed in deeply. "Life is the song of the sparrow in the summer, and the whispered word of the willow. It is the rain cloud that empties itself over the thirsty plains and is no more."

Aldric stood to leave, pausing as he thought. "It is the badgering of Bahir in the afternoon," he replied.

Bahir smiled, finally. "Gaiban Morrigan asked to see you, before you go."

Aldric raised his eyebrows. "Did she?"

"She's in the Sepulchre," Bahir said, nodding.

"What's she doing there?"

Bahir shrugged. "It's peaceful," he said, seeming to think that answered the question.

"As peaceful as a tomb can be," Aldric replied. He patted his leg and Cipher stretched, hopping down from the ledge to join him.

"Trust yourself, *Solani*," Bahir said. "Nothing else is important. Trust yourself. You are a good leader, a good fighter, a good pilot, a good brother and a good friend. You are gifted, my Prince. Trust yourself to know what is right. Then do it."

TEN

SANCTUARY

S trolling through leafy avenues of flitting sunlight, Aldric walked deeper into the Temple of Daor. The mossy stones breathed with an ageless rhythm, like a primeval god of the forest tossed upon Chaldrea's white shores. Dim passageways lined with hieroglyphics and sunlit courtyards mingled beneath the gaze of drowsy old trees murmuring in the afternoon breeze, patriarchs of a time long forgotten.

Aldric made his way through long corridors, running his hands over the faded bas-reliefs of ancient mythology. He saw the stories of how the Asaani gods, called the Aínir, had greeted the humans when they first arrived from the stars beyond. Even the story of the first emperors was there, beginning with Aronach the Great. They were tales Aldric had heard many times since he was a boy. His ancestry was tied to the creation of the world, his birth the evolution of myth to reality. *Am I not godlike?*

Pausing in a grassy courtyard, Aldric stopped to see a gathering of dryden kneeling before a reflecting pool. The fearsome head of a stone degren sent water gushing noisily into a pool below where red and orange and yellow fish swam. Cipher darted around Aldric as a butterfly fluttered past, leaping into the air to catch it. The black cat landed gracefully and peered under his paws, sitting to munch on his kill.

In voices barely audible above the splashing waterfall, the druids chanted together, reciting passages from the sacred Book of Caels. Dryden guarded the Asaani faith much as the warrior Valorí did, dedicating their lives to memorising and preserving the history and lessons in the Book of Caels. Their unshorn hair and drab brown habits had never changed in all the aeons the Temple had stood, and seeing them again transported Aldric far from Chaldrea and the outside world.

Parting a curtain of calirri vines Aldric stepped into a flagstone courtyard before the Adytum, the inner sanctum of the Temple. It was a hallowed place, second only to the high temple in Beluul; but that was nothing more than a snow-covered ruin now. A redented dome of mossy stone greeted the afternoon sun, and four Valorí in black *kilpani* stood beside the arched entrance, nodding as Aldric passed.

"Wait here," Aldric said, turning to Cipher. The cat sat back on his haunches and yowled. "I'll just be a minute buddy," he said, patting Cipher's head.

Aldric blinked as he stepped inside, his eyes adjusting to the murky temple. Shafts of sunlight poured down from high windows into a large, circular chamber. Spidery ocala roots dangled through cracks in the roof, and birds fluttered from their roost as his footsteps echoed from the walls. Statues with painted faces smeared by crushed red and blue berries returned Aldric's gaze, while incense smoked in dim corners around the chamber.

Finding a stairwell at the back of the chamber, Aldric descended to the Sepulchre. The Sepulchre was a great tomb below the Adytum, hollowed out by volcanic forces aeons ago. It was one of the most revered places on all of Errolor for the Asaani, and one of the few places where it was said the old gods still visited and communed with the faithful. He followed the winding stairs down, his boots scraping on grimy wet stones. Musty air filled his lungs, and he steadied himself on the slippery stairs, bracing the slimy walls that dripped with mineralised water.

The stairway ended in deep shadows, and Aldric kneeled and removed his boots before an enormous double door. He stretched his feet, gripping the cold wet stone with his toes. It felt good. The door was a porous, bluish grey metal and felt like stone as he pushed it open. Despite its bulk, it gave way without noise and he stepped into a vast cavern. Soft blue light diffused the gloom, revealing slender pillars rising spectral into the darkness above. Forbidden to all save the gaiban and the most senior Asaani druids, the Sepulchre was a sacred catacomb Aldric had visited occasionally for ceremonies and to speak with the old priestess.

Each of the slender stalactites and stalagmites rising around the chamber was actually the resting place of a former gaiban. After the matriarch died, her body was brought here and set upright in a modest throne of carved stone. The mineral rich water of the limestone cave would begin dripping down, and over the long years she would be entombed, creating an immortal statue. Eventually this pillar would grow upwards, becoming part of the foundations for the Adytum above.

Occasionally certain dryden and Valorí would be laid to rest here as well, their heroic deeds quietly sealed under the crystals that fell over them in a glistening sheen. The great Valorí warrior Anaxarian was said to be buried here somewhere. Aldric didn't know where, and there were over a thousand pillars in the cavernous mausoleum, the oldest no longer bearing any human semblance. Gaiban Morrigan would take her place here eventually, Aldric thought, wondering where her pillar would be.

Pausing before a column half hidden in shadow, Aldric studied the face of a nameless gaiban, resembling the caryatids carved around the temple above. Her face was lifted in serene repose, her hands folded in prayer above her stomach. He felt a sense of comfort at the thought of being forever preserved here, reclaimed by the nourishing earth.

In the centre of the room a dark pool was lighted by a ray of sunlight from somewhere far above. The black water rippled as drops fell from the ceiling, and Aldric walked to the edge and stared into the deep waters. Roots piercing the cavern above crawled over the white figures encased in the pillars, curling over their heads in mantles of ghostly mane and falling into the pool, drinking deep from its strange waters. All was still. Dripping echoed through the cavern and Aldric wondered if perhaps Gaiban Morrigan had left.

Yet she was there. Gazing at the pillars around the black pool, Aldric's eyes fell upon a familiar shape. He stopped and watched, his attention arrested as the shape coalesced from the shadows and light. Subtly he became aware that it was a person, and then a woman. It was similar to the feeling of noticing someone in a crowded room you had missed before, or when you stared at a painting and suddenly realised that there was something there, some hidden meaning you hadn't noticed, and it all came together at once. Aldric was startled at her appearance and blinked, unsure of his senses. But it was her, Gaiban Morrigan, the High Lady of the Rock, Mother of the Starborn, Seeress of the Asaani.

The Gaiban returned his gaze, unmoving. "Hello, young prince," she said. Her voice was deep and low, barely a murmur in the hushed catacomb.

"High Lady," Aldric replied, bowing his head in respect. "I didn't notice you."

"There are many things you do not see, *Solani*, because you do not look for them." Gaiban Morrigan stood, smoothing the creases in her sari as she rose. Her frame was small and willowy, the veins in her arms rising up like pale roots. Her long sterling hair was braided over her shoulder, kala feathers woven in places, and her grey sari was wrapped loosely about her waist. A silver *clamael* perched above her forehead, a clear, bright stone set in the centre. For all her years, Gaiban Morrigan retained the gentle aspect of youth. Her face was both joyful and sad, at once in awe of everything, yet never surprised by what she saw, as though she greeted every moment expecting to be amazed.

"I'm still practising my every minute awareness," Aldric said.

"Yes, we all are. It is like anything else, and will fade as it is left unused." She appraised him. "How are you, my Prince?"

Aldric considered the question. His body ached, but that was nothing new. But the weight of the Dhemorgal was pressing on his mind. He had thought a sparring session would clear his thoughts, but it hadn't; it had simply impressed upon him the monumental expectations that were being thrust upon him. He realised then with sudden clarity that for the first time, he didn't know what to do.

"Overnight, everything changed. The Raeth and the destroyer... My father, Arem, the Dhemorgal, the Coliseum, Chiron, Bahir, you..." He trailed off, gazing at her from across the still pond. "I'm tired, Gaiban. I want answers, and the more I question, the less everything makes sense."

"It is always so. When in doubt, you must act; it will stir the mind and sharpen the senses, and drive away the cobwebs."

"I was training with Bahir."

"Yes, I saw."

Aldric tried not to think about what she meant and said instead, "He said you wanted to speak with me?"

The gaiban nodded. "There's such little time for pleasantries," she said regretfully, touching the kala feathers in her hair. "I fear for the people of the city, my Prince; for the Asaani; for the emperor—for you. The old days are returned, and once again man is turning against his fellow man."

"Have you seen what will happen?" Aldric asked. He knew she wasn't actually prescient, but sometimes she just seemed to know things.

"We must be prepared," she said, giving Aldric a hard look. "We are human, and vain, and have forgotten what gifts the gods gave us, and what they asked for in return." She stepped around the pool to Aldric's side and took his arm in hers. "Walk with me." Aldric felt the iron in her sinewy grasp as she began walking, leading them back to the stairs.

"Yet we have endured, guardians for a time which may never come," she said. "It is a lonely vigil, Prince Aldric. And to see the days come down to this? Look at us, in our noble cities, filled with the memories of a thousand generations we've never known. We are the children of time, hoping to find some peace we can call our own. Yet when has such a time existed? When has there ever been peace?"

They strolled through the murky chamber, pillars growing up to the vaulted ceiling like the boles of a sleeping forest. "Our history is a palimpsest, Prince Aldric," she said. "The Asaani have endured the ages as the keepers of great knowledge, the caretakers of a struggling infant, fighting for his right to exist. The Dhemorahns have never been our allies, but we have learned to coexist. And the years pass, and civilisations make war and write their futile overtures at peace."

They reached the stairs and Aldric stooped to grab his boots. They climbed to the main level, continuing on to a rooftop terrace beside the central dome. Calirri flowers sweetened the hiemal breezes blowing down over the lake from the Enowyrth Mountains. Trailing from giant ocala trees in twisting ivy tendrils, they wrapped about the trunks in wreathes of pink and purple petals.

As they sat Aldric said, "Before I forget," and paused, reaching into his tunic pocket and removing a band of silver. He handed it to her.

She took the *clamael* and examined it, smiling. "Ah yes, Elder Khestor will be wanting this back, when he returns."

"You saw him then?"

"In a manner of speaking," she said. She tucked the *clamael* away and folded her hands on her lap, turning a questioning eye on Aldric. "You didn't also happen to save his basket of bread, did you?"

Aldric frowned, then blinked at the realisation. "You were watching?"

"I'm always interested in what Your Grace is doing. One can never be too careful."

Aldric wasn't sure how he felt she had used *aina* to watch him during his altercation with the Dhemorahns that morning.

"You said when he returns; where has he gone?"

This time it was the gaiban's turn to frown. "I don't know," she said. "I haven't seen him since this morning." A queer look came over her face then, and she turned away from Aldric to look across the rooftops. From their view atop the temple they could take in the entire complex. The temple sprawled out to the surrounding gardens and perimeter of jungle, the wide brown moat that encompassed the grounds, and finally the outer wall that held Chaldrea and the rest of the world at bay. Venerable grey moss spread over the crumbling stones in a living patina, ancient gods and goddesses vested in green garments, keeping tireless vigil over their ruinous estate.

"So what was it you wanted to discuss?" Aldric asked.

She folded her sari, shaking her head. "I am feeling the passage of time. Nostalgia for an age that has never existed. Another era is coming to an end, my Prince, and a new one is beginning."

"Gaiban, after all this time you're not becoming sentimental, are you?" Aldric asked.

"Oh my dear prince, if you only knew," she said, her back shaking with quiet laughter. She took his hand in hers, tracing the creases in his palm. "You know I remember when you were born," she said. "I was at your mother's bedside with your father and your uncle, the Duke. You didn't cry. I remember wondering at that. You gasped and gasped, as if you were choking on your new life. But you didn't cry."

Aldric wasn't sure what to think. "No one ever told me that," he said.

She shrugged, her shoulders thin and pointed beneath her sari. "You're right, I must be getting sentimental," she said, grinning. It was a strange look on her features.

"Does that mean something?" Aldric asked, wondering if there was some cryptic Asaani parable about babies that didn't cry.

She pondered for a moment. "Not really," she said. When Aldric looked disappointed, she continued. "Anaxarian did not cry when he was born. But he is said to be the son of the goddess Iivari."

Aldric considered this, staring down at the worn brown tiles of the temple roof.

The Gaiban studied him. "You like that, don't you?" she asked. Aldric looked up. "Such a proud connexion. It is the mark of a hero."

He frowned. "Well, we all like to believe we're different, better somehow, in whatever small way. I wouldn't mind thinking that was true, even if it doesn't make any difference."

"You are proud," she said, rather sternly. "But you are honest in your pride. There is hope yet."

"Bahir said the same thing. He said modesty was as much a fault as pride. Simple truth, he said, is what we aim for."

"And he's right." She sighed. "I remember when you began your lessons here."

"You certainly are nostalgic," Aldric said.

"You were among ten boys, all your age, around six or seven, from all across the empire. You weren't the tallest, or the biggest, and you tied your *kilpi* the wrong way so it bunched at your waist, which made you look even smaller." She smiled. "But you had courage. The other boys intimidated you, but you still fought them. You had strength. When I watched you that day, and on other days, I could see that there was something different about you."

Aldric tried not to take it as a compliment.

"But you were never serious," she said. "When your instructors would try to teach you the mantras or help you practise your discipline, you would laugh. It was always a game with you, never something to be taken seriously."

"I guess I still feel that way, a little," he said.

"I know," she replied. "The lessons, the histories from the Book of Caels, these are just myths to you. I know. *Craidath* is something real, because you can see it, you can feel it when Bahir hits you over the head with it. But the myths, the history of *craidath*—these are too vague," she said, waving her hand through the air. "You cannot experience them for yourself, so you dismiss them. I think this is why you have never mastered *aina*. You simply do not believe. There is no room in your heart for faith," she said.

"I have plenty of faith, Gaiban. But if I didn't have any doubts, it would be hard for me to believe anything."

The Gaiban pursed her lips. "There is a story," she began, "of a traveller who came to visit the temple one day, hoping to learn something from the druids. The master of the temple invited him to tea, and when the traveller sat down, the master began pouring his tea. When his cup was full, the master continued pouring, tea spilling out over the edges. The traveller watched, until he couldn't stand it and shouted, 'The cup is full, it can't hold any more!' The master stopped pouring."

Aldric picked up the story. "And the master said, 'You are like this cup, full to the brim with your knowledge. Empty your cup, and let us fill it again.'"

The gaiban smiled. "You remember."

"It's a good parable," Aldric said. "But my life is made of my experiences, I can't just forget them whenever I want to. I would just be an empty cup, and a cup is useless unless it holds something."

"But an empty cup can hold anything, young prince. A full cup can only overflow. You will learn someday that what you know and what you don't know are the same things," she said. "And when you do, you will see that your cup is always empty, and can never be truly filled."

"My cup feels empty enough as it is," Aldric said.

"That's because you don't know what to put in it."

"But you said I should empty my cup."

"I told you not to fill your cup, and to understand there's no difference between what is inside your cup and what isn't," the Gaiban said, her small face bright.

"Gaiban, you *just* said my cup is empty because I don't know what to put in it," Aldric protested.

"And yet you are still trying to fill it up."

"But if it's empty, what should I do?"

"Pour it out," she said.

"How can I pour it out if it's empty?" he asked.

"Then toss it out," she said.

Aldric thought about this for a moment. "I give up," he said finally.

"And your cup begins to empty," Gaiban Morrigan replied, smiling.

Aldric smiled too. He missed these conversations with the Gaiban. He glanced up as a squadron of pelicans flew by. "I've had a quote stuck in my head the last two days," he said.

The Gaiban nodded for him to continue.

"'It was not the youth within his face that marked his lonely age, but the beating of his titan heart that filled him all his days,'" he recited.

"Are you a titan, Prince Aldric?" the Gaiban asked.

"It's just a line from one of my favourite stories about Anaxarian," he said. "I always felt like he was lonely, separated somehow, and I like that about him. I feel that way sometimes."

"You may often feel lost, and even lonely my Prince. But it is only when you are lost that you will begin to understand your heart."

Aldric gazed into the courtyard below at the white roots of the ocala trees spilling down over the walls, prying the old stones apart. Hoary beards of mossy vines draped from fat old limbs, kala birds nesting among the deep foliage. Aldric could hear their warbling trills floating up over the roof.

"I suppose I'm trying to distract myself, I just keep thinking about the Dhemorgal and my fight in the Coliseum tomorrow."

A distant look came into Gaiban Morrigan's old eyes and she drew her mouth into a thin line. For an instant Aldric felt as though he could see her true age, and it astonished him.

"Have you ever heard of the Seven Regrets of the World?" she asked.

Aldric nodded. "But I don't know very much. It's mentioned early in the Book of Caels, but I remember Bahir saying it was really only explained in some texts found in the last few hundred years in some old temple in Erethya? He said the anagoge was too mystical for his tastes."

"Bahir has a very orthodox understanding of the faith," Gaiban Morrigan said. "His is a very pragmatic approach."

"I think it was probably just a little over his head," Aldric said.

She returned a knowing smile, her eyes warm in the early afternoon light. "He's an ascetic."

"He's Valorí."

She nodded.

"So what do these texts say, Gaiban?"

"Bahir was right, we have known of the Seven Regrets for some time, for five hundred years even, since Eochaid the Wanderer rediscovered and wrote of them in the Eldris Fane. But before that they were lost to time, and exactly what they were remained a mystery." A solemn look came into her eyes. "The Asaani religion is old, Prince Aldric," she said. "It predates every civilisation on Galinor, on Errolor. There is so much that remains unknown about its origins, but temples have been found nearly fifteen thousand years old." She paused. "Can you comprehend time on such a scale? What that means?"

Aldric simply looked at her. Of course it was impossible to understand what fifteen millennia actually meant, he wouldn't pretend to try.

"The Asaani are the servants of the Ainír, of the gods. From the beginning, we were tasked with maintaining the balance on Errolor—what was once *Eorathya*, in our tongue. The Ainír, the Great Builders, they were here first. They taught humans everything we know today, gave us the ability to channel Errolor's energy to power our cities, cities that they built for us. The Five Great Cities, even Chaldrea," she said, waving her hand across the white rooftops beyond the temple walls. "...they were built in a time when man was making houses from mud bricks and trees. These were gifts from the Ainír. They even came to dwell in our cities alongside us—to live with us, to help us, instruct us in things when we were too young to understand. They called us the *Ephriim.*"

"I've heard that name before," Aldric said.

"It's difficult to translate, but it means 'filled with wonder'. They gave us many of their secrets, and helped us to build much of the world, even what you see today. The Imperial Roads, the crystalline generators that give life to our great cities, these were their doing. Yet the Aínir were not of one mind."

"Victus," Aldric said. He'd heard the stories before and he knew the mythology. He had studied the Book of Caels for many long hours in his training with the Valorí. But like the gaiban said, to him these stories were just the colourful myths and legends that all ancient cultures passed on to their descendants. They were told back when societies lacked the knowledge to explain their world with science. But for the Asaani and Gaiban Morrigan, these stories were still very real.

The gaiban nodded. "Victus, the Golden God. He was not content to pass the ages in peace with the humans. He was an old god, one of the oldest, a remnant from the dreams of Daor before his wife Anneah could harness them and give them true life. Victus, the Wandering Chaos. He demanded worship, sacrifice, bloodshed. When the other gods would not listen, Victus came to Errolor and found Desedar, a lonely beggar living in the mountains beyond Ruador. Desedar gave himself to Victus, becoming his chosen prophet.

"Desedar travelled to the Great Cities, spreading his word, telling the people the Aínir were responsible for their famines, plagues, droughts, wars. Asaani who had once been faithful now turned against the Aínir, and blamed them for all their suffering. In our old tongue of Asaara, *Dhemorahn* means 'God-scorned.' They were led astray by Victus and began to follow false beliefs, enamoured of their own might and power. They believed that man didn't need the gods—that the Aínir were trying to make humans weak and enslave them.

"When the tyrant Victus sent Desedar to lead the Dhemorahns against the Aínir, the gods knew that Errolor would be destroyed in the coming battle. Rather than allow this, they chose to leave, bestowing the task of balance and harmony to the Asaani, until a time when they might return. They retreated, leaving the Great Cities for the first time in four thousand years, fleeing to their sanctuary in the north, Balog Mor. On the frozen plateau of Beluul they dwelt, forgotten by all but the most faithful."

A gust of wind sent leaves scurrying over the edge of the roof. "And what about the texts that Eochaid wrote of in the Eldris Fane? What are the Seven Regrets of the World?" Aldric asked, his scepticism turning to curiosity.

"I'm coming to that," Gaiban Morrigan answered, a glint in her eye. She enjoyed telling a story, and never came to the point before she needed to. "As you know, Aronach, the first emperor, had always been a loyal servant to the Ainír. When Victus learnt that the Ainír would flee the world rather than confront him, he became furious and sent the Prophet Desedar to meet them in Beluul, their last stronghold. Aronach was unwilling to see the Ainír slaughtered, and gathered an army to oppose Desedar, and they met on the rocky slopes of Torrn Borrus.

"But Desedar's legions were too many, and Aronach was pushed back to the grand temple of Balog Mor, the last refuge of the Ainír. The Ainír could have defeated Desedar's forces easily—what is the strength of mere mortals to the gods? But the Ainír were unwilling to harm the humans, misguided as they were, and deceived by the cunning words of the Golden God. The Ainír would not punish the mortals for the lies of Victus.

"At Balog Mor, Aronach held off the forces of Desedar until the last gods had escaped. But before they left, the Ainír bequeathed several gifts to the Asaani for their service. Aronach was named the White emperor for his courage and leadership, and the Asaani were charged with protecting him and all his descendants, until the Ainír might safely return. When Desedar saw that the Ainír had been defeated, he and all the Dhemorahns celebrated with a festival that lasted nine days."

"The Dhemorgal ," Aldric said.

"Yes. It means 'the banishment', in our tongue. It was celebrated for many years hence, until finally forgotten after the Warring Kingdoms divided the people. Despite their loss, and the millennia between, the Asaani have stayed true to the guidance of the Ainír. We were named the Asaani, or the *Ainír de Asaan*, meaning 'the remembered of the gods'. Yet the people of Errolor were no longer the *Ephriim*. We became the *Vandír*, 'those who wander.' This name has been passed down, and so are all the people of Errolor called today."

"And the Asaani and the line of Aronach were given the gift of *aina* to guard them against Victus and his followers," Aldric said.

"Yes, *aina,* the 'sight of the gods'. But there was another gift," Gaiban Morrigan said.

"The Seven Regrets of the World?"

"It was a book, given to emperor Aronach so that he might protect his people from the evils of Victus." She folded her hands in her lap, wetting her thin lips. "It was a history of Errolor, but a history that was yet to come. It was not complete, nor did it tell of how the events in its pages would come to pass. It merely told of the Seven Regrets that humans would commit to bring about their doom, and the triumph of Victus."

"It's a book of prophecies then," Aldric said, his eyes narrowing. "What became of it? Was Aronach able to prevent the seven regrets from taking place?"

Gaiban Morrigan shook her head. "The events explained in the book transpired over aeons. It would be impossible for one ruler, no matter how well prepared, to safeguard against such a timeline. The book was passed down through the imperial line and each generation tried to interpret its meanings and do what they could to prevent the prophecies, as they understood them."

"But then the book was lost?"

"Yes, it was stolen from the temple at Thrym, and vanished out of existence for thousands of years."

"No copies were made?"

"It was forbidden," Gaiban Morrigan said. "The knowledge contained therein could not be duplicated. It was a sacred text, and its warning was bound to its fate. It represented a second chance at redemption; if it was lost, then so was that chance."

"And what of the prophecies? Did they come true?" Aldric asked.

"In a manner of speaking," Gaiban Morrigan said. "The text is very badly damaged, and the language is more ancient than any tongue remembered by the Asaani, more ancient even than Asaara. But from what we have been able to learn, the events it predicted did come true."

"So what did it predict? What did the book say would happen? What's happened already?"

Gaiban Morrigan pursed her lips. "The Seven Regrets are all linked with terrible events throughout our history. They represent steps which have and will be taken to allow the return of Victus, and the annihilation of our world. They are too long to tell in full, but you have heard the stories before."

Aldric nodded. This is what he wanted to know.

"The First Regret," Gaiban Morrigan began, "was the banishment of the Ainír by the Dhemorahns."

"But that had already happened by the time they received the book," Aldric said.

"Yes. It was a lesson. Part of the path, the first stone in the road to our downfall. The Second Regret was the sundering of the kingdoms, and the Age of Treason which began the Thousand Years War. The Wasting of Aerethlore was another, and the Warring Kingdoms and the rise of the Illarien Empire was yet another. Yet these events took place over thousands of years, far longer than anyone might remember, though they changed our world and paved the way for the empire we know today."

"Those are very broad events," Aldric said. "Things like wars and global conflicts are bound to change the course of nations, there doesn't need to be a prophecy to predict something like that."

"Wars, yes," Gaiban Morrigan said. "But we have had many wars in our history; wars so terrible that entire people's and countries were lost forever. But these wars, these conflicts specifically, these were the seeds predicted by the book for what would come later, each necessary for the next thread to be woven, the next step to be taken."

"Well, then what happens next?" Aldric urged, trying his best to give the prophecy some chance at reason.

"As you know, those events took place over the last fifteen thousand years, sometimes hundreds and thousands of years apart from each other. However, the last two prophecies of the Seven Regrets have taken place just in my lifetime."

Aldric looked at her questioningly.

"The penultimate stone in the path of the return of Victus was laid only forty years ago." She stared hard at Aldric, prompting him.

"The War of the Dukes? It was something my grandmother did?"

Gaiban Morrigan looked down. "In her effort to reassert the power of the emperors and to quell the uprising in the north, the Dowager Empress Alexandra set in motion something terrible, something she could not have foreseen. It was her decree that the Dhemorahns must relinquish their seats of power, and that the Great Houses must abandon their armies, which brought about the anger and resentment which has created Mal'Dreghen."

Aldric considered this for a moment. It wasn't hard to see the connexion. The evidence was there. Until the Dhemorahns were banished from the royal palace, the two religions had coexisted peacefully, for the most part. They were never friendly towards one another, but a religious war hadn't been heard of in a thousand years.

"So if the Empress set in motion the sixth prophecy, what is the seventh, the last?" Aldric asked.

"It has been one of the most difficult to decipher," Gaiban Morrigan said. Aldric thought she seemed almost reluctant to continue. "The other prophecies were clearer because they had already happened, events could be connected to them. But the last prophecy has been the most clouded. It has been some of my life's most challenging work trying to understand what is written in these pages, hoping that I might prevent the return of Victus myself. Yet I have spoken with every *maegana* of the high temples, and they all agree." She paused, the wind ruffling the wispy strands of silver hair about her face. "The Seven Regrets of the World ends with the Dhemorgal tomorrow."

ELEVEN

THE WHITE TOWER

Mal'Dreghen sat up, stretching. He looked around at the three women who surrounded him, two naked and one wearing only a short leather skirt that was pulled up over her waist and covered nothing. The Mal was also naked, sweating and panting from his exertions, his black hair clinging to his face and neck.

One of the girls moaned softly as she laid back into the cushions and piles of blankets on the floor, another girl leaning against her and draping an arm over her naked breast. Mal'Dreghen ran a hand between the girl's legs and smiled as she moaned louder, biting her lip. He stood, pulling his robe on and fastening it without haste.

"The only beauty in the world is man," Mal'Dreghen said, but not to the girls. He savoured the words as he spoke them, licking his lips. The great white Ziggurat of the Divine Hall of Man towered above the rest of Chaldrea, nearly as tall as the grand Citadel itself, and as Mal'Dreghen walked to the window and looked out the slatted blinds he could see clearly across the entire city.

His pale yellow eyes scanned the streets, finally coming to rest over the lush island of Callas Waith. The prominent island jutted above the horizon in the distance, rising pristine on white limestone cliffs above the darkening waters of Lake Nimaine. In the afternoon light he could make out the glittering walls of Dur Enskai, the Imperial Palace, perched high atop the craggy cliff face. His eyes narrowed as he studied the distant island, the corners of his mouth becoming a scowl.

"On this one truth rests all our beliefs," Mal'Dreghen said, turning from the window. The flush of his appetites was still on him, and he swallowed, regaining his breath. "It is the first truth in the path to a pure and noble existence. Nature is empty without man, for man gives it life, distinction, awareness. For what is a mountain with no one to see it?" he went on, drawing a hand over his brow and wiping the sweat on his robe. "But we cannot forget that this truth exists with an undeniable parallel—that there is nothing truly ugly in the world but the weakness of men." The words sounded like poetry as Mal'Dreghen spoke, his voice soft and rich.

The Mal strode from the window towards a man kneeling in the centre of a high circular room. A column of white light poured down from a dome high above, reflecting off tall white pillars. Mal'Dreghen circled the man with deliberate slowness, his robe flapping open to reveal his nakedness as he walked.

The man in the centre of the room sat doubled over on his hands and knees, a tattered brown robe hanging loosely from one shoulder. The folds of a dirty white *kilpi* were just visible beneath, marking him for an Asaani druid. He was panting heavily, his back arching in spasms as he fought to regain his breath. A stream of blood ran from a livid gash in his temple and fell pattering to the polished marble. The sound echoed through the chamber. He spat, loudly, and sat back on his haunches. His round face, wide set eyes and light olive skin hinted at some vaguely western heritage, and a band of pale skin across his forehead suggested the tan line of a *clamael*.

The druid dropped his hands by his side and gazed upwards to the skylight far above. There was no fear in his brown eyes, only exhaustion. Closing them, he began reciting mantras to himself, his lips barely moving as he spoke. He was nearly inaudible in the stillness. "...I unbind the unknown and make the dark places light, and the emptiness whole. I follow where I fear to go, and am afraid no longer."

Mal'Dreghen laughed scornfully. "That! That is what I despise about you most, *druid,*" he said, spitting the last word. He stopped in front of the man and looked down, studying him. "If I hadn't seen for myself the craven, empty lives you heretics lead, I might have taken those words for true courage." His yellow eyes flashed dangerously.

"Man cannot wrong another man, not really. It isn't possible. Men are sovereigns unto themselves, and the only wrongs they receive are those they permit themselves to suffer. Men are kings, and no king would suffer the abuse of a peasant. So you see I have not wronged you by bringing you here. We each fight with the strength that is given us, that is all. The fight itself is not wrong. When men fail to see their own strength—when they cease their struggle—then they do wrong. Not to others, but to themselves. And you would encourage this! A passionless, gliding mediocrity that inspires no one to lift themselves up and strive for more!"

"You are satisfied that I am put here before you, stripped and at your mercy. But my joy depends not upon my circumstances. You may break this body, but I am not tied to it."

"You speak with such bravado, Elder Khestor," Mal'Dreghen continued, throwing his arms wide. The loose sleeves of his robe fell back to reveal bony forearms and rope like veins that rippled as he clenched his fists. "You sound like a true son of Desedar, but I shall make you wish you really weren't tied to this body," he said, stepping into the circle of light. His black hair fell in shinning rivers down his shoulders, framing a gaunt face with thin, purple lips and high cheekbones. His narrow yellow eyes peered out of sunken sockets ringed by the dark circles of many sleepless nights. He stank of flesh and sweat, and Khestor tried to lean away.

The Mal grabbed the druid instead, cupping his chin with his hand and wrenching his face upwards, his robe falling completely open. "You are a coward. You are lost without your wretched little gods. Your twisted devotion is a sad testament to the blindness which infects all your kind," he said, releasing Khestor's chin roughly.

Elder Khestor remained looking up at him. "Do not think," he said hoarsely, "that your beliefs are the whole truth, or even the only truth in this world, Mal'Dreghen. The only truth is the journey we are born into, without perspective or motive. What are we, compared to this?"

"What *truths* you speak, Elder," Mal'Dreghen spat. "And what will you leave behind, with all your humility? Your modesty writes no records. What mark have you left in this world to show that you were ever here at all, that you were any better than the mindless beasts of the forests?"

"I hope to leave nothing behind," Khestor said. "I hope to leave this world as unblemished as when I entered. I have faith that my spirit will return to Aminwyr and be reunited with the earth that made my flesh. This is my faith." Khestor spat out some of the blood that was pooling in his mouth. "And what is your faith?" he asked. "Is that it?" He nodded towards the girls lying together on the cushions.

"Faith?" Mal'Dreghen sneered, without looking back. "Faith is for those with no proof of their beliefs. The sons of Desedar need no such faith."

"And I say that only a tyrant would govern the faithless."

Mal'Dreghen sniffed, straightening. He regarded the druid for a moment. "Your fate is fitting then," he said. "You claim that I am faithless, yet it is *you* who have no faith. No faith in yourself, for you do not realise your own divinity, your own *strength*. Man is the only power in this world—the only one! Man and the *iron* of his will," Mal'Dreghen said, shaking his bony fist in Khestor's face. "You would rely on gods and on emperors, but I tell you it is man who is the true god. Man. Man alone stands among the beasts of this world and is aware, and with his might he defines the borders of his kingdom, creating beauty where once there was only a barren wasteland." Without taking his eyes off Khestor, the Mal called behind him, "Rasmus!"

A small man who had been standing in the shadows stepped forward. He was plainly dressed, and wore an open, faded red vest in the style of a deacon. He gave the Mal a questioning look, and Mal'Dreghen noted the eager, almost hopeful glint in his downturned, hooded eyes. The man's left eye was clouded by cataracts, and it glistened with a watery sheen. Greasy strands of greying hair hung from his balding head, and his leathery skin was pocked by old scars. He blinked expectantly.

"You see it is man who crafts this world and governs it," Mal'Dreghen resumed. "Desedar taught us this, and gave us the imperative to make this planet into our own domain—to sculpt it as gods do from the lifeless clay, and bring beauty into existence. Beauty, Elder Khestor, is the highest principle of man. Only man can understand beauty, so he must perfect it. Beauty is morality, those who cannot see it must be immoral," he said, licking his lips.

"Beauty is tyranny," Khestor replied meekly, too weak to lift his head anymore. "What is beauty when it must conform to your will?"

"Blasphemer," Mal'Dreghen hissed through clenched teeth. "Yet you will earn your redemption."

"I was not born to be compelled," the Elder druid recited. "By you, or anyone else."

"All men were born to be compelled, Elder," Mal'Dreghen said. "Every man is a god, but they would rain destruction and chaos down on their little lands without guidance."

"And it is *your* guidance they require?" Khestor asked with as much humour as he could muster.

"You presume to doubt, druid, but at least my guidance is *real*. I live and breathe in *this* world, not some ethereal plane of exile." He folded his arms patiently. "All your mantras and directives—they must make it so easy for you not to think. Your faith is a crux, a disease that cripples the true, glorious nature of man. It encourages weakness, and this is the true evil of this world. I will spread truth and purge that evil, and you will help me."

Khestor shook his head sadly. "What perversity of fate has led us to this path? The only good is knowledge," he said, "and the only evil is ignorance."

"Your mantras are endless," Mal'Dreghen said, a grim smile tightening his purple lips. "But we shall see. There is only one truth, and I shall soon reveal it." He turned to Rasmus who had been standing patiently by his side. "This heretic does not yet understand the salvation that waits with our Prophet Desedar. He still looks to his banished pantheon for absolution." The Mal stepped backwards into the shadows. "Instruct him."

Rasmus nodded and walked to the man, restraining his arms tightly behind his back with a metal clasp. He produced a small silver rod, ornately etched, with pointed forks at both ends. Khestor did not resist as Rasmus tilted his head back and tied the rod into place with one of the pointed ends projecting into his chest, the other jabbing upwards into the soft flesh beneath his chin.

When he had finished securing the prongs with a leather strap about Khestor's neck, Rasmus stepped back and surveyed his work. Both ends of the device were firmly held, their fine points already piercing the druid's skin as he struggled in this painful position. Mal'Dreghen watched without speaking as Rasmus moved around the druid, pulling Khestor's hair out of his face and straightening his robe. Rasmus pulled a white cloth from his breast pocket and gently dabbed at the spittle around the druid's mouth. He carefully wiped around the points of the fork where the blood was beginning to trickle, murmuring quietly all the while. Mal'Dreghen could not hear what he was saying, but he watched as Rasmus's fat, childlike hands fussed over the druid.

"Thank you, Rasmus," Mal'Dreghen said, inspecting the gasping druid.

Rasmus started, as if he were surprised to find himself not alone with the bound man. He looked up at Mal'Dreghen, bags drooping beneath his watery eyes. "He is ready to receive your benediction, Highest One," Rasmus said, his voice thin and faltering. Mal'Dreghen nodded, and Rasmus retreated a few paces, stepping outside the ring of light.

"This is the Truth of Desedar," Mal'Dreghen said, flicking the pronged forks. "Do you know why?"

Khestor began to speak, but choked on the words as the prongs dug into his chin, causing the blood to flow faster. He squeezed his eyes tight in a rictus of pain, his breath coming in short, snorting bursts through his nostrils.

"Ahh, I think you see now. You will find it lends certain, ah, *economy*, to your speech." The Mal smiled, but there was no warmth in his eyes. "Be wise about your words, *druid*, and you may find this conversation short," he said, his ashen face lurid in the cold light. "I have a message for you to deliver."

TWELVE

MAIDEN VOYAGE

From his vantage point on the bridge of the INV *Eidolon*, Raynard Sinclair had a spectacular view of *Torr Archus*. In the time it had taken him to eat, catch a few hours of sleep, and finally board the waiting *Eidolon*, the station had emerged from behind the shadow of the gas giant Victus and into the cold starlight of Daedrus. Escort shuttles and engineering teams flocked around the *Eidolon*, ferrying personnel from the shipyard and making observations as the cruiser pulled away from the station. The *Eidolon* was not a large vessel, but the dozens of smaller support craft looked like insects swarming in the sunlight.

Raynard paced the command deck. An elevated gantry looked down into the control room of the operations floor of the bridge, where he could monitor his crew. The gantry ran alongside an uninterrupted window spanning the width of the bridge, offering a 180 degree forward view of the *Eidolon's* bow, and Raynard found himself admiring the lean, efficient design. The *Eidolon* was the first of a new class of cruiser, lightly armed and built for speed, stealth, and manoeuvrability. It was his hope that her agility might come in handy against whatever new weapons the Raeth might possess.

There were nearly thirty personnel present on the command deck at all times, swelled to almost double that size as they made ready for departure. The murmur of voices sent a rush of excitement tingling down his spine, taking Raynard back to his early days as a leftenant aboard the battlecruiser *Sabre*. Raynard breathed deeply, absorbing the new life of the ship and feeling it surround him. He watched with pride as his handpicked crew attended their duties, rousing the cruiser from her long months of dormancy at the shipyards.

The timing could not have been more perfect, Raynard reflected. With the main fleet, gathering in orbit of Aera, a tiny moon of the ice planet Argoth, this would be the prime opportunity to test the *Eidolon* in combat. He'd hoped there'd be a little more time to test her before she saw action, but he was confident enough in the reports of her progress and in the development teams that there wouldn't be any problems. *Daor help us if there are*, he thought, stepping down from the gantry.

"What is our estimated time to rendezvous with the Sciphere?" Raynard asked a young ensign at the nearest terminal.

The man glanced at his screen. "My Lord, the trip to Aera will require approximately nine hours, at maximum speed."

Raynard nodded. "We're not in that big of a hurry, let's cut it back to three-quarters—don't want to overdo it on our first run," he said. "Where does that leave us?"

The ensign reviewed his screen again, replied, "At three quarters drive we should arrive with the rest of the Sciphere in twelve hours."

Raynard had decided to follow his instincts, and those of Captain Achres, and had designated two more destroyers for patrol duty around Errolor. He still thought it highly unlikely there would be any call for such precaution. Nevertheless, an uneasy feeling settled in his stomach when he thought about leaving the capital so defenceless. *Especially,* he thought, *with Evaine and Eleanor at the Dhemorgal.* Even with the firepower that brought down the *Malefactor,* he doubted the corsairs would set their targets on Errolor. But these were dangerous times. An archduke couldn't be too careful.

Raynard saw Captain Achres standing near the helm, giving directions to officers at every side. He doubted Achres had slept, putting the importance of this mission and his Duke's expectations above his personal needs. He was a resilient man, standing tall and alert amid a swirling sea of junior officers. Still there was something haggard in his eyes as he saluted Raynard.

"My Lord," he said, a note of restraint in his thin voice. "We will be underway shortly. Preliminary inspections reveal all systems in order, and the crew detail from the station are making their final rounds. I expect no more than twenty minutes until all the surveys have been completed."

Raynard nodded, allowing Achres to see the pleased look on his face. "I'm sure everything is fine, captain," he said. "So far I'm impressed with what I've seen. This is an excellent ship, and I expect she'll perform admirably." He ran his big hand over the gleaming console beside him. "She's one of a kind," he said, satisfied. "I've not seen finer."

Achres drew his mouth into a thin line, nodding. "No one has." He turned to speak with an engineer briefly, then, "I read the report you filed with the Admiralty earlier," he said.

Raynard had expected this. "It wasn't an easy decision," he said, frowning. "I've also sent orders to raise all able ships currently planetside. There will be well over forty vessels in orbit, in addition to *Arrus Athaban.* Only the Royal Wing will remain stationed at Chaldrea." He shrugged his big shoulders. "Besides, the Sciphere is nearly two hundred and fifty strong. Two more vessels will not determine the course of the battle over Drusus. And if they do? Well, then we're in worse shape than we thought."

Achres shook his head. "They may have a slight advantage in numbers, but they cannot contend with our training and firepower."

"Let's hope not," Raynard said. The old veteran in him was eager to see what awaited them over the rocky mining world.

Forty minutes later the last of the inspection teams disembarked. A dozen or so support vessels had retreated some distance away, observing the *Eidolon* before she engaged her Lantern drive for the first time. Raynard looked over the gleaming hull of the space station, searching for Alasdair's office. He wondered if the admiral were watching him now. *Have another drink on me, Al,* he thought.

The chaos of pre-flight examinations had subsided on the bridge and the crew took their stations. Raynard could sense the expectant pause of his crew as he waited for his chief of operations to report that the engines had completed their prep-cycle and were fully powered.

Captain Achres sat in the first officer's chair to the left of Raynard. For the first time since they had come aboard, Raynard thought the fastidious captain looked at peace. He was tired, Raynard could see that, but there was finally nothing left for him to do but sit and wait. For himself, Raynard was relieved to be underway. The next day would offer no rest, but he was excited to meet the Sciphere and discover what sort of enemy they would face. He never liked delay. *One can delay only to the advantage of one's enemy,* he thought to himself.

"My Lord Duke," the helmsman said, turning to face Raynard. "The chief reports all systems ready. The course is laid in. We await your orders."

Those crewmen not fixed to their consoles turned to look at the archduke, their faces bright with anticipation. Raynard nodded sternly, savouring the weight of the moment. This was the *Eidolon's* maiden voyage. There was no time for a christening. This was all the ceremony she would get for now, and he didn't intend to waste it. Raising his hand, he held it for a moment, and then said loud enough for all to hear, "Engage."

THIRTEEN

IN THE THICKET

Aldric gathered in the reins of his apala, pulling him to a stop on the verge of a grassy hillock. Thick rainclouds rolled away over the jungle treetops in the distance, and far thunder grumbled across the valley. His apala, a rare stallion he named Dravon, which meant 'fearless' in Dutharrin, stamped his hoof impatiently. He was eager for the chase, and he tossed his snow white mane and glared over the damp mead ahead.

Aldric patted his neck and Dravon flicked one of his ears towards him, staring off in the direction the degoll had disappeared. He snorted, flaring his nostrils and sniffing the wind anxiously. Aldric looked down into the long grass for any tracks. The breeze didn't make his task easy. Waves of grass stretched out across the rolling green veldt, tufted heads sagging from the recent downpour.

He hopped out of his saddle and knelt to the ground, holding the reins in one hand. He was sure he'd seen the degoll come this way. The short legged animal left a distinctive trail that wasn't hard to find. He picked at the soggy moss covered earth, rolling the black soil through his gloved fingers. The degoll wouldn't burrow here, certainly not after a rain.

He stood and looked down the valley. The native Thedarrans called it the Cwarri Glour, or 'Cloud Forest', and it stretched from Chaldrea to the Lyndron River two thousand kilometres to the north. Grey clouds of mist rolled out from the dales where the silver-green veldt met the ragged wall of jungle trees. The mist hung in the low places and swirled out from between the trees where it vanished in the long grass like ghostly fingers. Elcaern legends said evil wildwood creatures called *wyghe* came out to play in the fog at the forest's edge. They were servants of the forest god Wudu, and the Elcaern believed that anyone who wandered into the mist would never be seen again.

The sky was clearing in the east near Bailynn, and Aldric could just see Lake Nimaine over the dark treetops in the distance. Deep clouds still hung over the forest to the west.

"Over here!" A voice called to the right. Aldric leapt into his saddle and turned Dravon into a canter, his hooves thudding over the wet earth. The long grass slapped wet at Dravon's chest, smacking Aldric's legs and high riding boots. He paused on a ridge and gazed around.

"Here!" the voice called again. It came from behind a low brake of brambles, and Aldric eased Dravon into a trot until he spotted a riderless apala tethered to a branch. Aldric tied Dravon beside the tawny apala and snuck around to the other side of the thicket, his boots sinking into black mud. He came around the brake to find a mere of brackish water, tangled with underbrush and fallen branches.

The smell of rotting vegetation filled his nostrils. He looked around and made a low, warbling whistle. It was repeated, and he turned and made his way into the underbrush beside the black waters of the mere. After a minute of struggling through tangles of branches he emerged into a clearing. A small man with dark hair was kneeling in the mud and he waved Aldric over. He put a finger to his lips and motioned towards a thicket half a dozen metres in front of them.

"Iain," Aldric said as he knelt beside the man. "How did you get in here? I didn't see your tracks."

Iain nodded. "I came in the other side."

"Where is it?" Aldric asked, scanning the area around them. Iain pointed to a place a few metres away and Aldric spotted the slithering trail of the degoll leading into the bracken ahead.

"The mere is on the other side, he can't get out. He'll have to come this way," Iain said, his brown eyes wide with excitement.

"It'll be tough," Aldric said. The plants and vines grew close here; there wouldn't be much room to manoeuvre his hunting lance.

"All the better!" Iain said.

"I'll take left," Aldric said, looking around. "You go over there, and we'll flush him out." He reached over his back and pulled his lance from its sheath. It was a third the length of a normal lance, made for throwing or quick thrusts—perfect for hunting degoll. The black steel blade looked wicked in the dim light. "Be quick now," he said, his voice low.

They advanced together, taking up positions on either side of the small tangle of brush. With the pond behind the brush, the degoll would have to run towards them and they'd have him. Iain unsheathed his lance and they stood ready, their dark blades poised. The shadows in the thicket were deep and the black mud made it difficult to see into the underbrush. The degoll would have a hard time running from them in this mud, but degoll were wily, unpredictable beasts.

Aldric glanced at Iain, who nodded. Aldric removed his long hunting knife and lifted the leading edge of a large leaf that drooped to the ground. A roar exploded from the bracken and a russet coloured shadow leapt out towards Iain. Iain jabbed his lance forward but the degoll was already too close, slamming into his chest and throwing him to the mud.

Aldric cursed and scrambled to Iain who was wrestling with the degoll on top of him. The little creature was snarling ferociously and had its jaws locked around Iain's vambrace, swinging its powerful front claws at his face. Iain was using both hands to keep the creature from getting to his face and throat and couldn't reach down to pull out his own knife. They were moving too quickly, too close together and Aldric didn't want to risk thrusting his spear so close to Iain. He dropped his lance and grabbed the degoll's thick neck with one hand, his hunting knife in the other.

Feeling Aldric's hand on its neck the degoll released Iain's arm and swung round on Aldric, lashing out and dragging its razor like claws across his forearm. They grazed over his vambrace but the giant teeth clamped down hard on his knife hand and Aldric gasped as pain ricocheted up his arm and he dropped the knife. The degoll's fearsome black eyes glared at Aldric as he tried to ignore the pain and find his dropped knife in the mud. He suddenly felt the cold steel behind him in the muck and grasping it, jabbed it upwards, wrenching it into the degoll's gut.

The degoll howled angrily and released Aldric's hand, doubling over to attack his other hand. Aldric twisted the knife and the degoll screamed. Aldric tried to stand and get his boot on top of the thrashing creature but as he raised himself up the degoll tore itself off the knife and leapt for his face.

Before it could reach him the degoll was jerked sideways, yelping. A blur of black steel flew past Aldric's face, and Iain was standing at his side, the degoll writhing on the end of his lance. Iain let the lance down cautiously, dropping the degoll into the mud, where it struggled from side to side for a moment before wheezing and finally lying still. Aldric collapsed backwards into the mud, panting. Iain wrenched the short spear from the degoll and turned to Aldric, grinning. "That was a fine one, hey?" he said, nudging the lifeless degoll with the toe of his boot.

"You were never much of a hunter," Iain said as they rode back across the green swale of rolling grasslands. The storm had moved on and the sun was breaking low in the sky over the jungle treetops to the west. The limp body of the degoll was tied to the back of Iain's apala, its head flopping gently against the animal's mottled brown flank. Long shadows drew out from the jungle and spread across the hills, and the jungle insects began their evening chorus.

In the distance they could finally see Callas Andunn and the glittering white outline of Chaldrea. A score of retainers and four Valorí rode in silence some distance behind. They had caught up with Aldric and Iain as they were saddling their apalas, laughing and covered with mud and grime. The men responsible to the emperor for the prince's safety passed uneasy glances when they saw the deep cuts across his arms and his blood spattered jerkin; behind their mirrored helmets, the Valorí remained as inscrutable as ever.

Aldric laughed. "You were on your backside in the mud before I put my knife through his belly. But I guess your backside is where you're most comfortable."

"Oh you only tickled him a bit," Iain said, a frown turning down his full lips. "The critter was still wanting a good jab, and I obliged." He jerked his right arm forward, imitating the fatal thrust.

"You never miss a chance to jab a critter, eh?"

"Only your mum," Iain replied. Iain was a recent initiate into the nobility of the Erolan. He'd been born in the western province Ruador, and his round, youthful face and bronzed skin seemed out of place among the elegant countenances of the Chaldrean nobility.

Many of the nobility were descended from the Tir Annath—a tall, fair people who migrated from the north aeons ago. Iain, however, shared his people's stout, ruddy build, and had a fiery temperament to match. Aldric had met him when his family purchased their plantation on Callas Baltan and they had become fast friends, sharing in their mutual dislike for courtly pageantry. In all of Chaldrea, Iain was the one man Aldric thought truly understood the isolation he felt at court.

"Your hands are too soft, you see" Iain continued. "You've got used to servants wiping your arse for you, you've forgotten how to do anything yourself."

"You're probably right," Aldric conceded. "If I'd spent my childhood wrestling degoll in a mud hovel, maybe I'd be as good as you."

Iain laughed, though the fact his family hadn't been born into the Erolan was a sore subject for him. Despite their wealth, Iain's family weren't Erolan in the truest sense and would never be accepted as one of the blooded houses.

"Why'd you come out here, anyway?" Iain asked. Descending from the veldt they approached a close of low stone buildings. Centuries ago a manor had been built expressly for hunting on the plains, and lodgings were added for the emperor's hunting parties. However the emperor never hunted anymore, and the building would have gone to ruin if Aldric hadn't taken up the sport.

Aldric thought for a moment. "The same reason I went up in the Starling this morning," he said.

Iain glanced at him. "You were hoping to save Mal'Dreghen the trouble of killing you tomorrow?" His brogue was lilting and musical, and set him apart at once from the smooth Dutharrin accent of the capital.

"I was trying to take my mind off tomorrow," he said, chuckling. "It's just a game to everyone else," Aldric said. "Everyone is going to see the tournaments tomorrow, to see the games and competitions in the coliseum—it's all just a spectacle, they come and cheer and go home."

"It's entertainment," Iain said.

"But *I'm* the entertainment," Aldric said.

"Too bad you aren't entertaining," Iain replied, regretfully.

Aldric ignored him. "Tomorrow is..." he paused, trying to find the words. "I'm not sure you'd understand," he said finally.

Iain watched him. "I know you'll handle yourself tomorrow," he said. "The Draugor fight like animals, and that's how you'll finish your opponent—like the dog he is."

"Tomorrow could change everything, even if the Mal and I are the only ones who see it," Aldric said, swallowing. He didn't want to admit that he was afraid. Was he? He wasn't sure and he didn't want to lie to himself. This was like nothing he had felt in all the months he'd been training with Bahir in the temple. An icy fist grabbed his stomach, squeezing everything up into his chest, into his throat. If he could admit this fear to himself, he could also control it and keep it from showing.

Aldric forced a smile. "I've never fought anyone trained in *gho*. It's the opposite of *craidath*. Bahir told me what to expect, but it's all just academic at this point, it's all just in my head."

"You're right!" Iain said. "It is."

Aldric tried to think of something else. "What about you? You've been a little preoccupied yourself this afternoon. You're a bad shot, but I've never seen you miss a degoll sitting on top of you," he said.

"If I didn't get to watch you make an arse of yourself tomorrow, I'd finish you right now," Iain said. "But, since you asked, there has been something on my mind."

"Arianne?" Aldric asked.

Iain grinned. "Aye, she's the one I'm thinking of. You know, you're brighter than you look. I go on about her for months on end and out of the blue you guess what I'm thinking—all on your own! You'll box clever with that Draugor, you will," he said.

Aldric laughed. "Well? Are you going to see her after the tournament?"

"She's going to the gala at Aldon Court with her father."

"The Margrave? You better wear your best then. You know you can't just show up in your hunting trousers, right?" Aldric said.

"It's a shame, really," Iain said, looking forlorn at his blood stained breeches. "This is my best."

"In that case I'd say don't wear anything, but I think the clothes actually hide a bit of the musk," Aldric said, chuckling.

"One of my finest qualities, my musk," Iain said. "Drives Arianne wild."

"Now that I believe."

"No, but she's a real fine girl," Iain said, his eyes softening. "I never feel out of place with her, even with all the fancy courtiers. I can talk to her, you know—really talk to her—and I feel like she understands me."

Aldric didn't reply. He was pleased to see his friend so happy. Iain had always struggled in the role of a noble, and in truth had very few friends besides Aldric. Arianne was the first girl he'd felt comfortable approaching, and in the few months he'd known her, Aldric had seen his friend change dramatically.

"I'm taking her sailing next week, as well," he said, brightening. "She's agreed to come with me down to Brythanor on our sloop and see the red cliffs at Longarth."

"I'm not surprised."

"Really?"

"Of course not. It makes sense she'd want to go someplace where no one would see her with you."

"*Gaetha.*"

"You talk like that around her?" Aldric asked.

"What if I do? She says worse, you should hear her. Last week we sat together during the concessions, and you should have heard her carrying on about the Erolan at court. It was all I could do to keep from laughing. That girl is wicked!"

"You're a rogue, Iain. You always will be."

"What's that to do with anything?"

"Rogues don't love girls, they break their hearts. As soon as you know she's yours, you won't want anything to do with her."

"You're wrong," Iain said. His sincere tone took Aldric by surprise.

"Either way, I'm happy for you," Aldric said after a moment, realising he meant it.

Iain nodded. "I mean to keep this one," he said. "I'm twenty five, with a title and land—I deserve a noblewoman like Arianne—I'm finally a respectable man."

"Well, you've got a title and land, anyways," Aldric said.

"Oh and I suppose you think you're doing better?" Iain replied, suddenly defensive. "What've you got that I haven't? Hey? I put that to you, Your Highness. Besides the inheritance of a kingdom you don't want, and the promise of landing square on your arse tomorrow before the whole empire—I ask you: with all your success in love, what do you have that I haven't?"

"Hygiene," Aldric said.

"Much good it's done you. You're no happier than I am, even if you do smell like a girl."

"Oh no?"

"A man needs a woman Aldric. You're lonely, I can see that."

"I've got Dravon here, don't I boy?" Aldric said, patting the apala's thick neck. Dravon snorted and swished his tail.

"Yeah and a real fine romance that is, one for the sagas."

"I don't have time for romance Iain, I'm a prince."

"Oh I forgot, you're too busy blowing up ships, rolling in the sand with sweaty men and romancing your apala." Iain sighed. "Aldric, what good is a prince if not to keep romance in the world? That's what princes are good *for.* That's *all* you're good for! Princes aren't born to muck stables or bake bread. They're born to make people dream, dream of something better. So let them dream! Let them think romance is still alive, that a prince can marry a princess." He rubbed his chin. "And that they don't have to keep one eye on the stable doors at night. No offence, Dravon," Iain said. Dravon flicked his ears at his name.

"At least Dravon doesn't nag like an old hen," Aldric said. "What's your problem? You're awful preachy today."

A warm breeze sprung up through the grass and rushed down the shadowed side of the hill. The sun was breaking through the heavy clouds in the east and streamed in golden rivers across the jungle top.

"What is it about people that when they find romance they have to go and rub it in everyone's face?" Aldric asked. "Women are the solution to a problem a man doesn't have until he has a woman."

Iain shrugged. "You only say that because you haven't got one... And I don't think you would know what to do with one if you did."

"That's like saying I'm bad at being sick," Aldric said. "I don't need to be sick to get better at it."

"Arianne makes me happier than I've ever been," Iain said, shaking his head. "But I'm just as handy without a woman."

"You're all hands when you're without one, too."

Iain laughed. "That doesn't mean I don't love her comforts."

"If it weren't for women, men wouldn't need comforting," Aldric replied.

"You know, your brother's a scoundrel, but at least he enjoys himself. You could learn a thing or two from him."

"Damn your eyes, Iain, can't I come out here and ride in peace?" Aldric said. "Whose side are you on, anyways?"

"I just think you're avoiding confronting things you're uncomfortable with."

"You're damn right I am, tomorrow is gonna be hell, and I don't want to think about it right now." Aldric shifted in his saddle. "Or women, for that matter. Is that ok with you?"

"You think you're doing anyone a favour by ignoring what you have to do tomorrow?" Iain asked. "Whether you think about it or not, at this time tomorrow you'll be standing there in that arena, face to face with that Draugor. Will you think about hunting degoll then?"

"I'm trying to relieve some stress and you're being a pain the ass, I just want to take my mind off everything for a while. Didn't you just say I needed to enjoy myself more?"

"Are you enjoying yourself? Or are you avoiding your problems?" Iain switched the reins to his other hand, resting his arm on his leg. "Rest, lose yourself in the moment if you must. But trying to kill yourself twice in one day isn't my idea of relaxing. What are you running from?"

Aldric hopped down from his apala and swung the reins over Dravon's big head. "For now? You." he said. "I'll walk from here."

Dravon's hooves clopped over the stones in the stable yard. The smell of feed and manure and fresh wood chips drifted in from the open stable doors, and Aldric patted the apala's flank as he handed the reins to an ostler. Inside the manor he pulled off his boots and slumped onto a wide, comfortable divan of dark leather. The room was quiet, and for the first time that day he felt alone with his thoughts.

Without a sound, Cipher leapt up into Aldric's lap, balancing on his legs. He gave Aldric an expectant look and chirruped. Aldric had brought him along, though he'd never actually take him hunting. The razorcat was brave but he wouldn't risk him getting into a fight with a degoll. He scratched the big cat, rubbing his chin as he curled up on his legs.

Aldric found Cipher two years ago when he was hunting taebor in the highlands outside Innisglenn. The winter was particularly cold, and the wind that night tore through the fells, howling around the steep rocks and craggy bluffs on the barren braes. He'd heard a tiny mewling sound coming from somewhere up ahead, and followed it to a toppled cairn nearby. Stooping to look into a hollow under the rock, a scrawny black cub peered out at him, huddled against the cold, shivering in the back and crying for its mother.

The den appeared to be abandoned, and the cub half-starved. Aldric nervously looked for signs of the mother. Razorcats could weigh more than thirty-five kilograms, and he didn't fancy running into a mother who thought her den was being raided. He didn't see any sign of her however, and one dead cub half buried in snow on the other side of the cairn confirmed his suspicions.

So reaching into the den he'd picked up the quivering ball of fur and put it inside his jacket, carrying it back to his hunting lodge. Aldric named the mysterious black cub Cipher, and raised him at the palace, feeling sure he would have died that night if he hadn't found him.

When Aldric went on retreats to the highlands or hunting trips here in Bailynn, Cipher usually accompanied him, wandering off into the wilderness for days at a time. Aldric worried at first, but the razorcat always returned, happy as ever and fat from his own hunting ventures. He'd even escaped from Dur Enskai once when Aldric left him to go hunting alone. Cipher had somehow managed to descend the narrow paths down the rocky cliff face and swim across the lake to join Aldric at his lodge in the Bailynn grasslands. He was an intelligent cat, and Aldric appreciated his company more often than most humans. Especially now, he thought, remembering Iain's words.

Perhaps Iain was right though, Aldric thought, stroking the purring razorcat absently. Maybe he was running away from his fight tomorrow. He pulled off his gloves, noting where the fangs of the degoll had torn at the thick leather and revealed the fine mesh of silver galvonite polymer beneath. If these had been normal gloves, he reflected, he wouldn't have a hand anymore. As it were, his hand was bruised and sore, and ached when he made a fist.

Aldric laid the gloves on the table and stared out the window. The sun hung on the horizon, just above the peaks of the Enowyrth. He realised he didn't know if he could live up to the empire's expectations tomorrow. A cold knot wormed into his stomach. *Tomorrow,* he thought. *Tomorrow, and it will all be over.*

"It is, and will be, and that is all. There is nothing else," he murmured to himself.

"Sorry buddy," Aldric said, sliding Cipher gently to the side. The razorcat swished his tail at the interruption. Reaching for his boots, he picked up a cloth from a nearby table. He examined the boots in the light, wiping the muck and grime from between the tread in the soles. Removing a jar of oily paste from a drawer, he began polishing the boots with a stiff brush, rubbing the oil into the rich brown leather in long, smooth strokes. Cipher looked up at the sound, sniffing at the oil. He stretched and tried to lick the boot and Aldric tapped his nose.

"You wouldn't like it bud, I promise," Aldric said, chuckling. Cipher sat back and stared at Aldric, eyes wide, licking his lips. Aldric breathed deeply, inhaling the musky scent of the oil and the warm aroma of the leather. An old clock ticked quietly in the background and an apala whinnied in the yard outside. He finished polishing and set the boots down beside him, the leather glowing in the sun. Looking out towards the trees, he watched as the last rays of amber light passed over Chaldrea, the city falling into darkness.

FOURTEEN

THE DOLDRUMS

A young, sandy haired yeoman in a grey uniform saluted the archduke. "My Lord, the chief engineer reports it'll be another four hours until repairs are complete and we're underway." He handed a thin pad to Raynard who glanced at it before flinging it aside on his desk.

"Outrageous!" he bellowed. "The entire Sciphere is gathered and we're dead in the water. The largest operation in naval history and I'm left behind."

The yeoman looked down. "Your orders, my Lord?"

"The same as they were an hour ago dammit," Raynard said. "Keep the engineering teams on full duty shifts and let me know the moment there's any progress."

"At once," the yeoman said. He bowed and retreated from Raynard's briefing room.

"We should consider plotting a new course, Your Grace." Captain Achres spoke from a smaller desk at the other end of the room. The great cabin sat at the rear of the bridge and commanded an impressive view of the stern of the ship. Raynard unfastened the top two clasps on his uniform and let the collar drape open. He rubbed his eyes wearily and stared out over the lonely scene beyond. The mirrored skin of the *Eidolon* was invisible in the blackness of space, and rows of tiny glowing windows merged with the starlight reflected on the sweeping chrome hull.

Raynard clenched his jaw. "Gods of the Abyss!" His sanguine cheeks flushed the colour of his hair. "I've never missed a fleet engagement! These last twenty years, I've seen every major action of the empire, and now I'm scrambling to pull my britches up, waiting on those damned mechanics."

"This was unforeseeable," Achres said as he paged through a series of holocharts on the desk. "And we still have a five hour window to rendezvous with the fleet."

"Disasters like this have determined the outcome of battles," Raynard snarled. "If I can't reach the Sciphere, it'll be handed to Admiral Burns. That man doesn't know the galley from the orlop."

"With respect, your Lordship, we have the best engineers doing everything they can. There's really nothing you could have done differently."

"No, this is my fault, the damn ship wasn't tested! We take her out of dry dock and into stream space on day one without any preparation. It's reckless, she should have been at the Ahran proving grounds for months before today."

"It was necessary," Achres replied. "You're right, but there just wasn't time. The emperor won't postpone the convoy from Drusus. Every ship in the fleet has orders."

Raynard stared down at his paralyzed engines as the *Eidolon* drifted through the void. A knot worked itself around his insides. Burns wasn't prepared to command the Sciphere. The fleet would need an experienced, proven commander like himself. Burns was proud, haughty, and eager to fight. He pressed the attack when he should retreat, engaged the enemy when he was out manoeuvred. Raynard had saved him from being overwhelmed many times during the War of the Dukes. To Burns, strategy simply meant willing the enemy to lose, and engaging him with numerically superior forces. It had worked for him before, but he didn't have the upper hand now. Dogged determination was better left to boardrooms and court politics where it might impress someone who didn't understand strategy.

It had been six hours since the *Eidolon* dropped out of stream space, her engines collapsing under the strain. *Torr Archus* had informed him that he was too far out for any repair ships to reach him. He was stranded. Raynard had less than five hours to repair his floundering ship and meet the Sciphere at Aera or they would be forced to leave without him. He'd been in communication with the Admiralty and they had all told him the same thing: the fleet can't wait.

Dropping into his chair Raynard spun around to face Achres, still leaning over his desk. "What've you found?"

Achres pulled on his lip thoughtfully. "Nothing conclusive," he said. "I've been searching for possible routes of attack along the corridor from Drusus to Errolor."

"And?"

"And it's possible they've hidden a force around Khanos."

"The Drusus moon? We would have seen them."

"It's undefended and uninhabited and there are no monitoring satellites. We can't rule out possibilities," Achres said. "Knowing we'll be guarding this convoy more heavily than usual, they probably won't simply attack us head on."

"You suspect a diversion."

"I do, and because they have limited options for approach, I can't think of many alternatives besides hiding in plain sight. We've avoided deploying extra surveillance to keep from arousing their suspicion. They could use that to their advantage."

"Gods, I hope we're over thinking this," Raynard said. "The entire Sciphere? In our worst case scenarios, there's nothing that would offer genuine opposition."

"Do our worst case scenarios take the *Malefactor* into account?"

"We still don't have a clear picture of what happened," Raynard said.

"Have you read the reports?"

"I have, and I don't like it." Raynard tapped his fingers over his belly. "The captain was killed, and the officers can't seem to agree on how they were attacked. Some said they streamed through an asteroid field."

"They were nowhere near the system asteroids."

"I know. Others say they collided with a comet." Raynard frowned. "They all agree, however, that they were following alongside the convoy, all systems normal, and no indication of Raeth activity. Whatever attacked them came out of nowhere."

"Ship's logs report nothing unusual," Achres said thoughtfully.

"Until they were destroyed." Raynard gazed at the stars rolling past the expansive portal. He fancied he could pick out Victus in the far distance. Nearly five hours away at one tenth the speed of light, their maximum speed.

Raynard paced the great cabin over the next hours, studying the reports of the Sciphere massing around Aera and trying not to watch the clock. The entire designated fleet had arrived. His was the only ship missing. Engineering teams worked tirelessly to bring her engines online. The *Eidolon* would be one of the fastest ships in the fleet, and with her advanced weapon systems and new armour, he'd hoped that she could play a crucial part in the coming battle. Minute by minute his hope was fading.

With only one hour remaining to make his rendezvous, Raynard tried to quell the lump in his stomach and made the journey to the engineering bay one last time. The bay stretched back into the distance, the high, rounded ceiling and steel girders yawning like the belly of a whale. He gazed dismally around at the strewn engine parts, repair teams scrambling over the dismantled reactor core like ants. Blue jets of arc light flickered through the barren reactor canals and crews in heavy lifter mechs dragged around the massive coils from the damaged Lantern chamber. He felt his last vestige of hope vanishing somewhere between the copper piles of lifeless gauss stabilizers and mangled silo turbines. At least the thadium fuel cells hadn't leaked.

Raynard signalled a nearby deck officer as he trudged back to his great cabin. "Prepare to relay a message with the Sciphere command vessel."

The officer nodded, handing Raynard a data pad. The gold emblem of the *INV Monarch* flashed on the screen and the status bar blinked into transmit mode. At their current distance, there was still a twenty four minute delay between the ships, so real time communication was impossible.

Raynard braced himself for the words he knew he must say. "The Imperial Naval Vessel *Eidolon* will not make the rendezvous above Aera," he began, picturing the stern, narrow-eyed visage of Vice Admiral Burns as he received the message. "We will join you with the convoy over Drusus when we've finished making repairs." He paused, clenching his jaw. "The fleet is yours, Admiral."

FIFTEEN

PROPHETS

Mal'Dreghen shifted uncomfortably on his ivory throne. The chair was carved from the bones of some prehistoric behemoth. The Mal had discovered it mouldering away, forgotten in the bowels of an ancient northern monastery. He'd been delighted with the find, sending it to the great Ziggurat in Chaldrea to be restored. When the bones of the chair had been polished, Mal'Dreghen had spent hours studying the dragons and other nameless beasts of mythology that crawled over its ivory surface. The throne was grotesque, conjuring dread in all those who stood before its menacing panoply.

Men were fearful creatures, Mal'Dreghen knew. They dressed in fine clothes and lived in shining cities to forget the terrors of the dark jungles their ancestors called home. But nothing could make them forget, not truly, and when the shadows grew long, and the creatures of the forest howled in the night, they remembered. They knew that thunder was not the sudden expansion of heated air, but the voice of angry gods. That was the power of religion—to rouse the deepest terrors of the heart.

But religion was a kind of truth in itself, and Mal'Dreghen knew how to wield it—to bring the timid masses under heel and set them on the path to understanding: his understanding. There was no knowledge or scientific proof that could banish the fear of eternity, and so Mal'Dreghen would offer a nepenthe—the promise of immortality. Man was superior to all creatures, and Mal'Dreghen alone would bring the world to realise its error in worshipping the old heathen gods.

From his solarium in the great Ziggurat, Mal'Dreghen could look out to the mist shrouded peaks of the Enowyrth Mountains, their haunted spires looming above the dark waters of Lake Nimaine. The sun had set over Chaldrea, the bustling streets below shadowed in purple as the city lights winked on.

Three other men sat with the Mal in smaller stone chairs around a large circle. They were hidden in the deepening shadows, yet the Mal knew each of them well, and each would play a pivotal role in the days to come. One chair was empty.

The Mal's eyes narrowed as the guards on either side of the door stiffened. The pallanium door that barred the entrance was thick, passages from the sacred Dol Regas carved in fine script upon its silver surface. Nothing would penetrate that door unless it was opened willingly. Yet the crimson armoured Draugor dropped their hands to their weapons as someone unseen approached. Mal'Dreghen nodded, and the two guards swung the massive doors inward.

A young man stepped through, wearing a white half cloak over a simple grey uniform that bore the rearing white apalas of the Imperial house on his collar. He was a handsome man, though his youthful features and round face told that he had not yet grown into that handsomeness. He had alert, eager blue eyes and an air of surety that Mal'Dreghen was not certain he'd earned. The newcomer looked around the room, blinking, his eyes adjusting to the gloom, trying to see who his companions were.

"These men are of no consequence to you right now, Prince Arem," Mal'Dreghen said with a touch of humour. Arem continued to study their shadowy profiles. It was obvious he didn't believe him, but Mal'Dreghen didn't care. He only needed to listen.

"This is foolish," Arem said. "Spies must have seen me on my way over."

"And?" Mal'Dreghen asked. "After tomorrow, what difference will it make?"

"It could make a difference tonight," Arem said.

Mal'Dreghen scoffed. "You worry overmuch, young prince."

Arem bridled at the familiar tone. "I may not be heir to the throne, but I am a Danarean prince of the thirty-third dynasty, and you will use more respect when addressing me, Mal," he said, studying the Mal coldly. Mal'Dreghen wore a coat of rich fur dyed scarlet that gathered around his lean neck so that he appeared larger and more intimidating. Heavy chains of gold lay on his spare chest, and his raven hair hung thick about his face.

The Mal's eyes blazed, but a look of understanding came over him. "You expect such courtesy here, my Prince. Where is it you think you've come tonight? Aldon Court? Perhaps to an audience of ministers and courtiers?" The Mal let the words hang in the air.

Arem glanced around the room again, clearly uncomfortable with his disadvantage. "I am a prince, and you will do well to remember that," he said, not sounding as sure of himself as he had a moment before.

Anger flared once again in the Mal's eyes, but in the twilight the prince didn't notice. "But of course, Your Highness," Mal'Dreghen said. "You must forgive my abrasive manner, I seldom treat with such high born as yourself."

Arem turned to him, unsure if he was being mocked. "Who are these men, Mal?" He asked peremptorily.

"These are my colleagues. They'll be instrumental in our plans," he said.

Arem shook his head. "I will not confer with you in the company of strangers. Tell me who you are," he said, addressing the man nearest him.

"Your Grace," a gravelly voice replied. The man stood and removed the cowl of his robe.

"High Archon Vilimar," Arem said. "I suppose I'm not surprised you're here."

Archon Radul Vilimar bowed. "I may take that to mean several things, Your Grace," he said through ruddy jowls.

"I meant no offence," Arem replied airily.

"And none was taken, Your Highness." Vilimar smiled and sat down, his portly frame sagging into the seat. The elderly Archon composed himself once more and regarded Arem for a moment before resuming, "I am quite used to other's assumptions, and just as used to dismissing them," he said, his dewlap quivering. "Indignation has never served me well. Although," he said, moistening his fat pink lips, "it can be useful to *appear* indignant, from time to time. Men can be quite tractable when they believe they've offended you," he said, laughing to himself.

"Indeed," Arem replied.

"You see?" Mal'Dreghen said. "You are not among strangers."

"Who are these other men?" Arem asked, ignoring him.

"They are my confidants, and you will come to know them very well, I promise you that, dear prince."

"My terms for helping you are my own, Mal," Arem said firmly, finally taking his eyes away from Vilimar to stare at the Mal. "When you came to me with your plan, it seemed like madness. And though now I believe it's in the best interest of the people, you will not abuse my trust. We must be open, and I can't do that if I don't know who I'm speaking with."

Mal'Dreghen gritted his teeth. Did the little whelp actually believe he was doing this for the good of the people? The coward, Mal'Dreghen thought—he wanted to be given what he couldn't take on his own.

"Very well," the Mal said mildly. "You have met the Arch Inquisitor before, I believe?" He pointed to the man sitting next to Vilimar. "Rasmus, please pay your respects to the prince."

Rasmus stood and bowed. "Your Grace," he said quietly.

Arem nodded. "And him?" he asked, jerking his chin towards the last man.

"Him?" Mal'Dreghen said softly. "Him. Yes, I'm afraid, young prince, that even you must accept my word on this man. You know as well as I do the measures I have taken and the pains I have been through to ensure the success of our *arrangement*."

Arem glared at the Mal. "You forget your place, *Mal,*" he said, sneering the last word. "I must accept *nothing,* I am a *prince.* This ends here unless I know the identity of every man in this room. Do you understand?"

The Mal scowled, his face contorted in anger. Before he could speak, however, the last man stood, raising his hand towards the Mal.

"Please, Mal," he said. His voice was soft but commanding. "If it will satisfy the young prince, then I will gladly obey," he said, turning to Arem who eyed him suspiciously. The man had long, pale yellow hair that hung loosely over his shoulders. He wore a black uniform that Arem had never seen before, a coat with tails that stopped just short of his knees and red epaulets with a crest on his right shoulder that Arem didn't recognise: a red falcon ascending over a rising sun. His stern jaw and broad face were coarse but proud, and a livid scar ran from his jaw up to his right temple, just to the side of his eye. He had the grim appearance of a veteran, and piercing blue eyes swept over Arem. They paused without much regard.

"And your name?" Arem asked expectantly.

"I am Draccas, my Liege," he said, bowing his head slightly. "Draccas Ascagar."

Arem frowned. "Your name is unfamiliar. Who are you?"

"I am unfamiliar to you?" Draccas smiled strangely, his mouth twisting in a way that made Arem uneasy. "I suppose I am not surprised. The lessons of our fathers are all too soon forgot. I am, shall we say, a military advisor to the Mal. That is all."

Arem seemed unconvinced, but before he could press his questions further the Mal interrupted him.

"You see, young prince? There is no need to be concerned, you are among allies. Allies and friends," Mal'Dreghen said, his voice sinewy and gracious. "Now, if we may begin? The hour grows late, and as you said, you will have been seen coming here."

Arem sat, unbuttoning his vest. "Very well, Mal, but be brief."

The Mal's eyes twinkled. "As you wish, my Liege." He folded his bony hands over his lap. "Everything is in order," he said, turning to address the other three men. "So far, our plans have been executed flawlessly. Years of subtle manoeuvring have culminated in this very moment." He smiled. "There is every reason to believe that, by this time tomorrow, we will have succeeded in overthrowing the old regime and turning our *prince* into our new *emperor,*" he said. All four men turned to look at Arem.

"What of the attack on the *Malefactor* this morning?" Arem asked.

Mal'Dreghen waved his hand. "It's of no importance. It was unexpected, but perhaps this will only serve our cause."

"My Lord?" Rasmus said, raising his eyebrows. The milky blue cataracts of his left eye glistened.

"They now suspect that our firepower poses a far greater threat than before, which means they will probably strengthen their defences around Drusus," Mal'Dreghen said.

"Which means that we can destroy more of their fleet in one move, and there will be fewer forces to confront here around Errolor," Draccas said, leaning forward.

"It's true," Arem said. "I've seen the reports, the Sciphere is gathering around Aera and will be leaving for Drusus in the next ten hours. No one can agree on how many ships should be left protecting Home Space. Of course Attendant Fleet will remain, but the archduke is arguing for increasing the forces here, while my father insists on protecting the fleet and Drusus at all costs."

"The fool," Rasmus scoffed.

"Watch your tongue, Inquisitor, or I'll have it out," Arem said, flashing the little man a look of contempt. "He's still my father, and infinitely your superior."

Rasmus scowled and glanced at Mal'Dreghen, who remained unmoved.

"You speak highly of a man you've condemned to death," Draccas observed.

Arem shrugged. "Occasionally it is necessary to reform the dynasty," he said. "But that doesn't mean I'll listen to a sniffling sycophant malign my father as he pleases. He is still the descendant of a thousand generations of royal blood and the chosen of the Old Ones. And so am I. You will show respect."

A stiff silence filled the room. Mal'Dreghen contemplated the young prince from his throne, his dark eyes inscrutable in the gloom.

"Yes, well, be that as it may," Draccas resumed, "it's to our advantage that the largest part of the Sciphere will be deployed around Drusus. I don't expect numbers to be a problem in either regard, however."

"Once the main fleet is crippled at Drusus, there will be nothing remaining to withstand an invasion of Chaldrea," Mal'Dreghen said.

"But we must be careful to prevent our takeover from appearing to be an invasion," Draccas replied. "The tragic loss of an emperor and a prince are one thing, but an invasion is another. The Raeth are no match for the Imperial Army."

"Which is where our dear prince will come in," Mal'Dreghen said, directing an approving gaze towards Arem.

"If my father and Aldric are killed, I am second in line to the throne. I will be emperor. Any mandate I make will be legitimate and must be obeyed," he said with confidence. "I will order the Imperial Army to cooperate with the Raeth; after the tragedy of my father and brother's deaths, it will seem to be in the interest of the empire."

"They will rally around their new emperor and his army, seeking protection from the terrorists who murdered the royal family," Mal'Dreghen said.

"By terrorists you mean the Asaani, I presume?" asked Vilimar languidly.

"The Asaani, and Elcaern separatists. When the people learn it was Asaani rebels who killed the royal family, they will be outraged, they will demand justice."

"You mean revenge," Draccas said, his face stony.

Mal'Dreghen barely lifted an eyebrow. "As long as the guilty parties are discovered and brought before the emperor, you may call it what you like."

"And what makes you so sure the Asaani will be blamed?" Arem asked.

"After tomorrow, there will be no doubt in anyone's minds it was Asaani dissidents, angry with your father's lack of action against the Dhemorgal," the Mal replied. "I have something in mind for the festival that will help convince the public and the Erolan that the Asaani are to blame," he said. "In any case, they will not suspect us, nor certainly Your Grace," he said, looking at Arem. "And then we will finally be free of the heathenism that has plagued this city these last thousand years."

"The Asaani, Gaiban Morrigan—they hardly seem the real threat here, Mal'Dreghen," Arem replied. "We may wipe out the Imperial Navy, but the Imperial Army will remain, and if they suspect that I'm involved..."

Mal'Dreghen raised his hand. "Fear not, Your Grace. The Old Guard will be on our side."

"How can you be so sure?" Arem asked.

"Because," Mal'Dreghen said, revelling in the words, "we will give them something that will put them in our pocket forever. Something they've wanted for a long time."

Arem waited, but the Mal did not continue. "And what exactly is that?" he said finally.

The Mal smiled. "What has been the source of so much enmity between the Erolan and the royal family these past forty years? Why does the Old Guard even exist?"

Arem hesitated. "You can't mean..."

"You want to give the dukes their armies back," Vilimar said, amused. "Oh, my dear Mal, that is rich."

Arem narrowed his eyes. "The Imperial Army is not yours to dispense with as you please, Mal," he said scornfully. "They are my troops, and they will remain here in the capital."

"Ah yes, so they shall!" the Mal said, almost gleefully.

"Then what army are you going to give them? You aren't suggesting conscription?"

"Oh something much better, my prince," the Mal said, turning a knowing look to Draccas.

Draccas met his gaze without emotion. "We'll give them the Raeth," he said.

There was a pause as Arem stopped to consider this. The Raeth were nomadic pirates, living in hidden colonies throughout the asteroid belt and in small caravans of ships that clustered together to form mobile communities. They were not trained soldiers, but they were fierce, and after they destroyed the Imperial Navy, they would be the only other military force in the Aethian system. Not even the Archduke Raynard would have a force large enough to contend with them.

"Their loyalty is questionable," Arem said, clearly unconvinced.

"Their loyalty will be to you, my Prince," Mal'Dreghen said. "You are their liberator, you have brought them back from exile. Without your strength and foresight, they would still be languishing in the frozen climes of the asteroid belt, scavenging dwindling supplies from freighter convoys as the Imperial Navy grew more and more powerful. Truly," he said leaning forward, "you are their saviour, and they will be eternally grateful."

"Spare me," Arem said. "I am not so green in these matters that the simple promise of gratitude would convince me of loyalty from *pirates*," he said.

"The Raeth would never act against you, Prince Arem," Draccas said. "No matter what colours they fight under, they are yours to command. That you liberated them and restored their freedom will mean much."

"As will the generous donations from the treasury," Rasmus said. "These hounds may or may not be loyal, but they will be paid for, and well. Which is all pirates like them really care about," he said, chuckling.

Draccas gave the little man a cold glare, but Rasmus didn't notice.

"So we train and provide an army to the Erolan dukes and in return they offer their undying allegiance," Vilimar said thoughtfully. "They would certainly thank you for such a kindness," he added, his deep voice rumbling.

"Would they?" Arem asked. "Or would we simply be giving them the means for their revenge?"

Vilimar stuck out his lip. "Well, if they choose revenge, at least we could be sure that the Raeth know which side their bread is buttered on."

"That isn't much of a consolation," Arem said, though he could see the advantage of gaining the gratitude of the Erolan and at the same time acquiring another army which would be secretly loyal to him.

"It's more than you think," Draccas said.

"And we will finally have the means to eliminate the Asaani once and for all," Mal'Dreghen said. "With an army loyal only to you, Your Grace, there will be nothing opposing your reign—not even the pagan druids."

"I care nothing for your crusade against the Asaani," Arem said, frowning. "So long as my reign is secure, the people can worship as they will."

A queer expression came over the Mal's face. "The Asaani are rebels, Prince Arem. They have barred our progress as an empire for fifteen thousand years. Their idolatry and heathenism is responsible for the decay in this very city, for your father's weakness as a ruler, for your brother's arrogance and the ignorance of the people. Your father takes counsel from that Gaiban witch—she speaks lies into his ear and pollutes his judgment, as every Gaiban before her has. The peasants in the streets go with hands held open and praises for the goddess on their lips. If we permit these pagans to continue unopposed, the empire will fall. I will not sit idly by and watch this decay consume us, not when the answer is within our grasp. All we require is the courage to seize it," the Mal said, his voice hard as iron.

"We shall see," Arem said. "The Valorí have been the protectors of the royal family for as long as it has existed, for as long as the palace of Dur Enskai has sat atop Callas Waith, and they have proven themselves time and again."

Rasmus scoffed. "The Valorí," he said, hissing. "The Draugor are more skilled by far, they would obliterate the Valorí, if given a chance."

"And so they shall have that chance," Vilimar chimed in. "I am quite anxious to see the two warriors pitted against each other in the Coliseum tomorrow."

"As am I," Arem said. The Festival of Dhemorgal would officially begin tomorrow, and with it the fight between Mal'Dreghen's champion and his brother Aldric. Aldric was among the best fighters of the empire, trained from childhood by the Valorí, and taking to it with unrivalled dedication. Yet whether Aldric won or lost, he would be dead tomorrow night.

"I imagine that you are," Mal'Dreghen said. "And as much as I would love to see your brother humiliated and beaten before the watching eyes of the Coliseum, it is ultimately irrelevant. It's simply a distraction that serves as a launching point for our inevitable triumph."

"The arrogant princeling may be doomed in either case," Vilimar said, his thickly hooded eyes drooping. "Yet how delicious it would be if he were vanquished, dishonoured before his father, before the Gaiban. How much glory there would be for the disciples of Desedar, praise be to his name."

"There is still much to be done," Arem said.

"You almost seem reluctant, Your Grace," Mal'Dreghen said. "I should think you'd be happy to finally be rid of your do-gooding brother."

A clouded look came over Arem's face and he frowned, as if deep in thought. "Don't speak of things you don't understand," he said, raising his blue eyes to meet the Mal's. "Your mockery is an insult to everything I hold dear. You will not speak this way again."

Mal'Dreghen felt the rage burn inside him, the ache that had so long driven him and guided his every action. This whelp of a prince dared to speak to him in such haughty tones? Well, he would soon pay the price for his arrogance. The Mal sniffed.

"Very well, Your Grace," he said humbly. "I beg your pardons, and I hope this misunderstanding may not impede our progress?"

"Enough," Arem replied.

Mal'Dreghen couldn't help but catch the look of disgust that flickered over his young face. *There's fire in this one yet,* he thought to himself. "As you please, my Liege," he said. "Now, after the Sciphere has been crippled—"

"Is it really necessary to destroy the fleet?" Arem interrupted. "With the nobles and the Erolan on our side, we have the power to persuade the Old Guard to join us. Might we not do the same with the Navy?"

Mal'Dreghen shook his head. "The Navy is obedient only to the emperor. Leopold has seen to that. The new training academy he's built at Craic Achran is loyal to the royal family, the Old Guard has no influence, and they will be suspicious. We cannot risk their involvement."

"The Admiralty may be misguided, but they aren't stupid," Draccas added. "Craic Achran produces efficient officers; they may resist allowing their vessels to be commanded by the rebels they were so recently at war with."

"But I am their emperor," Arem protested. "They will listen to me if I command them."

Draccas shook his head. "And how will their emperor explain the dozens of Raeth ships suddenly in orbit, deploying troops in all the Imperial Cities?" He didn't wait for Arem to reply. "They will suspect what has happened and attack the Raeth. An enemy one day isn't suddenly an ally the next. The Admiralty may be gullible, but the archduke will not be. Raynard is a close friend of Emperor Leopold and your brother. He will be suspicious from the beginning, and certainly won't tolerate Raeth ships in Home Space."

Mal'Dreghen nodded. "I've also left a trail of evidence pointing towards Elcaern dissenters. They're unpopular enough that their support in the Erolan is worn thin. It won't be difficult to blame them for the attack on the *Malefactor,* and once prince Arem is emperor, we may deal with them as we see fit."

"The Elcaern?" Arem asked. "They're isolationists, why would they be involved?"

"They've long resented their treatment at the hands of the empire," Mal'Dreghen replied. "There have been several protests over the past few years, a few of the Elcaern thegns demanding secession from the empire."

"The Ardraigh Feradach is a lapdog of the emperor, he would never give in to those demands," Arem said.

"No, but he doesn't have the voice of the Elcaern thegns, or the Witan. They know he's been bought," Draccas replied, looking at Arem. "There're a lot of malcontents among the Elcaern clans, it wouldn't be difficult to make the suggestion they were involved with your father's death."

"Pagans and rebels," Archon Vilimar said. "The Witan is a council of peasants and outcasts, all they want is the return of their ancestral lands west of Berrond Duul. The Witan has argued for secession for many years, they seem likely suspects."

"They could raise the fyrd," Arem said. "If we press them too hard, that could mean rebellion. They've never been ones to submit lightly."

"That petty band of militia?" Vilimar scoffed. "No, I think not. Even if they tried, they'd be sorely outmatched."

Arem agreed that it didn't seem likely. "And what of the Asaani?"

Mal'Dreghen laughed. "The Asaani? My dear prince, the Asaani will no longer trouble anyone. I won't leave them any room to speak out against... *your reign,*" he said, drawing out the last words. "Perhaps you linger under the impression that if you govern justly, you will have no enemies?" He paused. "My Prince, we are taking control of an empire! This is no light affair. There will be those who doubt you, those who question your leadership, those who would speak against you and claim that you're unfit to lead. What would you say to them, I ask you?"

"They would not be allowed to protest," Arem said, uncertainly. "I would make public protests treason, and those who denounced me would be punished."

Mal'Dreghen nodded, inclining his head to the side in thought. "You have promise, young prince," he said. "But your inexperience makes you timid! You are unsure of your power, but you mustn't be! When the unbelievers demand proof, what will you tell them?"

Arem didn't reply.

"You will destroy them!" Mal'Dreghen shouted suddenly, startling Arem. "When your subjects lack faith, you must make them afraid."

"Fear affirms faith," Archon Vilimar agreed.

"And the people are faithless!" Mal'Dreghen half shouted. "They must learn to fear you! Your father believes that good food and entertainment will keep the people under his heel. If we are to be successful, we must show them that their lives are meant for more than idolatry and feckless whimsies.

They must command their existence. And we must show them how," Mal'Dreghen said, leaning back in his ivory throne.

"*I* will show them how, Mal," Arem said. He stared at the Mal, his face betraying no emotion.

Mal'Dreghen blinked, then nodded. "Of course, my Liege. *You* will guide the people. I am merely your faithful servant."

"You will do well to remember that, Mal," Arem said. "This is my empire, and I will shape it as I see fit."

"Even an emperor must take counsel on occasion," Vilimar said softly. Arem knew it for the reprove it was.

"Which is why I am here tonight, Archon," Arem said. "You are confident that the Elcaern will be blamed?" he added, turning once more to Mal'Dreghen.

"I am certain. Their recent restlessness is suspicious enough, but I have seen to it that several perpetrators will be brought forward in the coming days. The Ardraigh has assured me his full cooperation in hunting down any rebels."

"That pig is faithful as a degoll," Rasmus muttered.

"But he loves his coin," Mal'Dreghen said, smiling.

Vilimar laughed. "All the best do, don't they?"

"This appears to be a simple matter then," Arem said. "With my father and brother gone, there will be nothing to stop us."

"Simple, you say?" Draccas said, speaking loudly for the first time. "There is nothing simple about this, *prince,*" he said. "Words have been put in the proper ears; coin beyond your royal reckoning is lining more pockets than you have ever thought of. One slip, and it means doom for all of us— even you, *prince.*"

"I don't like your tone, *advisor,*" Arem said.

"And I don't like your recklessness!" Draccas said, no hint of fear or respect in his voice. "You think this will be easy, but it will be bloody. Tens of thousands will die—for *your* ambitions."

"And yours," Arem said coolly.

"I don't think of myself as a scion of the gods," Draccas replied. "People will die, their blood will run through Chaldrea—are you prepared for that, Your Grace? Are you prepared for the repercussions, the anger and outrage and grief of the Vassaryan Empire? Have you even thought of that?"

"What difference does it make?" Arem said.

Draccas laughed without humour. "Princes, they are all the same," he said. "Have you ever seen a lord dragged into the streets and torn apart by his sworn vassals?" He paused. "No?"

"I have an army, and the Valorí," Arem began.

"An army, he says." Draccas leant forward in his chair, his face coming into the light. Blue eyes pierced through the gloom. "And before the lords were torn apart, *who* do you think opened the doors to let their sworn vassals in?" He let the question linger for a moment, studying the disquiet on Arem's face. "You are not safe behind your walls, Prince Arem," Draccas said. "In the end, your fortress will only stop you from escaping."

"Then what can we do?" Arem asked, trying very hard not to show his concern.

"There must be a scapegoat," Vilimar said. "With so much carnage, the people must not believe you are to blame."

"And so we have the Elcaern," Arem said.

"And the Asaani," Mal'Dreghen added. "The Elcaern are querulous heathens. No one will miss them. The Asaani are the real culprits."

"I don't want a massacre, Mal," Draccas said, staring at Mal'Dreghen, a dangerous glint in his eyes.

The Mal waved his hand dismissively. "You needn't trouble yourself with such matters, my dear Draccas."

"These are my soldiers. They will not be butchers for your religious pogrom."

"Your soldiers?" Arem demanded.

Draccas frowned. "Apologies. *Your* soldiers, my Liege."

"The people must know that those responsible for their suffering have been punished," Vilimar said patiently. "Their anger must be satisfied, or they will lose faith in your leadership. You must show a firm hand from the beginning."

"We bring a new message, a message of obedience, of deliverance, of sanctity," Mal'Dreghen said. "Prophets who come in peace are murdered by the mob before they can speak. Revolutionaries have no friends. But," he said, waving a hand in the air as if gathering his words around an invisible spool. "But! Those prophets who come with swords, they are the prophets who conquer and dismay."

"Then we will conquer," Arem said. "Let us be the prophets of a new era."

When the prince had finally left the solarium and the others had departed, the Mal leant back in his throne, sighing deeply. The sun had set some time ago and moonlight was gathering over the high tower. He felt eager for the morrow. His mind was clear, sharp, his senses tingling. He walked out to the balcony overlooking the city below. The White Tower was nearly the highest building in Chaldrea, second only to the great stone Citadel a few blocks to the north.

The wind from the lake blew gently up over the stonework, a fresh, clean smell. The smell of change. This was a time of new beginnings, he thought to himself. The vile Asaani will be done with, and once the fool Leopold and his arrogant son Aldric were finished, he could install the eager little Arem on his throne. How blind Arem was! To think this was all his doing, that he had any say at all. He was egotistical, just like his father and brother. But he would serve his purpose. *And for that, I shall endure him, if only for a short while,* Mal'Dreghen thought to himself, a smile spreading over his thin purple lips.

The Mal breathed in deeply. "You haunt me like a shade, seneschal," he said, apparently to no one.

"And as a shade I must remain," a gravelly voice replied. A figure emerged from the shadows behind a marble colonnade beside the Mal.

Mal'Dreghen glanced at him, appraising the seneschal for a moment before returning to the scene below. "The city stands on the verge of a great precipice," Mal'Dreghen said. "Tonight, it takes the breath before the plunge."

"Are you ready for all that you bring down upon us?" Chiron asked, staring fixedly at the Mal, silhouetted against the moonlight.

"I'm not alone in this, seneschal—don't forget that. You've been invaluable to me all these long years. Whatever doom is wrought upon this city, your name must be recorded beside mine."

Chiron watched him for a moment, pondering his words. He joined the Mal at the balustrade looking down into the golden lights of the city below. "Prince Arem is not as blind as you believe him to be," Chiron said, almost sadly it seemed to the Mal.

"Is he not?" Mal'Dreghen replied, wondering. "He cares not for leadership, only for luxury and ease. If I make these things available to him, he won't trouble me."

"His brother is different," Chiron said.

"And what difference does that make?" Mal'Dreghen asked, turning to the seneschal. "In a day's time his brother will be dead, and the empire will see a new order to things. *My order.* Nothing else will matter." He gripped the balustrade, fingers tightening over the cold marble ledge.

"Men are simple creatures," Chiron observed. "So long as they are occupied with their daily wants and needs, it is not a difficult thing to deceive them. They will even follow you willingly, if only you will *promise* them everything they want. Yet you need only give them a little," he said, almost to himself.

Mal'Dreghen smiled. "You might have made an excellent inquisitor, Chiron."

"Me?" Chiron said, feigning surprise. "Oh no, not me Your Eminence. I'm far too dishonest."

Mal'Dreghen grunted, looking the wizened old seneschal over. There was something about the man that he distrusted, but he didn't suppose that mattered. Of course he shouldn't trust him. Any man who orchestrates the collapse of an empire bears watching, he thought dryly.

"Besides, Your Eminence, I find that religion, while useful for the ruler, is often harmful to the soul."

Mal'Dreghen laughed. "What soul? You're a fiend! Your soul is black as the damned Abyss."

The seneschal inclined his head thoughtfully. "Quite so, quite so," he said humbly. "But, I think it likely unwise to change sides this late in the game."

Mal'Dreghen watched as the seneschal turned and blended into the shadows. Far below in the streets, celebrants bearing torches had gathered in the great square before the Ziggurat and were lighting fireworks. Above the popping and cracking Mal'Dreghen could hear the chanting of passages from the Dol Regas, thousands of voices in harmony as they recited the lines. *"And in fire he shall return, and his light shall purge the darkness of decay."* Fireworks exploded, showering sparks over the plaza, shadows dancing like demons in the night.

SIXTEEN

THE WEIGHT OF AN EMPIRE

L eopold traced the misty shoreline of Lake Nimaine as it ran north to the Enowyrth Mountains. Steam from the dark lake hovered above the water, the jungle trees rising from a swirling cloud. Dawn dashed over the plains of Thedarras, greeted by a breeze from the snowy mountains that cooled the humid morning. Glassy wakes trailed behind small fishing boats, and trawlers and cargo ships bound for the docks sagged lustily in the cerulean waters. It would be a long day, Leopold thought to himself. He could feel it, the very air was latent with anticipation. It would be worse for Aldric, though.

From his balcony Leopold surveyed Chaldrea in the distance. The high curtain walls of the seven terraces shielded the city from the morning light, so that only the great Ziggurat and Citadel stood white in the growing day. Gaeliath, the stone bridge connecting the three islands, was festooned with colourful banners and pennants and even at this hour it was crowded with people. In just an hour's time, Leopold and his sons must be at the Coliseum to announce the start of the games. There he must stand alongside Mal'Dreghen in a show of fellowship, blessing a ceremony that celebrated acrimony and rivalries which ought to have been buried millennia ago.

But Leopold could not choose sides. All he could do was appear impartial, placate the ever growing demands of the Old Guard, the Erolan, the Dhemorahns and Mal'Dreghen. Only the Asaani were passive while the world exploded around them. Perhaps that was their secret, to remain uninvolved. Gaiban Morrigan merely smiled at him when Leopold had asked her for advice.

"This will pass," the Gaiban said as they'd stood in one of the temple arbours.

Leopold wasn't satisfied with her reply. "That's what you always say, Gaiban, but I need a better answer. I'm the emperor—I can't tell my people that their troubles will just go away."

"You can, but you wish not to. You are not responsible for their happiness."

"I am their caretaker. Gaiban, I need your advice." He was a stern man, unyielding in many things, as his father Theobald had been. It was an emperor's right to command, he believed, to be unwavering and steadfast in his decisions.

But not the Gaiban. She cared nothing of herself, and often seemed not even to care for the Asaani or the people of Errolor. Happiness was her domain; she tended to the moment alone and gave little heed for anything else. He had never known anyone to be as compassionate and also indifferent in his life.

Gaiban Morrigan smiled, her slender frame willowy beneath a thin blue sari as she knelt in the grass beside Leopold. Silver threads woven through her hair shimmered in the mottled sunlight beneath the leafy branches. Leopold watched as she ran her hands through the grass, her fingertips playing over the blades like she was speaking to them. She looked up at him finally. "You are not the first emperor I have seen who found his crown a little too heavy," she said, her voice hardly a murmur. "Nor will you be the last. You look to control your kingdom, command it; create order and structure and simplicity."

"And you would tell me that's wrong, that I should let order flow as water over the rocks, or some such nonsense," Leopold said. "Gaiban I need your support. The Mal wants to dethrone me and establish a theocracy with himself as the leader. What would be your order then?"

The Gaiban's smile faded. "I would not give you this counsel," she said. "The structure of one's own life is far different from those one must rule. You must live in the dark, and the light, for you are the sovereign. Yours is the balance of life, for you must do what others cannot. The people need your guidance, but you cannot give them happiness. That is up to them, not you. You must only give them that chance, they must decide for themselves."

"And what of Mal'Dreghen?" Leopold asked, kneeling beside her. His Valorí waited at a distance, their relaxed postures revealing much about their comfort and Leopold's safety.

Gaiban Morrigan looked at Leopold quizzically, tilting her head. "Do you know why the Gaiban of the Asaani is always a woman?" she asked. "Why men are the protectors of the royal line, but women are their guides?"

He shook his head. "I know that's always been the tradition, I've never thought to wonder at the reason," he said.

She nodded. "I suppose you think I'm going to tell you then?"

"Why else would you have asked?" He clenched his fist against his bent knee. This is not why he'd come to speak with her.

"To make you wonder," she replied. "You may be emperor, but you haven't been the only one, and there are some secrets not even an emperor may know."

"I didn't come to you for riddles," Leopold said. "I need to know what I should do about Mal'Dreghen. My counsellors tell me not to worry about his festival. But if I allow it to continue, it will incite anger towards the Asaani here in Chaldrea, and in the other Imperial Cities."

The Gaiban shrugged. "It is nothing," she said. "The people are fickle. They have short memories, they will not remember what they were angry about when it is over. But if you try to stop Mal'Dreghen, they will remember, of that you can be sure. The Asaani will endure."

Leopold rose to his feet. He pointed towards the Valorí waiting nearby, their armour gleaming like polished mirrors. "It is an insult to everything you stand for. It is an insult to them, those who follow you and pledge their lives to the teachings of the Ainír, to this building," he said, sweeping his arm across the green expanse of lawns and orchards of the temple. "Would you really do nothing?"

She shrugged. "It is an insult only if you are offended, Your Highness," she said. "The Valorí do not follow me, they are your men. Not mine. I have no men. I have no one. All who are here, are here because they wish to be. It is not me they follow, but the words of those who came long before me."

"You would have me lead by not leading," Leopold said, almost angry.

"*I* would have you do nothing. You must do what is in *your* heart," she said. "However, if you must ask me, I would tell you to lead by leading."

"And what does that mean, exactly?"

The Gaiban reached up and took Leopold's hand in hers, her tiny fingers squeezing his reassuringly. "Do what you must, my Liege. You are the emperor—the people will follow you."

And so he had, Leopold thought. The Gaiban had been right, there was no stopping something of this magnitude. He had learned the limits of his power. The Dhemorgal would go on, or he would be vilified by his people. Chiron had also told him as much. "The people have their emperor, and then they have their gods. You would do well to avoid making them choose," Chiron had said.

Well, let them have their gods, Leopold thought. A bile taste crept up his throat and he wrinkled his nose and swallowed reflexively. But the Dhemorahns had no gods. Their god was the Dol Regas, their sacred book. Their god was their own sense of superiority, their own self-service and self-worship. Entitlement was a dangerous philosophy. And then there was their prophet, Mal'Dreghen. His word was inviolate, and not even Leopold felt comfortable confronting the Mal when he could throw such words as "heretic" and "blasphemer" at him. Empty, meaningless words that carried so much weight with the wilful, ignorant people.

If he had the weight of the Erolan behind him, Leopold might have crushed the Mal and endured the unrest of the people, secure in the knowledge that the noble houses would stand with him. But he didn't. Rather, the Erolan were mistrustful of the royal house, suspicious of his every move. They were fearful that he might turn his army against them, the only standing army in the empire, levying new evils upon them as his mother Alexandra had done.

So the Erolan were polite, supporting him as they must and offering their services,as any good house should when called upon by their emperor. But they schemed against him, Leopold knew. His spies were everywhere, and he was sure theirs were as well, and the news they brought him of late was unsettling indeed. At least three of the five dukes were still his men, but the lesser houses were power hungry and eager to strike at any weakness.

Every noble house attended the rich galas that Leopold held throughout the year at Aldon Court. Even if he was not well liked, everyone wanted to be near the seat of power. Lords and ladies from all the provinces would turn out in droves, just hoping for a chance to be seen with the emperor. The royal court was the place to advance in society, to meet the rich and the powerful, to scheme.

It also gave Leopold the chance to know his enemies. When the Erolan were gathered here at court, then their devious little plots weren't spread across the entire empire. Leopold much preferred to play host and gather all the schemers into one place where he might keep an eye on them. The closer he was to his enemies, the safer he felt. *When all the knives are in the drawer, you know one isn't at your back.*

SEVENTEEN

THE GOLDEN EMPEROR

L eopold stood still while his lictors dressed him, taking his heavy fur robes and replacing them with a thin, woven achkan of white that fit snugly and was trimmed just below his knees. Fine gold tracery embroidered the fabric, and the rearing apalas of House Danarean were stitched across his shoulders. Beneath the coat he wore a loose sarong of the finest white silk—a traditional garment of Thedarras befitting its tropical climate. A purple sash was tied about his waist, and as he stood, Lord Robert Young of the Imperial Housecarl entered discretely.

Lord Robert bowed low, his galvonite scale armour clinking softly. "Your Grace," he said in a low voice. "If you'll pardon my intrusion, your sons are here."

Leopold nodded, and Lord Robert bowed again and opened the door. Prince Arem stepped in first, Aldric close behind. Arem nodded to his father curtly, flinging himself onto a nearby divan and sinking into tasselled silk pillows. Aldric entered and bowed, walking to the open balcony.

"It's a cool day," Aldric remarked, gazing off towards the Gaeliath Bridge. He felt something against his leg and looked down. Cipher was standing on his foot, gazing up at him, his nearly purple stripes glowing in the sunlight. Aldric wasn't sure where he'd come from, he was certain he'd seen him wandering off into the palace grounds an hour ago. He reached down to pet the big cat, but Cipher leapt up, scrambling up to sit on Aldric, balancing with his forepaws draped over his shoulder and planting his hind paws in Aldric's back.

"You may leave us," Leopold said to Lord Robert, who retreated, saluting. Leopold was about to speak when he glanced at Aldric and then up at Cipher. He paused, shaking his head. "I'll never understand," he said.

Aldric laughed. "What? Just because no one loves you," he said, scratching Cipher behind his tufted ears. "Good boy," he said. He could feel Cipher's chest rumble quietly as he purred.

Leopold turned back towards the lictors, flicking a hand towards the door. They filed out in silence, moving more like graceful dancers than servants.

Aldric walked over and sat down next to Arem, Cipher rolling off his shoulder and bounding out of sight. Arem was dressed in a similar coat as his father, with ancient medallions and badges of House Danarean upon his chest, and a gilded sabre worn through a scarlet sash about his waist. He tugged at the sash and it slid off, the sabre rattling to the floor.

"I hope this isn't a long affair," Arem said. "I don't care if the day is cool, I don't fancy traipsing about the streets of Chaldrea in an open carriage in the sun."

"I'm sorry if being cheered while you sit on your ass is tiresome, brother," Aldric said. "You want to trade places?"

"I wouldn't dream of stealing your glory," Arem replied airily. "Besides, we all know you're the one the crowd cheers for. Do I even need to be there today? I'm sure no one would miss me."

"Enough of this petty bickering," Leopold said. "I may as well have daughters." He smoothed the front of his coat, feeling the raised threads of the gold patterns.

Arem looked down, sniffing. "Well you're the emperor, you have to give speeches and look regal. And you," he said, tilting his head towards Aldric. "You have to be the valiant knight in your shining armour and stand proudly above your vanquished enemy. Someone has to bring honour to our noble house. But what's left for me? A gilded palanquin and this bloody sword?" Arem said, kicking the sword with his toe. "Everyone knows I've never used it, and probably never will."

"We all know which sword you're fond of using," Aldric said.

"Not all of us enjoy stabbing men so much," Arem replied.

"Arem I would forbid you to come," Leopold growled, "but I know you would take pleasure in that. No, you will join us, and you will play the part of a prince. Tell me what is so hard in your life? What? What inspires this petulance? No one harasses you or demands anything of you, only the most superficial pretences!"

Arem curled his lips into a queer smile. "We aren't all so comfortable with pretences, father—some of us would prefer some substance in our lives."

"And what would you know about that?" Aldric said, his temper flaring. "You live here in the wealthiest city in the empire without a care in the world—you have nothing but your pretences! You have no hardship in your life so you fabricate drama. You play your selfish little games and pretend that no one matters but you, what you want, right now. We tolerate you because we have to. If you were a duke's son he'd disinherit you for being caught in a brothel or selling heirlooms in the market. Gods what are you thinking? You have everything in the world and you treat it like it was nothing."

"You tolerate me?" Arem asked, a deep mote of anger welling in his throat. He swallowed hard.

"We tolerate your behaviour," Aldric said, correcting himself. "No, no, you were right," Arem said softly. "You tolerate me, because you must." He sat up, resting his palms on his knees, appraising them both. "I've never fit into this family, not ever, and neither of you have ever let me forget that."

"Spare us your woe and misery," Leopold said. "I have little enough sympathy for you today, when all you have to do is let the people admire you, surrounded by the comforts of your retinue. What indignity is so great you couldn't bear to suffer!"

Arem's eyes flicked upwards to meet Leopold's briefly before glancing back down. He clasped his hands together as if thinking for a moment, then, "What am I to you, father?" Arem asked, his face an inscrutable mask. "After Aldric, what am I? An afterthought?" He paused for a moment, waiting. "I am nothing, I inherit nothing—I am the postscript in the ledger of our house, an addendum to an appendix that no one will ever read. What will I be remembered for?"

"Your accomplishments speak more than your birth order, Arem," Aldric said. "Your life isn't predetermined because you're my brother; you have every opportunity to make your own name, even if you aren't the emperor."

"Your great-uncle Heidrich III signed Heidrich's Peace with the Elcaern and secured a truce with the north. He took the Elcaern ardraigh and turned it into a proper kingship among the Erolan—no small feat," Leopold said, his fierce blue eyes narrowing. "He paved the way for the colonisation of Allria, and was among the first with the builders to land on the planet and lay the groundwork for the fortress Cnoc Baegan where the archduke resides. You think that is nothing? You think he will be forgotten for that, just because he wasn't the emperor?"

"And how many worlds are there left to colonise?" Arem asked, his full lips curling down. "How many warrior chieftains are left to subdue, querulous dukes to suppress and steal their armies? There is nothing left for me."

"Dammit Arem you're my brother, that isn't nothing!" Aldric shouted.

"Perhaps," Arem said, turning to Leopold. "But you've never wanted me for your son."

"You're right. And you've never acted like my son, either," Leopold said. He turned from Arem and strode to the window, gazing out at the city beyond.

Arem slumped back in his chair. His eyes welled, but he blinked and looked away.

Aldric didn't know what to say. He looked from his brother to his father and was filled with hatred; for his father, for his house, for the Erolan and the nobility—the damning, insufferable nobility. He looked at Arem on the sofa, he seemed so small, so much like a child. Outrage burned in Aldric, and he wanted to strike his father, to shake him, to rouse some sympathy in him for the destruction he was causing, had caused in so many lives. He wanted desperately to wake something in his father, some emotion, some feeling of life, but there was nothing. His father was immovable, intractable, like a statue, hardened by he knew not what. There was a vast distance in his father's cold blue eyes, something remote that existed far away from anything Aldric or Arem could reach. Aldric knew there must be pain there, and fear, and that love, like compassion, was a dangerous emotion to his father, something akin to weakness. Showing love or compassion opened Leopold up, exposed him, left him vulnerable to an attack, so he shut it out, slammed the door, and locked the emotions away deep where they couldn't be touched.

Aldric had tried to reach him before, in the heat of the moment he had put his hand on his father's arm and begged him to see Aldric for what he was, to simply be truthful and forget the pretences and let down his guards, to trust Aldric. That touch on his father's arm had been electric, Aldric's entreaty stirring a fury in Leopold that had frightened Aldric in its intensity and suddenness. Leopold had turned on him in a rage, snarling, calling Aldric a fool for his plea with such ferocity Aldric though the emperor might strike him. But he didn't. Instead Aldric turned and left him, unable to bear his presence, or the depth of his anger and mistrust. The unspoken words were too much to carry, and his father's rejection had pierced him deeply. He had never looked at Leopold the same since then, always fearing any attempt to meet him on equal ground would be met in the same way.

He knew Leopold was afraid, knew that the old Emperor Theobald had beaten him mercilessly as a child, and that his mother, a strong woman who never tolerated weakness, had scorned Leopold's every failing. It had broken Leopold, bent his mind, and now he turned that warped understanding of the world on his sons.

Aldric was taken back to when he and Arem were only boys, he no more than nine and Arem probably seven or eight. They had been on an afternoon trip to the hunting manor near Bailynn and Aldric had goaded Arem into stealing one of his father's apalas and riding with him out into the fields.

"It isn't a big deal," Aldric had said, adjusting the saddle. He'd chosen the largest apala in the stable, a huge white stallion with thick shoulders and a long snowy mane. Arem squeezed his brother's waist, afraid of the big animal. Arem wasn't as capable as Aldric at riding so they rode together. The last time Arem had ridden he'd fallen off, and he'd been too afraid to try again since.

"It *is* a big deal," Arem said. "Father will be angry, and I'll get in trouble."

"No you won't!" Aldric said, feeling brazen as he cinched the reins and spurred the apala out of the yard and into a canter towards the fields. "You're with me, it'll be fine."

They'd ridden for no more than twenty minutes when they came to a stop along the crest of a ridge overlooking a small valley. The edge of the jungle rolled out beneath them, the misty treeline stretching into the distance as far as they could see, butting up against the mountains far and away to the north. Vast and empty grasslands wandered off to the south, and storm clouds lingered on the horizon. A herd of wild apalas grazed below them at the foot of the hill near the forest's edge, their mottled brown and black and white stripes making them difficult to tell apart from one another. Wild flowers bobbed in the swaying grass, sweetening the fresh country air.

"C'mon, just a little further then we'll go back," Aldric said, tapping the apala's flanks.

"I want to go back now, I can't see the manor anymore," Arem said, twisting in the saddle.

"We're fine, relax. Just a little bit more, I promise." Aldric liked feeling powerful and in control, it made him feel strong to know his little brother was scared and he was not. He liked the idea of being in charge and protecting him.

Aldric was about to nudge the apala off down the hill when a rustling noise from the tall grass nearby caught his attention. Arem heard it too and spun around, searching the grass for the source of the sound. There it was again, a little further behind them. Aldric's heart jumped into his throat. He reached down and undid the fastenings of his dirk, unsheathing the little blade and hopping down to the ground.

"What are you doing?" Arem asked, his voice high and faltering.

"Shhh, it's ok," Aldric said, patting the apala reassuringly. It whickered nervously, smelling something on the wind it didn't like.

"Aldy maybe it's a degoll, get back on and let's go!"

Aldric looked up at his brother, seeing the tears starting there in his pale blue eyes. Those tears gave him resolve, and he shook his head. "No, I have to see what it is."

"Aldy you're gonna die! Don't go, please!" Arem sobbed.

"Be quiet or you'll scare the apala," Aldric said. "I have to see what it is."

Moving as quietly as he could, Aldric stepped lightly on the balls of his feet, just as Master Bahir had taught him. His leather riding boots creaked, but he could barely hear them over the drumming of his heart in his ears. He held the point of his dirk outward and stooped low, the thick blades of grass reaching high over his head. He heard the rustling sound again, closer this time, and to the right.

He edged through the grass, all the while looking for the tell-tale signs that a degoll was near. He didn't see any, but that didn't mean it wasn't there. Behind him he could hear Arem sniffling, and a thud as the apala stamped the ground with his hooves. He hoped it wouldn't bolt, Arem wouldn't know what to do and would probably get thrown off.

The rustling noise stopped just ahead and Aldric paused, waiting for some sign. A light breeze hummed through the grass, and the smell of earth and sunshine and meadow flowers surrounded him. His senses were on a knife's edge, and he strained his ears for any unusual sound. But there was only stillness and the buzzing meadow insects. He waited for another minute before standing, looking around in frustration. As he turned to go back, he heard Arem scream.

He ran back the way he'd come, heart pounding. He heard the apala shriek and then its hooves pounding as it ran off. He didn't know if he hoped it'd taken Arem with it or not. When he reached the crest of the hill where he'd left Arem he found him lying on the ground coughing, the wind knocked out of him.

"What happened?" Aldric shouted, rushing up to Arem. "Are you ok?"

Arem coughed and clutched at the laces of his leather coat, his chest heaving. "Degoll," he cried, tears streaming down his red cheeks.

"A degoll? Where?" Aldric asked, looking around wildly. "Where did it go?" he shouted. Their lives might depend on Arem's answer.

"It went that way, I think," Arem said, lifting his arm to point to the right. Before he could finish the gesture Arem's eyes widened in terror and he screamed.

A horrible weight slammed into Aldric's back and he rolled over onto his side, claws digging into his thin leather armour. He remembered his training and tried to brace himself while kicking upwards to push off the ground. The degoll howled at him and swung onto his shoulder, its teeth sinking into his left arm—what moments ago would have been his neck. Aldric screamed and tried to stab it with his dirk but the ferocity of the attack threw him backwards onto the ground and he lost the knife.

A frenzy of tawny red and white fur whirled above him and he felt the creature's powerful hind claws tearing into his chest and shredding scales from his leather cuirass. He swung a gauntleted fist at the creature's head but it didn't even seem to feel it, savaging his shoulder and whipping its head back and forth. He could feel the teeth sinking into his bone. His mind reeled. He hit the degoll again, as hard as he could in the head, over and over again until the motion lost meaning and his mind faded, his vision blurring.

He didn't feel his shoulder anymore, and he watched his hand struggling to get a grasp on the degoll's thick neck and pull it off of him as if he were watching someone else, as if it weren't him who was doing it. He rolled onto his side towards the degoll, trying to make it release him but it only dug its claws deeper into his arm. He heaved himself on top of it in a final effort, and as his weight came down onto the creature it released his shoulder and snapped its bloody jaws at his face. It missed him by centimetres, but in that moment he dropped his dead arm onto the degoll's throat and pinned it with his elbow.

It gurgled and howled, glaring at Aldric with small black eyes that were filled with rage. But Aldric held it there, its head twisting and its jaws gnashing at his face. It buried its claws into his armour, worrying the joints free as it writhed. Aldric couldn't think, he couldn't even feel the hind claws kicking and scratching at his stomach. He thought he could feel the degoll getting weaker, its struggling less frenzied. If he could hold it here he might succeed. Its fierce gaze had begun to soften, its eyes rolling back into its head and its tongue began to loll over its fangs when the last fastening of his shoulder plate was torn loose and his arm slipped. Aldric's elbow rolled off the degoll's neck and into the soft dirt, and in that momentary lapse he watched, horrified, as the degoll shook its head and swallowed, twisting clear of his reach. It lunged at his face.

Aldric winced and closed his eyes, swinging his good arm up to shield his face. He heard the degoll scream and felt it land on his chest. He waited, tensed, but the degoll wriggled on top of him and rolled off, screeching. He opened his eyes to see the degoll lying beside him in the dirt, tossing and turning and rolling over on top of itself, an ivory handled dirk buried in its back. Aldric kicked away from the spot, scrambling backwards. Arem stood to the side, staring down at the degoll with a look of disbelief.

The degoll strained its neck backwards trying to bite the knife, but the effort was too much and it collapsed in the bloody dirt. As the creature finally lay still Arem dropped to his knees, shaking. Aldric just stared, too stunned to move. The degoll lay in a glistening pool, its dingy fur matted and stained with clumps of red soil and blood.

Arem began to cry, his body shuddering in silent spasms as he stared down at the lifeless degoll. He looked up at Aldric, an expression of helplessness on his face. Aldric heaved himself up and walked over to Arem. Stooping he pulled the knife from the degoll and wiped it on his trousers. His armour dangled in shreds from his chest and he fumbled with his good hand trying to take it off. It was useless and so he sat down next to Arem, unsure of what to do.

The apala had bolted off and would be long gone by now, and they were at least three or four kilometres from the manor. The tangy smell of blood was everywhere, crushed grass and black soil was thrown up all around them and as the adrenaline ebbed from his system Aldric felt the dead weight of his arm return, little pins of white lightning shooting up into his skull. He began to feel dizzy.

Aldric shook his head and looked at the degoll, overcome with something he couldn't understand. "Thanks," he said finally.

"You shouldn't have done it," Arem managed between sobs, his little chest heaving. "I didn't want to do it, I didn't, I didn't want to do it. You shouldn't have done it. You shouldn't have..."

"I know," Aldric said. "I know. It's ok, it's ok now."

"No it's not!" Arem cried.

"It is, I'm ok, it'll be alright. We're both ok, everything's ok."

Arem leaned into Aldric and put his head on his shoulder. "I want to go home," he said. "I want Mom."

Aldric swallowed. He missed his mother too. "Me too," he said softly. He tried to think of what to do but the pain was overwhelming. He looked down at his arm and quickly looked away, swallowing hard. Would they have to cut off his arm? Old Sergeant Bolverk only had one arm, he told Aldric they cut the other off in the war. But they had doctors now who could fix things like this, didn't they? He didn't know, but he felt suddenly frightened, wondering how they would get back and if his father would be angry and how they could save his arm and where the apala had gone and what he should do about Arem.

At that moment he heard the pounding of hooves approaching from the bottom of the hill. Aldric climbed to his feet and over the tops of the grass he saw a troop of soldiers and Valorí on white apalas approaching fast. His father was at the head of the party, his purple cloak swirling behind him as he galloped. Aldric shouted at them and waved, doing his best to pull Arem up to his feet.

His father reined up beside Aldric and leapt off, the soldiers and Valorí in their gleaming armour spreading out around the hilltop in a wide circle. "What happened?" Leopold shouted, kneeling down beside Aldric. "Oh gods, what happened?" he said, seeing Aldric's arm.

"It was a degoll sir," Aldric managed. One of the Valorí jumped down and skewered the degoll with his sabre, dragging the limp creature by his blade to the edge of the hill. He returned and knelt beside Aldric and lifted his visor, inspecting his shoulder.

"He needs a doctor immediately," the man said, his face grave. He pulled out a small pack from compartment in his belt and began pouring an oily paste over Aldric's arm. It smelt awful.

"Will he be ok?" Leopold asked the Valorí.

He nodded, his mouth drawn into a tight line. "Yes, but we must get him to the infirmary at the manor at once."

"How did you find us, father?" Aldric asked weakly. The grasslands were enormous.

"My Augures showed me where you were," Leopold said. "They knew exactly where to find you." He stood, his expression becoming severe. "You stole my apala, and went hunting for degoll? What's the matter with you?"

"Sir, we didn't mean—this wasn't supposed to happen," Aldric stammered. He was feeling nauseous now, it was becoming difficult to understand the voices around him.

"Get them back to the manor," Leopold commanded.

Aldric felt gentle hands lifting him into a saddle. "I'm sorry father," he said.

"I expected better of you, you're a prince, dammit," Leopold said. "Take him back to the manor, a ship will carry him to the infirmary at Dur Enskai from there."

White lights and a stone ceiling greeted Aldric as he opened his eyes. He looked around. He was in the sick room of the palace hospital, he recognised the low windows and white stone walls. The light hurt his eyes. He closed them and tried to move, but someone pushed him back down.

"Stay still," a woman said. Her voice was soothing. "You're ok, we mended your shoulder. You'll be alright."

He opened his eyes and saw a nurse standing over him, a long blue hospital gown wrapped tightly about her. She had blue eyes too, Aldric noticed. They were kind.

"You may leave us," another voice said. It wasn't kind. It was his father's. The nurse bowed and stepped aside, and Aldric saw his father and Arem standing behind her. His father's dark brows curled down and his jaw was set firmly, the muscles working back and forth.

"Hi Aldric," Arem said, his eyes darting up to meet Aldric's and then back down again.

"How are you feeling Aldric?" Leopold asked, pushing Arem aside.

"Well, sir," Aldric lied. His arm was numb, but his stomach was churning angrily and there was a pounding behind his eyes and they felt as though they might burst from his head.

"The doctors tell me you'll be alright," Leopold said. "You'll take a few weeks to recover, but your arm will heal and you won't have any permanent injuries."

"I'm glad, sir," Aldric said, wincing.

"As for what you did," Leopold said, his voice dropping. "You must be punished."

Aldric swallowed. "Yes, sir."

"I've never been more disappointed in you. I thought you would know better, that you would *do* better."

"We didn't think any of this would happen," Aldric began.

"Enough!" Leopold shouted. Several of the nearby nurses started. With a wave of his hand Leopold sent them away, their footsteps echoing off the high ceilings and trailing away until they were alone.

"Sir, we tried to—" Arem began. He was cut off as Leopold whirled around and sent him sprawling with a backhand across his face.

"I said enough! You rode out with your brother when you knew it was wrong? You stole one of my apalas, and then you thought you would go hunting? You could have been killed. You almost were!"

"But we didn't mean to—" Arem protested. He put a hand to his cheek, trying not to cry.

"You should have known better! I expected more of you. You can't ride, and so you wanted your brother to take you, isn't that right?" Leopold said, leaning over Arem who crouched on the floor.

"What? No, sir, no!"

"You were afraid to go by yourself, so you convinced Aldric to take you?" Arem backed away, shaking his head, his eyes wide. "And what did you do when your brother was fighting that degoll, eh?" He shouted, pointing towards Aldric's arm. "You turned and ran away. You let your brother save both of you, because you're a little coward."

"No!" screamed Arem. Aldric watched the scene in horror, unbelieving. He tried to speak but he could barely keep his eyes open, his stomach tightening into knots.

"Shut up! I can't believe you would just stand there and let your brother nearly die. No son of mine would run away from a fight. Why can't you be more like Aldric?"

"Father, he didn't!" Aldric rasped. "He saved me!"

"Silence," Leopold said, not even turning to look at Aldric. "Don't protect him. He's always lying, always trying to get attention, looking for an opportunity to get away with something." He stood, straightening his robes. "Neither of you are to leave the palace, you are forbidden." He turned to leave. "Arem, you will stay in your room, I don't want to look at you. I'm glad your mother isn't alive to see what a coward you are."

The intensity of the memory confused Aldric for a moment. *Aina* would occasionally bring on strong memories, and he blinked, shaking his head. He looked down at Arem, sitting on the divan, staring between his legs at the colourful Illarien rug. A flash of anger surged through him again, and he glared at his father, standing on the balcony with his back towards them, his proud shoulders firmly set as he gazed over his kingdom.

Arem sat back in the divan, a queer expression on his face. His brows were knit tightly together and his large blue eyes were red around the edges. He looked at Aldric, almost without seeing him, then to Leopold, whose back was still to them.

"Don't go," Arem said, almost too quietly to hear. Aldric frowned. When Leopold didn't respond, Arem said again, louder, "Don't go tonight father. To the banquet in Aldon Court. Don't go."

"And let the people think I am afraid of Mal'Dreghen? Don't be foolish."

"Please, just, don't go tonight. The people don't matter. They won't. They will forget, everyone will. Just don't go tonight."

"Arem, I don't know what you think you're playing at," his father said, finally turning around to face him. "But I won't have your little games interfere with the most pivotal moment of our lifetimes. My regency may very well hang in the balance, and if you think I'll just sit back and let him have his night?" He studied Arem for a moment, his jaw muscles working angrily as ever beneath his high cheek bones. "You must be mad."

Aldric just stared at his brother. He had never seen him this way before. There was something about him, something open and earnest that he hadn't seen since they were children.

"Father, Mal'Dreghen is crazy, his greed will destroy him, don't worry about him, please, don't go to the gala tonight. That will send a message that you don't care what he does, that—"

"You're just afraid," Leopold interrupted. "You're afraid of the Mal, and you're jealous that tonight isn't about you." Leopold's eyes narrowed as he looked Arem up and down. "You've always been afraid. You've always been selfish. You've always been *weak*. That I should have such a coward for a son." He turned and walked back to the balcony, the morning sun showering him in golden light. The Golden emperor.

Arem's mouth opened to speak, his eyes widening. Aldric had seen that expression before. It was as if Leopold had struck him again, as he had all those years ago. Nothing came though, only soundless protest in his unuttered words.

Yet as soon as it had come, it was gone. A hardness returned to Arem's pale eyes, and Aldric could practically see the mask falling back into place. Arem nodded, running a hand through his thick black hair. "Well, I'll just leave you two to your preparations then, shall I?" He said, standing.

"Arem, wait," Aldric said, reaching out to put a hand on his shoulder.

Arem backed away, shrugging off the gesture. "For what?" he asked.

"He didn't mean it," Aldric said.

"He didn't? Of course he did, you both did," he said. "You always have, nothing will change that."

Leopold turned around as Arem gathered his sword and left. "Let him go," he said to Aldric, waving a hand. "You can't help him."

Aldric wanted to follow him but he knew he wasn't wanted. His brother was humiliated, Aldric would only make it worse. He walked back to stand beside his father. "Why do you treat him that way? Why do you talk to him like he isn't your son?" he asked.

"I already said, because he doesn't act like my son. He is weak. He always has been."

"Maybe you've never given him the chance to be strong."

"We make our own chances," Leopold said, sniffing. "He's always been a disappointment, someone I couldn't rely on. I've given up expecting anything different."

Aldric stared at his father, seeing him as if for the first time. He almost didn't recognise him. The noble, handsome features and slicked back hair, glowing in the morning light. He was the very image of a god, regal and composed, all powerful and commanding. He was untouchable, unmoved, unfeeling—beauty and wrath written together in hard lines across his noble countenance. He looked at Aldric and the hardness softened, his blue eyes smiling.

"Don't let it trouble you, Aldric," he said, patting his arm. "You will make history today, and you will be remembered forever as my son, the emperor who conquered the tyrant."

EIGHTEEN

THE MESSENGER

The suspensors of the chariot floated noiselessly over the wide cobblestones of Gaeliath Bridge. Aldric shielded his eyes from the sunlight glinting on the water and tried to smile and wave at the hordes of people surrounding them. A *fianna* of Valorí strode beside the chariot, mirrored armour gleaming. Children climbed the statues that lined the bridge for a better look at the procession, while yachts and tall ships with onlookers crowding their topsails trailed along lazily at a distance.

As they left the bridge behind and passed under the massive main gate, they rode through a curtain of crimson petals tossed by people standing atop the battlements. People lined the rooftops, flinging basketfuls of red and blue flower petals into the streets. Behind Aldric on the chariot stood his father and brother, each wearing their finest silks and waving to the crowd. The chariot was joined by the Royal Cortege and a mounted regiment of cuirassier, tasselled lances held high.

The streets had been crowded the day before, yet Aldric couldn't believe the swell of onlookers today. Cracking the reins, the charioteer flexed his arms and gripped the chariot rail with one hand. His bronze skin and bare chest glowed in the sun, and he wore a gorget of patterned gold and gems draped over his shoulders and back, his black hair tied in a long braid. Four white apalas from the royal stables drew the chariot, their flowing manes braided tightly and their spiralling horns sheathed in silver.

Twisting aurancs blasted low, vibrating cadences as arba players drew wild melodies from their bows. Topless girls in flowing silks of all colours and hair woven with kala feathers and strands of silver and glittering necklaces twirled around, beating tambourines above their golden hair as they danced alongside the chariot. Men with painted bodies and faces and beards braided with gold danced beside them, picking them up and tossing them in the air like acrobats.

As they climbed Bael Dunmar towards the Coliseum, Aldric turned to stare back down the twisting parade route that trailed behind them like a colourful serpent. Behind the royal chariot rode the Royal Hagiographer Cyrus Nephellus, recording Leopold's every move so that it might be preserved and praised for all time. Maintaining the cult of the emperor and his grandiose persona were crucial for the invincible image the people all believed. Cyrus was followed by a contingent of Imperial dragoons—mechanised infantry in powerful mobile fighting suits. These were led by Lord Robert Young of the Royal Housecarl, a purple pauldron signifying him from the rest. The dragoons stood three metres tall, and with their chrome armour and smooth, featureless faceplates they looked like gods among the crowd.

The Grand Marshal Bruce Ramsay pulled his apala up beside Aldric's chariot and saluted, his dark eyes scanning the crowded streets. He had advised against this extravagant entrance, preferring a less exposed approach. The emperor had dismissed him out of hand. Leopold's passion for fanfare outweighed his sense of personal safety. Or that of his sons, Aldric thought.

"It'll be another hour to get to the Coliseum through this mess," Bruce Ramsay said, tugging on his apala's reins. The apala shied at a woman who danced too closely and Bruce swatted at her with his sheathed sword. "Infernal gods, this is madness, we should have taken the aerial."

"I'd have missed your smile," Aldric said, laughing.

Bruce grunted and swung his scabbard at another wayward dancer, slapping him across the neck. He was about to speak when his apala reared as two teenagers lit firecrackers beneath its hooves. They dashed back into the crowd and Bruce pulled away from Aldric's chariot, bellowing after them.

Aldric looked back over the crowd and glimpsed two apalas pulling an open palanquin with the archduchess and Lady Evaine. He'd hoped he could avoid her today, she'd been nothing but vindictive since his faux-pas at the gala years before. He'd kept hoping she might have forgotten after all this time, or at least forgiven him. But she was a brat, Aldric decided, and like as not took pleasure in her grudges. Chances were he'd have to see her tonight at Aldon Court, but he tried not to think about that now. He prayed silently to Daor that he wouldn't have to dance with her.

He glanced about at his brother. Arem was completely transformed, his beaming smile and enthusiasm betraying nothing of the morning's argument. He waved at the crowd happily, one hand resting on the hilt of his sabre. Aldric wondered at his abrupt change, unsure of what his brother must really be thinking.

Finally the streets began to widen and the buildings drew back as they approached the broad square before the Coliseum, still hidden behind rows of trees. The cobblestone road carried on through a great lawn, old trees towering upwards to join in the middle overhead. Aldric looked down the shady avenue and over the gardens beyond, every metre packed with people, many having slept in the parks and gardens overnight just to see the procession pass by in the morning.

As they neared the edge of the gardens the trees parted and the Coliseum reared up before them. The Coliseum was larger than life, looming over everything, its opal stonework radiating in the morning sunlight. A line of the Imperial Landser in black armour with white plumes stood shoulder to shoulder, purple cloaks drawn over their chests and sabre-rifles held to attention. They held the crowd back, opening up a wide alley for the chariot to pass through the shadowed tunnel and into the Coliseum beyond.

Yet before they could enter a man pushed his way through the crowd and past the Landser, stumbling into the middle of the cleared area ahead of the chariot. The Valorí darted towards him and the emperor raised his hand to stop them.

"Halt!" Leopold shouted. The Valorí checked themselves and the Landser pushed back the crowd as they surged to see what was happening. Everyone grew quiet, the sudden stillness making Aldric uneasy.

The man was perhaps six metres in front of them, his long grey hair braided neatly behind his back. He was dressed in the grey robes of an Asaani Elder, though he wore no *clamael*, and he stood with his arms open, facing the chariot. Aldric recognised him, he had seen him before. But where? Then it struck him. This was the man he had saved yesterday in the street, the one the Gaiban had said was missing. What was his name? Castor? Khestor? That sounded right. The man bowed towards the emperor.

"Elder, what are you doing here?" Leopold asked, his voice echoing off the stone walls.

"I am here to deliver a message, Your Eminence," the Elder said, his voice high in the still morning air. Even from this distance Aldric could see the beads of sweat on the man's forehead.

Without warning Aldric's head began to pound. It ached violently and he squeezed his eyes shut. A sudden flash of light tore across his mind, bright colours, faded images, ghostly shapes moving around him. He shook his head, trying to block it out. A vision of *aina*, but what was it? For a second he saw the Elder in his mind's eye, lying on the flagstones, his face twisted in agony. Then flames, flames everywhere—green flames and screaming. As quickly as it had come the image was gone and his mind cleared. Aldric blinked and rubbed his temples, disoriented. It had all happened in an instant.

"And what is your message?" Leopold said, his eyes narrowing.

The Elder bowed low to the emperor. "The Dhemorgal cannot be permitted to continue," he said, loud enough for all nearby to hear. "It is an abomination to the goddess Anneah, and it must end now."

"You're wasting your breath Elder," shouted Arem.

Leopold silenced his son with a jerk of his hand. "This is a festival of the people, Elder," Leopold said in measured tones. "It is not my province to obstruct their wishes."

"I beg you to reconsider, Chosen of the Gods," Khestor said, using the old Asaani name for the emperor. "You are our protector, you must lead us into light, not into darkness."

"I am the guardian of all people," Leopold replied. "I give favour to no one. The festival will proceed."

The Elder nodded, a look of sadness overcoming him. "If that is your will," he said. "I take my leave of you then." He bowed again. Then, straightening, he lifted both his arms into the air.

"He's holding something," Aldric said in a whisper.

"What?" Arem asked, giving him a confused look.

"Stop him!" Aldric shouted. Leopold turned and reached out a hand to silence his son. Aldric shoved his hand away. "*Stop him!*" he repeated, leaping from the chariot.

"*Tuá vyth amon, éya vaé non ruath ésah,*" Khestor proclaimed loudly to the sky. The Valorí rushed towards the druid as he smashed his tightened fists down into his chest. A burst of light erupted from his hands and he was engulfed in a pillar of green flame. The Valorí stopped short and Aldric shielded his eyes from the sudden flash of heat. People in the crowd screamed and rushed backwards, trying to get away. When Aldric looked again the druid was sunk to the ground on his knees, his darkened silhouette framed by a roaring fire, his arms outstretched to either side in an appeal to the heavens above.

NINETEEN

THE COLISEUM

It took only half an hour to remove all evidence of the Elder's demonstration. The Landser held the crowd at bay, directing them through a second entrance in the Coliseum and away from the scene while an efficient clean up crew erased all traces of the immolation. Bruce Ramsay was already busy conducting an investigation and tightening security around the Coliseum. Bahir added an additional two dozen Valorí to stand watch around the emperor and at strategic locations throughout the stadium. Lord Young erected barricades at the entrances and stationed heavy patrols around each of them. Military aerials droned above the streets, offering support to the gendarmerie that were stopping people for questioning.

The emperor's Augures were busy reading the crowd for any disturbances, but their *aina* revealed nothing unusual, though the panic made it more difficult for them to see clearly. Leopold didn't believe the druid's protest was anything more than an isolated event, but Bruce was adamant that more would follow.

"You heard his last words," Bruce Ramsay said, eyeing the crowd below suspiciously. People were filing into the Coliseum in droves, the empty stadium gradually filling with colour. Bruce still wore his gleaming ceremonial cuirass and high black riding boots, though his polished helmet was set aside on a table.

"'And he opened the gates, and saw the darkness descend,'" Bahir translated. He sat beside Aldric in his brilliant phase-armour with his close-helmet under one arm. Inside their private booth there was no noise from the outside. The walls were built with treble reinforced pallanium, and the glass was made of ferranite. A bomb could detonate on the roof and they wouldn't even hear it.

"And yet the Gaiban remains silent," Bruce said. "You think she might take a keener interest."

"The Mother of the Starborn is not responsible for what her children do," Bahir said.

"And if thousands of Asaani druids take to the streets and start torching themselves?" Bruce snarled. "What then?"

"They won't," Bahir replied.

"You seem awfully sure of that," Aldric said, not feeling as confident as Bahir. "Would you have thought an Asaani Elder could have done this before you saw it this morning?"

"It goes against everything we believe," Bahir said. "Elder Khestor was respected, he was a senior druid, and I cannot explain what he did. But I know it won't happen again."

"The implications are intriguing, but I think it improbable the Asaani will turn riotous," said Chiron. He had joined them at Leopold's request after they were hurried into the safety of the emperor's Booth. "They are pacifists by nature. There's never been a violent Asaani protest in the history of the empire."

"This is exactly what I didn't want," Leopold said, a distant look in his eyes as he watched the stadium fill.

Aldric looked at him. "And you took such great pains to prevent it."

Leopold glanced up, seeming not to have heard. "The festival must continue," he said. "I won't let him beat me."

Aldric shook his head. "Maybe *you* should go down there and fight with Mal'Dreghen, instead of me."

Leopold smiled. "Such a spectacle it would be!" he said, almost laughing.

Arem and Aldric exchanged glances. No matter what happened today, there would be a spectacle, and that was exactly what the emperor wanted.

Bruce Ramsay left to see to the security measures and Bahir stood at attention next to the armoured glass keeping an eye on the stadium below. Chiron spoke in low whispers with the emperor while Arem sat and fidgeted, kicking his legs over the edge of a sprawling couch. For Aldric it was simply a matter of waiting now. All the ceremony and games were just the preamble before the grand finale, his final showdown. Aldric's match wouldn't be until near the end of the day, and he already imagined it would be a very long day.

Twenty minutes later when the Coliseum had finally filled a blue robed lictor entered and nodded to the emperor.

Leopold rose. "It's time," he said.

The lictor stepped back from the doorway and two Draugor in carmine armour entered, followed by Mal'Dreghen. Aldric stood, quelling his anger. Two inquisitors in white robes stepped in behind the Mal, their veiled faces concealed and mysterious. The Mal inclined his head respectfully towards the emperor. "Your Highness," he said.

"Mal'Dreghen", Leopold replied.

"It is a terrible shame about the good Elder," the Mal said in the deepest tones of sympathy. "I met him once or twice, I understand he was something of a pillar among the other druids at the temple."

"His dedication was inspiring," Bahir said. "He will be missed."

"Ahh…" Mal'Dreghen said, appraising Bahir. "Well, it is fortunate that his… passing… has not proven incommodious to our purpose on this glorious day."

Bahir looked down, almost sadly Aldric thought.

"It'd be a tragedy for anything to get in the way of your celebration, Mal," Aldric said.

Mal'Dreghen turned his yellow eyes upon Aldric. "You are generous, my Prince." He wore his long black hair over his shoulders, falling freely above a deep red robe with blue and gold embroidery. He smiled. "Your closeness with the Asaani must make it especially difficult for you."

"Any senseless death is a tragedy," Aldric said, refusing to rise to the bait.

"Senseless? You think his death was without meaning?" Mal'Dreghen asked.

"Why he died—why he felt the need to take his life will always remain a mystery," Aldric replied.

"He died for his principles," Bahir said, looking up.

"Yes, his principles. Something I've never understood about you Asaani," Mal'Dreghen said, inclining his head to the side. "What use are principles you must die for?"

"What use are principles you only live to break?" Aldric replied.

Mal'Dreghen smiled. "Perhaps that is a principle in itself?" he said, looking at Aldric intensely.

"It is far better to die for your principles than to live and betray them," Aldric answered, holding the Mal's gaze.

"You make it difficult to disagree, my dear prince."

"Perhaps we might continue this repartee at the banquet this evening?" Leopold said, interrupting.

"Yes, of course Your Highness!" the Mal said, finally turning from Aldric.

Leopold straightened his achkan. "We are about to begin. You will join me?" It was not a question.

Mal'Dreghen nodded and stepped aside with his Draugor escort to make way for Bahir and the four Valorí guard. As they passed, Aldric noticed one of the Draugor casually slide his foot in front of one of the Valorí. Before Aldric could say anything, the Valorí lightly stepped over the foot without even looking down, carrying on out the door as if nothing had happened. Mal'Dreghen kept his head bowed. If he noticed, he made no sign.

As they stepped out onto the balcony beyond, trumpeting music began to play and pounding drums thundered through the Coliseum. Aldric stepped up beside his father, Arem standing to the other side. Mal'Dreghen stood respectfully at a distance. The events of the morning didn't seem to have dampened the enthusiasm of the crowd. The music could scarcely be heard over the sudden roar of the onlookers as they caught sight of the emperor and his sons.

The emperor nodded approvingly, raising his hands into the air. The tumult crescendoed, and Aldric sucked in a breath, feeling suddenly overwhelmed. Even for the emperor's son, he wasn't accustomed to anything of this magnitude. The monthly games held in the Coliseum paled in comparison, and he had to admit to himself that he was a little awestruck.

Flowing banners on the ramparts of the Coliseum whipped against the blue sky, and enormous tapestries hung from the uppermost tiers and rolled gracefully in the wind, portraits of the prophet Desedar thirty metres high making the purpose of the day impossible to forget. And the tragedy this morning, Aldric thought bitterly. There were banners featuring Aldric as well, depicting his heroism of the day before and proudly proclaiming how noble and brave he was. Yet it struck Aldric as sort of pathetic in light of Elder Khestor.

At an unseen command the crowd fell quiet. "It is an historic day," Leopold began. "A thousand years ago our ancestors dedicated this day to their beliefs, coming together from across a divided empire to join with one another in a celebration of their history and heritage. Our history has since seen many traditions rise and fall. Yet in spite of adversity, rivalry, and war, we have managed to reunite as one people, to form the most powerful, enduring civilisation in the history of Errolor." Leopold waved down the chorus of cheers. Aldric watched Mal'Dreghen from the corner of his eye, but his rapt expression revealed nothing.

"Though we share a multitude of beliefs, I am proud that we can, as one people, join together on this day and commemorate our ancestors' struggles and triumphs. Our origins are diverse, but our purpose is unified, and it is through traditions such as these that we will remain steadfast in our unity. Now, and forever."

Aldric marvelled at his father. Every bit an emperor, regal, dignified, and handsome—no one could mistake him for anything else. His every movement proclaimed his nobility, and Aldric couldn't help but admire him for that, in spite of all his shortcomings.

A royal herald took the emperor's place and waited patiently until the cheering crowd had subsided. "It is my pleasure to present the eminent Mal'Dreghen."

"People of Chaldrea, of the Vassaryan Empire! I welcome you today," Mal'Dreghen said grandly, stepping up to the balcony. He waved and looked even more proud than the emperor had, Aldric thought. The Mal gestured with an open palm to Leopold. "Your gracious emperor has introduced this magnificent day more eloquently than I could ever hope to," he said, smiling. Aldric noticed the not-so-subtle emphasis on 'your emperor'.

"I must only express my gratitude, to you, the people, who have so faithfully stood beside me during our many trials and tribulations," the Mal continued, "and have shown Errolor that we are ready for the return of the Dhemorgal! Here, in this glorious Coliseum, where man has tested his strength against man for millennia, proving his own divinity. May the brilliance and wisdom of Desedar shine eternally! Let the games begin!"

The cheering and applause following the Mal's speech lasted a full five minutes. Aldric resumed his seat beside his father in the Emperor's Booth. Below them in the arena Aldric watched a troop of Dhemorahn girls performing an elaborate dance to start the ceremonies. When they had finished, two teams of apala riders entered the Coliseum and began circling each other. One man on a black apala rode to the centre of the arena and collected large gold rings from each of the riders, placing them over the tip of his lance. It was an old Illarien game, and was popular among the nobility and those who could afford an apala. The game grew in complexity once the rings were collected, but Aldric found his attention drifting elsewhere.

Lictors kept a steady stream of exotic foods on silver platters moving through the booth, and Aldric absently plucked at a bushel of bright orange grapes. Iain joined him on a nearby cushion and Aldric tossed him the grapes. Four teams of Elcaern dramads in battle gear were now squaring off, each vying for a trophy at the centre of the arena—a mythical sword called Crodan.

The sword was renown among the Elcaern for having slain a god at the hands of the hero Artagan, and was said to be so vicious that it must always be kept in a cauldron of blood to slake its terrible fury. This was only a replica, but it was still placed in an iron vat of urocha blood, which the victors would afterwards pour over themselves in grisly celebration.

Today two men from the Glengaeligh tribe stood triumphantly atop the altar, each with a fist gripped tightly around the hilt of the bloody sword. "*Dom nach tael cadugg baen glasgoth! Faeda Glengaeligh!*" shouted one of the red bearded dramads as he upturned the cauldron and disappeared under a crimson wave.

"Magnificent," Lord Robert Young said, watching the two Elcaern dramads thumping their shields and bellow at the crowd. The sixth Baron of Affonweare, Lord Robert was the youngest captain of the Housecarl Aldric had ever heard of. In his late thirties, Lord Robert was sandy haired and trim, a close cropped blond beard framing a strong, good-natured face with hard blue eyes that ever seemed full of mirth. "I wouldn't mind a few more like them in my garrison," he continued, his highland brogue soft and merry.

"Savages," Bruce Ramsay replied. "They'd as soon die and go to the Land Beyond to drink with their damned gods than stand in your ranks," he said.

"The Land Beyond is actually Dulannan; that's their hell."

"Is it now?" Bruce said absently.

"Aye, it's Fíadamor you're thinking of."

"Well, either way, they're far too undisciplined to be of any use in combat," Bruce replied.

"Just because they didn't train at Braigh Ardunn or the Auldor Royal Academy doesn't mean they aren't handy on a battlefield," Lord Robert said. "You know the Illariens didn't build the Wall at Berrund Duul for nothing."

"Quite so, quite so," Bruce said, obviously unconvinced.

"I'd like to see your officers go through the *Comrath Andach*," Lord Robert replied. "You don't train from the age of seven and not know a thing or two about discipline."

"Wouldn't that be a sight!" Iain said. "The Grand Marshal—running with a hornet's nest through Chaldrea."

"They carry a hornet's nest?" Bruce asked, suddenly interested.

"And they're beaten bloody if they drop it, and have to start again," Bahir said.

"Or quit in shame," Lord Robert added. "How many of your Old Guard could do the same?"

"Then they're branded on their face for life, a sign of the warrior. Much discipline to endure such pain," Bahir said.

Bruce Ramsay furrowed his brow, watching the bloody dramads laughing and cheering one another as they paraded off the field.

Next a team of charioteers from Elidan vied off against a team from Laithlynn and began a race to collect flags from around the arena. The crowd roared and cheered as the chariots crashed and collided with one another. Those who lost their chariots and were forced into the sandy arena on foot ran the risk of being run over by the other chariots rushing around the course. One unlucky man stumbled and was caught beneath a spiked chariot wheel. A bloody smear across the sand marked his remains. The crowd roared with applause.

Huge damadrons in battle armour—lumbering beasts with massive leathery shoulders of muscle and two large horns—were driven across the field by skilled riders in golden armour. They wielded spears three meters long with points tufted in colourful feathers and shrieked strange battle cries as they attempted to dismount the other riders, careening into one another, riders thrown under foot while gold capped horns tore into flesh.

Afterwards the arena was cleared, and an assortment of trees and rocks and other bits of vegetation were brought in until the once sandy ring resembled a jungle. A team of hunters armed with short swords, spears, and bows and arrows entered the now forested arena and moved together to a clearing in the centre where they stood back to back, forming a tight circle. A few moments later several gates around the arena were opened and a dozen degoll were released from their cages. Aldric's jaw clenched tightly as he watched.

Brown plains degoll—the stout, burrow dwelling creatures he had faced as a boy and on his hunt with Iain—were thrown together with the leaner, tree climbing degoll found in the northern forests near Galhane and Laithlynn. The tree degoll were much slimmer, with long bodies and white or grey fur. Both species were ferocious, however, and they were lost to sight in seconds as they darted into the underbrush. The centre of the arena was clearly visible to everyone in the Coliseum, and Aldric held his breath with the audience, waiting to see what would happen. The first attack came from a tree degoll that lunged at one of the hunters from a nearby bush. It flew through the air but the man managed to catch the attack on the rim of his targe, throwing the snarling creature to the ground where he impaled it with his spear.

His companion, distracted by the attack didn't see a plains degoll dart towards him and fell to the ground as it savaged his leg. The degoll howled as it was suddenly pierced by an arrow, the crowd screaming with delight. Another brown plains degoll ambushed the party as they attempted to rescue their comrade, leaping onto the back of the woman with the bow and arrows. It sank its teeth into her neck and she barely managed to cry out before falling to her knees, her scream cut short. As one of her friends turned to help, a tree degoll sprang up at his face. He raised his short sword in time for it to skewer itself, growling and hissing at the end of his blade. He threw it off and ran to the archer, slicing down into the degoll that was still worrying at her neck.

Four of the original eight hunters were now dead or incapacitated, the remaining four huddling close together as they awaited the next attack. Aldric wasn't sure how many degoll were left, he thought that perhaps a dozen had been released. He couldn't imagine being there in the arena right now. One degoll was a nightmare, let alone a dozen.

"This is barbaric," Aldric said to no one in particular.

"You disapprove, brother?" Arem asked.

"This isn't a noble death," he said. "This isn't grand or pure or honourable. Where is the honour here?"

"These men and women are hunters," Arem replied. "This is their passion, their pursuit, their highest ideal. You might argue they are fighting for their *principles*," he said, with wryness in his voice.

Aldric wrinkled his nose. "This isn't principled, it's blood sport, and they're dying for the entertainment of the crowd, not their ideals."

"And what of your little scuffle today, hmm? Are you fighting for anything so grand as your sacred beliefs?"

"You know I don't want to fight, Arem."

"Then why do you? No one is making you, you could decline and no one would stop you," Arem said, smirking. "You're just like father—you just want the chance to put the Mal in his place and to hear the crowd cheer for you."

Aldric couldn't express the sadness he felt at those words. "I go because my emperor asks me to, and because more is at stake than my own personal desires. I go because I must. The Mal thinks he's invulnerable. I have to show him he isn't."

"Your damnable duty," Arem said. "It doesn't matter what you do here today, nothing does."

"What do you mean?"

"Nothing," Arem said. "Forget it."

The audience laughed and jeered and clapped and screamed the names of their favourite combatants. Aldric had never seen such brutality, not on this scale. It was an orgy of violence. Yet the crowd was enthralled. 'Religion and blood,' Chiron had once told him. 'These are the tools of statecraft. A successful ruler understands his people's fear of religion and their thirst for blood. Both are endless, and they will distract the people. Pity the nation whose ruler is so blind that he can see nothing else. Empires will collapse under the burdens of blood and religion.'

The words rang through Aldric's head over and over again as he watched the spectacles before him. Mal'Dreghen knew how to hold the people in thrall. He was better at being an emperor than his father was. But the Mal was motivated by hatred, and Aldric knew that such hatred could not endure for much longer without exploding.

The games carried on all morning and through lunch, people coming and going as they pleased. In the afternoon the arena floor was cleared and the Coliseum was filled with water. Wooden warships of ancient times were brought in through gates at the rear of the stadium, benches of rowers straining at the oars as the ships rammed each other, oars cracking and snapping as they collided and warriors in shining armour clashing through the thunderous applause of the spectators. Some of the ships were set aflame with burning arrows, and the smoke from their wreckage billowed through the Coliseum until they sank sputtering and hissing below the water.

As Aldric was stretching he noticed a nearby booth where the Lady Evaine Sinclair was sitting. She sat with her mother wearing a light blue sari wrapped tightly around her slender figure. Her golden hair was pinned up with silver fastenings and revealed a long, graceful neck which rose to meet a proud jaw with small, pouting lips. Aldric hated to admit it, but she was captivating.

She chanced to glance up towards him and their eyes met. Fighting his instinct to quickly look away, Aldric held her gaze. She looked at him coolly, but did not flinch. Her mother finally leaned in and whispered something to her and she was forced to turn her head. Aldric pursed his lips, thinking perhaps he might forgive whatever had passed between them before, even her arrogance. She was certainly comely enough, though he knew she must be aware of this, and that knowledge somehow diminished her beauty. Beautiful girls were never so beautiful as when they had no idea they were.

One of the last two ships was finally sunk and a cheer came up from the surviving crew. The Coliseum was cleared of wreckage and the water drained from the arena, and Aldric stood to make ready for his contest, though it was not for another hour. His father rose to meet him, taking him aside.

"You will not lose," he said, holding Aldric's shoulder. He spoke in a low tone, his blue eyes fierce. The determination Aldric saw there startled him. "This is the moment we have all waited for, and I know you will not fail."

Aldric took his father's hand from his shoulder and let it fall. "I will, or I will not," he said, surprising himself. Were those Bahir's words? "I will do what I must, and only the gods know if it will be enough."

"It will be," Leopold said. "You are my son, and I love you. You will be victorious, and today we shall see Mal'Dreghen shamed before everyone— on his own day of veneration."

Aldric could find nothing to say, so he merely nodded. He searched Leopold's face for some sign of his father. The noble eyes and proud cheekbones they both shared, the jet black hair and long, straight nose. He had so much in common with this man who stood before him, but he could not see his father. He saw only his emperor, the ruler of an empire bent upon the conquest of his foes. Aldric was not his son, but a means to that end. Aldric forced the thought from his mind before he could dwell upon it further.

"I am proud of you, for all that you have done," Leopold said. "This is the beginning of the end."

Aldric pondered the words as he followed his Valorí escort down the steps and into the many pits below the Coliseum. The winding tunnels were eroded from centuries of wear, the steps themselves worn and smooth in the centre from countless footsteps of forgotten warriors. They emerged into a large stone chamber with a high arched ceiling and rough dirt floor, racks of weapons hanging from the walls.

Other combatants stood in various stages of readiness, some returning from their fight, others bruised and bleeding from numerous lacerations and awaiting the attention of medics. Still others were dressing in their armour, giant Elcaern dramads sliding heavy mail or boiled leather coats over their big frames. One man towered head and shoulders above the rest, his dark brown hair braided and beard woven into pleats strung with hieroglyphic beads. A bronze torq around his neck suggested he was noble born, and the intricate scar running down his temple marked him as a warrior of the *Comrath Andach*. He lumbered to a corner and knelt, drawing an inscription in the sand and muttering to himself.

An iron portcullis at the far end of the chamber led to the arena, and Aldric walked over to see two armies crashing together beyond. Elcaern dramads were allied with the painted warriors of Brythanor in an historic re-enactment of an assault on Durengol. The soldiers of Illaria and Perendur held the fortress and were defending valiantly, though historically the battle resulted in the capture of Durengol and the slaughter of all the forces within. A small stone castle had been built in the centre of the arena, and Brythic warriors were scaling the walls on wooden ladders, the soldiers above trying to push the ladders off the battlements.

Aldric stood still as his steward dressed him for his match, weaving the off-white *kilpi* around him in tight folds. Atop this his page secured his armour, segments fitting into place so he could move more easily. In Aldric's opinion there was no finer armour than Valorí féthabban. This armour would stop a blast from plasma rifle or even a ballistic weapon, to say nothing of a sword or powered blade. It could even take a few hits from a sabre-rifle, but the highly explosive rounds would eventually shatter the armour's casing. The reflective silver pieces slipped snuggly onto his chest, moulded especially for his body for the closest fit. Typically this would be the phase-armour the Valorí wore during combat, but camouflage wasn't necessary in the arena, so he would be fitted with regular amour.

Bahir joined him when he'd been suited up. "It fits you well?" he asked, inspecting the joints and tugging on them to make sure they were secure.

Aldric shrugged, flexing and stretching his arms. "Yes, perfectly," he said, slapping the large plate fitted over his thigh. The metal was polished to a mirror finish, inscriptions from the Book of Caels traced into the silver. He gazed at his reflection behind the fine script, surprised at the lack of emotion he found in the grey eyes that returned his stare.

They sparred lightly, Aldric practising with the *cobran*—the small targe with a razor's edge used by the Valorí as both a shield and a weapon. It was light enough he barely felt its weight upon his arm. Bahir scored only two hits, but they weren't serious and Aldric doubted he would have been hit at all if he'd been fighting in earnest. The other combatants in the chamber who weren't preparing for their own fights or mending wounds gathered around to watch. *Craidath* was an elegant fighting technique, like watching skilled dancers in a deadly ballet.

The hour passed quickly, almost too quickly for Aldric. He rested with Bahir on a bench while the last of the warriors returned and the arena was cleared. They recited mantras together, and Aldric tried to quell the knots that were growing in his gut.

Slipping into his white surcoat, Aldric buckled the clasp over his waist. The surcoat was a garment carried over from medieval times and had retained its versatile functionality. In the tropical clime it helped to keep the wearer dry, and for regular troops without the sophisticated cloaking phase armour, it kept the sun from baking them. However Aldric's féthabban suit was hermetically sealed and a finely tuned ventilation system constantly kept his body at the optimal temperature. Aldric's surcoat was snow white and bore the sigil of House Danarean, two heraldic apalas rearing.

"Remember, you are not the outcome of this contest," Bahir said, putting a gloved hand on his shoulder. "Win, lose, it makes no difference."

Aldric nodded. "*Ém fáh Valorí annú*," he said.

"*Té fán Aldric, fán Valorí, fán bráith sythríc annás*," Bahir replied. "You are Aldric, you are Valorí, you are eternal."

A path was cleared before him and the heavy iron gates swung inwards. His steward handed him his helmet and he wiped a layer of dust from the crest before slipping it on, securing the padded straps to the bevor above his neck. The close-helmet covered his head and face entirely, its smooth surface broken only by a slit for his visor no more than half a centimetre wide that ran nearly ear-to-ear. The slit sat above a protruding lip in the helmet, and was actually a sensor strip, artificially projecting his surroundings on a display inside the helmet.

The projection was a complete illusion, so that to the wearer it seemed as if he weren't wearing a helmet at all. This gave Aldric total protection as well as an unobstructed view of his environment. In modern warfare, this heads up display would be augmented with real time battlefield data— remaining ammunition, troop movements, and enemy locations—but today it only registered his bio-readouts—heart rate, blood pressure, body temperature and so on. He switched those off as well.

A scimitar was strapped into a scabbard on his back, and his steward handed him his *darrac*, a long spear used by the Valorí to keep an opponent at a distance. The point was flattened so that it wasn't lethal, as was the blade of his shortened scimitar. He shook his shoulders, clanging his spear and *cobran* together. "I'm ready," he said. Bahir patted him on the back but said nothing.

The sensors in his visor dimmed the harsh sunlight as he stepped into the arena. The crowd had been silenced before he emerged, but as he appeared from the chamber the Coliseum exploded in a wild roar. He gazed about. Every seat in the Coliseum was filled, even the uppermost tiers were crowded. It hadn't seemed as big from the royal booth, but here from the arena floor the Coliseum was gigantic.

His opponent had not yet entered the arena, and so Aldric walked to the centre and stood with his spear at his side, doing his best to look princely. Was he looking princely? He didn't know. He stood up a little straighter and tried not to look around. His face was hidden, and no one could hear him, so it didn't matter what he said or did, he would look regal all the same.

The uproar of the crowd had begun to subside when a moment later it resumed, nearly as loud, and Aldric turned to see his opponent emerge from a gate opposite him. He was clad in crimson plate armour, segmented like Aldric's, and wearing a black and red surcoat emblazoned with a black fire beneath eight stars, encircled with a pattern of fine script; the emblem of the Dhemorahn Sect. His helmet was broken by a single vertical slit that ran from his chin to his crown, his features hidden as Aldric's were. Aldric could picture him nonetheless: dark haired and lean of face, as were all the Draugor of Mal'Dreghen, and eyes black as his surcoat.

He carried no shield, but instead hefted two long swords with vicious downward pointing hooks at their ends and smaller, pointed blades extending beneath the pommels. They were called *tamka,* and they were the perfect weapons to counter Aldric's *darrac.* He had expected this however; it was a typical Dhemorahn weapon, blunt and practical.

The man stopped short of Aldric and seemed to be appraising him from behind the narrow slit in his visor. Aldric initiated the *beol,* the traditional salute before combat and the Draugor reciprocated, clenching his fist tight above his heart as he bowed low. They stepped backwards, lowering the points of their weapons to the ground in deference. Aldric could hear the herald announcing the event, and he heard his name, but he wasn't listening. The man before him was huge, a full head taller than Aldric and almost half as broad. He was a monster, Aldric thought. No matter, though. He would tire sooner, and he would fall. More trumpets blew, and a great ceremonial *auranc* seven storeys tall blasted long and low across the Coliseum. Aldric stilled his mind, banished all thoughts, and lifted his spear.

TWENTY

THE ROCK AND THE SWORD

The Dhemorahn was huge, but he moved like a wargren. They backed away from each other and began circling. Aldric watched his feet: light, quick movements, no dragging or shuffling. This was a non-lethal fight, victory would be determined when one man was on his back and in a position that would kill him if they were using real weapons. That wouldn't be easy, but Aldric had known that before he ever set foot in the arena. This was a contest to end all, and everything was at stake.

The Draugor looked fearsome in his scarlet armour, contrasting Aldric's shining, argent panoply. The Draugor twirled the heavy *tamka* as he circled Aldric, his shoulders low, prepared to strike. Aldric held his spear well above the haft, pointed loosely at the Draugor. He was a brute, and manoeuvrability would be key here.

Without warning the Draugor leapt off one foot and darted towards Aldric, swinging his *tamka* down to deflect Aldric's spear point. Aldric dashed aside easily, ducking below a hooked blade that swung centimetres above his head. Before he had even finished moving out of the way Aldric was turning, his *darrac* aimed at the Draugor's back.

The Draugor spun around and pushed the spear point to the side, locking the hook of his *tamka* around the shaft and pulling Aldric into him. Shots to the body with fists would be useless against all this armour, Aldric knew, and he dropped the spear, freeing his right arm to grab his opponent's shoulder. As the Draugor closed Aldric pulled his shoulder down and swung his *cobran* up into his helmet, smashing it across his face at the same time he brought his armoured knee into the man's stomach. It was a blunt attack, but the Draugor reeled backwards, dropping his tangled *tamka*. Aldric pressed the attack.

As the Draugor stepped backwards, Aldric sprinted to the side and locked his calf behind the Draugor's knee, jamming the targe into his helmet again. The Draugor staggered to the side and Aldric heard the crowd erupt in wild cheering. Before he could recover Aldric leapt behind him and prepared to land a kick into his lower back when the Draugor suddenly spun, ramming his giant forearm into Aldric's helmet. It was like being hit with a tree and before Aldric could react the Draugor swung his remaining *tamka* behind him, hooking it around Aldric's neck.

With a mighty jerk he pulled Aldric down, landing on one knee. Aldric tried to roll forward out of the hook but an enormous boot connected with his face, jarring his senses. He tasted blood; he must have smashed his nose because it suddenly ached fiercely. He saw the Draugor shift his weight, lining his leg up again for another kick and without thinking Aldric gripped both armoured hands onto the blade of the *tamka* and pushed off the ground then dropped again quickly, pulling the Draugor off balance. The Draugor heaved forward, stumbling and Aldric rolled to the side.

Before he'd managed to recover Aldric was back on his feet, pulling his scimitar out. The Draugor turned to meet him and Aldric pirouetted high in the air, landing a kick across his helmet. The Draugor lunged forward and Aldric slipped to the side, smashing his blade across the back of his helmet. His opponent didn't seem fazed and reeled around with his *tamka* as Aldric leaned backwards out of his reach. He parried the blade away with his scimitar and thrust forward, aiming once again for his opponent's face.

In the dirt and dust of the arena they clashed, Aldric meeting the Draugor's blows and parrying them, the Draugor lunging at every opening he found. It was ferocious, Aldric had never faced an opponent of such savagery. What would have been heedless in other fighters was calculated recklessness, and Aldric felt himself wearing down. He was much lighter on his feet than the Dhemorahn, and this saved him many times, but his lightness was more evasion while the Draugor was able to drive home several devastating attacks.

As the crowded Coliseum watched on, Aldric landed pointed blows with his scimitar, weakening his opponent but not finishing him. All the while he felt his strength draining. Even the comfort of the suit could not completely combat the growing heat of the afternoon, the sun now directly overhead and beating down intensely. Aldric's muscles had begun aching long ago, and the ache was now a shooting pain that ran from his calves through his shoulders and into his neck. Each blow he caught on his targe shuddered through him, fresh bolts of pain arching through his body.

Aldric shut out all sensations except what was necessary in the moment. Valorí mantras streamed through his mind, cleansing him of his pain and banishing thoughts of weakness. Yet every swing of his scimitar was a struggle to maintain his precision against the scream of his protesting muscles. Even when he could drown out the pain it felt like fencing underwater, slow and clumsy, and the energy required to stay alert and keep his motions tight and focused was overwhelming. He had lost track of time, but judging from the shadows on the arena floor they had been fighting without rest for at least forty-five minutes, and the Draugor seemed just as determined as he had at the onset.

Aldric had never considered that defeat would be a reality, not really. He had worried he might not win, he had worried what might happen, that it would be difficult, but he had never truly believed that he would fail. Yet now he found himself fighting back the idea as it began to creep into his mind. Using every focusing technique he knew he pushed it back away from his consciousness, suppressing the pain of the blows and fighting on with all his strength. Several times the Draugor's blade left bloody trails across Aldric's *kilpi* where it slipped through his armour. The blades were dulled, but with enough force they would open skin. The Draugor was bloodied as well, though his crimson garments hid his wounds more than Aldric's snow white *kilpi.*

Aldric swung his scimitar downwards across the Draugor's chest, but the Draugor caught the blade with his hook and for a moment they were locked. Before the Draugor could pull away Aldric leapt forward, untangling the blades and swinging his *cobran* into the Draugor's helmet. But the Draugor caught the edge of the targe and yanked Aldric's arm out away from him, exposing his chest. With their blades free the Draugor jabbed his fist towards Aldric's stomach. Aldric rolled into the attack so that the fist fumbled harmlessly across his back. With the Draugor pressed up against him Aldric dropped and hooked his arm behind the man's knee, standing quickly to throw him off balance.

His muscles screamed as he tried to lift the Draugor. Suddenly his vision flickered and with his mind's eye he saw the pommel of the Draugor's *tamka* flying down towards his head. He shifted to the side just in time for the blow to glance off his helmet and crash into his shoulder. Disoriented, he tried to throw the Draugor off his feet yet he only managed to grasp his calf, rising to face the Draugor with his leg held at the knee under Aldric's arm. The Draugor was standing on one leg now, and as Aldric stood up the Draugor swung his *tamka* full into Aldric's face.

The force sent Aldric spinning backwards to the ground. As Aldric rolled over to stand up, he realised he couldn't see. His visor had gone black. The external sensor strip must have been damaged, he couldn't see a thing. *Impossible!* he thought, disbelieving. *This can't happen.* It was pitch black, and in a moment of panic Aldric dropped his scimitar and fumbled with the clasp to remove his helmet. But it was dented, hinged under his bevor so his armoured fingers couldn't reach it.

He managed to stand up, trying to remove his helmet when an incredible blow to his head sent him sprawling into the dirt. Flames licked through his skull and he screamed in pain and anger at the unfair attack. As he came to his knees another blow landed on his head from behind and his vision went fuzzy for a second and through the blackness of his helmet he saw stars. His ears were ringing and he stumbled through grogginess. He tried to stand again but he fell over, landing on his side. A tremendous force thudded into his back and he gasped as bolts of white lightning shot through his brain.

He couldn't think, he couldn't focus, he couldn't concentrate on anything except the pain. The sensors in his helmet had ceased transmitting sound as well, and Aldric was trapped in a black void of heat and pain and confusion, broken only by the sounds of his grunts and rapid breathing. Blows rained down on him, to his head, his neck, his stomach and back. Every time he moved to defend himself a blow would land in an exposed area. One hit drove his head into the ground and he bit his tongue hard. He felt his mouth begin to fill with blood and he tried to swallow but he coughed instead, blood spilling over his face, trapped inside his sealed helmet.

He tried to remember something, anything that would help him stand up, help him get his helmet off, help him to do anything at all. He managed to climb to his feet, and in a delirium he began walking, stumbling, he didn't know where, just somewhere away from the pain. He tripped and fell, landing hard on his face again. He lay there breathing for a moment, and miraculously, the rain of blows ceased.

Lying prostrate on the ground, Aldric was submerged under wave upon wave of nauseating agony. He didn't know if his eyes were open or closed as darkness descended over him. Darker than the blackness of his helmet, darker than his pain; it was a pure, empty darkness engulfing his senses. It was bliss, serenity, and he welcomed the darkness with a mindless acceptance that was all he had left to offer. He felt himself give up, accepting the darkness.

But the darkness wavered then. Something, somewhere, broke through the emptiness and called his name. A tiny point of white light, smaller than a star, flickered though his consciousness and called him back from his surrender. He felt anger at the light, anger at being pulled back into the pain he wanted to escape. He tried to send the light away, but it grew brighter. He tried to blink, still unsure if his eyes were open or closed, but it made no difference. The light was there, and it was growing brighter and more intense.

Aldric began to forget his pain, to forget the darkness threatening to consume him. As the light grew brighter, he thought perhaps his visor had been restored, that he could see again. But it wasn't his visor. The light came from somewhere beyond, outside his vision but also inside his mind. The light kept growing, consuming his entire vision, so intense he tried to squint and look away, but he couldn't, and the brightness suddenly resolved into clarity. He could see.

Aldric gazed into the Coliseum, but he wasn't looking out of his own eyes. He was somewhere above, overhead, hanging a dozen metres above the arena floor. He saw his body lying there on the ground, white surcoat tattered and hanging in ribbons, armour still intact but his *kilpi* beneath it torn and bloodied. Behind him stood the Draugor, pacing back and forth, swinging his *tamka* and holding his fist high in the air. Aldric tried to shake his head. What was this? Was this real? Was he actually seeing this?

Yet Aldric could see so much more. He looked up and there was his father and brother in the booth above him, and suddenly he was there next to them, sitting beside them, his father's face twisted in anger, his brother's in fear and wonder. Then he was outside the booth, above the Coliseum, looking out over the rooftops of Chaldrea. He could see the blue waters of Lake Nimaine and the deep green jungles beyond, and far away to the south he could even see the great ocean beyond Gwynngalas Bay. There was nothing he couldn't see.

The vision became even more focused, and Aldric heard the voice calling his name again. It was faint, but he listened intently, and he recognised the voice. It was Bahir, calling him, telling him to get up. Abruptly Aldric was back in the arena, staring at his body lying in the dirt. Aldric pleaded with the voice. *I can't,* he said, his own voice muffled inside his helmet.

You can. You must, Bahir said, his voice strange and distant, like a voice from a dream.

Aldric coughed and tried to sit up. *I can't!* he said again. His muscles refused to obey.

You are Aldric, Bahir replied. *You are eternal. There is nothing but you, and you, and you, and you. Forever. This moment is you, and there is nothing else.*

There is nothing else, he repeated to himself. *I am eternal.* Aldric tried to roll over but his body simply would not respond. He groaned in anger and frustration.

Darkness began to grow once more, and he felt his vision fading. He began to settle into his body again, inside his helmet, surrounded by blackness, lost in a haze of pain and confusion. He screamed in protest, but there was nothing he could do.

He heard a new voice then, speaking to him softly, soothing, as from a long forgotten memory. It was the Gaiban's voice. *Only when you are lost, can you begin to understand your heart.*

At these words Aldric's pain began to fade, calmness coming over him. The blackness of his helmet fell away like a curtain, and he was suddenly there above his body once more, the torment of his muscles vanishing. He felt clear and empty and bright, the pain receding away and becoming a distant noise that he could barely hear. It was all the lessons of the Valorí coalesced into this moment, all the years of training and practise forging his mind and body into a weapon with a single purpose: to defeat this Draugor before him.

Aldric got to his feet, and looking down he pulled the tattered remains of his surcoat aside. Rather, he *saw* himself looking down and tearing off his surcoat, as if he were watching someone else. But the colours were different; everything was brighter, clearer, more radiant. His body glowed like a prism in the sun. He watched himself turn around to face the Draugor. An aura enveloped the Draugor as well. Yet instead of the white prism shimmering around Aldric, red and orange flames leapt above the Draugor, as though he were on fire.

The Draugor stopped when he saw Aldric standing, and if Aldric could have seen his expression beneath his helmet, he was sure it would have been one of dismay. The Draugor raised his *tamka,* lunging forward, striking at Aldric's face. Aldric leaned away from the attack, jumping to the side. He ran over to his scimitar and picked it up, turning to face the Draugor who was charging after him.

The Draugor raised his arm and swung downwards in a blow that would have crushed steel. Aldric darted away and the blow fell harmlessly into the dirt, though Aldric could feel the force of the impact through the ground. He watched himself from a few feet away, dodging and parrying and striking at the Draugor. He could see everything, every movement the Draugor made— the very instant the Draugor's muscles moved Aldric could see it and he moved to counter them. It was fighting like he had never known, he felt weightless, as if he were in a dream, and he struck at the Draugor and cut him between his segmented plates until his blood ran in streams over his crimson armour.

Rounding in anger, the Draugor put all his weight into a lunge and dove towards Aldric, furiously swinging his *tamka* towards Aldric's helmet. Sword still in hand, Aldric hopped away and kicked out with his right leg, sweeping the Draugor off his feet. As the Draugor fell, Aldric reached out and caught his leg. He gripped the Draugor's calf tightly, squeezing his ankle up under his armpit, dropping to the ground with him. As they landed Aldric wrenched the Draugor's leg upward with all his strength, locking his leg over the man's armoured groin for leverage. As the ligaments popped and tore, Aldric could feel the man's kneecap explode inside his leg. Despite his helmet, Aldric heard the Draugor scream. He *saw* the Draugor scream.

Without hesitating Aldric bounded up and grasped his scimitar, landing on the Draugor's chest. Aldric seized his shoulder, and raising his arm high above his head, he brought the pommel of his scimitar smashing downward as hard as he could squarely into the Dhemorahn's visored faceplate. The helmet crunched loudly as the faceplate cracked beneath the blow. Aldric released his shoulder and the Draugor fell back into the dust. Aldric watched, fascinated, as the flaming aura around the Draugor flickered, changing from red to yellow to white to green, then fading back to a dim red, as the embers of a dying fire.

Kneeling on top of him, Aldric pressed the blade of his scimitar against the man's throat. The Draugor lifted his arm and clutched at Aldric's wrist, but Aldric brushed it off. He suddenly became aware of the crowd roaring all around him. It sounded like the crashing of waves in the ocean. Black shards of the Dhemorahn's broken visor fell away and Aldric glimpsed his face through the sliver in the helmet. Blood ran down the man's broken nose and across his lean face, and in the sunlight Aldric saw his eyes blinking away the blood. They were black.

TWENTY ONE

ALDON COURT

Aldric was barely aware as a score of lictors escorted him from the arena. His strength was gone, exhaustion flooding through him. He gazed back at the vanquished Draugor, his crimson armour broken and surcoat smeared with dirt. Bahir congratulated him, though Aldric couldn't remember what he said. His head swam as he tried to focus on what was happening around him.

As he was carried from the ring, his vision faded once again and he was left blind inside his helmet. Helping arms lifted him up, leading him away from the field. He collapsed when his lictors released him, and when his page removed his armour and unwound his *kilpi* there were gasps from those around him. His chest was a patchwork of bruises, his back and arms faring no better. Aldric's armour had protected him from the worst of the Draugor's *tamka,* but the tremendous blows had taken their toll.

Bahir walked beside Aldric, following a team of royal physicians to the medical bay beneath the Coliseum. Aldric's nose was tender, and there was a deep cut above his right eye that fascia stimulators only partially healed. He held his mouth open as medics applied a biotorch to his swollen tongue, mending the severed tissue. Subdermal rejuvenators repaired much of the bruising, but his body ached, and he was weak and exhausted and nauseated and ravenously hungry, hungrier than he'd ever been in his entire life.

When his superficial wounds had been seen to, medics helped Aldric into a stainless steel Ohm Chamber. He fell onto a cushioned bench, too weak to even sit up as the heavy door was sealed behind him. Aldric felt the machine hum to life, dim blue lights glowing overhead. Warmth filled his limbs as his battered body was saturated with biogenic radiation. An Ohm Chamber was similar to a biotorch, but on a much larger scale, promoting rapid tissue and cellular regeneration.

The Chamber worked by inducing accelerated endogenesis, encouraging the natural healing response at hundreds of times the normal level. The body could begin to repair serious injuries in minutes and hours, rather than days, weeks, or months. There were no more than two dozen such chambers in the entire empire, incredible cost and upkeep prohibiting their widespread use. Normally he wouldn't use an Ohm Chamber, feeling it cheapened the experience of what he had earned through his struggle. But with the gala tonight at Aldon Court he didn't have the time to wait for his body to heal on its own. He tried to breathe deeply but he caught his breath short, wincing at his bruised ribs.

What happened in the arena? Aldric wondered, closing his eyes. He wanted to tell Bahir about his vision, but he couldn't yet, he still didn't understand it himself. He'd never experienced anything like that before. Was it *aina*? Could it really be? It couldn't, he thought, but he didn't know how else to explain it. He didn't have *aina*, he simply didn't. What would Bahir say? What would his father say? The Gaiban would know what to say.

He wondered if this was how others perceived *aina*, if this was something the Gaiban and Bahir and his father's Augures and others could simply turn on and off at will. He tried to see himself again as he had in the arena, but nothing happened. He focused and cleared his mind, straining to find that colourful vision that so miraculously transported him outside his body. It was no use. All he saw was the darkness behind his eyelids.

It had been such a release, weightlessness and absolute freedom. He couldn't imagine having that ability whenever he wanted it, just being able to fly up and out of his body in an instant. And the colours! He'd never seen colours like that before, everything glowing and shimmering with a rainbow-like aura. He wondered what it meant. Maybe that was the *alu* that Bahir had always told him about, the spirit energy that surrounded the body. What did the colours mean? Why had his been glowing like a prism?

So many questions. He wanted answers now, but he didn't even know how to ask the questions, the experience was so far beyond anything he could relate to or understand. How could he explain what it had felt like? *Like being limitless,* he thought. What had Gaiban Morrigan called it? 'The sight of the gods.' Yes, that was it. He'd felt like a god, looking down on the world as he floated above it.

There were other questions too. How had his visor failed? That should have been impossible. It was impossible. Valorí féthabban armour never failed. As far as he knew, it had never happened before. He remembered watching the treads of a light armour culverin roll over a close-helm at a demonstration, and when he'd picked it up, the visor still worked. They were damned near indestructible. *Sabotage?* Would the Mal have sent an agent to damage his visor? That was the only possible answer. He tried to remember. Who had handed him the helmet? His steward. He knew the man, he was totally loyal. Who had handed it to his steward? Questions rattled through his mind until he drifted off to sleep, the chamber humming peacefully around him.

When he awoke two hours later, the pain in his chest was gone and his head no longer ached. He looked down at the faded bruises on his bare chest, still tender to the touch. He lifted a hand to his face, feeling how the cuts had healed. His nose was still sore, but nothing compared to before. His tongue felt a bit swollen as well, though he could talk now and there was no pain. His body tingled as he stepped out of the chamber, similar to when an arm or leg fell asleep, but he knew this would pass. It felt like that every time he used the Ohm Chamber.

After some final examinations by the royal physicians, he received nutritional supplements specifically to help his body recover, dressed, and joined his father and brother back in their private booth. The games were still in progress, though the afternoon sun was dipping low over the Coliseum. Arem saw Aldric first, and a look of surprise passed over his face before he managed to smile.

"The triumphant hero," Arem said.

Leopold turned to look at Aldric over his shoulder, a smile breaking out over his face. He stood and embraced Aldric, kissing him on his cheeks. "The hero of the Fatherland!" he said, beaming. "This is a day that will never be forgotten."

"I don't suppose so," Aldric replied, not sure how he should feel.

"What happened out there?" Bruce Ramsay asked, coming over to inspect him. The Grand Marshal was also personal chief of the emperor's household security, and he was very aware that something had gone wrong in the arena.

Aldric hadn't mentioned his visor's failure to anyone yet, and so he didn't know how to simply explain what had happened. "My visor was damaged, and," he began.

"Damaged?" Bruce said, interrupting.

"When I was hit with the *tamka* my display went out."

Bahir shook his head. "Your suit was fashioned by the Valorí, féthabban armour does not malfunction," he said.

"The Mal," Bruce growled. "I didn't think he would stoop to sabotage."

"I want a full investigation," the emperor said. "Bring me that helmet, I want to see it for myself. And round up Aldric's retinue, I want every page and steward interrogated."

Bruce nodded. "At once." He turned a quizzical look on Aldric. "If your visor went out, how did you...?"

"He could *see*," Bahir answered for him. There was something in the little man's face that gave Aldric pause.

"What does he mean?" Bruce asked, looking from Bahir to Aldric.

"He's right," Aldric said, not knowing how the words would come out. "It just happened. My visor was black, and then all of a sudden, I could see again."

"You mean your display switched back on?" Bruce said, unsure.

Aldric shook his head, but before he could speak, Lord Robert Young, who'd been listening, spoke up. *"Aina,"* he said, wonderment in his thickly accented voice. "Heavens to halberds, the lad found his *aina!*" Everyone stared at Lord Robert.

"Is that true?" Bruce said, turning back to Aldric.

Aldric could think of nothing to say, so he simply nodded. "Yes."

"But you don't have *aina,*" Arem said from across the room.

"I don't think I do," Aldric confessed. "It just came on suddenly, and then vanished. I haven't been able to do it since."

"That doesn't matter," Leopold said, grasping his son's shoulder. "You were gifted with far-sight when you needed it most. The gods favoured you, and you carried the day."

Aldric didn't know how to respond to that. "I think I just got hit on the head a little too hard," he said, trying to smile.

"A gift from the gods," Bahir intoned, reverence in his voice.

"Oh, sure, that Draugor whacks your head and it's a blessing from heaven, but when I do it you just piss and moan," Iain said.

Aldric touched his finger to his temple and closed his eyes. "I see... I see Arianne, walking in a park—"

"You do?" Iain asked, suddenly serious.

"Yes, she's quite lovely. But wait—who's that tall, blond man she's holding hands with?"

Iain sat back, chuckling. "You had me going there, but Arianne fancies her men short and dark."

"Who prefers swarthy little midgets?" Aldric laughed.

Bruce Ramsay shrugged. "There's a fetish for everything."

"How's your wife anyways?" Iain asked.

"I will feed you to degoll," Bruce said.

"Honestly why do you keep him around?" Lord Robert asked, shaking his head.

Aldric raised his hands helplessly. "You know how sometimes you take in stray dogs off the street, just to feel better about yourself?"

"No," Bruce said.

"Oh aye, treats me like a mutt too he does," Iain said, elbowing Aldric. "Always kicking me about."

"Let me tell you what I would do to you," Bruce started.

"Are you asking me if I have plans tonight? Cause I'd hate to cancel on your wife again," Iain said.

"Can't we have his assets seized?" Lord Robert asked, smirking.

"I'll tell you who knows a thing or two about seizing assets," Iain began. "Bruce's wi—"

"Enough," Leopold said, waving his hand. He straightened his achkan and returned to his dais.

"My Liege," Bruce Ramsay bowed towards the emperor. "I have suspects to interrogate, I'll inform you if I make any progress," he said, striding from the room without a second glance at Iain.

"You have unlocked your far-sight, my Prince," Bahir said, putting his hand on Aldric's arm. He had changed out of his armour and now wore loose white breeches and a short, ceremonial robe of the Asaani that came just short of his knees and resembled the royal achkan.

"Not yet," Aldric said. "I really don't know what happened, or why; I don't know how to explain what I saw."

"You shared the vision of the gods," Bahir said. "Your entered a place of *no thing*, your mind was empty."

"I felt like I was dead," Aldric replied.

"Precisely, your mind was finally free, free to see without seeing. We must be driven further than we believe we are capable, driven by desperation sometimes, before we understand *this*," Bahir said, tapping the middle of Aldric's forehead. "It is always thus."

"Well I hope I can learn to use *aina* without the help of a Draugor."

"He really was kicking your arse," Iain offered helpfully.

"Is that what *aina* is like, Bahir?" Aldric asked, ignoring Iain. "Can I leave my body and experience far-sight whenever I wish?"

Bahir frowned. "It is different for everyone. For some, yes, we may travel with the gods at will, and see what we wish to see. Some may see very far, some only a little ways. Some may only see what the gods choose to show them, and may not travel where they please."

"I could see everywhere," Aldric said.

"Your *aina* is very strong," Bahir replied. "But you are chosen by the gods. You are the descendant of Aronach, of the Fael Danar, and your strength is bound by the will of the Ainír."

Aldric sat, reflecting on this. His *aina*, the Dhemorgal, his sabotaged helmet, the Seven Regrets of the World... He watched the swirling commotion around him without feeling like a part of it. Why did he have *aina*, but Arem didn't? Well, he hadn't always, he thought. He still didn't, not really.

He heard voices and drifted back into the conversation. "That's just like him," Lord Young was saying, snorting.

"What's just like who?" Aldric asked.

"The Mal, leaving without congratulating you on your victory," Lord Robert said.

"Did you really expect the Mal to come up here and the two of them would shake hands?" Iain asked.

"I suppose not," Lord Robert agreed. "I know you had your own personal reasons for going out there this afternoon," he said, looking at Aldric. "But you gave the Mal quite a black eye today, and I take that as a personal kindness."

"I've never seen the Mal in such a fit," Iain said, moving to sit beside Aldric as they watched the last of the games.

"You saw him?" Aldric asked, somewhat surprised.

Iain nodded. "As I came in, he was leaving with his cronies, a bunch of those Draugor shoving the crowd out of his way. I think you may have upset the man," Iain said, plucking an apple from a platter as a lictor walked by. He took a bite.

"I'd be disappointed if I hadn't," Aldric replied.

Iain wiped some juice from his mouth with the back of his sleeve. "That's all well and good," he said, wagging his finger at Aldric, the apple still in his hand. "But I might not sleep as well knowing the Mal had it out for me."

"The measure of a man may be taken by his enemies," Bahir said. "If Prince Aldric can count Mal'Dreghen among his enemies, he is quite a man indeed."

Aldric cast a sidelong glance towards Iain, raising his eyebrows. "Well there you have it," he said.

"Yeah, take advice from him why don't you, the very model of sociability," Iain scoffed. "Bahir wakes up scowling; he'd stab you as soon as shake your hand, you want to listen to him?" He took another bite. "You know what your problem is? You Asaani types are all so damned stoic. What's the matter with having a little fun now and then, eh? Arem's got the right idea," he said. "Isn't that right, Arem?"

"Leave me out of it," Arem said from his dais without looking over.

"I mean you won," Iain continued, ignoring Arem. "Would it kill him to smile?"

"He just saves all his love for you," Aldric said.

"What'd I ever do?" Iain asked.

"You're an arseling," Lord Robert said.

Aldric laughed. "Bahir's only happy when he's pinning someone to the ground."

"Sounds like me," Iain said, winking.

Bahir folded his arms, turning his back to Iain.

"See?" Iain said.

"You should try *craidath* sometime," Lord Robert said. "Might finally make a man of you."

Iain rolled his eyes. "Tell me how tossing about with a bunch of sweaty blokes will make me more of a man?" He turned to Lord Robert. "Now, if we threw in Lady Young—" Iain began, and then suddenly yelped. The blade of a black throwing knife protruded from the apple he was holding in his hand. He stared at the blade, then looked wide eyed at Lord Robert, who leaned back in his seat, smiling.

"Mind the apples boy," Lord Robert said. "They're pointy."

Iain swallowed, then flipped the apple around and held it by the knife, taking another bite. "Thanks!" he said. Aldric hadn't even seen Lord Robert's hand move. He made a mental note to never insult the Captain of the Housecarl.

"I'll be glad when the day's over anyways," Aldric said, breaking the silence. "I could sleep for a week."

"You bested a Draugor twice your size and had your first vision of *aina*, in one day," Lord Robert said. "And humiliated Mal'Dreghen to boot. I'd say you're entitled to sleep the rest of the month."

As the sun crept behind the Coliseum and the flapping banners dipped into twilight, the final games came to a close. The seven storey auranc vibrated through the arena once again, signalling the end of the day. The crowds poured into the darkening streets, costumed dancers twirling through the gloaming. Young and old alike danced and sang together beneath blazing braziers, clouds of incense billowing through the warm summer air. Sylphic, painted girls cast wild shadows as they danced in the torchlight, and strange music from distant lands filled the air. Somewhere over the lawns drifted the sad sound of Elcaern mouth music, and Aldric stopped to listen for a moment before climbing into the waiting carriage with his father and brother.

Aldon Court was several blocks away, and the crowds were thick in the streets. Aldric smiled, seeing all the people and the lights and colours and music. As the carriage drove through the darkened park, people were throwing handfuls of fennywisp into the air—colourful, phosphorescent powder that flickered and glowed in the dark. Glowing clouds of pink and blue and green and yellow floated through the trees, lingering on the branches, fading as they fell. He glanced towards Arem who sat in a shadowed corner of the carriage, hiding in the plush cushions and gazing out the window distantly. Leopold had logged into the royal comnet and was reviewing Bruce Ramsay's security report on the investigations. One of Aldric's pages had vanished after the fight in the Coliseum, and Bruce's men were tracking him down.

The netspan was buzzing with news about the day, particularly the self-immolation of Elder Khestor. The feeds were heavily monitored by the Circle of Amren and other Imperial agencies, so spurious rumours were kept to a minimum. So far no one had claimed any inside knowledge into the Elder's death, with protestors and Asaani mostly expressing sympathy for his passing. A few extremist Dhemorahn groups announced there'd be more such burnings in the days to come, and Aldric laughed to himself as he imagined the looks on their faces when Imperial agents showed up at their doors later tonight.

The sky was a deep blue scattered with stars by the time the cortege arrived at Aldon Court. A great throng of onlookers were gathered, and a cry went out as Leopold descended from the carriage. He gripped his ceremonial sabre with one hand, waving to the crowd. Rows of white plumed Landser stood to attention in their obsidian armour, sabre-rifles held across their chests. They flanked either side of a carpet of purple kormorah, holding back thousands of people clamouring to see past them. The emperor and his sons made their way down the wide avenue and through the massive plaza of encircling colonnades, Arem and Leopold basking in the adoration of the crowd. Aldric felt yet again more like a celebrity than a statesman.

Lords of the Erolan flocked to greet them as they entered Aldon Court. Aldric was suddenly overwhelmed by courtiers eager to congratulate him on his victory, while Arem separated, laughing and conversing with the lords and ladies and doing his best, Aldric thought, to pretend he didn't have a brother. When Aldric's hand and arm were numb from being shaken and squeezed, they finally moved into the rotunda gallery where waiting servants presented drinks on silver trays. Supported by statues of kneeling giants of red granite, the rotunda stretched a hundred and fifty metres to a glass domed roof and was hung with yellow tapestries from the Eldris Fane.

Aldric escaped the coterie of nobles to a quiet balcony where he could observe in peace. The aristocracy swarmed below him—the most powerful people of the empire, gathered in one place, Aldric thought. A gong was finally sounded and the assembly made their way into the great hall. A high ceiling was braced by carved pillars, and long windows of stained glass were illuminated from the outside. Long tables were arranged around the outside of the room, and in the centre a great fire was burning in a wide stone hearth. The emperor entered first, followed by Aldric and then Arem. They took their seats at three high backed thrones at the far end of the hall.

Once they were seated, a herald announced the arrival of the other guests. He called out in a clear voice, loud enough for all to hear, "His Grace, the Duke Bannan of Chaldrea!" A tall, regal looking man in his sixties stepped forward, a small band of gold worn above his fading yellow hair. He wore a long coat of muted gold and blue, with fur tufted sleeves and a silver brocade around his chest. He was a large man, and even hidden under his cloaks, it was clear he was still a warrior.

Many other dukes and nobles were called, and so they came: from Arangath, Durengol, Aryngia and Orath Rund, from Tara, Brythanor, Thedarras and Erethya, and from the far western province Ruador and south to Ewerdon and to the eastern Isles of Thallas, Wysst and Wyth and Sundon and from the far north in Dyffendell and Droos Agan and the icy climes of Thrym, all the great lords and ladies presented themselves in their finest raiment.

When the last was announced, a hundred waiting servants brought in steaming trays of food. The male servants wore bright sarongs and collars of interlacing gold and gems above their bare chests, while the women wore flowing shalwars that tapered narrowly at the ankle, and saris of colourful silk that Aldric found pleasantly transparent.

Acrobats from across the Brythic Sea in Cymbryth were performing on a stage in the centre of the hall, followed by a troop of gypsies from the Välborg forest leading a tame wargren onto the stage. The wargren padded through the crowd without making a noise, four hundred kilograms of giant cat on muscled legs with claws longer than Aldric's dirk. It swished its striped tail, scanning the great hall with luminous green eyes and sniffing at the myriad of foods being passed around. The Landser nearest the stage stepped back as the wargren yawned, revealing rows of glistening fangs. Aldric chuckled, thinking on how men would rush into battle against sabre-rifles that would disintegrate flesh in seconds, yet they were terrified of a simple beast. *A lesson to remember someday*, he thought.

A gaily dressed man bowed to the emperor and began strumming a bocalyn as black haired dancers from Nuorri moved around the fire pit. Long skirts swished about their feet and tinkling jewellery glittered over snow white skin flowing with tattoos. A drummer began and the dancers lifted their arms and twirled, dipping low and sweeping the floor with their hands. A sensual poetry coursed through every movement, lean muscles igniting in the firelight. As the drummer crescendoed, the dancers swirled around and fell to the floor, leaning backwards with arms outstretched like a flower unfurling.

Aldric glanced down the long table. The Archduchess Eleanor Sinclair sat two seats away, and the Lady Evaine sat beside her. The Royal Hagiographer Cyrus Nephellus sat nearby as usual, his hawk-like gaze observing and recording every detail of the evening. Aldric didn't trust the man, but he did respect his formidable memory. In fact that was probably why he didn't trust him, he thought. Normally the Archduke Raynard would have been beside the emperor, but he was gathering the armada for battle. A noble man, the archduke, Aldric thought. He wondered what Raynard would find when he reached Drusus. He wished he were there with him on the bridge of the *Eidolon* right now, instead of here at this banquet.

Trays of roasted game, braised uroch flanks, scallops and seared fish and buttered crabs and fruit platters were set before them. Stuffed caebryn, arranged with their wing muscles outstretched, were set upon the table. Their long head feathers were left untouched, giving them the queer look of being half alive. Courses of eel and giant muscles pulled from Gwynngalas Bay that morning were presented in trays of ice, and hoji eggs—considered a rare delicacy—were offered hardboiled in sterling stemmed glasses. There were even jars of Skogmarra honey, famous for its rich, buttery sweet flavour. Wines from the vineyards of Lotharraine were served in silver chalices, with stronger spirits and intoxicants for those of sterner constitutions. The assortment of food was overwhelming, a hundred savoury aromas blending together and filling the hall with the smell of cooked meat and sautéed vegetables and freshly baked sweet bread. Yet Aldric found his appetite somewhat dulled after the nutrient supplements he'd taken earlier. He'd only had a couple to dull the ravenous hunger he'd felt after his fight, but it left him feeling full even hours afterward. Now the bewildering array of food didn't stir his hunger and he only picked at his plate, feeling disappointed. Peering down the table he saw that the Lady Evaine didn't appear to have much appetite either, nibbling at her food with disinterest. She must have been accustomed to large feasts. It would probably take a lot to impress her, he thought.

As a group of performers vaulted across the floor, Leopold leaned close to speak to Aldric. "What a glorious day," he said, surveying the hall.

"Is it?" Aldric asked, not sharing his father's obvious enthusiasm. "Many good men died today. They may have died for the applause of cheering crowds, but the crowds have gone home, and the men are still dead. Who will remember them?"

"It is our custom," Leopold said. "They went willingly, no one drove them into the Coliseum."

"Of course they were driven," Aldric said. "You and Mal'Dreghen sent them there."

Leopold flashed Aldric a dangerous look. "Do not compare me to Mal'Dreghen," he said.

"Then be better than him," Aldric replied.

Leopold sat back in his throne, a sullen look falling over his handsome features. "Nothing will diminish our triumph today," he said.

"Not even the death of an Asaani Elder?"

"His memory will fade. Your victory, however, will not. Mal'Dreghen won't soon forget this day."

"Khestor's death wasn't just inconvenient," Aldric said, galled. "He was a figurehead for the Asaani."

Leopold frowned. "And what if he was? The Dhemorgal is over, Khestor sacrificed himself for nothing."

"You can't believe that."

"You think he didn't? What did he die for?" Leopold asked. "The games went as planned, there were no threats, no accidents, and we're here celebrating your victory. The day is ours."

"The day belongs to Khestor, to all the Asaani—to your own Valorí, who you seem to have forgotten about. It doesn't matter that I won," Aldric said, believing it for the first time. "This whole day was about Mal'Dreghen and his spectacle, and you've gone along with all of it. You think this party of yours makes the day any less of an insult to the Asaani?"

"This is a glorious night, for you, and for the empire!" Leopold insisted. "We have beaten Mal'Dreghen at his own game, and if I'm feeling indulgent, who's the worse for it?"

"Indulgent? Father you're a libertine."

Leopold laughed, swirling his goblet of wine. "And if I am? The people don't care. They are libertines too! In fact, the people love a leader who shares their vices: it makes them feel safer, less worried about their own hedonism. They only care that their needs are met, that they have enough distractions: food and wine, good entertainment and warm beds at night with warm women. Monotony—that is the true danger. Keep them entertained, self-serving, and corrupt."

"If both you and the people are corrupt, then does it even matter who sits on the throne? Anyone could be emperor, there is no moral authority." Aldric said.

Leopold sat back in his throne, sipping from his silver chalice. "Am I not emperor because they cannot be? I pose as their servant, and so I become their master."

"You would sacrifice your son, your empire, for your own glory?"

"I sacrifice nothing!" Leopold hissed, anger flaring in his blue eyes. "The people must be ruled, must be led! Mal'Dreghen thought he would best me today, but I've shown him the House of Danarean is not so easily beaten—that it is *I* who rule the empire, and not him. That it is *I* who sit in this throne, and not him. That it is *I* who command the people, and not *him*!"

Aldric stared at his father. He suddenly looked small and powerless. Aldric couldn't help but feel pity for him. "He has led you here by your nose father, every step of the way," Aldric said. "This whole day, the Dhemorgal? This was his idea! And the people celebrate his generosity, not yours. Nothing can change that."

"No!" shouted Leopold. Those nearest the emperor paused to glance at him, and he quickly composed himself. "No," he said again. "No. He is beaten, and this is only the beginning. I will ride him down until he is nothing and there is no place left for him to spew his poison. And you will be there with me," Leopold said, putting his hand over Aldric's. "We will drive him out together, and show the people that there is no power that can contend with that of the Imperial Throne."

Aldric could find nothing to say. He nodded, withdrawing his hand. Chiron was right. Pity the ruler who sees nothing but blood and religion.

An ensemble of the finest musicians in Thedarras began tuning and arranging their instruments, discordant melodies ringing through the hall as they tuned their strings. The floor was cleared and an open area was made ready for dancing as the lords and ladies of the empire discussed their favourite tournaments of the day and the politics and affairs of their provinces. Aldric watched them strut about the room, the ladies parading their dresses before one another and the gentlemen flashing their medals.

Iain made his way over to Aldric.

"Quite a ball," Iain said cheerfully.

Aldric nodded. "Are you dancing with Arianne?"

"Of course! I asked her earlier and she said she couldn't think of anyone she'd rather dance with." He slapped Aldric's arm. "Can you believe it?"

"Not an imaginative girl, is she?" Aldric said. "Better keep her."

Iain laughed. "You excited for your turn on the floor with the lovely Lady Evaine?"

"Shut up," Aldric grumbled.

"That's the spirit!" Iain said happily. "Smile just like that, you'll melt her little heart."

Aldric glanced over to see Evaine speaking with her mother. When the dancing began, he would be expected to open the floor with Evaine. As the Crown Prince, Aldric was the most eligible suitor in the empire, while the Lady Evaine was the most eligible of the Erolan, and the two of them would have to put on good show together. He knew that for many of the noble houses he and Evaine would be a natural pairing, though he also knew they all secretly hoped he would choose their own daughters instead.

Aldric wasn't particularly interested in the ambitions of other houses, and he was loath to perform for anyone, especially with the Lady Evaine. He'd been fortunate in years past, she didn't usually attend these galas, and the last time he'd danced with her was when all the trouble had started between them. Now he must dance with her again, alone on the floor, in front of nearly every member of the Erolan. *Black gods of the Waste,* he thought.

Once Iain had put that thought into his mind, Aldric could think of nothing else. A knot wormed its way into his stomach, one he hadn't even felt earlier today when he was locked in combat with the fearsome Draugor. He chided himself for reacting to this little wisp of a girl, but he couldn't make his apprehension any less bearable. In fifteen minutes the musicians had finished setting up and the floor was his.

He was announced by the herald, along with Evaine, and the music began. A score of arbas whispered sweetly as Aldric descended the stairs to the gleaming wood of the dance floor. He glanced briefly at his father, who returned an imperious gaze. Across the hall he spied Evaine also making her way to the floor. It might have made it less awkward to speak with her before this moment, but he'd decided it would be best to just get it over with. She appraised him icily as they met in the middle of the dance floor.

She wore a long silk gown of violet under a pale green sari that was fastened above her breast by an ornamental silver clasp depicting her coat of arms. A collar of interweaving silver strands criss-crossed her slender neck and in the centre a large green emerald was set. Where each strand met a tiny diamond was affixed, so that she glittered at every movement. Her hair was worn up, exposing elegant collarbones, her golden braids held in place by a carcanet of silver studded with pearls. Had Aldric not known her for the spoiled duchess she was, he might have said she was beautiful.

Aldric decided he'd do his best to put her off balance, and so he smiled warmly. "It's lovely to see you, my Lady," he said, taking her hand and bowing.

She inclined her head ever so slightly and curtsied. "Is it?" she asked. She had a graceful figure, skin the colour of cream, and soft red lips that were full and alluring. However there was no forgiveness in her green eyes as they stared into his. He wondered if she thought the same of him.

"It has been far too many years."

"They were not short enough for you?" Her soft voice cut like steel. *She isn't making this any easier,* he thought.

They began to dance, Aldric holding her left hand in his right, walking side by side towards the high table where his father and her mother were seated. They spoke quietly, concealing their candour.

"Six years is a long time," Aldric continued.

"How it flies."

They reached the end of the floor and bowed together before the emperor. Leopold nodded his approval and they turned, switching hands. When they reached the centre of the floor they faced each other and Aldric pulled her close, placing his hand just below her neck and holding her right hand lightly in his left. They began to dance in a large, slow circle as the musicians played a sweeping melody from the classical era of Thedarras.

"You're even more beautiful since we last met," Aldric said.

Evaine glanced at the faded cut above his eye and on his nose. "And you look as though you've been in the wars," she replied.

"I have."

"Playing with toy swords isn't a war," she said.

"They cut deep enough, but I don't need to tell you that."

"Meaning what?"

"Nothing, I'm sure you've seen much hardship, my Lady."

"It isn't my fault I was born an archduke's daughter," Evaine bristled. They spun around and Aldric held her waist firmly as he lowered her in one arm. He drew her up hard, pulling her into his chest. She met his eyes for a moment and quickly pushed away.

"Besides," she said, as they resumed their dancing. "What would the Crown Prince know of hardship?"

"Have you met my father?" Aldric asked.

"Have you met my mother?" Evaine replied.

"The archduchess is a great woman," Aldric said, dropping her hand and putting his arms around her hips as she leaned back. "My father cares only for titles."

"Yes," she said, leaning forward again. "Titles are handy for those who can't achieve anything on their own." The jewels at her neck sparkled as they turned.

"You're right," Aldric said, deciding he'd had enough. "We ought to ask the survivors of the *Malefactor* what title would be more appropriate for me." Evaine looked away, unable to meet his gaze. Aldric felt very pleased with himself then, for once Evaine didn't know what to say.

Before she could think of a response, the floor was opened and the lords and ladies of the realm joined them as the music became livelier. Aldric saw Iain leading Arianne onto the floor, his face bright and happy as he held her hand. Arianne was a lovely girl, Aldric thought, her long hair dark and wavy, a close-fitting green dress worn tightly around her enticing figure. Arianne smiled up at Iain as they began dancing, and as Aldric turned back to Evaine, he thought not for the first time that Iain was a lucky man. Iain was smiling just as happily at Arianne, and together they seemed the perfect pair.

Iain made his way with Arianne over to Aldric. "Lady Sinclair," he said respectfully. "You have my sincerest condolences."

Evaine gave him a questioning look. "I beg your pardon, Lord Baird?"

"Oh, a lovely lady such as yourself, that you should be made to dance with the likes of him?" Iain said, nodding to Aldric.

"Thank you, Lord Baird, but a lady learns to endure such things." She turned back to Aldric. "One learns much of a man from his friends."

"You could endure them quietly," Aldric muttered under his breath. Evaine shot him a questioning look, her eyes narrowed.

"It's wonderful to see you again, Lady Amond." Aldric continued, ignoring her.

Arianne bowed her head. "Your Highness," she said, smiling prettily.

"And dear Aldric!" Iain exclaimed. "Why you almost looked like a prince for a moment!"

"You're young and beautiful," Aldric said to Arianne. "You really don't have to settle."

"I wouldn't settle for anything less," Arianne said, looking up at Iain and beaming.

"You couldn't if you tried," Aldric replied, smiling. "Iain, hold on to this one."

"I intend to," he said. "And don't worry my Lord, we'll have you home in time to kiss Dravon goodnight."

Aldric returned his attention to Evaine, who was staring off over his shoulder somewhere. If only he could have what Iain had. But did he really want that? He looked down at Evaine. She was beautiful, he couldn't deny it. She turned and caught him looking at her, and behind her icy gaze, just for a moment, he thought he saw something in her eyes. What was it? Anger? Curiosity? Desire, maybe?

He realised she wasn't as invulnerable as she tried to appear. There was uncertainty in her eyes. Why did she have to be so stubborn? She looked away, and that haughty demeanour of hers fell into place once more. *Still...* He studied her, trying to see her for who she really was. There was something enticing in her refusal, something charming in her pride. He realised suddenly that he admired her. He still couldn't stand her, but he admired her strength. What a strange creature, he thought to himself. So beautiful, and so cold.

At that moment the heavy wooden doors at the back of the hall were thrown open and a tumult of voices jarred through the room. Aldric couldn't see what was happening through the crowd of people, but he heard shouting and one woman cry out in surprise. Five Valorí sprang from sight unseen and surrounded Aldric in an instant, and he noted at least a dozen more were now stationed around the emperor's table. The Landser who had been standing at the corners of the room took up formation in front of Aldric and the people who had been dancing were now scattering to the sides.

It had all happened in a matter of seconds, so quickly Aldric had to look around to make sure he wasn't imaging it. One moment the dance floor had been full of happy couples, the next it was bristling with soldiers. He pulled Evaine in protectively as he tried to see what was happening. The crowd in front of Aldric parted and a score of Draugor in scarlet armour pushed their way through, stopping before the Landser. Black armour squared off against red armour. The Landser levelled their sabre-rifles and probably would have fired if the emperor hadn't called out at that precise moment.

"Stop!" Leopold shouted, his voice echoing off the walls. No one moved. "What is the meaning of this?"

Silence filled the hall, and the Draugor abruptly stepped aside. Mal'Dreghen stood before them, a black robe clinging to his wiry frame, his gaunt face proud and dark beneath his coal black hair. The Mal was only a few paces away from Aldric and he glared at him with his fierce yellow eyes. He smiled then suddenly, turning to the emperor.

"Good evening, Your Highness," he said graciously.

"Mal'Dreghen, what is this?" Leopold demanded.

"It seems you are celebrating, I didn't mean to cause a commotion."

"Then you should have left your henchmen at the door," Leopold said. The Landser kept their sabre-rifles trained on both the Draugor and Mal'Dreghen. The Draugor carried rifles of their own, but they wisely kept them lowered.

"My *henchmen?*" the Mal said, considering the word. "Yes I suppose they must seem so. But these are dark times, what are magnates to do without their *henchmen?*"

"You're no magnate, Mal," Aldric said.

The Mal turned a menacing glare to Aldric. "I will deal with you, prince," he said.

"Like you did today in the Coliseum? Deal with me now," Aldric replied, stepping between the Valori. "Come, let's be done with this."

The Mal laughed. "So eager! But your time will come soon enough," he said.

"Explain yourself, Mal," Leopold commanded.

The Mal turned back to the emperor, a surprised look on his face. He laid his hand over his chest in a mocking gesture. "Explain myself? Me?" He shook his head. "No," he said loudly. "It is *you* who must explain." He examined the crowd around him, then turned to Aldric again. "You all act as though you won a great victory today," he began. "The triumph of a prince over the people."

"Is that what this is Mal?" Aldric said. "Did you come here to protest your defeat?"

"I could not be defeated by the likes of you, princeling," the Mal sneered. Aldric was taken aback. The Mal had never dared openly insult him.

"You may have bloodied an emissary of the people," the Mal continued, "but you did not defeat him, nor did you win yourself any eternal glory by your so-called victory."

"Are you claiming I didn't win? Bring your man back here and I'll break his other leg." Aldric said. "And this time, I'll do it blindfolded."

"No one is impressed with your little tricks, my Prince," Mal'Dreghen replied.

"Tricks? Even you must have been *surprised* when I got up after my helmet *malfunctioned,*" Aldric said.

"Did it?" Mal'Dreghen asked. "How fortunate you weren't injured."

"You were beaten, you think you can change that by coming here tonight with your cohorts?"

"You cannot *win* by defeating the people," Mal'Dreghen said angrily.

"You aren't the people, Mal—you're insane."

"Ha!" the Mal shouted. "And there you see," he said, waving his hand around the room. "The heretic admits it! He is not one of us, he is not of the people. He thinks he is above us!"

"Let me show you how far above you I am," Aldric said, taking another step forward.

"I needn't suffer the vanity of your threats, princeling. That one such as yourself even believes he is capable of speaking as you do proves how blasphemous this empire has become." He pointed at Aldric. "He wears a crown of lies and imagines he'll sit on his rotting throne one day and be a lord of nations. How could a free people be happy under such tyranny? You, who are gods unto yourselves! This heretic believes the gods have chosen him to lead you! But I tell you this," the Mal shouted. "There are no gods or princes or emperors, there is only man!" he said, pointing to the crowd. "Man is the only god, and he needs only his own strength to guide him. I tell you now, *there are no gods but man!*

"Look around you!" Mal'Dreghen waved to the rafters in the hall. "Gods did not build this—faith in the divine did not lay the mortar between these stones; man did! Men a thousand years ago built this hall that we stand in today—that is *true* immortality. Breathe the air that ripens under this eternal roof. This is the power of man, the power at your fingertips— the very signature of your forefathers, written in these stones. Deny this, and you deny your very soul! We have forgotten what it means to be men, and so we give honour today to mere pretenders.

"Maybe they *are* kings! But they are not the kings of *men*, for no man would suffer himself to be led like an animal. They are the kings of swine! This madman," the Mal said, looking at Aldric, "weaves sticks and grass into a crown, and he wears it proudly too, and sits on his throne of manure and declares himself your lord! And worse, he's made you all happy to share his little dream, to believe that the likes of him could ever be a king. His delusion consumes him, but not so you and I. Once awakened, we cannot believe his lie again. Men must lead themselves, and I would not deny you this." He turned his cold yellow eyes upon the emperor. "He would," he said, pointing with his long, bony finger. "If there are any among you who still call themselves men, let them leave now, for there will not be a second chance." With that he turned and the Draugor closed in behind him. The crowd parted and before anyone could think he had left the great hall.

Aldric was stunned. The Mal had given him the opening he needed. People began chattering all at once, voices filling the room. Looking around,

Aldric took stock of the situation. The Mal would have to expect reprisal, which would probably mean there'd be a good chance of people getting hurt. "Stay here," Aldric said to Evaine. "The Valorí will keep you and your mother safe."

"I don't need protecting," Evaine said angrily.

"I'm not asking you," Aldric said, gripping her shoulder. "I don't care what you think of me, I'm your prince, and you will remain here with the Valorí. Watch her," he said to the Valorí nearest him. Evaine looked like she was about to object, then shook her head in disgust. That was fine, Aldric thought, as long as she was out of the way. He thought of her giant father. Aldric didn't want to have to answer to him if something happened to her.

Pushing his way through the crowd, Aldric joined his father at the dais. "It is madness," Leopold said, his face flushed with rage.

"It's war," Aldric replied, scanning the room. The people were in an uproar, shouting amongst themselves and being herded by the Landser who were trying to restore order. "We have to go after him."

"Go after him?" Leopold said, incensed. "I want him flayed and quartered for treason! He will not live the night!"

"So do I, but he knew what you would do, he isn't foolish enough to sign his own death warrant. He must have had a plan when he came in here."

Leopold turned as Bruce Ramsay approached, breathless. "We've scanned the immediate vicinity, he's vanished," he said. "We're tracking the surveillance feeds, but he's not showing up."

"Are you saying you can't find him?" Leopold demanded. Aldric thought he might leap out of his chair and start looking himself.

"No, but it's hard with all the people rushing around. I've locked down the building, no one is getting out."

"I want him found, *now*." Leopold said. "Are you saying the palace security is blind?"

"It's not blind, but Mal'Dreghen just isn't there," Bruce replied. "I'm having my men go back over the footage, if we see how he came in it might help answer where he went."

"Could the feeds have been compromised somehow?" Aldric asked, afraid of the answer.

Bruce shook his head. "On a night like this we've taken every precaution, I've got trusted men in the control room. If surveillance was tampered with, it would either have to be from the outside-in, or we've got a bigger security problem than we thought."

"Maybe you'd better bring in some new men, just to be sure," Aldric said. "And keep an eye on the ones who are in there."

Bruce furrowed his brow. "Of course Sire," he said. Aldric could see he didn't like the suggestion either. "I have monitors on every person from here to the exits, there's no way we'll lose him. I've also set a contingent of the Landser outside guarding the perimeter and I've dispatched an attachment from the army to sweep the streets; the aerials were already on standby and they're scanning the streets quarter by quarter, just in case he managed to get outside the building already."

Before Leopold could respond an officer of the Landser in black armour rushed up and saluted. "Your Highness," he said. "We have Mal'Dreghen's men, we have his Draugor."

"And where is the Mal?" Leopold asked, fire in his eyes.

The officer hesitated. "The Mal wasn't with the Draugor, but Lord Young has ordered their interrogation. We'll know shortly," the officer said.

"I want to know now!" Leopold shouted.

"Have Lord Young put the palace guard on alert," Aldric said, looking at Bruce.

Bruce nodded. "The Housecarl is on full watch."

"Somehow I don't think the Draugor are going to tell us much," Aldric said. Bruce gave him a look that said he felt the same. "And what about the Gaiban?"

"I wouldn't worry about her, Sire," Bahir said, joining them. "She is safe."

"Where is the Archon? Find Radul Vilimar! I'll have his fat ass hanging from the rafters next to the Mal's," Leopold shouted. Aldric had never seen his father this angry, but he'd also never been publicly humiliated in his own palace.

Aldric looked around suddenly. "Where is Arem?" he asked.

Leopold shrugged. "Who gives a damn! I want that man brought before me on his knees!"

Aldric tried his comsig. Arem didn't answer. "Can you track his comsig, Bruce?"

"Give me a minute, I'll try," he said, tapping into the comnet. He looked up after a moment. "He's under the Circle's surveillance now, it shouldn't take long."

Aldric gazed about the room. He felt suddenly uneasy as he looked around; so many ranking members of the aristocracy in one place. He didn't like it. "I'm worried about all these people," he said to the Grand Marshal.

"I agree," Bruce said, nodding. "The Erolan must be kept safe. I have Landser at every door, but if you could try to keep the Valorí in this room it would go a long ways to setting my mind at ease," he said, looking at Bahir.

"The Valorí will not leave the emperor's side," Bahir replied. "And what of the Old Guard here tonight?"

Leopold scoffed. "They can take care of themselves, and so much the better if they don't."

"Even with the added protection, I want you to start getting these people out of here Bruce," Aldric said. "Take them out the side entrance and have transports waiting for them." He nodded towards the Archduchess Eleanor and the Lady Evaine. "And make sure they get to safety," he said. The archduchess had moved to stand beside the Grand Marshal, listening to them speak.

At this last she started. "I will not leave," she said.

"Archduchess Sinclair, it isn't safe here," Aldric replied.

"With respect, my Prince, this is probably one of the most heavily guarded locations in the empire right now," Bruce said. "There're over a hundred Valorí in this room alone."

"I don't care," Aldric said. "Bruce, I want you to take the archduchess and her daughter to Dur Enskai, immediately."

"I told you I'm not leaving," Eleanor said.

Bruce reached towards her. "My Lady, you must—"

She stopped him with a glance. "Grand Marshal, if you wish to keep your hand you will not lay it on me." Bruce stopped, withdrawing his hand.

The archduchess turned to Aldric. "The archduke would not leave his emperor's side. And neither shall I," she said. "My place is here. Evaine may go if she would like."

Aldric regarded the archduchess, the iron determination in her noble eyes. He nodded finally. "As you wish, my Lady," he said. *Now here is a woman,* he thought to himself. *What an empress she would make.* He glanced at Evaine who stood nearby, and he thought he saw the same look of wonder on her features that he felt as she stared at her mother.

"I'm staying too," she said. Aldric thought she didn't look quite as formidable as she had earlier.

"Very good," Aldric said. "Make sure they're protected," he told Bahir.

"We're wasting time," Leopold said, glaring about. "What of my Augures? I want to know where that bastard is!"

"My Lord, the Augures cannot see the Mal when he is with his Inquisitors, they are blind," Bahir replied.

"Damn him." Leopold slammed his fist into the arm of his throne. "Damn him!"

"Any luck on Arem's comsig Bruce?" Aldric asked.

"No, my Liege. I'm scanning the Imperial Comnet but it isn't showing up. The Circle can't trace his signal either; it's possible he's turned his comsig off."

Why would he turn it off? Aldric wondered. "Bahir, I want you to organise a party and look for Arem. Have your men help Bruce's team to evacuate these people, and then search the grounds."

"I wouldn't advise that, Sire," Bruce said, his face anxious. Ever the watchdog of the royal family, Bruce would sooner die than see Aldric come to harm.

"I'll be careful, Bruce," Aldric replied. "But I'm not going to let other people put their lives at risk while I sit here and do nothing. Arem's my brother; this is my duty."

Sliding through the crowd Aldric surveyed the room. It was chaos. People crowded and pushed and shoved together trying to get somewhere, anywhere, and the confusion was maddening. There was no rank or social order when panic struck. Performers and acrobats and dancers alike mingled with the very upper crust of society, dukes and barons bumping elbows with fire breathers and belly dancers. Aldric even saw the wargren sitting by a feasting table, surrounded by the jostling crowd. It appeared placid enough amidst the uproar, but he couldn't help but wonder what would happen when someone eventually stepped on the poor beast's tail.

Aldric scoured the hall, but he didn't see Arem. Looking around he noticed a side corridor that turned off by the rear of the great hall. He thought he'd seen Arem standing near there when the commotion began, but he wasn't certain. It was worth a shot, anyways. Two Landser parted for him as he passed, and he realised it was an entryway leading to the kitchens where the food was brought to the main hall. It was a wide hallway, dimly lit, and he'd taken only a few paces when he heard a voice shouting behind him.

"Aldric!"

He turned around and saw Iain trying to push his way through the Landser blocking the entrance. "Let me past, you *geth guan dahl!*" Iain shouted as the Landser held him back.

"He can pass," Aldric said. The Landser released him and Iain stumbled forward, catching his balance. He straightened his achkan and came running up.

"Where are you going?"

"Stay in the great hall, I'm looking for Arem."

"I'll look with you, we'll find him faster."

"What about Arianne?"

"She's with her parents, they volunteered to stay and help the others evacuate."

The hall wound around into the kitchens and then took a circuitous route behind the palace. High windows looked out over Lake Nimaine, moonlight streaming through the darkened corridor. Aldric glanced out the window, looking down the sheer cliff face below. The rear of Aldon Court formed a portion of the city's outer curtain wall, and sat perched atop a nearly vertical cliff at the far end of the island. He looked down both ends of the hallway, feeling uncertain.

"You think he would have come this way?" Iain asked.

"I don't know. The hallway has to loop around and reconnect at some point, so we'll just keep looking." They came to a branch in the corridor, one which led off into darkness and the other winding away to the right where it disappeared. "You head down that way," Aldric said, pointing down the darkened hallway. "I'll go this way. Meet me back at the great hall if you don't find him in five minutes."

The hall was lined with old portraits of long dead monarchs and noblemen. There were some Aldric recognised, and others whom he'd never seen. The hallway seemed endless, and he was beginning to feel like coming this way was a bad decision. *Hahka! Where is he?* He dialled his comsig. "Bruce, is there any sign of Arem?"

Crackling, a confusion of voices, then, "No my Lord, we haven't seen him. I have the lictors searching the palace. He's still not responding to calls."

"Right then, this is useless. I'm coming back, we'll think of something else."

As he turned a corner and prepared to head back, Aldric heard voices. In the quiet of hallway, the voices seemed loud, though whoever was speaking was talking in whispers. Aldric couldn't quite hear them and moved closer. They were coming from somewhere around the next corner.

Aldric carefully peeked around the corner and stared down the gloomy hallway. Two figures were standing in a doorway conversing about half a dozen metres from where Aldric crouched. The voices sounded angry. Aldric moved around the corner, keeping to the shadows. One of them was a tall blond man in a black uniform, someone he'd never seen before. The other one though... Arem! He realised suddenly. Arem was gesticulating wildly, and thumped the back of his hand over the blond man's chest. The blond man threw his hand off and grabbed Arem's coat, shaking him.

The blond man whispered something too quickly for Aldric to understand and released Arem, storming off through the doorway behind them. What was Arem doing? Why hadn't he answered his comsig? Arem shook his head and was about to follow the blond man when he glanced down the hallway and saw Aldric.

Aldric stood up, unsure of what to do. A look of shock passed over Arem's face, and he was about to call out when Aldric was wrenched to the side by a pair of strong hands. He staggered as he was pulled violently through the corridor and out the open window. He struggled, lashing out and landing a solid blow across his attacker's chest as he fell, tumbling into a bush.

Aldric was free of his attackers, and standing, found himself in the gardens below the palace, some two and a half metres below the window he'd been pushed through. He dropped into a fighting stance and looked around him for his assailants. Two men in faded *kilpani* were standing up, brushing themselves off and looking around, almost as if they were frightened. Aldric was confused. The Asaani?

"My Prince, don't be alarmed!" one of the men said, raising his hands. "There was no time, we must get you away from here."

"Get me away?" Aldric asked, lowering his guard. "Away from what, what's going on?"

"There's not time to explain, my Prince, we must hurry! Your life is in danger!" one of the druids said, taking his arm and turning to leave.

Aldric pulled away. "Who is? Tell me what's happening," he demanded.

The man looked desperate. "Everything will be explained, but you must come with us now!"

"What about Arem?"

"He is being looked after, we have sent others to bring him as well, and your father. There is simply no time; every second puts you in danger!"

Aldric looked back at the darkened window he'd fallen from. Arem was back there somewhere, and so was that strange blond man. Answers were back there. But there was something in the desperation of these two druids that compelled him to trust them. "Very well, let's go," he said.

Aldric kept his head low, skirting through the bushes. The lights of the city were bright, but the palace gardens were dimly lit and they moved behind trees and brushes until they were near the outer wall. "Where are we going?" he asked as they paused beneath the bole of a great cannoch tree.

"We must get you out of the city," one of the druids replied. He was a young man, roughly Aldric's age, perhaps twenty five, and clearly unhappy at having such a large responsibility. The other druid was a little older, in his forties Aldric guessed. He seemed more composed.

"What's happened?" Aldric asked. "Who sent you?"

"The Gaiban, my Prince," the older man said.

Aldric felt an icy fist grip his stomach. Gaiban Morrigan would never act except in absolute fear for his life.

"Our Elders could see that you were in peril, and so we came to remove you to safety," the older druid said, scanning the area hurriedly. There were many people in the streets celebrating. Aldric doubted anyone would notice them.

"In peril from what?" Aldric asked.

"They would not say," the older druid said. "It's possible they could not see the danger itself, only that harm was meant for you."

"And what of the Erolan? Of the dukes and the archduchess? The Lady Evaine?"

"I do not know, my Prince," the older druid said. "We were told to find you specifically and bring you back at all costs, but the other druids have members they must save as well. We will take you back to Dur Enskai. You will be safe there."

Sudden movement caught Aldric's eye and a rustling noise in the bushes nearby revealed more figures moving quickly in the darkness. Aldric sat up, ready to fight. He relaxed when he saw the outline of more druids. And Iain! His heart leapt.

"Iain, what are you doing here?" he asked, patting him on the shoulder as they joined Aldric and the other druids.

Iain looked surprised as well. "These oafs threw me out a bleeding window!" he said, looking resentfully at the two druids he'd come with.

"We apologise, my Lord," said one of the druids. "As we explained, we thought he was your brother, Arem."

"Do I *look* like Arem?" Iain rasped, trying to remain quiet.

One of the druids shrugged. "In the dark, one man looks much like another."

"It's a wonder you didn't nab the cook," Iain said, brushing dirt from his trousers.

"If you brought Iain," Aldric said, "then where's Arem?"

"Others will be searching for him my Prince," said the older druid. "He will be brought here when we find him." He stood and beckoned to them. "For now, we must go, you will be missed soon, and then they will come looking for you."

"Who will?" Aldric asked, suspicious.

"The Draugor," the druid replied. Before Aldric could question him further he was off, leaping over a low wall and vanishing into the shadows of a nearby alley. They followed him quickly, moving through the darkness and avoiding the crowds and bright streets. Nothing of the events in Aldon Court had reached the rest of Chaldrea, and the celebrations were still in full tilt. After ten minutes of ducking through alleys and weaving through crowds, they paused at a corner to wait for a group of Dhemorahns to pass. The Dhemorahns wore bright sarongs and laughed as they joined arms and began singing.

"You really think they'll care if they see us?" Aldric asked, more sceptical of their escape now than he had been at the start.

"It's impossible to say," the older druid said. "I would not risk anything; there is no knowing who's watching whom."

"Really, this is a bit much," Aldric said. "For the gods' sake, they're drunk!"

Iain drew up beside Aldric and leaned against the wall, panting. "So, are we going to run the whole way, or…?" he asked, trying to catch his breath.

"No, we have a carriage waiting for you at the Temple," the older druid said. "From there, we'll—" he was cut off by a deep rumbling sound from far behind them.

They stopped and turned as the rumbling sound grew, and suddenly cloud of light erupted into the night sky and the crack of an explosion shattered the air around them. The ground shook and Aldric ducked instinctively as a tremendous shock wave tore over them, sucking the breath from his lungs.

Coughing, Aldric stood and ran back down the alley to look around the corner. Between the buildings there was a clear view leading up the hill through the streets, and as he stood staring in the direction they had come, a second explosion rocked the ground. A tower of white flame burst into the sky, shooting a cloud of black smoke and debris high into the air. Aldon Court was in flames.

TWENTY TWO

OLD GLORY

Vice Admiral Sebastian Burns gazed across the wedged prow of the super battleship *Monarch*. The distortion effect of stream space glazed over the viewport, giving the stars beyond an iridescent sheen. Inside the slipstream bubble the hull of the battleship remained unaffected by the warping illusion, and Burns clenched his jaw in grim approval, surveying the domed turrets of the mighty guns stacked upon the deck. The *INV Monarch* was one of the largest ships in the fleet, though not quite as large as the massive dreadnoughts that were following close behind. *She'll make short work of any Raeth we find,* he thought.

Walking over the gantry above the quarterdeck Burns revelled in the exhilaration that came before an engagement. This would be one of the brilliant marks of his career, vanquishing the rebellious Raeth corsairs and bringing glory to his emperor. The Fatherland would herald him as a hero. What a stroke of luck it had been that the *Eidolon* was immobilised!

Since the War of the Dukes there had been no major naval engagements. The Raeth were a constant threat, but they were just bandits, marauders— pirates who would strike fast and hard and be gone before a retaliation could be mustered. They'd been a thorn in the side of the Admiralty for the last thirty years, but they didn't pose any real danger. Not the kind Burns longed for, anyways. There was no great honour or glory in fending off a few rusty buckets when they swooped in to raid a convoy.

With the rebellious dukes stripped of their power, there was no hope of another grand war and Burns had resigned himself to a career forever in the shadow of Archduke Raynard. Raynard: the heroic commander of the Sciphere who had saved the emperor and defeated the ducal fleet above Errolor when all hope seemed lost. It was a farce for Burns to pretend he might rival that feat, and he'd resented Raynard all these years that he hadn't had the same opportunity himself.

Burns had only been a captain at the time, his ship merely a light cruiser stationed on the far side of Allria in the off chance that rebels would seize that moment to attack the nascent colonies there. It was an absurd backwater assignment, with no real chance for any action, and Burns cringed when he read the reports of the fighting over Errolor. He knew what it had meant at the time, and he had festered on it these past forty years.

Now, however, the day would be his. The time was finally right, and he would make it clear to the Admiralty and to the emperor himself that he, Sebastian Burns, was the saviour of the empire. He tried to convince himself that he wasn't settling a personal score, but rather fighting for the glory of his Fatherland. As a military man raised among the Erolan and groomed to be the epitome of an aristocratic soldier and commander, he knew this wasn't true, and he felt ashamed to harbour such petty ambitions. It didn't matter though, and he smiled as he looked out into the starlit blackness ahead of them, thinking of the victory that would finally be his.

"Admiral, we are minus fifteen minutes from D-Point Zero," a sandy haired yeoman reported from his side.

"Prepare for standard shock formation," Burns replied. "Inform the rear wing of the echelon that we will disengage last."

A confused look ran over the yeoman's face. "Sir, the battle formation indicates that the *Typhoon* drop last, our orders—"

"I'm well aware of procedures and protocols, Yeoman Bates," Burns interrupted. "This is the *flagship* of the Sciphere. I will not be outdone by some lumbering dreadnought. There is an order to these things, it must be done with elegance." Burns said, sniffing. "You have your instructions."

The yeoman saluted. "Sir!" he said, and turned on his heels.

Burns scoffed. Who did they think he was? This was his fleet now. It mattered little enough if the dreadnought *Typhoon* could bring more guns to bear once it dropped out of stream space. He would be the last ship to deploy, this was his battlefield and the honour of overseeing the fleet from the rear would be his.

"Admiral, the corvettes and frigates have assumed formation at the head of the fleet, and the destroyers and cruisers are moving up. We will be in full battle formation in approximately eight minutes."

Burns nodded. The strategy was a simple one. When deploying into an unknown combat zone, the smaller ships such as the corvettes and light cruisers would drop out of the slipstream first, providing the waiting enemy with a multitude of vectors. The smaller ships were more agile and presented more difficult targets. While the enemy attempted to engage the more manoeuvrable ships, the heavier ships of the line would fall out of stream space behind them and pick off the confused enemy being harried by the littler ships. It was called a shock deployment, intending to stun the enemy and keep them off balance.

"T-minus five minutes to D-Point Zero, admiral," a deck officer reported. "The Sciphere is in full battle formation and awaiting your command."

Burns clenched his jaw. This was it. The moment weeks of preparation had built towards. The moment he'd been anticipating for more than half his career. This was the tipping point. *Before the raging eye of the storm, my little vessel ploughs. Beyond the foaming trough ahead, beyond the bucking bows,* he recited to himself. It was a very old poem, passed down by ancient sea captains who faced the terrible forces of the old ocean's fury. He felt a kinship there, between himself and those captains of bygone eras.

He smiled then, sure of his readiness. "Send word to the Sciphere: the first four echelons may deploy in standard deviation pattern and disengage stream space in formation. Stagger D-Point Zero to five marks—I don't want the fleet pilling up on itself. Wing commanders can deploy at their discretion. I want the marines prepared for boarding, have the dragoons on standby." If they could successfully board a Raeth vessel, they would have all the intel they'd need to ensure this was the last engagement they'd ever face.

"Acknowledged," the deck officer replied.

Burns surveyed the command deck, appraising his officers. Men in neat grey uniforms sat in consoles arrayed in a semi-circle, the open end pointing towards the rear of the ship. Steel grey girders braced the interior, the multi-reinforced hull of the bridge protected by additional layers of new, highly ablative armour. Low whirring sounds filled the air and a faint aroma of diluted chemical cleaning solvents, coffee, and ventilated air filled Burns's nostrils. These were the little details he absorbed before deployment: the murmuring voices, the shuffling feet, the nervous air of excitement that filled every action—the minutia that made the moments more palpable, more real. He breathed in deeply. After they arrived at Drusus, there wouldn't be time for such indulgence. It would be chaos and orders and delegation. Now was his moment of reflection.

Indicators at the fore of the command deck blinked red. "Sir, the first echelon has dropped from stream space," his deck officer reported. "We're in black-com." Communication with stationary objects became impossible during stream space; the signals couldn't penetrate the folds of the slipstream. As a result, there was a momentary period of communications silence that occurred during deployment, when the transmissions from the front couldn't reach the back. It was a tense and dangerous moment, and formations were staggered as efficiently as possible to minimise this blind spot.

Burns gave a curt nod. "Very good. What is our drop time?"

The officer glanced at his console. "T-minus one minute."

The stars ahead swirled in the iridescence of stream space. The mirror finish hull of the *Monarch* was poised, ready—eager to greet the coming storm. *Beyond the foaming trough ahead, beyond the bucking bows.*

"Echelon five has deployed, we are dropping in fifteen seconds." All but the last indicator had clicked over to red.

Burns counted down. He hadn't seen Drusus in over ten years. He was almost giddy with excitement, but he controlled himself. *Incredible*, he thought. The Raeth had never attacked an Imperial planet before, what would they find? Even the convoys rarely required an escort closer than one million kilometres out. He thought of the echelons already deployed, wondered at the sight that would greet them when they arrived. *Beyond the bucking bows.*

The last indicator buzzed and glowed red. "Disengaging from stream space admiral."

With a sudden moan, the deck of the *Monarch* shuddered beneath Burns's feet. The whirling, iridescent sheen of the stars faded. Real space returned suddenly, and Burns gripped the gantry railing as they slowed to normal speeds. He looked out the main viewport, expecting to see the fleet deployed before him, the six echelons of the Imperial Sciphere in orderly shock formation.

Burns gasped, sucking in his breath. The excitement of a moment before was gone, replaced by sudden confusion and dread, cold fingers gripping his spine. He stared the madness before him, trying to comprehend what his eyes told him was impossible. Knuckles white, Burns squeezed the steel railing, distantly aware of blaring klaxons and angry red lights.

TWENTY THREE

BURNING FIRES FOR OLD GODS

Raynard stared at the navigation display from over the shoulder of the helm officer, tugging at his beard in agitation. There were no transmissions coming from Drusus. There were no transmissions coming from anywhere. It was conceivable all communications had been knocked out on the refinery station, and even on the relay station on Drusus' moon, Khanos. But among the two hundred ships of the Sciphere? Not one of them was responding? They should have been engaged for over two hours now. What would prevent the fleet command ship from broadcasting?

"I want a report!" he snapped, trying to hide his frustration and failing.

"Sire, there's no word from the Sciphere. Communications are silent."

"What of the relay station above Khanos?"

The pennant master shook his head. "Nothing, my Lord. Nor from the orbital refinery station."

The *Eidolon* had restored power six hours earlier, and they had rushed at three-quarters drive to arrive here at Ahran, a barren planet only an hour and half distant from Drusus in stream space. Communication with Errolor was cut off at the moment as they were on the far side of the sun. Raynard assumed there would still be fighting around Drusus, but even a full scale engagement of this magnitude wouldn't last more than a few hours. It certainly wouldn't prevent communications with the rest of the system.

"Realign our trajectory for Khanos, and stream in at full speed," Raynard snarled at the helmsman. "We'll come in from behind. If something's happened, I don't want these bastards catching us by surprise."

Raynard strode to the operations terminal at the centre of the room and gazed about, gathering his thoughts. He was angry. This shouldn't be happening. There were less than a handful of reasons he could think of to explain comms-blackout, and none of them favoured the Sciphere.

The Raeth must have had something to surprise the fleet, he thought. *And I'll bet Burns stormed in like a battalion on parade, no regard for caution.* It would be just like him, to insist on ceremony where tactics were needed.

The Admiralty had ignored Raynard's recommendation of a divided approach, preferring the tried and true shock deployment. *That only works on an assembled, entrenched force,* Raynard thought angrily. The Raeth were anything but organised—there's little chance they'd just sit there in orderly columns and wait to be killed. It was like the ancient battlefield volley fire formation—and just as ineffective when the enemy was shooting at you from hidden positions. *Damn the fool!*

The navigation officer approached Raynard, saluting. "My Lord, we've realigned and are now on a course for the dark side of Khanos. We're beginning the engine manifold purge." It was impossible to change directions during stream space, so periodic course corrections were necessary.

"Excellent, what is our jump time?"

"At full speed, we will reach the moon in a quarter hour."

"Will our approach be seen?"

The navigation officer shook his head. "Our angle takes us past the edge of the sun's photosphere, as you ordered. We will be undetectable until we've disengaged stream drive, and only then if they have ships on the dark side of Khanos."

"Very good," Raynard said. "Relay these coordinates to the helmsman." He turned to the Master-at-arms, Grigor Eiden. "Grigor, coordinate with Colonel Urquhart: I want the marines prepared for any contingency, and I want all non-essential personnel in lock down. The ship is on full alert, and I don't want any mistakes."

"My Lord!" the older man barked, saluting. Eiden was a surly bear of a man, with keen blue eyes and a perpetual scowl. He was no more than fifty, fifteen years Raynard's junior, yet his creased, sun beaten face and grey hair added unevenly to his years. Raynard thought he looked the sort who might stab you in a darkened alley for the fun of it.

Grigor Eiden had spent seventeen years in the Varic Skirmishes, however, and was more decorated than any officer aboard. He was as coarse as they came, but he'd received his training on the battlefield, not some classroom, and Raynard respected his instincts. Here was a true warrior, he thought, not some preening noble of the Old Guard. *Those pantywaist boat lickers aren't worth a fart in a whirlwind when it comes to real fighting.*

"Do you have orders for the *fianna*?" Grigor asked gruffly, spitting out the words half-chewed.

Raynard shook his head. "Fedann Andros knows his business, he'll see to the Valorí."

Grigor nodded, saluted again, and strode from the bridge, barking orders at two marines who flanked the door as he passed. That was one thing he didn't need to worry about, Raynard thought, glancing at the Valorí Captain, or *fedann* in their tongue. Andros was a dark haired man, clean shaven and with the high, hollow cheeks and solemn blue eyes of the Tir Annath. He stood in one corner of the bridge in his phase armour, impassively gazing out the viewport. The Valorí never needed looking after.

At least we can outrun anything we find there, Raynard thought. There were only a handful of ships in the entire navy that could match the *Eidolon* for speed. "Inform me when the engine has finished recycling and we're prepared to jump," Raynard said to a tech sergeant at his side. "I'll be in the great room."

Captain Achres stood leaning over his desk, a holographic representation of Drusus and Khanos spread out before him. Raynard joined him, studying the positions of the refinery station and the last known formation of the convoy. The convoy was a long line of small blue shapes like tiny bricks, filed together in neat rows beside the refinery.

Achres sighed, putting a hand to his lower back as he stood. "I don't have an explanation, my Lord," he said. The frustration in his voice was plain. "I believe as you do, that the Raeth hid a part of their force behind Khanos and flanked the fleet when they arrived."

"That wouldn't account for the complete lack of communications," Raynard said, peering at the display. "Bring up the Sciphere." Achres touched a pad beside the display, and suddenly the entire Sciphere was displayed at the far end of the map. "Put them in formation." Another touch of the pad. Raynard gazed at the overlay. The full force of the Imperial Sciphere should be more than a match for any host the enemy could muster. *Except, there's the Malefactor,* Raynard thought, feeling his stomach tighten. *Nothing can account for that.*

"Do you suppose they have some weapon we haven't heard of yet?" Achres asked.

Raynard frowned, shaking his head. "I think it's more likely that they've developed a tactic that can defeat our methods of combat. But it would have to be damned impressive. I've never seen conventional weapons that can bring about the kind of destruction we witnessed on the *Malefactor.*"

He straightened, tugging at the collar of his uniform. It suddenly felt stifling. He hated the way it clung to his body, and the way the cloth didn't breathe and how it made him sweat. He hated how the displays were too dim and the overhead lights were too bright and how small the "great room" was. He hated the stale recycled air and reprocessed water and preserved foods they served, and he hated how fat he'd gotten. What was he doing? He was distracted. He was tired. *Always tired,* he thought. *Well, it's no more than my men are facing.*

Raynard looked at Achres, seeing the tired lines on his sallow face as well. The rigors of command and worry were written there in hard creases. Achres took his station as seriously as any man Raynard had ever served with. *When we're finished here,* he thought, *I'll order him on shore leave. A long one, someplace warm.* Raynard chuckled inwardly. Achres would probably hate that.

Raynard bit his lip, returning to the moment. "There's nothing we can rule out at this point. Without contacting Chaldrea, I don't want to jeopardise our position by putting us in the same situation that may have brought down the Sciphere."

"Sire?" Achres said, a touch of alarm in his voice.

"Like I said, we can't be certain, and the fact that we're out of range of Chaldrea makes me feel like the cautious approach is best." He reached into the holo display and moved his fingers around Khanos, spinning it so that the dark side faced them. The entire map rotated accordingly. "We'll approach from here," he said, drawing his finger past the side of the star Daedrus, represented by a glowing semicircle at the edge of the map. "And stop here," he said, moving his finger past the sunward side of Khanos, stopping at the rear.

"The relay station above Khanos is tidally locked with the moon's surface, so we won't have to worry about them reporting our presence."

"And what do you have planned when we reach Khanos?"

Raynard compressed his lips, blowing air out in a long, thin, hissing noise. "Survey. We're not equipped to deal damage on large scale, and as we learned earlier, most of the ship's systems are untested. We run the risk of stranding ourselves in harm's way if we're not careful."

Achres studied him for a moment, then returned his gaze to the map. "You seem to have taken the view that the fleet is out of action."

Raynard jutted his chin, his brow furrowing. "I don't like it. There's no reason for them not to reply, and I don't want to assume nothing's wrong when the lives of this crew are at stake. And I pray to the unholy gods it's only our *crew* we need to worry about."

"Errolor?" Achres asked, his voice hollow.

"Errolor." Raynard replied.

In ten minutes the engines had finished recycling the waste from the six hour hot burst through stream space. They didn't need to recycle the radioactive waste yet, but after the last engine failure, Raynard didn't want to take chances. He settled his giant frame into the commander's chair at the aft of the bridge and watched with a grave expression as the crew readied to re-enter the slipstream.

"All stations report blue," the operations officer sounded from a terminal beside Raynard.

Raynard pursed his lips. *Now we learn the truth,* he thought, finding no satisfaction in it. "Engage," he said, nodding to his helmsman.

With a faint shudder, the *Eidolon* hummed to life, the stars beyond the viewport sliding into an iridescent sheen, swirling like oil on water.

"T-minus seventy-five minutes to D-Point Terminus," the nav officer reported.

The time passed quickly, Raynard turning over the various scenarios they could encounter. Here was a thing he dreaded, something unlike anything he'd faced before. When the emperor was besieged during the War of the Dukes and Raynard arrived with his forces to smash the ducal armies, he'd known what to expect. There'd been precedent. It was warring armies, and he understood that. This was guerrilla, this was something unknown, unforeseen. He watched the display in his palm console moving towards the fixed destination. Thousands, millions of kilometres were passing by outside, and he sat up as they approached the drop point.

"My Lord, we're at the Terminus threshold."

"Bring us out of the stream," Raynard said, imbuing his voice with all the steadiness and command that his years as a veteran could summon. He fought down the uneasiness he felt, presenting the calm demeanour he knew his men expected. Simply composing himself this way made him feel more relaxed. The persona became a reality.

The ship slowed, shuddered, and then a shimmer ran over the stars. It reminded Raynard of someone drawing their hand across a pool of rippling water, smoothing its creases. The shadowy hulk of Khanos reared up before them, its pocked surface clear even through its murky umbra. Raynard peered out, searching for some clue. Nothing was visible, not with the moon blocking their vision.

"Take us above the pole," Raynard ordered. "I want to get a better look."

"Aye my Lord," the helmsman replied.

"But be damned discrete," Raynard growled.

"Maybe it's time to burn some fires for the old gods, eh?" Achres asked, coming up to stand beside Raynard.

Raynard grunted. It was an old tradition of the Elcaern. After the Illarien invaders conquered the Elcaern, they tried to convert them to their religion, banishing the worship of their heathen gods. The Elcaern paid tribute to the new rites and rituals, and over time some of them even began to embrace the new gods. But in times of hardship or when they were desperate, or when the fears of their ancestors pounded in their blood, and the nights grew long and cold, then they would light fires for the old gods and say a prayer, and hope they hadn't been forgotten.

"I'll light the bloody fires when I'm desperate," Raynard grumbled. "Right now we have a mystery to solve."

The *Eidolon* drew up above the north pole of Khanos, settling just above the horizon. "Begin a long range sensor sweep," Raynard said, studying the empty field of blackness beyond. Drusus was visible there, about the size of a silver guilder from this distance, mostly beige with deep swathes of dark brown running in ragged lines across the entire planet. Nothing else was to be seen, certainly not from this range.

"Perhaps if we move closer," Achres said, though his tone suggested he didn't think much of the idea.

"I'm as keen as you are to move into a trap," Raynard said, glancing at Achres. "Try raising the Sciphere. See if you can hail the *Monarch*. I want to know what the hell is going on."

After a few moments his pennant master turned in his chair, a puzzled look on his face. "My Lord, there's no response from the *Monarch*."

"What about the rest of the fleet? The command ship? Can you raise anyone?"

The officer shook his head. "No, my Lord, there's no response, I have complete silence on all military frequencies."

"Is there a transponder? Can you locate any distress signals?" Raynard asked, restraining his anger.

"I'm getting nothing, Your Lordship. We have absolutely no reception of any incoming signals, and no transponders are emitting."

Raynard clenched his fist, his leather gloves creaking. His ruddy cheeks flamed red. "Officer Carmichael, give me some information. I need something right now, report something useful to me. Are you picking up any signals at all, of any kind? Are we certain the communications array isn't malfunctioning?" Wouldn't that just be his luck today? *Gods, let it be the array*, Raynard prayed.

The officer checked his screen briefly, nodding. "Sire, I'm detecting a lot of local radio chatter, communications from the orbital refinery station to the surface."

Hahka, Raynard cursed. "And?"

The officer paused, listening, pressing one hand to his earpiece. The whole bridge seemed to be listening with him. Carmichael frowned. "It doesn't make sense sir, it's badly distorted, but they appear to be communicating with someone in the military."

Raynard allowed himself a momentary sigh of relief. *Well that's something*. "What's troubling about it Mister Carmichael?"

Carmichael continued to listen. "Sire, they're talking about the movement of troops, transferring soldiers from the refinery station to the surface."

Raynard saw Achres glance at him from the corner of his eye. "Occupation?" Achres asked.

Raynard shook his head. "Why would the Sciphere deploy troops to the surface? It'd be impossible for the Raeth to land and attack the mining colony directly, that's suicide, and they know it."

"A last ditch offensive?" Achres said, though his voice was tinged with scepticism.

"Sire, I'm not sure which division this is, but they're using names I'm not familiar with, and the language is... well, it's highly unorthodox," Carmichael said, still listening.

Raynard felt his stomach tightening again. "Have you anything to report from the sensor sweep?" he asked the tech officer at the terminal nearest him.

"It's difficult to decipher," the man replied, staring at his console. "There's a lot of interference, it almost looks like I'm sweeping an asteroid field, or like a fleet of garbage scows dumped their load out here. I don't know, Your Lordship. I've never seen anything like it."

This is maddening, Raynard thought furiously. *Nobody knows anything!*

"Can you detect any ships, at least, Mister Wright?"

"Aye sir, there's a great deal of ship movement, but it's hard to read through the interference. The ships don't conform to our military designations."

"The convoy?" Raynard hoped perhaps the convoy was scattered for some reason, maybe confused by the absence of the Sciphere. He chided himself before he'd finished the thought. *Of course it's not the bloody convoy.*

"If I had to guess Sire, I'd say they look like Raeth ships."

Raynard swallowed. "How many do you count, Mister Wright?"

"One hundred fifty-eight," Wright replied.

Raynard clenched his jaw. *Impossible.* "I want a scan of the area. Bring up a visual feed," he ordered, his throat tightening. He could feel Achres looking at him, and he ignored the urge to turn and meet his gaze.

A lucid projection flickered over a holo-projector in the centre of the room. It gradually solidified and became opaque, the view behind it fading away. The scene that coalesced from the projector was one of total carnage. Wreckage was strewn about in every angle of the projection, pieces of ships and debris floating and spinning in all directions. Fragments of what looked like asteroids whirled though the scene, colliding with the remains of the ships and spinning off in new directions. Behind the debris field was the planet Drusus, its orange and black colouration a hellish backdrop to the desolation that floated before it.

"*Daor above,*" one of the officers gasped.

"That's the Sciphere?" someone else asked in a hushed voice.

"That's enough," Raynard said. He wouldn't allow this atrocity to interfere with the performance of his crew's duties. *What in all the infernal gods could have done this?* He clenched his jaw and thought quickly.

"Scan for any survivors, life pods, ejection terminals, any support systems still active, I want to know if there are people still out there," he ordered. "Put the ship on silent run, disengage the heat sinks and put the stream drive in standby, we're running on batteries for the time being. But I want to be able to jump at a moment's notice." *We don't know what's out there,* he thought warily.

"Aye my Lord!" the operations officer replied, already busily carrying out his commands.

"Tactical, I want an assessment of the ships in this space, and I want targeting solutions on every one of them, I don't want to be surprised."

"My Lord, you mean to attack?" Achres asked, startled.

"No, but I'm not leaving until we understand this situation better, and I want to prepare for any contingency." He turned to the pennant master. "Can you raise Chaldrea from here?" He was afraid to ask, he had the sickening feeling that he didn't want to know the answer.

"We're having trouble penetrating the debris field with the dat-tran, it appears to be scattering the signal Sire, but give me a moment to work on it."

"Use the conventional network if you have to, I don't care if there's an eight minute delay, I want something, anything. We need answers."

"The Attendant Fleet?" Achres asked.

"Gods, what was I thinking? Leaving a handful of destroyers over Errolor? What could they do against this?"

"My Lord, nothing could have prepared us for this, clearly the entire Sciphere wasn't enough."

"We don't know that yet," Raynard said, resisting the feeling growing in his gut. "This could be just a partial debris field, it's impossible to tell how much of the fleet was lost. We can't know anything until we can get some kind of communications established, with Chaldrea or otherwise."

"There appear to be a large number of asteroids in that debris," Achres said, peering at the holo-projection.

Raynard nodded, he'd noticed that as well. It didn't make sense, there was no reason for there to be rock fragments drifting around Drusus. It didn't even have a ring system. One more problem that needed to be answered, but it could wait until later.

He glanced up from the holo-projector. The scene beyond the main viewport starkly contrasted with that of the projector. Beyond the viewport was empty, black space, Drusus hanging stilly in the void. No evidence of the grisly wreckage was apparent from this vantage. The entire Sciphere could have been spread before them, and it wouldn't have been visible. *Deceptive isolation,* Raynard thought. It was easy to miss something in all that blackness.

"My Lord!" the tactical officer shouted. "Hostile ship, approaching from under the south pole," he said, punching the data into the holo-projector. A small, one man raider appeared beneath the horizon, artificially illuminated by the projector. It was a mean, asymmetrical looking craft, one of the typical vessels used by the Raeth in their sorties on convoys.

"Have we been detected?" Raynard asked, fixated on the little vessel.

"I don't believe so Sire, but if we stay here much longer we will be."

"A scout," Achres said, taking a seat next to the archduke.

"Performing routine patrols," Raynard replied. "Keep us on stealth and take us over the rim of Khanos. Edge us out there, into that debris field," he said, pointing at the projection.

"Aye sir," the helmsman responded.

"My Lord?" Achres asked.

"We have no option other than to turn tail and run, and I'm not willing to do that without knowing more about what we're facing here. We don't even know if there are any survivors yet."

"I do not wish to seem callous, Your Lordship, but I think it is extremely unlikely, given the nature of the wreckage, that there are survivors."

"If there are," Raynard said in a low voice, "I will not be the man who left them here to die."

The sun's light moved across the bridge, sweeping through the broad forward viewport and casting long shadows over the consoles. "We've lost line-of-sight with the raider, my Lord," the tactical officer reported.

"Keep us moving forward," Raynard ordered. "I want an active eye on any threats in the space ahead, and I want to know if anyone is coming up behind us. Don't lose track of that little *scatha* back there," he said. They drifted out beyond the moon, passing through the night line and over the many valleys and craters on its barren surface. They picked up speed and in a few moments the moon was left behind, the debris field approaching rapidly.

"Easy," Raynard cautioned the helmsman. "I don't want to attract attention. We want to blend in." Small pieces of asteroid began colliding with the hull, bouncing harmlessly off and rolling away past the main viewport. The command deck was nearly twenty metres wide, and the main viewport stretched from one side to the other, giving over two hundred degrees of uninterrupted visibility. The debris field enveloped the cruiser, small bits of wreckage thudding into the deck, careening soundlessly away over the viewport. Dull thumps and thuds echoed from the larger pieces colliding on the outer hull around the bridge.

"Keep her smooth," Raynard said. Standing, he climbed the gantry at the front of the bridge and stared out at the carnage, still disbelieving. "Have you finished scanning the area?"

"Nearly Sire, there's a lot to process with all the pieces of debris constantly moving, but another five minutes and I'll have a report for you," the operations officer said.

"Lay in a course for Errolor," Raynard ordered. "As soon as we've finished here, move us out of the debris field, and take us into the stream. We might alert the Raeth to our presence, but it won't matter. They can't catch us." *I hope it won't come to a game of cat and mouse,* Raynard thought to himself, considering what their options would be if they really had nowhere to go.

They continued through the field, pieces of twisted metal wheeling past them. A large chunk of housing from an engine drive whirled past so close that officers standing by the main viewport instinctively ducked. It collided with the armoured roof of the bridge, ringing like a gong before scudding off over the aft superstructure.

An eerie stillness settled over the command deck, Raynard watching his officers working with calm efficiency, the quiet anticipation of the bridge punctuated by the muffled thuds and clangs of the debris outside. *We're floating through a graveyard,* Raynard thought. The disquiet grew as they began to pass through fields of bodies. None ever came close enough to see clearly, but they were obvious at fifty metres and the effect upon the crew was instant. Raynard knew that whatever had done this would not hesitate to destroy his ship as well.

"Steady on," he said, standing and making a tour of the bridge. "Is the scout following us?"

"No, Sire," the tactical officer replied, his voice uneasy.

"And the Raeth in the area? Any indication we've been spotted?"

"Ship movements have remained local and isolated, there's no suggestion we're being monitored or will be intercepted. But," he hesitated.

Raynard paused and turned to look at him. "Yes, Mister Hornsby?"

"Our sensors *are* having trouble in this debris cloud. It's the same thing with our communications; it's not easy interpreting all the signals we receive."

Like picking out a fly in a sandstorm, Raynard thought. "Very well, I want spotters in the forward observation posts and I want to know the moment it looks like we're going to have company." He turned to the pennant master. "Any luck getting through to Chaldrea?"

"No, Sire, our signals are being deflected by the debris. I've sent a standard transmission as you requested, but there's been no response yet. It's possible those channels aren't being monitored at the moment, my Lord," he said uncertainly.

Not likely, Raynard thought, trying to ignore his growing misgivings. "Keep up your efforts, Mister Langley." He did his best not to think of Chaldrea at the moment. He wouldn't allow himself to start wondering and worrying about his Eleanor and darling Evaine. No, he couldn't start that. *Stop,* he told himself. *Stop!*

Glancing across the bridge he caught Captain Achres' gaze. The lean man was watching him, his penetrating blue eyes full of concern. Raynard was wary of that look, at a time like this it would be dangerous to admit to such fears. There would be time for doubts later. *Concentrate on the moment at hand.* He would master this situation, and all those that followed. His men relied upon his ability to command, and that reliance gave him strength. He knew what his duty was.

A sudden flash of light blazed past the main viewport. An instant later, klaxons blared and red lights filled the bridge. "Report!" Raynard shouted, gripping a nearby handrail for support.

"Sire, two ships are closing on our position. I'm reading com-dispatches from the forward ship, it appears they've alerted the other ships in the sector. I believe reinforcements are en route," the tactical officer said, pouring over his screens.

"Battle stations," Raynard said, the calm forcefulness of his words settling over the crew. "Enemy ship class, Mister Hornsby?" he asked, taking his seat and turning to the tactical officer.

"Two corvettes, Sire—four-thousand tonne."

"Firerats," Raynard said, musing.

"Mister Langley, can you jam their signals? Maybe we can stop them from telling the rest of the ships we're here," Raynard said.

The pennant master dialled through his terminal, working for a solution on the signal, racing against time. "It's no use," he said, shaking his head. "The signal's already been sent." *Damn,* Raynard thought. "What about their weapons, can you shut them down? Engines?"

Langley worked furiously over his console. "I can disrupt their secondary systems, possibly take their gravity offline, but weapons and engines will take longer—they're using a scratch system, I've never seen anything this primitive, it'll take me a while to figure out where their systems are."

"Get on it," Raynard said.

"They're no match for the *Eidolon*," Achres said, examining a data pad. "Those ships are at least fifty years old."

"As am I, Captain," Raynard replied. "Likely they've been upgraded since then. I doubt they'll attack with welding guns and core drills. Mister Cormac, what is our ETA through the debris field?"

The navigation officer performed a quick calculation and turned to the archduke. "My Lord, at this speed another seventeen minutes. However, if we increase to full thrusters we can escape the field in two minutes."

"And when do you estimate the reinforcements will intercept us?"

"Presently they are on course and will reach us in approximately nine minutes," the tactical officer replied.

"Mister Cormac, do you suppose at full speed we'll suffer any damage moving through this debris?"

"It's possible, Sire, though probably not serious."

"Probably? Well then by all means, use your discretion and get us out of here. I don't want to be around when a hundred and sixty Raeth ships arrive."

Another bolt of energy streaked past the viewport. "They're having trouble acquiring a lock, Sire," Hornsby reported. "Our hull is deflecting their sensors."

"Clearly it wasn't their arclight cannons that took out the Sciphere then," Raynard said, glancing over at Achres. "Return fire, evasive manoeuvres."

The *Eidolon* rolled upwards and then down in a smooth arc, coming to bear on the approaching corvettes. They were just dots of light at this distance, but the plumes of cannon fire streamed past the bow at steady intervals, none landing a direct hit. "Target the lead vessel," Raynard ordered. "Fire when you have a solution." He stared out beyond the silver bow of the *Eidolon,* the green balls of phosphorescent energy reflecting on the mirrored skin of her hull as they rocketed past.

Raynard watched as the four mounted cannons emerged from their domed housings and swivelled about, coming to bear on the distant corvettes. The enemy fire continued to pour over and around them. He waited anxiously for the guns to fire. "Mister Hornsby?" Raynard asked, glancing over at the young tactical officer. He kept his voice calm. "As you please."

"Aye my Lord, firing now," Hornsby replied.

Jets of white light suddenly burst from the mouths of the cannons, propelling unseen shells at the incoming Raeth. Raynard heard and felt the concussive vibrations through the deck even here in the bridge. A moment later explosions erupted across the hull of the lead corvette, and it tumbled downward out of formation, spewing gas and streams of fire. The fires were doused almost instantly in the vacuum of space, looking like fireworks bursting over the hull of the ship.

"Well done Mister Hornsby, let's add a little wreckage of our own to this debris field," Raynard said, keeping his tone even. The two heavy, treble barrelled coil guns in the forecastle were joined by two lighter twin-barrelled protocannons higher up amidships. "A full barrage please, Mister Hornsby, we don't want to be sparing with our affection," Raynard said, allowing himself a moment of grim satisfaction as he watched the heavy guns pounding away in their turrets.

The shots vanished into the gulf between the closing vessels, and for a moment Raynard thought they had missed somehow. The continuous stream of arclight fire from the corvette poured forth, shots flying wide on all sides, balls of green energy whirling past the bridge.

A jagged beam of light suddenly tore open the corvette, slicing it down the middle and exploding outwards in all directions. The stream of cannon fire cut short and the corvette began tumbling end over end, gouts of fire bursting into space, extinguishing in flickering silence. The great guns of the *Eidolon* went quiet, and Raynard and the rest of the bridge crew watched the spinning hulk of the corvette drift past, its bow completely split in half, enormous gashes laying open the inner decks. Raynard was impressed with the *Eidolon's* performance, despite the gravity of the moment.

"Excellent work, Mister Hornsby," Raynard said. "Excellent work all." This only added to the mystery of the Sciphere, however. His little cruiser had just destroyed two corvettes without taking a single hit, in a matter of minutes. How could this ragged fleet of aging derelicts be the force that destroyed the entire Imperial armada? A glance at Captain Achres revealed he was thinking the same thing. It didn't add up.

"Now take us out of here," Raynard said, resuming his seat at the aft of the bridge. "That was handily done, but I don't want to test our luck a hundred and fifty six more times."

"Aye sir, resuming course, three-quarters Ram."

Another klaxon blared through the bridge, and Raynard glanced at the helmsman. "What's going on?"

"Collision detection!" Davits shouted, swinging the ship around. "We're in the path of—"

Suddenly the *Eidolon* bucked wildly to port, sheering to the side and rolling over almost a hundred and eighty degrees. Raynard was thrown from his seat, sprawling on the deck. A monstrous grating sound reverberated through the hull, followed by what sounded like sand falling on metal.

Raynard groaned as he collided with a nearby terminal, feeling the air sucked out of him. He coughed, pushing himself to his knees and sucking in deep lungfuls of air. He looked around, trying to get his bearings. All around him the crew were in a similar condition, many on the floor, disoriented, a few still strapped in their chairs.

Raynard shook his head, climbing into his seat. "The hell was that?" he roared, fighting with the chair straps. An aid came running to his side to help, Raynard swatting him away angrily. "I want to know what the devil just happened! Now!"

"Sire, it looks like we were hit," Leftenant Davits reported from the helm, a red gash running the length of his forehead.

"Hit?" Raynard repeated, disbelieving. "Hit by what?"

"I can't tell, my Lord," Davits replied, frantically searching through the console. "By an asteroid, I think."

Raynard stared at him. "Did you say an asteroid, Leftenant?"

"Aye, my Lord," Davits said, almost apologetically. "An asteroid, about fifteen tonnes, if these logs are correct."

"Where the hell did an asteroid come from?" Raynard demanded, looking out past bow into the empty space beyond. "I want to know exactly—"A whirling grey rock suddenly flew past the bow of the *Eidolon*, spinning away to the port side. It was massive, missing the bow of the ship by metres. Raynard stopped midsentence and stared with the rest of the crew as the rock sailed away into the night. Collecting himself he shouted, "Damage report!"

"The asteroid collided with the ventral shielding, there's minor damage to the hull and two starboard turrets."

"Did a comet blow through here I don't know about?" Raynard said, flicking on the display in his chair.

"Sire, the composition of the asteroids matches the rock found in the debris field," Leftenant Commander Boer reported. "It's identical to the makeup of Khanos."

"Are you telling me Khanos is blowing rocks into space?"

"No, my Lord, but the composition is the same."

Another giant asteroid appeared from over the starboard bow, flying away to port. It was immense, at least a thousand tonnes. Raynard watched it go, looking around the wreckage of the fleet. A field of debris, strewn with broken rocks and mangled ships. *We're being shot at,* Raynard realised suddenly. "Get us out of here," he ordered. "Whichever direction we can jump through the field quickest, never mind Errolor—just get us out of here now." *This is what happened to the fleet.*

The *Eidolon* shuddered violently, swinging wide from an unseen force. Raynard gripped his chair from the violence of the spin, deafened by the titanic explosion of noise through the hull. Another sound like raining sand followed the impact, and Raynard glimpsed the fate of the Sciphere in a blinding clarity.

"Damage report!"

"Hull breach in crew quarters Sire, it's sealed off—the flight deck is compromised and pressure's lost in the munitions bay. All breaches contained."

"Do we have stream drive?"

"Aye my Lord, engines are undamaged—we can jump as soon as we clear the field."

"Change course, evasive pattern theta, I don't want to give them a clear target," he said angrily, gripping the arm of his chair.

"Sire? Give who a clear target?" the helmsman asked.

"Just get us through this field!"

The *Eidolon* darted forward, dancing through the maze of debris in a zigzag pattern as detritus bounced off the hull. An asteroid nearly the size of the *Eidolon* whirled past the starboard bow, no more than fifty metres away. Raynard swallowed hard. How was this possible? *Defeat is found in failure to anticipate your enemy,* Raynard recalled. It came from a book called the *Parables of War,* written by the ancient Thedarran General Brude. *Improvisation is deadlier than proven strategies. Rely on your old strengths and you shall find new weaknesses.*

"Where are these coming from?" Raynard heard someone say.

"It's the Raeth," Raynard said, bracing his chair. This was their secret weapon. This explained the massive damage to the *Malefactor.* It explained the complete decimation of the Sciphere. He knew that now, beyond a doubt. It seemed impossible, but the reality of it was before them—they were flying through it right now, chunks of the fleet and their comrades all around them. The sudden realisation was horrifying. The Admiralty, the Sciphere—no one—had been prepared for this. And they had been destroyed.

Raynard watched as the last of the debris slipped behind them. "Engage Lantern drive," he ordered. A low humming noise vibrated up through the deck and the stars began to swirl. Raynard felt the sudden jump as they were pulled into the slipstream, and he breathed a sigh of relief. Yet he felt certain that this had far greater implications, and his stomach twisted as he imagined what awaited them in the skies over Errolor.

TWENTY FOUR

GREEN FIELDS NO MORE

The return to Errolor required dropping from stream space five times. At this point in the planets' rotation, Errolor sat on the opposite side of the sun from Drusus, and Raynard ground his teeth as they fell out of stream space to make the fourth and final course correction. It had taken nearly three hours already, and there remained a further forty minutes before they reached home space. Even at a tenth the speed of light the trip took four hours and Raynard stared out the main viewport unblinking, watching the bow of the ship swing around to their new heading. A moment later and the deck hummed, the stars outside shimmered, and they jumped back into the slipstream.

Repairs to the *Eidolon* were underway, but after inspecting the damage Raynard knew they would need to put into a dry dock to recover completely. Sections of the outer hull would need to be replaced, and portions of the crew quarters, including Wardroom B, were uninhabitable for the time being. They'd managed to restore enough of the hangar that the flight deck was operational, but one of the Starling fighters had been shot through by rock fragments and was inoperable. That left them with eleven fighter craft. There'd been no casualties.

Considering the circumstances, Raynard was amazed they hadn't been obliterated. Reports showed the first asteroid had clipped them at over nine thousand kilometres an hour, while the second, larger asteroid had been closer to eleven thousand. That was faster than ram speed. *You'd almost need to be in stream space to escape those*, he thought. And even so, there would only be seconds to respond. He couldn't imagine the horror awaiting the Sciphere when it dropped from the stream. Even the *Eidolon*, advanced as she was, had nearly been destroyed.

The *Eidolon,* code named *Poltergeist* during development, was unique in the Imperial fleet, heralding a new class of cruiser. It was Raynard's flagship as the archduke, and had been specially modified for his purposes. It wasn't the largest or most heavily armed ship in the fleet, but it was far more powerful than most ships in its class, with enough firepower and armour to go toe-to-toe with a battleship. It was also designed with a lean, wedge shaped bow to create a slim profile from the front. Raynard had even lent some of his own designs to the project. It was fitted with turrets both on the main deck and on the sides of the hull, with the command superstructure situated near the stern. This allowed it to bring all of its guns to bear on targets directly ahead, without exposing its full profile during a broadside attack. *Smaller target, more firepower.* As Raynard had seen earlier, it was a lethal configuration.

It was also equipped with the latest Lantern drive, something only a handful of ships in the Sciphere had. And now with the Sciphere destroyed, it was the last example of this technology. Even if they couldn't take on the entire Raeth fleet, Raynard knew there was no one who could catch them. Gods willing the Attendant Fleet hadn't been overwhelmed. If *Arrus Athaban* had fallen? Raynard pushed the thought aside. He needed more information; he simply couldn't work without data. They would have to arrive and discover for themselves the extent of this insurrection, and hope they weren't too late.

In the stillness of his great room, a moat was forming in his mind, a moat between him and the world he knew. Even without knowing what had befallen Errolor, Raynard knew there would be no going back. Everything was changed. The Sciphere was destroyed. A hundred thousand people had just lost their lives, and Errolor was practically defenceless.

The emperor still maintained his army, and the unbreachable citadel would remain guarding Chaldrea. But when the soldiers of Vassarya walked the battlements, who would they see in the skies above them? There was nothing stopping the Raeth from orbital bombardment. Perhaps the Attendant Fleet had survived. Perhaps it hadn't.

No more the green fields of my fathers,
no more the furrow or the glebe.
I set them all behind me,
and look out towards the sea.
For my dear old home is empty,
and my hearth fires frozen over.
The meadows are a'wilting,
and the lark, he calls no longer.
Bring back, bring back, the wheat ripe wind,
and the laughter of the mill stream.
For the flowers all are dying,
and I ken not whither my road may wend.

The lines of the poem came to him unbidden, and he found himself speaking them softly. It was an old poem his father had told him when he was a boy. He had a sudden image of his home back on Errolor growing up, a low stone building with a peat roof tucked away in the highlands of

Galhane. From peasant to archduke. He frowned, feeling out of place. *This is no time for sentimentality, old man,* he thought, shaking his head.

Raynard reached into a drawer and pulled out a red vial. It was a stimulant, and breaking off the cap, he swallowed it quickly, screwing up his face as the drink churned down his throat. *There will be no more mistakes today,* he thought. The time for mistakes was over. His duty lay clearly before him, and he would be damned if he would go down without a fight.

"Report," Raynard said, returning to the bridge.

"My Lord, we're preparing to drop from stream space now," the helmsman said.

Raynard nodded, strapping himself into his seat. This was the moment of truth.

The *Eidolon* dropped in from over the rim of the moon Landas, the red-brown rock charging past them. Colours blurred and shimmered with a crystalline brilliance and suddenly Errolor appeared in the distance, blue and tiny, no bigger than Raynard's thumb. He watched it grow rapidly as they decelerated.

"Report," he said, staring at the little blue planet.

"We're picking up a large debris field," a nearby tech officer replied.

Raynard swallowed, glancing at Captain Achres. "Are there any ships in orbit?" he said, maintaining his composure. How he responded to this situation was almost as important as the situation itself. If they discovered they were the last ship in the Imperial Navy, how would his crew react? Morale must be maintained, even in the face of utter defeat.

"Aye, my Lord," the officer responded. Raynard detected the uneasiness in his voice.

"Attendant Fleet?"

"No, my Lord," the tech officer said, shaking his head. "Scans are detecting hull signatures from what appears to be the Attendant Fleet. But they are heavily fragmented."

Raynard stared hard at the sandy haired officer. "Are there any ships remaining?"

The officer studied his console, then, "Sire, I'm picking up the signatures of over two hundred vessels, none of them matching Imperial configurations."

Raynard tried to digest that information. Suddenly the command deck seemed very loud, the droning of machines and the humming of the engines through the deck plating almost overwhelming. His temples were throbbing. He tried to swallow and found his throat was too dry. "*Arrus Athaban?*" he asked. "Can you raise the Admiralty?"

"Your Grace, *Arrus Athaban* is still in orbit, and it appears to be undamaged," Leftenant Langley replied from a terminal nearby.

"Can you raise them?"

"I'm attempting now, Sire."

Raynard stared out at the expanse beyond. Errolor was still quite small, probably two hundred and fifty thousand kilometres away, but he could pick out the debris from this distance, glittering in the sunlight like some strange starfield that had settled over the planet.

"My Lord, they're responding, would you like to take it in your great room?"

"No," Raynard said, shaking his head. "Let's hear it."

A tenor voice piped through above the terminal, clear in the sudden stillness that enveloped the bridge. "*INV Eidolon,* this is pennant master Brannan of *Arrus Athaban,* respond."

"This is the Archduke Raynard Sinclair, what's the situation? What is the status of the Attendant Fleet?"

"Archduke Sinclair, you are ordered to bring your ship to dock and come aboard for questioning at once."

Raynard blinked. "I'm ordered to what? Where is the Attendant Fleet?"

"I repeat, by command of the Glorious emperor, you are hereby ordered to surrender your vessel at *Arrus Athaban* and report for questioning by the Council of Ministers immediately."

The emperor? Raynard thought, with mixed feelings. He was alive then, and Chaldrea was still under Imperial control. But what was this nonsense? "Answer my question," Raynard said, ignoring the man. "Where is Attendant Fleet?"

"*INV Eidolon,*" a new voice cut in. It was harsh and commanding. "You are to report to *Arrus Athaban* immediately and surrender without resistance or you will be fired upon."

Surrender? "Surrender to whom? I'm the archduke, this is an Imperial vessel of His Majesty's navy—we surrender to no one. Who is this, and where is Attendant Fleet?"

"Attendant Fleet has been destroyed," the voice replied, unconcerned. "They defected to the rebels. Unless you are defectors and wish to be destroyed as well, you must surrender yourselves at once and come aboard for questioning."

Raynard sat back in his chair. He turned to find Captain Achres beside him, a look of cold fury on his narrow face. This was absurd. "Who is station commander?" Raynard asked, knowing already he wouldn't like the answer.

"This station is under the command of Draccas Ascagar, Grand Overseer of His Majesty's army."

Raynard shot a glance at Achres, who mouthed a silent, "*Who?*" Raynard shook his head. The name wasn't familiar. What was a "grand overseer"? There was no such title.

"I don't recognise the authority of any grand overseer," Raynard replied. "The only orders I take are from his Highness Emperor Leopold, and as his loyal servant I will not surrender my ship to you, or anyone else, under any threat."

"Emperor Leopold is dead," the voice said, static momentarily cutting through the transmission. "His Glorious Majesty emperor Arem Danarean has succeeded him, and he has ordered all remaining vessels of the Imperial Navy to return to *Arrus Athaban* and their crews and commanders report for questioning by the Council of Ministers at once."

A cold wave swept over Raynard. The emperor was dead. He stared at the terminal, a row of tiny lights blinking, flashing at the corners of his awareness. The emperor was dead. He said it to himself again. He couldn't understand it. The words didn't make sense. The emperor was dead. The emperor was dead? How could he be dead? It wasn't possible. The emperor was dead. His worst fears realised in a moment of incomprehension. Arem was the new emperor? What had happened to Aldric? Was he dead as well? *Oh gods! Gods of the Abyss!* Another darker fear gripped him then, shaking loose all other thoughts and possibilities. *Eleanor,* he thought—empty, hollow fear welling up inside. *Evaine!*

"My Lord," a voice said to him from beyond an immense gulf. The sound echoed without meaning, a horn blowing from a distant mountain top, trumpeting through the canyons and gullies and fading away into emptiness. "My Lord!" it said again, more insistent. Raynard stood up from the terminal, his body automatically searching for the source of the voice, rote instinct answering as his mind fought for some purchase in the nothingness around him.

He had the sensation that he was wanted, that someone needed him somehow. "Your Grace, there are ships approaching," the voice said again. A drumming filled his ears, and he turned finally to see his tech officer standing beside him, urgency written on his face. *Eleanor. Evaine. Evaine!*

"Sire, what are your orders?"

A black curtain fell over his senses—oceans washing over the ramparts of his consciousness. And then in an instant the shrouds vanished and the sounds of the room returned suddenly, and all there was before him was this yeoman and the grey rows of bright metal terminals and the swirling blue ball hundreds of thousands of kilometres away. There was nothing else. *Orders.*

"Have the engines finished their coolant recycling?" he asked, his voice calm. *Duty. There is only duty.*

"No, Sire, they're at fifty percent, I estimate another five minutes before the cooling sequence is complete."

"Much can happen in five minutes," Raynard said, feeling Achres' eyes on him. He would know what he was thinking.

"Sire?"

"What of the approaching ships?"

"There are approximately two hundred ships on a direct intercept course, Sire. They will reach us within three minutes."

"How close is the lead ship?"

The tech officer glanced at his console. "One hundred fifty thousand kilometres, closing. Sire, its hull matches Raeth configuration," he added hesitantly. "A heavy cruiser, by the looks of it."

"And the rest of the fleet?"

"Mostly frigates and gunboats Sire, though a few larger cruisers and heavy corvettes."

A chasm stretched out before Raynard, black and empty, yawning endlessly into an abyss from which there seemed no return. What was this path before him? These steps that trailed into the void, where would they take him? There was no going back, he knew.

"Resume the channel with *Arrus Athaban*," Raynard said. The officer pressed a switch, looked up at him and nodded.

"*INV Eidolon*, this is your final warning. Declare your intentions, do you submit?"

Raynard glanced at Captain Achres. The captain's brow was knotted tightly, his arms folded over his lean chest. His resolve was written in every taught line of his face, in every tensed muscle.

"*Arrus Athaban*, this is the Archduke Sinclair," Raynard said. He looked around at his waiting bridge officers. Young, expectant faces, untried and unsure of themselves. Their lives were in his hands. Would they live to see tomorrow? Would they ever see their families on Errolor again? Would he? He gazed at the silver bezel of the transceiver. *Gods, forgive me,* he said to himself in a silent prayer.

He took a deep breath. "We submit. We will rendezvous with you at your designated coordinates."

There was a hesitation, crackling of static. The voice returned. "*INV Eidolon*, on behalf of the Glorious emperor and the Grand Overseer Draccas Ascagar, we accept your surrender. Proceed en route to the station. You will be under escort."

"Understood," Raynard said. He glanced at the officer at the terminal and drew his fingers across his throat, cutting the transmission. "Are you prepared?" Raynard asked, looking at Achres.

Achres met his gaze. "We are with you, Sire."

Raynard compressed his lips, nodding. "Good. Good. It is good." He turned to the tactical officer. "Mister Hornsby, target the lead ship," he said, striding to the gantry at the front of the quarter deck.

"Sire? What of our orders? The emperor—"

"Damn our orders and damn the emperor," Raynard said sharply. "We are on our own gentlemen, and we submit to no one. The Imperial Navy is destroyed, and we're to be escorted by a Raeth fleet?" He almost smiled. "No, we take no orders today—I will not surrender this vessel to a Raeth commander, or some *grand overseer,* whoever he might be. We are at war, and there is no turning back." The tiny blue planet hung motionless beyond, the blackness threatening to swallow it. "Do you have the lead ship acquired?"

"Aye, my Lord."

Raynard stared at the little planet. Everything he had ever loved was on that tiny speck of rock. It seemed so small now, so fragile. He took a deep breath, and let it out. "Fire, all guns."

With an explosion that could be heard throughout the ship, the great guns of the *Eidolon* roared into life, white fire tearing out into the darkness, flashing over the mirrored hull in a blinding eruption. The shots vanished, and Raynard stared out after them, moments drawing into an eternity. *Eleanor, my dearest Eleanor. Evaine, how I love you.*

A tiny burst of light twinkled in the distance. "Direct hit my Lord, the cruiser has been destroyed."

"Target the next ten closest ships," he said.

"Sire, we are being hailed by *Arrus Athaban.*"

He nodded. "Put them through."

"*INV Eidolon,* what is this? What are you doing? Surrender, now!" There was panic in the voice now.

"Long live the emperor," Raynard shouted. "*Fire!*"

The guns of the *Eidolon* bellowed, great bursts jetting out into the night, flame ripping through the darkness as the massive cannons reverberated in their housings. Shot after shot tore through the void, streaking out to find their targets, still invisible at this distance. Raynard watched as little burps of light marked where the deadly shells found their homes.

"What is the status of the engines?"

"Eighty five percent recycled, my Lord."

"Very good. Keep targeting the next closest ship and fire as ready," he said.

"Sire, the fleet is approaching. I read two hundred and twenty vessels en route," the tech officer reported from behind him.

"Good," Raynard said. Bitter resolve filled his stomach, numbness emptying his heart of all concern but for the moment. Raynard could see his reflection in the viewport, his red hair glowing with each explosion. The fury of battle was upon him, and there was nothing inside of him but cold, empty hatred. Achres joined him on the gantry.

"If they want to come, let them," Raynard said. "We shall meet them as men."

"For the emperor," Achres said.

"For the emperor."

A bright flash of green light whipped past the bridge, followed by another, and another. "The closest ships have opened fire, my Lord!"

"Stand ground, and inform me when the engines finish recycling."

More and more green balls of crackling electricity blazed past the bridge. With a faint shudder a shot crashed into the base of the command tower, green tendrils of light and sparks exploding outwards.

"We've been hit Sire!" someone shouted behind him.

"Continue firing," Raynard said. "Our armour will hold." Another shot exploded on the bow, green electricity dancing over the hull. Two more collided on the deck, searing the hull into a white hot glow.

The main battle line of the Raeth fleet was now visible, hundreds and thousands of flashing lights piercing the darkness as the enemy guns poured out their deadly barrage. The great deck guns of the *Eidolon* continued firing, hammering out round after round, rocking the deck plating, the sound of explosions pounding through the bridge. Raynard watched as the fusion rounds left ghostly pink trails through the cold void, bursting in vivid gouts among the growing wave of Raeth ships. He counted five, ten, sixteen explosions among the enemy lines—sixteen ships that would never go home. *Sixteen ships, for the two-hundred of the Sciphere.*

More and more enemy rounds were thudding into the *Eidolon*, burning white hot trails across the hull. There seemed to be as many rounds of enemy fire flying past the bridge as he could see stars beyond. The Raeth fleet was close enough that he could clearly see individual ships now, and he watched as the *Eidolon's* guns tore them apart, one after another.

"What is our status?"

"Engines have finished coolant cycle, we've dumped the chambers and are prepared for jump."

"Very well," Raynard said. He gazed out at the massing fleet before them. It was too large for him to count, the ships spread out from horizon to horizon. *So it comes down to this,* he thought.

"Set a course for *Torr Archus*," Raynard said. "Maximum speed." *For the flowers all are dying, and I ken not whither my road may wend.*

The giant guns on the *Eidolon* burst one last time and fell silent. Raynard followed their line of fire as the *Eidolon* came about. The lead ships of the

Raeth fleet were visible now, and Raynard smiled as he watched the flickers of light that marked their doom.

Moving sidelong into the incoming fire of the fleet, more and more shots exploded against the hull. One detonated just below the bridge and Raynard gripped the gantry railing as the deck bucked under the impact.

"Fire a broadside," Raynard said suddenly, observing the approach of several Raeth ships. The deck guns quickly swung about to face the oncoming fleet, and with a thunderous roar jumped to life once more. Half a dozen explosions pocked the night, like stars bursting and winking out suddenly. Raynard studied the havoc his guns had wreaked among the enemy ships, four more vessels shearing off from the main fleet, ripped apart by gouges of white flame.

"We're ready to jump Sire," a tech officer reported.

"Very good. Engage," Raynard said, watching as the moon glided past the bow and they settled on their alignment. A tremor rumbled through the bridge from an unseen impact, Raynard rocking with the ship from dozens of hits. "Get us out of here, Mister Davits, if you please."

"Aye my Lord."

The stars began to shimmer, and with a sudden lurch they were gone.

Raynard swallowed hard. He suddenly realised he was covered with a cold sweat. It wasn't from the battle, he knew. He had been in many battles, more than he could even remember. The Raeth must pay for what they had done. *What have they done?* He asked himself, not even knowing how to answer.

All his years as a general of countless battlefields had not prepared him for the feelings that engulfed him as he thought of his wife and daughter back there on that little blue planet behind them. His emperor was dead, his long friend of many years, and now he must leave his family behind as well. He didn't even know if they were alive or not. The swirling stars beyond merged together, and a terrible emptiness opened up inside him. *Eleanor, my beloved, I will find you.* He clenched his jaw. *Evaine, I will find you.*

THE ENCYCLOPAEDIA OF ERROLOR

A

Achkan – A snug fitting, long-sleeved robe that comes just short of the knees. It's worn by the aristocracy in Thedarras and for formal occasions.

Aelswyth – The traditional language of the Elcaern, spoken by a large percentage of the population in Galhane and the outlying territories. It is seldom used in the rest of the empire.

Aerial – Any type of flying or hovering vehicle used for carrying passengers, but not capable of space flight.

Aina – The unique, clairvoyant ability bestowed by the gods to the royal family and certain among the Asaani. It permits an individual to see events from far away, though the strength of the power varies from person to person. Only the smallest fraction of people are gifted with *aina*. It's also called *Faetha*, "farsight" and known by the Asaani as "the vision world." Alternately called "The sight of the gods," or "God-sight", in the Asaaran tongue.

Ainír – the gods of the Asaani. Believed to have helped humans to construct the five Imperial Cities, they are known as "The Great Builders", the "Old Men".

Aldonn Court – The palace in Chaldrea for the emperor.

Alu – the Asaani "spirit", a person's soul, visible through *aina*.

Aminwyr – The afterlife for the Asaani, in which they return to the world as spirits to help their loved ones and heal the planet, helping nature flourish.

Anaxarian – A famous Valorí soldier who died defending the emperor against impossible odds. He is said to be the son of the goddess Iivari.

Apala – A large, quick moving herd animal with two spiralling horns pointing backwards behind its head, and used for mating. Apalas are indigenous to Thedarras, and wander wild in the grasslands. Mythology speaks of a larger breed now extinct. Apala have been used for riding for thousands of years, and are integral in the history of the empire. Many apala are mottled colours of brown and black, but the apalas of the Royal stables are pure snow white.

Arba – A five stringed instrument with a long neck, played by drawing a bow over the strings.

Archon – the Dhemorahn religious leader of a large city, usually an imperial city.

Ardraigh – the elected chieftain of the Elcaern. Previously only a position held by a warlord, it is not officially recognised by the Erolan.

Aronach the Great – The first emperor, chosen by the gods.

Arrus Athaban – The military battle station above Errolor.

Artagan – mythical hero of the Elcaern, said to have slain a god with the sword Crodaen.

Asaani – Also known as the "*Ainír de Asaan*", or "the remembered of the gods," the Asaani are followers of a peaceful religion that promotes a deep spiritual connexion with the land and all living things. They speak an ancient language called Asaara.

Asaara – The unique language of the Asaani. The word means "the god-echo". It is generally only spoken among devout Asaani, and is thought to be a dying tongue.

Ascendancy – The battle which brought the ducal armies into ruin and elevated Raynard to his Archducal status.

Augures – The clairvoyant advisors to the emperor.

Auranc — An ancient Elcaern instrument, the auranc is a twisting horn of bone and wood and ivory that originated in the plains of Erethya.

B

Bael – Asaani prefix for "street".

Bael Alar – The street which runs outside the Temple of Daor.

Bael Dunmar – Known as the "street of heavy steps' in Asaaran. It is the main thoroughfare through Chaldrea.

Balog Mor – The last northern stronghold of the Ainír before they fled the planet.

Battlemaster – The highest rank of the Valorí. Above a *fedann*, there is typically only one or two battlemasters alive at any given time.

Beol – A traditional salute before combat

Biotorch – A device used for repairing and stimulating the regrowth of tissue damaged by serious injuries, such as a gunshot or a knife or broken bone. Utilises biogenic radiation.

Bocalyn – A seven stringed instrument plucked with the fingers.

Boma – A snake from Brythanor whose eggs are a delicacy.

Book of Caels – The collected wisdom and histories of the priestesses and monks of the Asaani, it is their primary religious text.

Braigh Ardunn Academy– The training academy for the military Old Guard, located in the mountains near Durengol.

Brude – Arethian general of ages past who wrote the famous "Parables of War".

C

Caebryn – A large bird that lives in the grasslands west of Chaldrea, considered a delicacy.

Calirri flowers – Purple and pink flowers that grow on vines in the tropical rainforests of Thedarras.

Cannoch Tree – A large deciduous tree with sweet smelling yellow and red flowers that grows in Thedarras.

Cnoc Beagan – The fortress on Allria where the archduke and his family reside.

Clamael – A circlet of silver worn on the heads of Asaani elders. They are very rare, and are rumoured to enhance the abilities of *aina*.

Cobran – A small shield unique to the Valorí, used on the defending arm. Sharp edges, can deflect blows and as well as attack. It is a specialised weapon which wraps around the forearm and must be gripped, folding over the entire hand.

Comnet – The communications network, similar to the netspan, but localised and for personal use between individuals.

Comrath Andach – An Elcaern ritual for boys destined to become warriors.

Comsig – A small, personal communications device, usually worn on the wrist.

Craic Achran – The military naval academy near Chaldrea. The personnel here are generally considered loyal to the emperor, and not the Erolan.

Craidath – The combat technique used by the Asaani, emphasising fluid movements and quick strikes.

Crodan – A famous Elcaern sword that was forged by the old gods, so powerful and vicious that it must be kept in a cauldron of blood to tame its fury. It was used by the Elcaern hero Artagan.

Culverin – A mobile, lightly armoured, one man, all-terrain tank that hovers.

D

Damadron – A large, powerful beast with two horns and thick, leathery skin. A herd animal of the western savannah, it was ridden in ancient times as a war animal, knocking over and trampling foes with its massive hooves and goring enemies with its horns.

Darrac – A long spear used by the Valorí.

Dat-tran – A long range signal relay used aboard ships.

Degoll – A carnivorous mammal, degoll have several species that dwell either in burrows in the grasslands or in the treetops of jungle forests. With long tufted ears and blue or silver eyes, degoll are solitary creatures known for their tremendous ferocity and aggressive behaviour.

Degren – Degren are beasts of ancient mythology, said to belong to high forests and mountains. They once were thought to be the spirit animals of the Ainír.

Deveron – The flight academy where navy pilots and officers are trained.

Dhemorahn – "God-Spurned", the followers of the Prophet Desedar, and adherents to the spiritual leader known as the Mal. They believe in the divinity of man's willpower to conquer his inner and outer world.

Dhoti – Baggy trousers worn by the Thedarran men, loose at the waist and tied with a knot of fabric, they have a narrow fit at the ankle.

Dol Regas – The sacred book of the Dhemorahn's spiritual teachings, written by the Prophet Desedar. Dhemorahn doctrine holds that Desedar was inspired to write the book from the innately divine humanity. However, the Asaani believe that he was a mouthpiece for the old god known as Victus.

Dramad– An Elcaern warrior. Few choose this profession in modern days, as the training is rigorous and the lifestyle austere, but they are feared and respected as some of the most formidable warriors in the empire. They are often used as mercenaries.

Draugor – The chosen elite warriors of Mal'Dreghen, also known as the Red Guard. Little is known of the Draugor, save that they are trained from an early age in the combat technique known as *gho*. They are devout adherents of the Dhemorahn sect.

Dragoon – A specialised soldier in powered battle armour. They are a mechanised branch of the imperial army, and not considered regular infantry.

Dryden – The men who become monks of Asaani, yet do not go on to become Valorí. They are responsible for maintaining the faith, and are the custodians of the temples throughout Galinor, alongside the Maedes.

Dulannan – The land of hell in Elcaern mythology, a place of swamps and marshes, always in darkness and full of stinging flies where the traveller is forever lost, yet hears the voices of his loved ones calling him.

Dutharrin – The standard language of the empire, and the native tongue of Chaldrea and Thedarras. It's also known as the "Imperial Tongue", as the emperor and the court at Dur Enskai have spoken Dutharrin for many thousands of years.

E

Elcaern – Called the *Cuirith* or sometimes *Gal Galheal* in their own ancient tongue, the Elcaern are a group of tribal people who adhere strongly to their traditional background. They live in the central northern plains and highlands of Galhane, and observe a modicum of self autonomy. The Elcaern speak a language called *Aelswyth*.

Eldris Fane – The book of collected mythologies from around central Galinor. It was collected by Eochaid the Wanderer in the year 689.

Eochaid the Wanderer – An ancient scribe who collected many of the stories from the earlier mythologies of Galinor. He wandered about the Eastern plains and created a great literary work now known as the "Eldris Fane".

Erolan – The political body of all the noble houses as a whole.

Eorathya – See *Errolor*

Ephriim – The name given to the people of Errolor by the Ainír, meaning "those of wonder". The first name they used at the beginning of the world.

Errolor – The main planet, once called "*Eorathya*" in the old Asaaran tongue of the Asaani. A temperate world with many jungles spread over a vast central continent. It has one moon.

F

Fascia Stimulator – A medical tool used to regenerate skin tissue and other injuries.

Fedann – A Valorí commander, beneath a battlemaster.

Fennywisp – Colourful, phosphorescent powder that glows in the dark, used for celebrations and parties.

Ferranite – Used to reinforce glass in warships

Féthabban – The armour of the Valorí. Also known as phase armour, it has unique properties of strength and durability not found in the general army. When activated, it also serves as a cloaking device, camouflaging its wearer with his surroundings, to a certain degree. Its construction methods are a closely guarded secret, and none save the Valorí are permitted to wear it.

Fiadamor – The Elcaern afterlife, believed to be a misty island to the east where the gods live with the people. There is no sickness or disease or hunger, and life is much the same as it is on Errolor.

Fíanna – A platoon of Valorí, no more than thirty soldiers, no less than sixteen. Valorí are seldom seen in groups larger than this, for any reason.

Firerat – A class of Raeth corvette, converted from old cargo frigates.

Fyrd – The militia of the Elcaern, composed of individual families and men willing to fight. It's not considered part of the standing army of the Elcaern, which is merely a token gesture for traditional purposes, but is considered the "unofficial" army, with a root in the culture dating back thousands of years.

G

Gaeliath Bridge – The ancient bridge between Callas Andunn and Callas Waith, built at the same time as Chaldrea.

Gaiban – A gifted seeress and the spiritual leader of the Asaani, the Gaiban is always a woman, chosen by the previous Gaiban from among the Maedes and Maegana who dedicate themselves at the cult temples across Galinor. Also known as the High Lady of the Rock, Mother of the Starborn, the Seeress of the Asaani

Gal Galheal – The ancient Elcaern name for themselves, from their native tongue Aelswyth. It's rarely used as a demonym except in historic texts or by anthropologists referring to a specific timeline. It's also used infrequently as a reference point for racial backgrounds, referring to a distinct stock of people from that region with specific characteristics.

Galhane – The traditional northern region of land that is home to the Elcaern people. Its borders have been heavily disputed for thousands of years, until a consolidated territory was outlined and agreed upon in Heidrich's Treaty in 1177.

Galvonite – A very fine, durable, lightweight metal alloy. It is often woven into a mesh that is used to strengthen fabrics and sometimes armour.

Ghinni Peas – A vegetable that grows along marshy river banks and in low lying wetlands to the north near Galhane. Renowned for its bright yellow colour and distinctively sweet flavour, it is now enjoyed in homes around the empire.

Gho – The specialised combat of the Dhemorahn Draugor.

Glengaeligh Tribe – A tribe of the Elcaern who fought in the Coliseum at Dhemorgal .

H

Hagiographer – A court appointed poet and historian who records the life and events of the emperor with an embellished, flamboyant style.

Hoji – A large bird of the eastern savannah with enormous red feathers whose eggs are considered a delicacy.

Housecarl – Palace troops of the emperor.

Hyperflight – The speed at which much civilian space travel occurs, much slower than stream space, yet still relatively quick at roughly 100th the speed of light. Hyperflight is the next stage of space travel after ram drive, beginning at around 10,000 kilometres per hour.

I

Imperial City – One of the five original fortified cities built on Errolor, all on the continent of Galinor. The five are Orath Rund, Arangath, Durengol, Alyria, and Chaldrea. According to Asaani beliefs, the five cities were built with the help of the Ainír.

Inquisitors – The advisors of Mal'Dreghen, they are a secretive group of men chosen personally by the Mal himself. Little is known of their origins, and their ability to repel the clairvoyance of those gifted with *aina* has long been a mystery.

K

Kala bird – A bright, tropical bird known for its vibrant plumage and unique, warbling call.

Kilpi / kilpanii – Tight, form fitting clothing worn by the Asaani for fighting. Its dense fibres help protect the wearer from cuts and scrapes. It's applied by wrapping it in folds around the arms and legs, and is worn tightly across the torso in a snug tunic. Given its density, it surprisingly breathable, and is comfortable in the hot southern climates.

The Old Guard – The officers of nobility in the Imperial Army, composed of aristocratic families.

Kormorah - A dense, hand woven fabric made by a reclusive order of monks and produced only in Erzog Koth on the Otthon peninsula far to the north. It shimmers in the light and is very soft to the touch. Rare, and extremely expensive.

L

Landser – The royal guard and shock troops of the emperor. An elite body of infantry pulled from the general army.

Lictors – Servants and personal attendants of the emperor, they are born for their duties at the palace. Each lictor is hand chosen by the emperor for his service. All are male, and all are deaf and mute.

M

Maedes – The women in the temple, those that have devoted themselves to the Asaani.

Maegana – The high priestesses of Asaani temples, always women.

Magael – A blindfold used by the Valorí to help teach acolytes how to focus their *aina*.

Medara – A swift rushing manoeuvre in *craidath,* intended to surprise.

Dhemorgal – "The Banishment" in the old Asaaran tongue. The great festival of the Dhemorahns celebrating the defeat of the Asaani gods by the Prophet Desedar and his army.

N

Naedras Marr – A military station in orbit of the frozen world Hellas.

Nebrian Drive – A type of space flight at a 20th the speed of light, used by the last generation of military naval vessels.

Netspan – A network of information and communication for business and personal use, a medium for sharing information and videos, heavily monitored and controlled by the government.

O

Ochla Tree – A type of thick jungle tree that has massive roots.

Ohm Chamber –A large medical device that induces rapid healing through the saturation of body tissue with biogenic radiation. Cellular growth and regeneration are greatly increased, though patients require an increased amount of nutrition to compensate for the accelerated growth.

P

Parables of War – The de-facto military manifesto compiled by the ancient general Brude.

Pallanium – An immensely strong alloy that is nearly indestructible and is used in building materials that are required to withstand great forces.

R

Raeth – A band of marauding corsairs who live in nomadic colonies around the star system.

Ram Drive – The baseline drive for most modern space faring vessels. Much slower than Lantern or Nebrian drive or even Hyperflight, ram drive is used for low-speed manoeuvring and general combat purposes. Maximum ram drive speed is approximately 10,000 kilometres per hour, at which point Hyperflight begins.

Razorcat – A medium-sized predatory cat native to the highlands of Galhane and the eastern plains and forests of Laithlynn. They can reach twelve kilograms and are exceptionally good hunters. They are mostly solitary, though some claim to have seen packs roving through Dranmoor Wood. Few are kept as pets due to their feral and frequently savage nature.

S

Sabre-Rifle – The rifle issued to the Household Guard and elite military units. It fires energy based cartridges relying on micro-fusion technology.

Sari – A loose wrap of usually colourful, light-weight fabric, worn over the shoulders and sometimes around the waist. Saris are a traditional piece of clothing in Thedarras, and the custom has spread throughout the empire wherever climates are warm. The fabric can be wrapped in many different ways, sometimes worn open-chested, sometimes completely covering the chest. They are worn mostly by women.

Sarong – A traditional article of clothing in Thedarras, it is similar in style to the sari except that it is only worn around the waist and may be worn by men and women. Light and loose, it provides comfort and ease of movement in the hot, humid, tropical climes of the south-central province, and is favoured by aristocrats and commoners alike.

Schiphere – The term for the main battle fleet of the Imperial Navy when it is assembled for operations.

Shalwar – A loose fitting trouser worn by women, tapering to a narrow fit at the ankle. It is a typical part Thedarran fashion.

Sooling Tea – A very expensive and difficult to procure herbal tea from the eastern empire. It is highly refined and infused with spices.

Stream Space – The tunnel-like phenomenon which ships using Lantern drive manoeuvre through. Stream space represents the fastest sublight flight speed of military vessels, at approximately 1/10th the speed of light.

Subdermal Rejuvenator – A non-invasive medical device for rejuvenating bruises and damage beneath the skin.

Subterminal – An underground transit network linking transportation hubs around the city for easy access to key points in Chaldrea and other Imperial Cities.

Surcoat – A fabric skirt worn about the waist to protect the leg armour and display heraldry or garrison insignias.

T

Tamka – A hooked sword used by the Dhemorahn Draugor.

Temple of Daor – The sacred temple of the Asaani in Chaldrea. It is one of the oldest and most sacred temples on Errolor, second only to the high temple in Beluul far to the north.

The Circle of Amren – The name of the secret intelligence agency for the Imperial House. A bureau entirely devoted to subterfuge, espionage and counter-intelligence. Named for a mythological stone that grants its possessor omniscience.

Thegn – An Elcaern nobleman, officially recognised as a member of the aristocracy, though generally not part of the Erolan or ruling class of Errolor. Thegns are responsible for their own demesnes and answer directly to the Ardraigh of Galhane.

Tir Annath – The ancient people of Thedarras, migrated south after many generations from Beluul.

Torr Archus – A military space station orbiting Victus. It is used as a shipyard and civilian trade port for the families living with the military personnel stationed there. As the most remote station in the system, a large scientific presence is maintained to study astronomical phenomena and conduct military research.

Transcaster – A broadcasting device with a screen for accessing videos and information from the netspan.

Tserpal – A medium sized, domesticated herd animal, used as livestock. The wool from their coats is made into many items of clothing.

U

Uroch – A large draft animal, thickly built and more sturdy than an apala. They are used as domesticated livestock and for hauling goods in more rural areas.

V

Valorí – The elite warrior guards of the emperor and his household. All are born members of the Asaani religion and are sworn defenders of the imperial family. They are dedicated to a disciplined existence as warriors, and while they are devout Asaani druids, they are loyal to the emperor and his family first, and to the Gaiban second. There are roughly only a thousand Valorí in the empire, and each is gifted and exceptionally talented in the use of *aina*.

Vandiir – "Those who wander", the new name of the people of Errolor, given by the Asaani gods after the first Dhemorgal .

W

Wargren – A large, predatory cat native to many western jungles.

Witan – Members of the high Elcaern ruling council.

Wyghe – A malevolent creature of Elcaern mythology, the wyghe are servants of the forest god Wudu.

The Aethian Star System
- Planets in order of closest to furthest from the sun -

Daedrus – A yellow, main sequence star.

Drusus – A large, rocky planet that is closest to the star Daedrus. It is largely uninhabited, but it is heavily mined. No permanent civilian inhabitants.

- **Khanos** – A small, barren moon around Drusus.

Errolor (*Eorathya*) – The home planet of the Vassaryan Empire.

- **Landas** – The moon of Errolor.

Allria – A smaller sister planet to Errolor. It is a temperate world with several moons and a ring system.

Ahran – A medium sized, barren planet with no atmosphere.

Argoth – A rocky ice world with frozen oceans and no atmosphere.

- **Aera** – A small moon around Argoth.

- **Hellas** – A stormy, frozen world with a thick atmosphere and several smaller moons.

Daedlon – A standard gas giant with a number of moons that boast atmospheres of their own.

Daor – A standard gas giant with two ring systems.

Uhrias – A standard gas giant, with the exception that its axis runs parallel to the ecliptic plane.

Victus – A standard gas giant and largest in the system by a significant measure. It is notable as the last planet in the system and the orbiting military shipyard *Torr Archus.*

Kor (*Morath*) – An eccentric planet with an unusual, elliptical orbit that creates an exceptional orbital period of nearly a thousand years.

About the Author

Pearson Sharp grew up in the woods of Ohio, which is where much of the imagery in *The Sovereign* comes from. After living in England, Pearson combined his fascination with Celtic and Norse mythology, as well as ancient history, to create the backdrop for the novel. He now lives in Southern California, where he enjoys sailing, snorkelling, and hiking in the mountains near Laguna.

You can find more information about the book and the world of Errolor, including a full sized map of Galinor, on the author's page at pearsonsharp.com.

Made in the USA
Middletown, DE
29 August 2015